I0583242

MAYAN RUINS

A NOVEL

BRANDON HASTINGS

Copyright © 2026 by Brandon Hastings
All rights reserved.

No part of this publication may be reproduced,
stored or transmitted in any form or by any
means, electronic, mechanical, photocopying,
recording, scanning, or otherwise without written
permission from the publisher. It is illegal to
copy this book, post it to a website, or distribute
it by any other means without permission.

ISBN (paperback) 979-8-9933378-0-7
ISBN (ebook) 979-8-9933378-1-4

ACT 1:
EXCITEMENT

THE LAST SUPPER

She basked in the afterglow as she stepped back outside on the clean-swept wooden walkway, the cool smoothness of the planks grounding her with each barefoot step. Waves crashed in rhythmic crescendos, carrying the warm ocean breeze that wrapped around her like a lover's embrace. The moonglade shimmered and rippled across the water, its jagged luminescence stretching hungrily toward the full orb perched low on the horizon. Flickering flames from tiki-style torches cast golden halos over the banquet table, their smoky tendrils curling like ghostly fingers in the night air.

She closed her eyes and drew in a deep breath, letting the scent of dying embers swirl through her—familiar, haunting, and stirring something deep inside. The aroma of the lamb hung heavy in the air; its tender flesh, stuffed with vegetables and nuts, had spent the day absorbing the caresses of cinnamon, cardamom, and cloves. The lamb had lain buried all day in the large pit, a makeshift altar surrounded by glowing coals, soaking in the embrace of smoke and heat until it emerged transformed, its surface caramelized and shimmering with juices.

Nearby, the Mayan temple they had built to sacrifice her gleamed in the moonlight, one side facing the ocean, the other facing the jungle.

Quzi was a dish to impress in her youth, reserved for feasts and festivals where the all-day process of roasting the lamb was paid back in communal appreciation. Here it was made by unfamiliar hands, previously unknown to all others but prepared in her honor all the same. One last, glorious supper.

It was from her home country that the first cookbooks were discovered, clay tablets thousands of years old unearthed in Mesopotamia, the birthplace of civilization. She had declined the traditional masgouf—barbecued fish cooked vertically, a recipe that went back to the Babylonians and Sumerians, who had fished carp out of the Tigris. Quzi took more effort but offered more to savor in its symphony of contrasts—the softness of the lamb against the golden rice that cushioned it, plump raisins bursting with sweetness, the crunch of toasted almonds that engaged the senses with every bite.

The rice, yellowed from the richness of the lamb broth, carried an earthy, buttery depth, a note of umami that seemed to anchor her. The flavors mingled and unfolded, each spice unveiling itself slowly on her tongue like a whispered secret.

Her memories of quzi were fragmentary, like shards of glass catching the light. She couldn't remember what it did to her young taste buds the last time she had it, but in her mind's eye she could see her father preparing the pit, sweat glistening in his beard as he labored over the coals, and her mother carefully seasoning the lamb, her face a portrait of quiet resolve framed by her hijab.

Her parents had made the dish with reverence, as though making quzi was more than a meal. It was an act of tradition, a thread that connected them to generations long past. It all felt so far away now, but she wanted to taste it again, those long-repressed memories of a life she'd spent a lifetime hiding from.

The best description she had heard of her birthplace was a land of *too much* history, and she'd spent decades trying to run from her own history.

Finding quzi took some time inside that door, buried inside the deepest recesses of whatever it meant to be her. Once she decided to search for it (in her dreams, for she had buried it too deep for her waking self to find) she first had to battle the nightmares that guarded it. It took some time before she had enough practice to spot *quzi* again, but when she found it, she recognized it instantly as the dish associated with her happiest childhood memories, full of friends and family and laughter, weddings and births, surrounded by date palms in the beauty of her homeland.

You can run from everyone but yourself. Someday you will have to face your past.

The qatayef was a memory from her past she was happy to face: a sweet dumpling, warm and tender, its delicate folds cradling a luscious filling of cream, nuts, raisins, and unsalted cheese. She rolled her tongue over the top of her palate behind her teeth, searching for traces of it. She could taste some of the sweetness of the sugar, mixed with vanilla and cinnamon, and licked her lips to taste the lingering kiss it had placed upon her.

She was certain there must have been a touch more purity to it in her youth. Probably it was fresh free-grazing goat cream, with a cheese of similar provenance. She wanted to remember having dates with the qatayef of her childhood, common as they were, but was skeptical that her wanting them clouded her memory. In any case, she thought dates would have been a welcome addition to what was, on balance, the most perfect meal of her life.

"Can I have a glass of wine?" she had asked as the chef laid out the mezze on the banquet table while the lamb finished roasting on the smoldering embers of the now open-air pit, spreading its aroma over their private beach. The mezze made for a playful array of contrasts: the cool juiciness of fresh melon beside the salty sharpness of white cheese, the tangy brightness of pickled vegetables cutting through the fiery depth of chili paste, balanced on the crunch of walnuts. Each bite was a flirtation, a delicate balance between indulgence and restraint.

"Well, technically you *are* the queen," Julia had said. "But I'm still gonna do what you brought me here for and keep you to just one glass, so you'd better enjoy it." The Pinot Noir unfurled its velvety warmth on her tongue, eventually dancing with the savory lamb and sweet raisins like a chord to resolve the dish's symphony with its notes of vanilla and oak. She had swirled the wine in her glass, watching the silky tendrils of its legs slide down the sides, saving a few final swigs to wash down the qatayef.

It was, in retrospect, a careless mistake, walking out of the bathroom looking like that, her cheeks flushed, her eyes glassy, wearing a dreamy expression on her face, standing still in front of everyone.

"Did you just masturbate?"

The surprise of the accusation woke her from her stupor like a violent shake. She went to respond, to retort—to rebut, surely—but in her shock, she couldn't find any words. So she just stood there, her mouth slightly agape, paralyzed.

Julia looked now to her ex-husband, the one person whose judgment on the matter everyone there would trust. "She just masturbated, didn't she?"

Desperation shone through her eyes as she turned to look to her ex-husband. He looked back at her, studied her patiently, before his eyes closed and he nodded his head down with mournful solemnity, the brim of the fedora hiding his face, his unfortunate verdict visible to all.

Her heart sank.

The Italian was the first to speak in the ensuing astonishment, his mustache braying in annoyance. Everyone knew she favored him the most. They could sense it in how she looked at him when he spoke, but now the look she wore was that of a child caught with her hand in the cookie jar.

"I thought we agreed-ah to draw names to pick the order!" he bellowed, his accent undulating like a wave, his face behind the mustache reddening with betrayal. His fingers pinched together in that classic gesture of Italian outrage, his whole body vibrating with righteous umbrage.

She turned her full head to him, feeling the whiplash, panic mounting like a deer frozen in the headlights of an oncoming Ferrari.

"Yeesss, we talk-ed about making it random," the Brazilian added, his tattooed serpent flexing and shifting as he shrugged.

"Why does it matter?" Julia asked casually, despite being the one to notice originally, shrugging her shoulders like it was No Big Deal. She felt a momentary surge of hope that Julia's gambit would end this inquisition.

"WHY-ah?" The Italian's mustache practically took flight, like a gust of wind through the leaves of a tree. He took an exaggerated breath, preparing for what was surely going to be an *explanation*, his voice dripping with that infuriatingly sexy accent that made her squeeze her thighs together.

"Let me esplain you!" he thundered, pointing a dramatic finger in her direction. "It *matters* because *SHE* asked-ah for it!"

"It's true honey, that was your request," her ex-husband said, a gentle tone in his voice.

"To not let her know who was where," the Black man added smoothly, his Jamaican accent booming with a piercing calmness that instantly claimed the metaphorical conch shell whenever he spoke. He locked eyes with her, and she felt a heat at the back of her skull. Unlike the others, there was no judgment in his gaze. Just knowing.

She held her breath in the somewhat desperate hope everyone would accept silence as repentance and move on to the next topic.

"Well, I suppose now's as good a time as any to pass out male ego support pills," her ex-husband sighed, somewhat petulantly, pulling out a packet of singly wrapped blue pills. "25, 50, 100 mg, your call. Each pill is 100 mg, which is both the maximum daily dose and the amount I'm taking for good measure."

"Yes," the Black man boomed without hesitation. "I will take one."

"I will, mmm, split one," the Brazilian said.

Her ex-husband popped a blue pill out of its packaging and into the Brazilian's open hand, before he put it in the pill splitter and cut it in half.

Her ex-husband looked at the Italian. The Italian shook his head.

Her ex-husband raised his eyebrow. The Italian looked away.

"Just to get past any performance anxiety," her ex-husband offered. "In case, like me, you've never performed in front of an audience before. No one's judging."

The Italian waved a dismissive hand, his bravado so effortless it was suspicious.

"Just so you know," Julia cut in, tone dry as sandpaper, "fluffers are a thing of the past, and I guarantee you there are none here tonight."

The Italian gave her a polite, tight-lipped smile, followed by the kind of solemn head nod one gives to a flight attendant explaining how a seat belt works.

"They still use fluffers, don't they?" her ex-husband asked, cocking his head at an angle in that way he always did when he found himself surprised and curious.

"They *use-ed* to," the Brazilian said. "Now we have pills."

"We?"

"They."

"It's a whole new world of enlightened male independence," Julia said. "Men can now go-go-gadget-dick on their own, even in the absence of a female mouth giving it a warm-up first."

"I think you just had a sarcasm, Julia," her ex-husband said, somewhat indignantly.

She stood nervously in the détente.

The Brazilian broke the silence first. He squinted at her, wrinkling his nose like he'd just gotten a whiff of something highly suspect. "Did you actually go to the bathroom to…?" He trailed off, then made a vague, almost delicate motion, one she realized with mounting horror was supposed to communicate the word *masturbate*.

Julia folded her arms, utterly unfazed. "Seems like the boys have a pretty solid case. Don't think you were supposed to jump the gun, girl."

"Technically, she *is* still queen, though," her ex-husband said, exploring a defense that she realized may have real merit.

She opened her eyes wider as she studied it like a ray of hope.

Julia's brow furrowed in thought. "Can still do what she wants…"

For the first time, she felt the tides turning in her favor.

The Brazilian exhaled, the serpent relaxing slightly. "Yeesss, well, I suppose is okay since it was just you doing to yourself."

She took a mental vote tally. Worst case, three against two. She felt the guilty weight lifting off her.

The Italian huffed a little into his mustache and looked down at the ground, acknowledging defeat but refusing to give her the satisfaction of hearing him respond.

The Black man untied the kitchen apron looped around his neck and bowed his head at her. "I'm honored that you chose me first," he said as the other men turned to glare at him.

BOWERBIRDS AND ANGLERFISH

When Matt was done, he lay limply over her, his weight pressing her into the mattress as he wrapped his arms around her. His breath was warm and damp against her neck. "I love you," he whispered, his voice soft and vulnerable.

She stared past him, her gaze fixed on the darkened ceiling and said nothing.

The next day, she signed a lease on a furnished apartment. She always traveled light. Its sterile simplicity formed a sharp contrast to the cluttered warmth of Matt's apartment. She told him she was leaving him that evening, her voice calm but resolute.

He cried. Big heaving sobs that shook his shoulders as he sat hunched on the edge of their—his—bed. She stood awkwardly by the door, waiting for him to tire himself out. Then she moved on.

For weeks, she'd felt it coming. This restless feeling deep in her chest. This familiar pull of an urge she could never entirely suppress.

This primal need to run.

In retrospect, she wished she could have waited a week or so to avoid this bit of awkwardness. As the Uber approached the house, her phone buzzed. She glanced at it, her expression clouding.

"Matt again?" Julia asked.

She nodded tersely. "Third time tonight."

"You know, most people have actual conversations before walking out," Julia said, her tone gentle but direct. "It's this weird thing called *closure*."

"I gave him closure," she insisted. "I told him I was leaving."

"Ah yes, your special recipe: 'I'm out, don't call me, have a nice life.' One day you're going to run from someone and actually miss where you were standing."

She silenced her phone and put it back in her purse. When the Uber arrived, she paused on the cracked driveway before walking the familiar path to the house. The Texas sun hung low, casting long shadows that stretched across the neatly trimmed yard. She reached forward and rang the doorbell.

"Mom!" Hannah opened the door and wrapped her in a loving embrace.

"Happy birthday, baby," she said, her voice soft and warm as she reciprocated the hug.

As they pulled apart, Hannah studied her mother's face with those perceptive hazel eyes that always saw too much. "You look tired. Matt stuff?"

Her smile faltered slightly. "Nothing worth discussing on your birthday."

Hannah gave her a knowing look, one that suggested she understood far more than her mom gave her credit for. "Some things never change," she said, but the gentle squeeze of her hand took any sting from her words.

"Hi, Julia! Ah, I'll take that." Hannah said with a grin, reaching for the bottle of wine that was wrapped neatly with a bow. "Come on in. Dad! Mom and Julia are here!" Hannah swung her head over her shoulder and shouted, "You two want wine? I've got a bottle of Pinot Grigio open."

She hesitated on the threshold for a moment, her gaze sweeping over the familiar doorway. The house still looked the same: the cream walls she'd painted herself, the scuff marks on the doorframe where she'd measured Hannah's height over the years. The rug was new. She followed Hannah over it into her old kitchen.

"Richard," she said, her voice steady as her eyes found her ex-husband standing by the sink, a glass of beer in his hand.

"Maya," he replied, his nod curt but not unkind.

Their eyes locked for a beat too long, that familiar, loaded gaze that spoke of years of intimacy, arguments, and unresolved feelings. She was the first to look away, her fingers instinctively brushing a strand of hair behind her ear. Richard took a long sip of his beer, as if to wash down words better left unsaid.

When they walked out back, the first thing Maya noticed about the patio was how little it had changed. Mesquite smoke, piped out the charcoal grill's vent, lingered in the air and painted the patio with its aroma. Flames danced in the fire pit Richard had built with his own hands years ago, their flickering light illuminating the rustic stonework and casting long shadows over the arrangement of couch, loveseat, and chairs encircling it. He'd always loved this patio—the fire pit especially—but mostly he loved having people to sit around the fire with him. Somewhat guiltily, she wondered how long it had been since he'd had this type of experience.

Maya sat cuddled next to Hannah on the loveseat, both women cradling a glass of white wine as the flickering light of the fire danced across their faces. Richard manned the grill while Julia curled her feet under her on one end of the couch and rested her elbow on the armrest. When Richard moved to sit on the other end, Maya shifted imperceptibly. It was the kind of automatic adjustment you make only around someone whose proximity once meant everything and now means something undefined. Richard noticed, of course.

Charles Ruddick sipped his dark beer from an open glass ("I like to get my nose in it," he'd protest when handed a bottle). He was wearing, as was his wont, a ridiculous-looking ascot, two triangles of silken red and yellow decanting from a loop around his neck.

"What's that on your shirt, Charles?" Maya asked.

"Oh, this?" he said in his proper English accent that seemed immune to the casualness of the evening. He tilted his head down to examine the shirt, as if seeing it for the first time. "Ah yes, Civil War battle maps. This one here appears to be Gettysburg… see the Pennsylvania flag… and let's see… here's Antietam, halted the Confederate invasion of Maryland."

All three women were smiling good-naturedly at the eccentricity sitting in their midst. Hannah had known him all her life, a colleague and close friend of her dad's despite being nearly a generation older. Charles Ruddick wasn't wearing an ascot and a button-up shirt detailing military maps of specific Civil War battles because it was Hannah's birthday.

He wore the ascot because he always wore an ascot, and he wore that shirt simply because it was next in line. Maya imagined it nestled in between a shirt that broke down the Standard Model of modern particle physics and the wrinkled blue shirt he saved for weddings and funerals.

"That looks like Harpers Ferry, there, no?" Richard wandered over, beer in hand, drawn into Charles's orbit as he often was. He bent down slightly, studying the map on Charles's chest with a level of genuine interest that never failed to tickle Maya.

Charles squinted down at his shirt, tapping the general area with his finger. "I, well, I'd need my glasses, but that looks about right."

"If memory serves, that's the battle that cost McClellan his command," Richard said.

"Yes, turning Lee back wasn't enough for Old Abe. Evidently thought McClellan was a…" He looked at Hannah. "I believe your generation calls it a 'pansy-ass bitch.'"

"*Charles!*" Hannah shouted, nearly spilling her wine as everyone burst into spontaneous laughter.

"Where's that new man of yours now?" Charles asked, looking at Maya.

And there it was, the question Richard had been too polite to ask. Charles, with his customary lack of filter, had stumbled right into the elephant in the room as effortlessly as only he could.

Maya shrugged, lifting her rounded cheeks into a pained smile. "Another one bites the dust."

"Sorry to hear that," Richard said, nodding in her direction, his blue eyes soft and kind. To the best of Maya's knowledge, Richard had not been with anyone else since the divorce.

"Meh, fuck him. He was a slob." Everyone laughed, even Maya. While Julia could be as serious as anyone when needed, she could always be counted on to burst any unnecessarily awkward conversation bubbles at parties. Especially after a glass of wine or two.

"Didn't you have a Mexico vacation coming up with Matt over his spring break?" Julia asked.

"Mmm-hmm," Maya replied, swirling the wine in her glass. "What are you doing in three weeks?"

Julia smiled. "Hosting a marketing roundtable for female executives that Wednesday. Sorry, but… nope."

Maya looked over her shoulder at her daughter and raised an eyebrow. "You sure you can't change your plans?"

Hannah shook her head. "Still can't, Mom, swamped at school.

Besides, you wouldn't want your daughter around on your Caribbean rebound. I'd ruin all your fun!"

"Fine. I'll ask Mom." All three ladies laughed. Maya reached over and refilled everyone's wine.

After dinner, Maya wore a sleepy smile as she snuggled her daughter on the loveseat, enjoying this rare moment of intimacy, this reunion serving as a brief respite from their usual sparring. Julia had her midnight-black hair pulled up in a loose bun and idly swung an empty patio chair back and forth in its circular base with her foot.

A pleasantly cool breeze whistled through the trees, rustling the fire pit's embers into brief flares of light. It had been some time since they had all sat together like this, but the haze of alcohol and the comfort of this old patio made it easy to fall back into familiarity.

Charles tugged gently at the loop of his ascot, as if for the first time realizing the constriction around his neck. "If you'll excuse me, I need to use the WC," he said, carrying his beer with him as he went inside.

Hannah pulled out her phone to check a notification. "Sorry, just my study group."

"Whatcha' studying?" Richard asked.

"We're giving a presentation on gender dynamics in post-colonial Arab literature." She glanced up to catch Maya's surprised expression. "What?"

Maya's eyes widened slightly, and a shadow passed over her face. "I had no idea you were going that deep."

"There's a lot you don't know about my studies, Mom," Hannah said with a small smile that held both challenge and affection. Maya never spoke Arabic to her daughter growing up. Hannah had hired a private tutor in high school and was now fluent. Maya would occasionally engage in superficial conversations with her daughter in her native tongue, and they always made her feel uncomfortable.

Richard leaned back in his chair, swirling the remnants of his beer. "Seemed like you had a long chat with Grandma earlier," he said, glancing at Hannah. "How's she doing?"

"She's good! And I'm sure she'll be excited to go to Mexico." Hannah gave her mom's thigh an affectionate pat before turning to Maya with a mischievous grin. "She was telling some *stories* about you at my age. I mean, I always knew you had a rebel streak, but wow."

"Oh, God," Maya said, putting her head in her hands.

"I'd heard about Tommy Nielsen and your mean streak before, of course. But your mom told me how… *flirty*… you were at my age." Julia and Richard laughed.

"At *your* age?" Richard teased. "I think Nancy's Victorian tendencies held her back from that conversation by about a decade…"

"Oh, that's nothing, honey," Maya said, her cheeks flushed with wine. "Did I ever tell you that Julia paid her way through university as a dominatrix when she was your age?"

"*What?*" Hannah exclaimed, her wide eyes darting to Julia.

"Close," Julia clarified, without embarrassment. "I was already out of college. I did it for about four years in my mid-twenties."

"*You?* A dominatrix?" Hannah let her jaw drop to show her surprise.

Julia leaned forward slightly. "I think what I learned from that job is more valuable than any corporate training I've had since."

"Oh?" Hannah asked, clearly intrigued.

Julia smiled, swirling her wine. "People think being a dominatrix is about control, but it's really about perception. You learn to read what people really want versus what they say they want. You develop this sixth sense for the truth beneath the surface." She cast a knowing glance at Maya that made her shift uncomfortably in her seat. "*That's* why your mom trusts me so much. I can spot a lie from a mile away, especially hers."

Maya laughed. "I call her my therapist."

"Honey, I've been giving you free sessions for years," Julia said with a wink. She turned back to Hannah. "Most people think dominatrix work is all about leather and whips. Really, it's about reading people, learning how to play with power dynamics and status."

"There are whole animal species built on those dynamics," Richard said, taking a sip of his beer.

Maya raised an eyebrow. "You're not about to talk about penguins, are you?"

Richard sat up, gesturing enthusiastically. "Penguins? Please. Too pedestrian. I'm talking about bowerbirds. They literally build these elaborate structures called bowers and decorate them with blue trinkets. It's all about putting in the effort to impress potential mates."

Charles walked back outside and stood momentarily by the fire as he sipped his beer. Everyone quieted, making for a momentary break in the conversation.

"Hey Charles," Julia said, motioning at the wet spot on his pants. "You might want to untuck Tennessee."

"Uh oh," he moaned, looking down. "The Old Man and The Pee." He shrugged and pulled the Battle of Shiloh down to cover it up. "What's this about bowerbirds?"

"We were just talking about how Richard never built me a bower," Maya pouted.

Richard laughed freely. "I streamlined it to a smile and a compliment. Charles, tell me, why aren't men out here building bowers like bowerbirds? Seems like an evolutionary step backwards."

"Well," Charles said, scratching at his imaginary beard, "seems like the Taj Mahal was the last human-made bower. Why collect blue trinkets when you can just say, 'Nice shoes, wanna grab coffee?'"

"Or swipe right," Hannah teased.

Richard lifted his glass of beer toward Julia in a mock salute. "But then you lose the flair. The drama. That ineffable *je ne sais quoi* dressed up in black latex with a whip in hand."

"Oh, come on, Richard," Julia narrowed her eyes, as if she were challenging him. "I know you're just trying to distract the conversation away from what the alternatives to bowers are."

"Oh God," Maya said, shaking her head in an imitation of mournfulness even as a smile wrapped itself across her face.

Richard let out a slow exhale and nodded his head slowly. "I almost didn't even want to mention the OG peacocking with those ridiculous tail feathers. A little egocentric for my liking, kinda like a dick-measuring contest."

"*Dad!*" Hannah shrieked.

"Exactly. Not my style," Richard continued, the firelight reflecting flecks of gold in his daughter's hazel eyes, shining as if they smiled at him. "And still, fundamentally, about impressing a mate— just in the peacock's case, it's looks over effort." He thought for a moment. "I think the deep-sea anglerfish is more pure power dynamics."

"What's the male anglerfish do to get laid?" Julia asked.

"Well, the males are tiny compared to the females, and they lack the ability to hunt effectively on their own; I think their jaws and teeth are too underdeveloped. Plus, they don't have those bioluminescent lures—those are just for the ladies. So really, their only purpose in life is to find a female and bite into her skin. He has some enzymes that dissolve the tissue at the point of contact and fuses his mouth to her body, creating a permanent attachment."

"I think I'd rather the bower," Maya said, wrinkling her nose.

"Over time, he effectively becomes a living appendage of the female, completely dependent on her for survival. And in return, the female is guaranteed sperm on demand."

"Um, you realize you're describing like half the fantasies from my old client base…" Julia said. She gave a wicked grin before continuing, "… totally owned by a BBW, who uses him for his mouth and his cum."

Everyone laughed—everyone but Charles, that is. He looked quizzically at Julia. "What's a BBW?" he asked.

It took a minute for the hilarity to settle before Hannah could blurt out the answer—big, beautiful woman—the ripple of humor settling into a comfortable quiet.

The conversation's pause felt like an exhale, a moment suspended in the glow of firelight and long-forgotten comfort. Maya let it wash over her, leaning her head against Hannah's shoulder, savoring the rare peace of simply being close to her daughter. The wind rustled through the maple leaves, harmonizing with the crackle of the fire like a gentle serenade.

Dreamily, Hannah stretched and sat up. "As much as I'd love to sit here and talk about sex all night, I have an early flight, and I'm not as young as I was yesterday, you know."

After arranging an Uber, Julia hung back to help Richard clear some dishes.

"How is she, really?" Richard asked quietly, nodding toward Maya, who was saying goodbye to Hannah.

Julia considered the question. "Running scared, as usual. Matt was getting too close." She stacked plates with efficient movements. "She called me at 2 a.m. last week, you know. Just to talk. Said she couldn't sleep."

Richard raised an eyebrow. "That's new."

"Not really. She's been doing it since college," Julia said. "I'm her emergency exit plan, her confessional, and her reality check all rolled into one." She glanced at Richard. "She trusts me because I've seen her at her worst and never tried to fix her."

"Unlike some of us," Richard said with a rueful smile.

Julia nudged him with her elbow. "You tried to build her a home. I just offered her a place to crash when she needed it. Different approaches."

Maya was the last to leave when the Uber came. She offered Hannah one last hug. "Bye honey, happy birthday. It was so great to see you."

"Bye Mom, great to see you, too."

She turned to Richard next. "Thanks so much Richard, I had a lot of fun."

"Me too. It was great to see you, Maya. Have fun in Mexico. Tell your mom hi for me." He gave her a hug, and after a moment's hesitation, she allowed herself to fall into it.

ON HELL

"I want to read today from Matthew, chapter 10, verse 26. Please stand." Pastor Lawson spoke in a soft voice, but everyone in the church that day knew it wouldn't last. He paused, inhaling slowly with his nose to embody the gravity of the Word.

He read methodically, precisely articulating each word, his wrinkles exposing a deathly concern sculpted onto his face. "Fear them not therefore: for there is nothing covered, that shall not be revealed; and hid, that shall not be known." He conveyed punctuation through the length of his pause and his head movement—short with a slight head twist down and starboard for a comma, longer with a slight twist down and port for the semicolon (preceded by a slight elongation of the word's articulation—*reveeeeeled*), and so on.

"What I tell you in darkness, that speak ye in light: and what ye hear in the ear, that preach ye upon the housetops. And fear not them which kill the body, but are not able to kill the soul: but rather fear him which is able to destroy both soul and body in *HELL!*"

His voice crescendoed on that last word, imbuing it with a drawn-out, emphatic resonance.

He paused again and looked up. "Father, add your blessing to the reading of your Word and give me the wisdom to preach this now. In Jesus' name, amen. Be seated."

Pastor Lawson stood elevated on the polished oak platform, his hands gripping the edges of the ornate pulpit that bore the carved image of a lamb. Behind him, the baptismal pool waited like a still, silent promise, covered for now, but visible enough to remind the congregation of its purpose. A large wooden cross hung suspended from the ceiling above him, perfectly positioned to catch the light at particular moments, as if heaven itself were adding emphasis to his words.

Madison held the hem of her blue dress as she sat to prevent it from wrinkling. The fabric had to stay perfect; messy clothes made her feel itchy inside. Besides the orange belt (opposites on the color wheel), she wore the contemplative face she had learned from her mom and the other women currently around her—focused eyes, straight-lined lips, hands resting on her lap. She thought of it as her Attentive mask.

"These verses describe the commands our Lord Christ Jesus gave to His disciples." He paused, letting the weight of his words settle over the congregation. "Before these verses, Jesus directs His disciples as He sends them out to share the news of the Kingdom of Heaven with the lost sheep of the house of Israel." He shook his head solemnly. "Now, liberals like to focus on the Kingdom of Heaven, but they may not like this sermon."

"Preach," someone from the crowd called out. Sunlight streamed through the stained-glass windows, casting jewel-toned patterns across the congregation and turning the sanctuary into a kaleido-scope of colors that shifted with each passing cloud.

"They preach on how Jesus went to Calvary, to the cross, and died, so that we may be saved. They examine the parables Jesus left us so that we may understand, and be awed by, the Kingdom of Heaven. And they are right to do so.

"Liberals and many others—Catholic, Methodist, and so on—preach on the compassion of Jesus, the shepherd, carrying His lamb." The pitch of his voice increased ever so slightly, a subtlety Madison noted. Her dad, who occasionally did some work for the pastor, talked about his ability to modulate pitch and volume and body language to drive the sermon forward, almost as if he were a composer.

It was the way her dad talked about Pastor Lawson that caused her to study such things, to decompose them, like a kind of math. She catalogued each element of his performance and added it to her growing mental library of behaviors—his wrinkled brow, his commanding gestures. She thought of this collection as her Charisma mask, though she wasn't brave enough to wear it herself.

"They call out how Jesus told His disciples to heal the sick, cleanse the lepers. They, too, are right to do so. Many point to Jesus's words to raise the dead and cast out devils, and rightly so. Freely ye have received,"—the volume of his voice slightly elevated now to meet the pitch—"freely give. But in this day and age, it's not popular to take *everything* Jesus Christ said and preach on it. For it was the Son of Man who told us to fear Him who is able to destroy both body and soul in HELL!"

Madison looked over and saw many in the congregation nodding their heads. Pastor Lawson had a way of wielding vocal inflection like a weapon to swat away inattention. He carried himself with authority; the etches formed by the wrinkles on his face, the powerful boxer's jaw, and the silver hair gave him the appearance of steel. It was this magnetic charisma and moral authority that filled the church every Sunday, his booming voice filling the airwaves on other days. He was one of the most universally respected Southern Baptist preachers in the nation, with many famous sheep in his flock. While his sermons undoubtedly attracted her father, she knew he also appreciated the proximity to so many rich potential clients.

"In this day and age, most churches have stripped the Bible of all references to Hell." The preacher pushed both his chin down and his volume up at the word "stripped," almost like he was yelling in a military drill instructor kind of way. "The entire Seeker Friendly movement says that if you preach on hell fire, you alienate folks and run 'em off."

He slowly shook his head in a demonstration of empathy. "I understand the temptation. Talkin' 'bout hell makes people uncomfortable. Talkin' 'bout hell forces us to exclude people, to divide folks, for some go to heaven and some go to hell. But according to the *direct* words of our Lord Jesus Christ, hell exists. The reality of hell means that some people will be excluded from the Kingdom of Heaven. This is the message Jesus sent to his disciples. So, to those Seeker Friendly folks, I ask: where do you think you're running everyone off to? There're only two choices in the Bible—the Kingdom of Heaven, and *Hell*!

"If you doubt this, Jesus *describes* hell elsewhere in the Bible. Matthew chapter 5, the famous Sermon on the Mount—liberals *love* the Sermon on the Mount—verse 22." His voice began its slow rise in volume as he quoted Scripture from memory. "*Hell fire*—he calls it 'hell fire.' Two words, not one, the second describing the first. Hell is a place of fire. In Mark, chapter 9, Jesus describes hell as the fire that shall never be quenched. Matthew, chapter 25: 'And these shall go away into everlasting punishment.' Into *everlasting punishment!*"

The crowd was worked up now, enraptured. Every eye was on Pastor Lawson, the volume of his stentorian voice silencing out every shopping list, every to-do list, every thought that wasn't directly engaging with his sermon. It was as if he spoke from the mountaintop, the thunder of his voice booming through the valley floor of the church, its rounded walls serving as an amplifier.

"You don't wanna talk about hell? Well, I got news for ya! Our Lord Savior Jesus Christ, the Son of Man, spoke of hell. He spoke at length of hell. In fact, He spoke more 'bout hell than He spoke about heaven. In fact, He spoke about hell more than anyone else in the Bible!"

As Pastor Lawson's voice rose, the church itself seemed to contract around them. The rounded walls that had once felt protective now pressed inward, channeling his booming words directly into Madison's chest. She wished he would soften, just for a moment. Even the cushion beneath her felt harder, less forgiving, as if the physical world were aligning itself with the sermon's unyielding message.

"Why? Why did Jesus speak more about hell than heaven? Two reasons, I think. One is simply because most folks are *headed* to hell. We know this because Jesus told us in some of His most famous words in the Sermon on the Mount: 'Strait is the gate and narrow is the way which leadeth unto life—into the Kingdom of Heaven. And FEW there be that find it. Wide is the gate and broad is the way that leadeth to DESTRUCTION, and MANY there be which go in there-at.'"

He paused, staring at the crowd, who certainly felt the gravity of the Word now. Madison suspected the pause was part of the Charisma mask, although she wasn't sure she understood how yet. The heat of the crowded room felt heavy, like it was pressing her into the pew. The scent of old wood and faint cologne mingled with the damp warmth of too many people sitting too close together. Madison tried to focus on Pastor Lawson's voice, loud and rhythmic, cutting through the murmur of *amens* and the occasional cough.

He lowered his voice. "So, according to the Scriptures, according to Jesus Christ *Himself*, hell is a place that truly exists. It don't matter if you're a Baptist or a Lutheran or a Methodist or a Catholic or a Jew or a Muslim. It don't matter. There's nothing you can do 'bout it. Hell exists. Many argue this is but a metaphor, a bit of poetic license, when Jesus says 'fire,' but they're wrong, my friend.

Do not allow others to dull the sharp edge of His Word. If Jesus revealed to us this fiery place named Hell, we should take him just as seriously as we do when he speaks of the Kingdom of Heaven. We can't pretend that one exists and the other doesn't, just because it makes us uncomfortable to talk about.

"Hell exists as a place that awaits those among us who are unprepared to meet God. And the Bible tells us that Hell wasn't simply a place some folks go. It was designed for punishment, a lake of fire that shall never be quenched, everlasting punishment." Madison could detect a slight vibrato every time he spoke the word *hell*, his hands punctuating the word with decisive thumps on the lectern, each thump making her heart quicken. The sound reverberated in her ears like a drumbeat. She squeezed her eyes shut for a moment to gather herself.

Heads nodded vigorously. A few men and women shouted their approval of the preacher's challenge. "*Mmm-hmm*"s and "*Amen*"s and "*That's right*" wove their way as musical backdrop to his sonorous preaching.

"Remember the parable of Lazarus and the rich man? At least some call it a parable. I don't think God would have revealed the very *real* name of Lazarus if it was merely a story. No, this was not some metaphor. This was a very real account of what happens to those who reject the truth."

He placed his hands on either side of the pulpit and leaned in, his voice quieting, but intensifying, drawing his audience forward with him.

"The rich man was buried… and lifted his eyes in *HAY-ELL*…" The word rumbled through his chest, vibrating with a force that made the room seem smaller, heavier. His voice, so controlled before, now carried a deep, unwavering edge. It was a word that did not end cleanly, the syllables stretching, trembling, until they settled into a distant silence.

"… in *eternal torment!*"

His fist came down on the pulpit—not in anger, but in conviction, the kind that sent a ripple through the pews.

"O Abraham! O Lazarus!" he cried, throwing his hands up in the air dramatically. "Free me from this torment, from this *FIRE!*"

The plea rang out through the sanctuary, echoing from its rafters, as if the very walls bore witness to its desperation.

"The rich man became aware of the presence of hell, and there was nothing—*nothing*—he could do about it. There was *nobody* who would change his situation. For once you're in hell, you're always in hell. There is no forgiveness in hell. *Hell is eternal!* Whosoever goes to hell, stays in hell.

"Note that the rich man still had *all* of his senses. He could see, smell, taste, hear, and feel the agony. He could see Lazarus, this leper he turned back at his gates when he had plenty, hungry no more, dining at the table of the Lord.

"The fires of hell will not be quenched. Because it is God's fire, you cannot put it out. In hell, you'll find no respite day or night. There is no freedom, no peace, no hope. Hell is a place of extreme hopelessness. And Jesus will not save you in hell."

He let the crowd quiet down, staring through those steely eyes, before resuming, *sotto voce.* "Without God, you're going to hell. It don't matter if you're rich. It don't matter if you're powerful like Caesar."

Following the pastor's attention, Madison's eyes drifted toward Governor Callahan, who occupied the center of the front row, the unofficial reserved section where the deacons had strategically left space open despite the packed house. His security detail stood discreetly by the side exit, their earpieces barely visible. The governor sat with perfect posture on the polished pew, his leather-bound Bible open across his knees, nodding at precisely the right moments, as though he and Pastor Lawson were engaged in a choreographed dance of power and piety that everyone in the building recognized without acknowledgment. Her dad told her that Callahan was hoping to replace *governor* with *president*, but it wasn't yet an election year.

"That's what it means that the guilty go to hell. We *need* hell. Proverbs tells us that fear of the Lord is the beginning of wisdom. We need to understand what turning our back on the Lord means so that we may fear it. That deep discomfort you feel in the pit of your stomach when people talk about hell is a reminder to embrace the narrow way, the path of our Lord Jesus Christ. That, my friends, is why Calvary was so horrible.

"Jesus died on the cross so that we may follow Him into the Kingdom of Heaven. Jesus died so that we may stay out of hell. There's but one path to avoiding hell, but one path to salvation, and that, my friend, is the path of our Lord Jesus. Hell is a place you go when you are without God. He destroyed this land once with the waters of the flood. Next time, he's coming with *FIRE*! That's in the Bible, my friend."

Pastor Lawson pulled a handkerchief out of his jacket pocket and wiped the sweat from his brow. "Now let's get real. Let's bring this home." He continued in that soft voice that quieted the crowd, commanding silence. Madison was thankful for the decrease in volume but still felt hot and uncomfortable. "Some of you are going to hell." He looked suddenly sad.

Heads nodded, all in the same direction, eyes transfixed on the preacher.

"You're going to hell. And the sad truth is that, once you get there, it's too late. Hell comes at the end of a Christ-rejecting life. Jesus Christ is the only way to the Father. He who hath the Son hath life. He who hath not the Son hath not life. Are you ready?" His question pierced the silence, once again inviting affirmations as heads nodded. "Are you sure you're ready?"

Yes. Mmm-hmm. Amen.

"How can I hath the Son, you ask? How can I join the Kingdom of Heaven? Well, let me tell you. There's only one way to enter the Kingdom of Heaven, and that's through our Savior Jesus Christ, to be *baptized* for Him.

"Are you ready? Are you ready? Let me tell you where hell is. It will be at the end of your life if you don't know the Lord. It will be waiting. Father, in Jesus' name, I preached what you gave me, Lord. I preached the Word. Now Lord, use it for whatever purpose You intend to do with it this morning. In Jesus' name, we pray. Amen."

CARIBBEAN REBOUND

You can make art out of anything.

Some people paint, and some people sing. Some dance, some cook, and some sculpt their bodies into something beautiful. The street performers on the bustling Quinta Avenida of Playa del Carmen on the Mexican Caribbean coast made art out of some combination of these things—music, movement, bodies, and infectious enthusiasm. Soccer balls balanced on knees and heads. Mariachi quartets bounced from table to table. Performers dressed as Mayans in traditional garb danced their fire dance by the ocean.

"What's a Rumble with Chuck Norris?" Maya asked.

"Oh," the waitress said. "It is, um, mezcal with slices of orange and chili salt, Oaxaca cheese, and crickets, but multiple types of mezcal."

Maya blinked. "I'm sorry, did you say crickets?"

"*Sí*. Fried in oil."

"Oh. So, it's like a mezcal flight?"

The waitress looked confused and squinted her eyes as she parsed Maya's question. "Flight, like…?" she asked, finishing the sentence with arms stretched out sideways, opting for the airfoils of a plane rather than the flapping wings of a bird.

"Oh no," Maya laughed. "A flight of alcohol is like a variety of it, so you can sample different types."

"Oh! How do you spell?"

"It's spelled the same way."

The waitress wrote it out on the pad she used to take orders and showed it to Maya, who nodded. "I'm so glad you teach me this! I never know this word before. What is your name?"

"Maya."

The waitress's eyes lit up. "Maya! Like," she wrote it out on her pad and showed Maya, who once again nodded. "Like Chichén Itzá!"

"What's that?"

"Oh, it's very beautiful. It is… um… an ancient Mayan city. They have this, um, temple, with a sculpture of the head of their god on one side, who is a serpent. Somehow, they designed it to catch the shadows so that it looks like the entire serpent is winding down the… um… the side by the stairs during the, oh, I don't know the word! When the sun and the earth are in position, so that day and night are equal?"

"Oh, I think that's the equinox? One in spring and one in fall?"

"Yes, equinox!" The waitress looked at Maya's mom. "And what is your name?"

"Nancy."

"Nan-see, like this?" She showed her pad to Nancy.

"No, C-Y at the end. N-A-N-C-Y."

"Ah, thank you very much, Nancy! I am Mariana." Mariana was young, but Maya judged she must also be new at waitressing. The endearing eagerness she showed in meeting new people seemed hard to keep up over the long run.

"Nice to meet you, Mariana. I'll have a glass of chardonnay."

"Ah!" Mariana scribbled once again on her pad. "And you, Maya?"

"What do crickets taste like?"

"Oh… um… better than you think!" She laughed. "Crunchy, I think you will like."

"Better give me Chuck Norris then."

"Ohh-K. Give me some minutes, and I come back with your chardonnay and Chuck Norris. Nice to meet you, Nancy and Maya."

"Nice to meet you, Mariana."

After their drinks were served and they ordered the octopus to share, Nancy took a sip of her wine as her daughter surveyed the glory in front of her. She sipped the mezcal furthest on the right and chased it with an orange slice dipped in Tajín. "Wish me luck, I'm going in," she said as she grabbed a cricket by the body, brought it up to eye level, and stared at it.

"I think it's best if you do it all at once rather than nibble by nibble."

"I think you're right." Maya looked tentative. She breathed in, steeling her nerves, and popped the cricket in her mouth. A couple of chomps on her molars was all it took to swallow it down.

"Huh. Not too bad." She tried another one.

"How's Hannah?"

"Oh Mom, she looked so happy. I think she's enjoying Arab studies at school. Wants to be like her grandfather." She winked at her mom.

"That's great! I'm sorry I couldn't be there for her birthday."

Maya waved her arm. "Don't be; she understood. Richard had a low-key event for her in his backyard."

"And how is the good doctor Richard Russell these days?"

"Pretty good, I think. Charming as ever. He and Charles Ruddick are a hoot once you get a few beers into each of them."

"Is Charles Ruddick the one who wore that ridiculous-looking ascot?"

"That's him! The older fellow."

"Well, I wouldn't say that. I mean, we're probably the same generation!"

"Yep, the older generation."

Nancy smiled. "He still loves you, you know, Richard."

"Mom, don't."

And there it was. Before his death, Harry had called it her *fuck you response*—the sudden change in vocal intonation, the narrowing of the eyes, the hardening of the face. The dark side of it, Nancy thought, was that she dipped into it too readily when loved ones tried to probe about something vulnerable or offer help, but as with everything as complicated as a personality trait, there were two sides to that coin, and the flip side was Maya's unflappable confidence and fierce independence. It was part defensive battle armor to rebuff any prying eyes from digging into those awful parts of her she didn't want anyone to see, and part a powerfully animating force as it led her to overcome obstacles that would have crushed most people.

Nancy knew better than to push and lifted her hands in defense. "Okay, okay, I'm sorry, honey." After a pregnant pause, she changed the subject. "Well, this is a lovely change of pace. Not bad spending time in the sun with a nice warm breeze sipping wine outside."

"And getting some pretty amazing people watching in, too." Two men in full body Spider Man and Venom costumes walked past, pausing when a tourist wanted a picture with them. "The number of tourists wearing white pants is truly appalling."

"What do you have against white pants?" her mom asked with a laugh, following Maya's disapproving gaze at a woman walking past wearing them.

"Look—you can see her pocket liners!" Maya turned to face her mom, a wicked grin on her face. "Did I ever tell you about my book idea?"

"No."

"I call it *White Pants and Other Crimes Against Humanity*."

"Oh, God."

"Look at this one passing. I'm sure even your old eyes wouldn't have trouble spotting her panty line."

"*Maya!*"

"The number of people who know how to actually wear white pants is at least twenty times less than the number of people who wear white pants. Maybe a hundred times less. Check that guy out by the shop across the street. What's in his pocket?" She slipped another cricket into her mouth, no longer hesitating.

"Oh, I see what you mean!" The two women shared a light laugh and took another sip of their drinks. "So, what other crimes against humanity are you cataloging?"

"Well, those Crocs and socks on that guy walking over there are on the list, for sure. That's true of all sock-sandal combinations, but Crocs are the worst. Oh! This guy doesn't look like a criminal."

She lowered her voice as a shirtless man approached with a battered boombox and laid it on the ground in the middle of the pedestrian-only street. His chest was a canvas of ink—a winding serpent coiled across his ribs and slithering down his left arm, its scales etched in intricate detail, its eyes glaring menacingly just above his elbow. Beneath the tattoos, his muscles moved like liquid, every flex and shift revealing lines of inscription sculpted into his abs. He set the boombox down, pressed play, and the street filled with a pulsing beat that sent ripples through the crowd.

The other performers joined him, clapping in rhythm and shaking their bodies to the music, their infectious energy drawing a loose circle of spectators. Maya watched from her comfortable seat as the crowd pressed in closer, people craning their necks and raising phones to capture the scene.

A man wearing elbow pads sprang into the center. Effortlessly, he flipped upside down, balanced on his hands, his legs moving to the music as if defying gravity. His body shifted fluidly from one position to the next, his weight transferring from hand to forearm, then back again, each movement precise and deliberate. The crowd erupted in cheers when he transitioned into a one-handed handstand, his legs forming sharp angles, his strength and control on full display. Maya watched, mostly unimpressed, stealing glances at the tattooed eye candy by the boombox.

When it was his turn, the tattooed man launched himself into the circle with a powerful spinning flip that seemed to defy physics. He landed with a fluid crouch, his hands brushing the ground before springing into a push-up that sent him airborne. The crowd gasped as he reversed his momentum in midair, landing lightly in a seated position with his legs hovering just above the pavement. Like a living pendulum, his legs swung in hypnotic circles, his hands shifting seamlessly to keep time with the beat.

"Hey!" his fellow performers chanted, clapping to the music. The tattooed man leaped to his feet, his bare torso glistening in the streetlights.

The beat shifted, faster now, as two performers grabbed a thick rope and slapped it rhythmically against the ground before swinging it like a jump rope. The tattooed man reentered the circle, timing his jumps perfectly to the twirling rope. He moved with a confidence that seemed effortless, flipping into a push-up position midair before transitioning onto his back in one smooth motion. He arched his hips into a bridge, lifting his legs clear over the spinning rope, his body curling and uncurling with precise control. Each wave flowed into the next like a river carving its path, powerful yet fluid.

The crowd roared in approval, their cheers blending with the pounding beat. Maya clapped along, her body swaying to the rhythm despite herself. When the tattooed man rose to his feet, he turned toward her, his eyes locking onto hers with startling intensity. His lips curled into a wide, toothy grin. The serpent on his chest seemed to flicker in the streetlights as he held her gaze.

"Hello, Nancy. Hello, Maya," Mariana said, glancing down at her pad to confirm her memory. "Are you okay or do you need more drink?"

"I'll have another Chuck Norris, please."

⁂

A sea of uppercase omega symbols on butt-hugging Lycra greeted them the next morning as they unrolled their borrowed mats. Maya had a slight hangover, but her mom had talked her into going.

"Oh!" her mom said, a note of surprise in her voice.

Maya looked up and froze. There he was, the tattooed dancer from the night before, strolling confidently to the front of the room, the sleeve of his tattoo spilling out of his tank top.

Maya widened her mouth into an exaggerated "O" and shot her mom a knowing look, mirth dancing in her eyes. Her mom arched an eyebrow but said nothing, her lips twitching in a barely concealed grin.

As she struggled through warrior poses and shaky pyramids, she kept stealing glances at the instructor. His balance was perfect; his movements deliberate and controlled.

"Move slowly and with intention," he said in heavily accented English. "Breathe in and feel your body expand." He raised his arms in a slow arc, gazing upward. "Breathe out, and let your body come back." He brought his hands to his chest in a fluid motion.

Maya wobbled on her one bent leg as he demonstrated an eagle pose, his arms wrapping gracefully, one leg hooked around the other. "Learn to be calm in the struggle," he said, holding the pose with ease. Maya's leg trembled. She tipped forward and fell, catching herself on the mat with an embarrassed huff.

After class, she caught up with him as he packed his bag. "I saw you moonlighting last night," she said.

"Moonlight?" he repeated, his head tilting in confusion.

"Your other job, with the jump rope."

"Oh," he laughed. It was the kind of boyishly pure laugh that could only come from someone who taught yoga to support their life in paradise.

"How did you get into that?" she asked, rolling up the studio's yoga mat.

"Oh, I talk-ed to my friend who live here," he said, audibly pronouncing the -ed as a separate syllable, "He mov-ed here before me and was part of that group. He wasn't there last night, but he was the one who got me into that back home."

"Where's home?"

"Brasil. Hee-oh de Janeiro."

"Rio?"

"Yes. We say it with an *hache* sound."

"Never been. Hear it's beautiful though."

"Yes, it's very beautiful. Like your eyes."

It was the kind of pickup line that would have sat firmly on the cheesy to creepy scale from most people, but against the backdrop of that boyishly pure smile and his broken English, it caused Maya's eyes to light up and a grin to spread across her face.

"Oooooh," her mom said, wrapping up her mat and conspicuously minding her own damn business.

"I'm Maya. This is my mom."

"I am Rafa." He pronounced the R with an *hache* sound. An awkward silence lingered before Rafa broke it. "Are you hungry? I am walking to, um, to *desayuno* at this cafe on 10th avenue. Really good."

Her mom spoke before Maya could answer. "Honey, I think I'm going to just relax on the beach a bit if you wanted some time to yourself today." Maya gave her mom a sweaty side hug and told her to enjoy herself. "You too, but not *too* much," she said, smiling.

"Where are *you* from?" Rafa asked Maya as they walked to breakfast.

"I grew up in Canada." He nodded the way you would expect a Brazilian living in a tourist spot in Mexico full of Americans and Europeans would nod. "What type of music do you like?" she asked, mainly to change the subject.

"In Brazil, we have different kinds, like bossa nova and chorinho, which I like. But I also like a lot of American music."

"Oh yeah? Like what?"

"Mmm, I like pop music. Taylor Swift. I also really like hippy hop."

She belly-laughed as they walked through the crowds, the sun beating down on her.

PAPA BEAR

Madison hated the perfume Mrs. Marsh wore. It radiated like billowing wisps of noxious gas that invaded her senses uninvited and made her eyes water. She imagined its odor sticking to the sides of her nostrils like the sticky pads her mom once used to rid her kitchen of pantry moths. It was tacky and made her head spin. She forced herself to inhale through her mouth and occasionally exhale as hard as she could through her nose to try to force the smell out—cloying, like rotting fruit.

Katie Preston tapped the eraser of her pencil on the desk in staccato bursts—*rat-a-tat-tat, rat-a-tat-tat*—like she was drilling into Madison's skull. Overhead, the air conditioning hummed with a slight whistling noise. Madison looked up and saw the same paper airplane in the vent that Zach had slipped up there last week as a joke when Mrs. Marsh stepped out of the room. Zach had a slight cold this week; she could hear his heavy breaths as he too breathed through his mouth, and the occasional garble of mucus when he forgot and drew breath through his nose.

It didn't stop him from constantly shifting in his chair. She blinked every time he dragged its plastic legs against the vinyl floor. Outside, the lawn crew's weed eater whirred and buzzed, muffled by the closed window but still too loud, like bees trapped in her brain.

"Madison," Mrs. Marsh said, directing the room's attention toward her. "Is there a reason you're rocking back and forth?"

Madison froze and shook her head. The movement had been soothing, grounding her against the storm of smells and sounds, but now it was a spotlight. She hated that the whole class was looking at her now.

Someone tapped their fingers on the desk in rhythm behind her. That was probably Hector. He liked to hide one of his AirPods behind his cupped hand, elbow resting on the desk as if he was resting his head and stupidly tap out the beat with his other hand. Madison didn't know why Mrs. Marsh let him do that. She was supposed to be the one to fix those kinds of things.

"Madison?"

Madison thought she had already given her answer by shaking her head. "No, ma'am," she said, realizing that wasn't enough. She felt her cheeks flush as the heat of embarrassment washed over her. She felt exposed with her mask down.

"Is this class boring you, Madison?"

"Yes, ma'am."

Mrs. Marsh sighed. Madison hated it when grown-ups sighed like that. She wished they would just use their words. She could hear the borborygmi from Katie a couple of seats over—borborygmus is the name of that gurgling sound of the gases and fluids moving in the intestines. She could almost follow Katie's digestive tract, one borborygmus at a time. The latest one sounded like the slow creak of a door closing in a haunted house.

"Madison, is something bothering you?"

"Yes, ma'am. I don't like the smell of your perfume. It makes me feel sick inside."

Mrs. Marsh pursed her lips and hardened her face as someone giggled. "Are you trying to start a fight?"

"No, ma'am!" Madison suddenly felt very hot. She wished everyone would stop looking at her. She wasn't sure what Mrs. Marsh wanted her to say.

"I thought I told you to stop rocking!" Mrs. Marsh raised her voice. Madison felt scared and wrapped her arms around herself.

"Do you want to go see Principal Simmons?"

"Does she wear perfume?" Madison asked.

Madison heard Katie Preston snort as Hector let out a noise that sounded like an extended owl's coo. She felt like the world was getting smaller and she was losing control. She felt like she was choking on the syrupy saccharine smell of the perfume. Her ears started ringing. Mrs. Marsh surveyed the room as blood flushed through her cheeks.

"Madison Quinn, get up right now!"

Two students whispered behind her. She wished Mrs. Marsh would get the paper airplane out of the vent. She wished Katie Preston could just fart so her stomach would stop rumbling. The other students were clamoring and getting restless. *Everyone* was looking at her. She didn't understand why Mrs. Marsh was yelling. "Stop rocking and get up now!"

Madison clapped her hands over her ears. She nearly gagged on the smell. When she felt Mrs. Marsh try to peel her hands away, she screamed.

~⌒~⌒~

Madison was on her phone with the window open when Travis walked back to his truck after talking to Mrs. Marsh. She didn't look up as he opened the door and climbed behind the wheel. He let out a sigh and started the engine.

She didn't show any interest in the outside world until they approached the graveyard. She swiveled her head and seemed to contemplate it as they passed.

"Daddy?"

"Yes, honey?"

"Do you think Mommy went to hell?"

Travis squinted, caught off guard by the question, a tightness forming in his stomach. "Oh, honey, why would you say that?"

"Pastor Lawson said that most people go to hell."

A wave of emotion washed over Travis, a mix of melancholy and empathy. "Oh, Madison," he began gently. "He was talking about people who haven't been baptized. Your mom was baptized a long time ago. She's at peace in heaven now." He felt the weight of the silence as they drove, pulling his shoulders down as he stared out the windshield and let the sadness wash over him.

"I haven't been baptized. Will I go to hell if I die?"

Sometimes she could analyze something to death, but analyzing death itself made him feel sick inside. He pulled over to the curb, put the truck in park, and stared at her. "Do you think Papa Bear would ever let that happen to you?" He unbuckled his seatbelt and wrapped his arm around her, giving her the tightest hug the confines of the truck would allow.

LA PETITE MORT

"Do you want the… mmm… happy ending?"

"I guess that depends on how good you do on the lead-in." She lay face-up, naked and undraped on a massage table in Rafa's apartment. She'd never been bashful, but this had the feeling of adventure, and she was soaking up its playful nature.

He folded a small hand towel in thirds and draped it over her eyes. A small slit of light emerged from the bottom, but she found it more comfortable to close her eyes. She inhaled through her nose and smelled the incense from the stick burning on the chest of drawers against the wall.

"So, how does this work?"

"Is like yoga. You focus on your breath. Become present in your body. Here, the table supports you, so you can close your eyes."

"And you sex me?"

"Mmm… when you translat-ed tantra from Sanskrit, it's nothing to do with sex. It means web, because everything is connect-ed."

"What connects us?"

"*Shakti.*"

"What's *Shakti*?"

"Energy. Power. The goddess. There's nothing more powerful than sexual energy. It can create life."

"So it *is* about sex?"

"No. Tantra is the worship of the goddess, because that is where life and energy come from. They saw that orgasm is energy. Tantra helps you guide and control that energy throughout your body."

"That sounds like sex."

"Maybe I do not explain it good."

"But you teach this to others?"

"Yes, but in my native language. I explain it better there."

"You have Portuguese-speaking clients in Mexico?"

"No. I have an… mmm… website. I write and people can subscribe."

"Nice! How many subscribers do you have?"

"It is very new. Not many."

"How much longer are you going to make me wait for the happy ending?"

"Do you have hurry?"

"No, just checking."

"Okay. Then it takes as long as it takes."

"Do you want me to tell you when it's happy ending time?"

"No, I want you to focus on your breath and to fall inside your body."

"How will you know when it's happy ending time?"

"Because your body talk-ed to me."

"Impressive. So you speak Portuguese, Spanish, English, *and* female body?"

"Yes. Is because I am *babe magnet*."

She felt her grin try to touch her ears as she let her head sink into the pillow. She felt like she had been laughing the entire time she'd been with Rafa.

"Now just breathe." He rested one hand on her forehead and one on her belly. She breathed and felt the warmth and the grounding pressure. He left his hands there in perfect stillness as she tried to breathe intentionally.

"Just so you know, I'm okay with a happy ending now, if you are."

She felt him smile. "Imagine, mmm, breathing in from my lower hand and follow your breath up your spine to my upper hand." She lifted his hand with her belly and felt the breath fill her chest as she imagined sending it to the hand on her forehead, an impish smile still pulling her cheeks back and lightening her closed eyes.

"Good. Now, in reverse as you breathe out." He lifted the hand on the forehead over her nose briefly, just long enough so she could feel him reflecting her exhale, and then floated his hand down toward her belly, inviting her to follow, leading her breath back to her navel. His hand stayed above her skin, but he grazed just enough landmarks—his pinky barely touching her chin or exposed throat, maybe brushing the small hairs—that she could judge its altitude and speed even with her eyes closed, and therefore to track its location in space and time.

"Breathe," Rafa said softly, his voice a low hum that seemed to vibrate in her chest. She inhaled deeply, following the path of his hands, her belly rising as the warmth of his palm hovered above her navel. The heat was palpable, magnetic, pulling her awareness inward. She felt her breath climb her spine, guided by the slow ascent of his hands, until his fingers brushed the air just above her collarbone, pausing like an artist considering his next stroke.

"Now exhale," he murmured. His hand floated back down, tracing her breath in reverse, each slow descent leaving her skin tingling in its wake. Though he never touched her directly, she could feel the faint currents of air stirred by his movements, a delicate pressure that made her tingle as if innervated by electricity. It was as if his hands were tuning her body, each pass drawing her deeper into herself, closer to him, blurring the boundary between self and other.

Time slowed. The space between his hands and her skin felt electric, her breath stretching to meet him. She followed his rhythm, a wave rising and falling, filling and emptying her. Her mind quieted, every thought evaporating as her focus narrowed to the heat radiating from his palms and the pull of her breath.

"Slower," he said. His hands hovered just above her chest, fingers spread wide, tracing invisible lines that seemed to connect the swell of her breath to the steady beat of her heart. She arched slightly, her body responding as though he were touching her, the ache in her chest spreading downward in a slow molten ripple. Her nipples tingled, the air brushing over them like a whisper, and she felt the flush of warmth spread across her skin.

She let herself sink into the rhythm, her body pliant under his unseen and ethereal touch. His hands moved with deliberate care, circling above her abdomen, down the curve of her hips, then back up the inner plane of her thighs. Each movement sent waves of sensation rippling through her. Her breath caught as she chased the energy he created, feeling it pool deep in her belly before radiating outward.

Her breath grew deeper, her body rising to meet his. She could feel the heat of his hands without them touching, an unspoken language written on her skin. Her awareness expanded, stretching beyond herself to encompass the space between them, the magnetic pull of his presence grounding her as her mind unraveled into pure sensation.

And then...

...the wave broke.

It started in her chest, a quiet pulse that blossomed outward, filling her body with warmth and light. She arched instinctively, her breath catching in her throat as the energy cascaded through her, a current that flowed from her belly to her fingertips and toes. She felt her body tremble, not in sharp spasms but in slow, rolling waves, each crest dissolving in the next. Her head tilted back, her lips parting as a soft, involuntary moan escaped her, a sound that seemed to rise from the very center of her being.

His fingers hovered above her forehead, the lightest touch of warmth pressing down on her skin, grounding her as her body writhed beneath him. She felt the energy between them, invisible and undeniable, wrapping around her like a lover's embrace. Her breath came in slow, deep pulls, each exhale sending another ripple of heat through her body, each inhale drawing him closer into her soul.

There was no friction, no urgency, just the steady rhythm of breath and energy, a dance that blurred the line between them. Her body felt weightless, suspended in a state of pure connection, moving in harmony with his unspoken commands. She was no longer sure where her breath ended and his began, only that she was utterly, beautifully consumed by the moment.

He shifted to rest his left palm firmly on her belly, grounding her as his right hand cupped her vulva, radiating warmth and energy. With deliberate precision, his left hand lifted, curling his fingers upward, as if coaxing her breath to rise. Her inhale followed instinctively, her belly lifting to meet his touch. His right hand moved with equal care, gently squeezing her labia and pulling upward, the oil on his skin creating a glide that ignited every nerve. She exhaled slowly, feeling the weight of his touch as his fingers slid back down, exploring her with reverence.

His left hand set the rhythm of her breath, each motion deliberate, each sensation profound. She heard the faint squirt of oil from the holster on his hip before the slick warmth returned to her skin. His well-lubricated middle finger teased her slit, moving with exquisite slowness, building anticipation like embers waiting to ignite.

As his left hand subtly shifted the tempo of her breathing—fast, deep inhales followed by slow, deliberate exhales—his right hand mirrored the rhythm. He entered her as she exhaled, his movements timed to the rise and fall of her breath. First one finger, then two, each motion patient, each sensation layered with intensity. Her body hummed, the hair on her skin standing as though charged with static, her nipples hardening as they peaked toward the heavens.

More oil fell in warm, silken rivulets down her skin as he added a third finger, then a fourth, his movements slow and exploratory, pushing past her initial resistance. She gasped, her body trembling as she worked to match his rhythm, exhaling her moans in long, vibrating waves. His thumb brushed her clit, sending a surge of electricity through her, and she arched into him, surrendering to the pull of gravity and desire.

Don't think, don't think, she thought, and sucked in the deepest inhale up the straw of her spine she could in the time he gave her. She arched her hips up toward him on the exhale, pushing into him as he rotated his hand slowly into her. As his thumb descended down her vulva, she felt more oil drip, while his fingers supported her from within. She moaned the air out slowly, feeling and hearing its vibrational quality, an echo of the wave inside. She pushed into him as he rotated some more and arched his thumb so that the top of it explored her opening, which squeezed defensively and reflexively, tightening and narrowing the passage inside her as she thought about not thinking and breathed and felt her body buzzing.

He rotated a few degrees clockwise and counterclockwise as more oil spilled over his hand, exploring her, pushing in slowly. She tried not to think as he rotated back and forth and pushed slowly, pausing as she inhaled sharply, letting her work into him on her exhale, slowly merging her body into his with each breath until she felt a POP! and gasped and bit her lip and held her breath.

He rested his left hand gently on her belly again, reminding her to breathe.

The single orb of heat radiating from deep inside consumed her body, mind, and everything within her. The sensation bordered on unbearable—fear, ecstasy, and surrender mingling until they became indistinguishable. Her head spun, her skin flushed with heat as the orb inside her expanded, sending concentric ripples of energy through her body, wave after wave of pure sensation.

He moved with impossible slowness, expanding his fingers so gently that the motion was only recognizable to her because she had previously studied it with such attention. She felt herself teetering on the edge, each rotation of his hand pulling her closer to the brink. The room around her dissolved into streaks of light and shadow, her vision a kaleidoscope of brightness and void. Time itself unraveled, stretching and contracting with every pull, every push, every subtle shift of his fingers. Her body trembled, caught between explosion and implosion, the vibrating hum of her release building in the marrow of her bones.

She could no longer keep the rhythm of the breathing, collapsing into moans and gasps and proto-screams and *ohgods* and *omygods* and *ohgodohfuckohgodohfucks.*

And then: POP! The dam inside her burst, and all thought evaporated.

Her entire body convulsed in a series of ecstatic waves. Her cries filled the room, her moans rising and falling like the tide, until all she could hear was the steady drip of her release, cascading off the table to the tiled floor below.

When she could move again, her mouth able to form sound between the paralyzed circle of her lips, her eyes open wide in amazement and uncertainty and wonder (the towel having fallen off her), she made just enough of a small neck movement to watch her orgasm drip onto the floor. She struggled through the mental gymnastics of taking a desire to be polite and apologetic about the wet tile and thankful and appreciative and to explore the wonders of the universe through the power of speech.

"Huh," she said.

❧

Nancy Bennett flipped idly through the photos on her phone, leaning back into the creaking wicker chair on the Airbnb's balcony. A warm breeze played through the dense jungle foliage, swaying the fronds just enough to obscure her from any curious passersby below. In the distance, two monkeys darted across the skeletal frame of a partially constructed apartment building.

She watched them, their small bodies scaling the exposed beams like mischievous acrobats. They stopped at the top, perched with inscrutable expressions, staring out at this strange liminal landscape where concrete collided with jungle, where rebar jutted up like artificial trees and roots cracked through the pavement below.

Nancy took a long sip from her bottle of sparkling water, the carbonation sharp against her tongue. She had debated pouring herself something stronger but thought better of it—her headache from last night's wine reminded her to rehydrate first. Maya had texted earlier, checking in, saying things with Rafa were going well. *Enjoy yourself,* she had replied. *Responsibly…,* she added, though the word felt like a humorous attempt to assert some maternal authority over a woman who had long outgrown the need for it. The silliness of it made her smile now. Maya had not been a woman in need of protection for a very long time.

Her finger lingered over an old photo, one of the Russells taken at her house a couple years before the divorce. Hannah was, what, a sophomore? Nancy's breath caught briefly as she studied her granddaughter's face. Hazel eyes, flecked with gold, caught the light with an almost otherworldly glow, her wide smile radiating the unabashed confidence of youth. Hannah's chestnut hair fell in natural waves down her back, and though she carried Maya's elegance, it was the subtle tilt of her chin and the mischief in her expressive brows that betrayed her father's easy humor. She was, Nancy thought, a perfect blend of both parents, both charming and formidable in her way.

Richard wore his carefree smile under that chocolate-colored fedora he loved because, he said, it made him look like Indiana Jones. Nancy could hear his voice now, that mix of sharp wit and good-natured absurdity he wielded so effortlessly. He could find the humor in almost anything, no matter how ordinary or strange. *An occupational hazard,* he'd say, shrugging it off with that glimmer of self-awareness. His graying hair and faint crow's feet betrayed the years he had on Maya, but his energy never seemed dulled by time.

Whereas most people would seek a polite exit when conversations exposed wide chasms in values or beliefs between them and their co-conversationalists, Richard leaned in—with curiosity, not confrontation. He wasn't sparring; he was exploring unfamiliar territory. Where most people would see irreconcilable differences, he saw opportunity. In retrospect, he would have made the perfect diplomat.

It was more like the opportunities to explore these new perspectives that walked into his life fascinated him, probing their boundaries and internal contradictions without judgment, fully aware of the absurd contradictions that informed his own worldview. It was never the case that he did so to challenge a particular point of view; he was legitimately just *curious* about damn near everything. He was the type of person who opened his arms to the full breadth of humanity. She loved him dearly.

She had tried many times to imagine anyone else who could have domesticated Maya, even for a little while, and failed each time.

It took some near mythical combination of traits: humor sharp enough to dull her attacks, intelligence keen enough to keep up with her wit, a patience deep enough to accept her flaws, a knack for cooking up to her high standards, a gift with children to cover for her own maternal challenges, and—yes—being tall. Those piercing blue eyes probably didn't hurt, either. She did not hold out hope for Maya to find a future long-term partner.

He had his arm wrapped languidly around both ladies in the photo. Nancy smiled back at her daughter's radiant grin. She loved seeing Maya happy like that.

It had been one hell of a journey to get to that smile.

There had been a few separations over the years—quiet, temporary ones, mostly unspoken outside their closest circle, but they'd always managed to patch things back together for Hannah's sake. Richard, especially, had shouldered the weight of Hannah's emotional turbulence through high school, playing the steady parent while Maya drifted in and out. By the time Hannah left for college, even Nancy could see how much her daughter wanted out. They had split amicably, or as amicably as anyone could expect under the circumstances.

A shadow crossed over Nancy's face as she contemplated her grand piano in the picture's background.

Maya's feet had always kept perfect time, even as a nine-year-old whose legs barely reached the pedals. *Tap, tap, tap* against the piano bench, her little metronomes marked each beat with unwavering precision. Over the months, then years, Nancy watched her daughter's rigid posture soften as Maya learned to feel the music in her body, finding the sweet spot on the bench that let her sway with the melody. Her fingers, once stiff and deliberate, began to curve and flow like water over the keys, discovering the subtle dynamics between forte and pianissimo.

The last song Maya had ever played on it—or, as far as Nancy knew, on *any* piano—was Chopin's "Ballade No. 1 in G minor."

She had come home early and, hearing the piano, walked in to watch as Maya's teenage hands floated above the piano softly during the early rests, how they fell like raindrops on the keys, how the gentle melancholy of the opening bars transmuted into something heart-racing and scary, how the resolution seemed to float ominously in the air before Maya opened her eyes and saw that Nancy had been watching her.

"Oh, honey…" Nancy had said, overcome.

She saw something dark and stormy staring back at her, something angry at having been seen without permission. And Maya never played the piano again.

Nancy let out a melancholy sigh and flipped back in time through the digital photo album until she found an old picture of Harry. Now, she thought with a wistful smile, *that* was what an ambassador was supposed to look like.

Harry Bennett, her ex-husband, radiated the kind of dignity that seemed to belong to a bygone era. The immaculate tailoring of his double-breasted suit perfectly framed his expensive white shirt, magnetic collar stays snapping the edges into place. A dark blue tie ran down the center like a river cutting through a pristine landscape. The narrow loops of cufflinks at his wrists caught the light just enough to hint at his quiet affluence. His graying hair gave him an air of stately authority, but it was the warmth in his eyes, kindness tempered by wisdom, that had always set him apart.

In some ways, she could see shades of Richard in him. Both men had the same gentle curiosity about the world, the rare ability to explore its contradictions without judging too harshly.

This particular photo was from one of Harry's final diplomatic trips to the Middle East before his retirement. An American film crew had been in Kuwait City at the same time, chasing a story about *The Girl from Dujail*. Maya herself, of course, had either told them to go fuck themselves or had simply ignored them altogether.

Harry, however, had declined the interview with more diplomatic finesse.

But the film crew, aiming to capitalize on their good fortune to be filming in Kuwait City at the same time Harry was there, had no intention of missing out on their luck. They awaited him as he exited the Canadian embassy and filmed him like paparazzi at various stops.

Nancy had snapped this picture at their favorite Mediterranean restaurant in the city after having been harassed by the film crew outside. Harry's famous ability to bounce back from annoyance into good cheer was on full display. He leaned back in his chair, a glass of wine in hand, laughing at some joke she could no longer remember. Looking at the photo now, Nancy could still hear the warm timbre of his laughter, a sound she had missed more than she cared to admit.

She scrolled forward in her album until she found the photos from Harry's funeral. One photo showed Adam Lewis, Harry's best friend and Canadian ambassador to the United States, holding Maya in a deep embrace. The camera caught the moisture in Adam's eyes and the tension in his jaw. Maya pressed her face into his shoulder, her dark hair spilling across his suit. Even through the screen, Nancy could feel the weight of the moment pressing down on her chest. She felt her own eyes welling up and put down her phone.

Of all their friends and colleagues, Adam had been the one who stepped in the most. He was the one who flew to Kuwait to bring Harry home after his heart attack, and the one who had used his own connections to help Harry and Nancy settle into retirement in Phoenix, despite Harry's lack of US citizenship. Harry complained about the radical shifts in weather on his trips, and decided that, when forced to decide between them, he much preferred the heat to the frost.

She looked up at the skeletal pile of concrete and rebar in the distance. She could see only one monkey now. It sat monk-like on one of the concrete beams on the highest point of the unfinished (and potentially abandoned?) building, its legs making a V shape as it squatted between them, its hands resting peacefully on its knees. She couldn't make out its face from this distance, but she had the distinct impression it was staring back at her.

The monkey held its ground in the staring contest, unblinking, its stillness almost serene. She narrowed her eyes in defiance, unwilling to cede until her phone buzzed, breaking her concentration.

"Things going well. REALLY well. Need me or OK if I stay out late?"

Nancy couldn't help but smile. This was her daughter's vacation anyhow; she was just a last-minute add-on. And if Matt couldn't be here to enjoy the escape, it seemed Maya was more than capable of finding someone who was.

She texted back. "I'm fine honey. Got a bit of a headache anyway so probably gonna call it in early tonight. Love you. Be careful!"

A momentary flash of light sparked in her peripheral vision, there and gone so quickly she wasn't sure she'd seen it at all. She blinked several times, but everything looked normal. She looked back at the monkey and stuck her tongue out at it. It stared back without moving, calm, and perhaps a little arrogant, in its staring contest victory.

Maya had not been a woman in need of defense for some time, but on that day, she needed Adam's embrace. It was Harry, more than anyone, who had pulled Mayyada al-Rahbani out of whatever hell she had crawled through, guiding her one determined step at a time until Maya Bennett emerged. Once she had, she never looked back.

The filmmakers wanted the obvious story, the one that had captivated the media for years. It was Harry, after all, who offered sanctuary to this mysterious seven-year-old survivor who had stumbled, alone and starving, across the Kuwaiti border. He had been the one to meet her immediate humanitarian needs: food, clothing, medical care, a safe place to sleep, and the luxury of a warm shower. It was Harry who navigated the labyrinthine bureaucracy as only a talented insider could until, eventually, Mayyada became their own daughter, an orphan of Iraq with a new Canadian father and American mother.

But the filmmakers could never grasp the full weight of Harry's role in Maya's transformation. Nancy had willingly changed out bandages and provided food, and over time, the burns healed and the malnutrition eased. But her limited language skills made her ill-equipped to heal the psychic damage behind Mayyada's famously mysterious journey from Dujail to Kuwait. *It was for that purpose that Harry was put on this earth,* she thought, for who else could have possibly possessed the combination of language mastery, a nuanced understanding of the political and bureaucratic landscape of the various governments involved, a deep network, and decades of experience with patient diplomacy to help Mayyada travel from Kuwait to Ottawa to Harvard? Whatever indomitable spirit propelled that little girl's journey away from massacre and through a war zone, it was Harry who propelled her forward in a world that had tried and failed to abandon her.

Despite Harry's gentle encouragement over the years, Maya had never gone back to Iraq. The past was a weight she refused to carry. When news of Dujail resurfaced during Saddam's trial, headlines screamed about *The Girl from Dujail,* pairing grainy, intrusive photos with the sparse details known of her story. They recounted the final, defiant words of Maya's renowned biological mother—the only woman Saddam Hussein had ever feared, and the one he held responsible for the assassination attempt in Dujail—uttered moments before Saddam himself pulled the trigger: *she will bury you.*

The "she" in question had never uttered a word about it. Maya's response to prying journalists was legendary: water in their faces, a shove into the nearest wall, a string of expletives that left no room for ambiguity. That chapter of her life wasn't just closed. It was locked, sealed, and thrown into the abyss.

Nancy felt a strange tingling in her right arm, as if thousands of tiny pins were gently pressing into her skin. She shook her arm, trying to restore normal circulation. The monkey turned its head. She followed its gaze and saw the second monkey return. Her staring nemesis moved down from the beam gracefully, and the two monkeys ambled out of sight as the sun made its glorious descent behind the building.

Nancy was only half paying attention to the show on her iPad. Mainly, she used it as an excuse for being up. She liked it because if she chose to, she could see some of Maya's reflections in the main character, an orphaned girl who became a chess phenomenon. It was the subtle things—that unflinching gaze daring the world to try its worst, the brittle veneer of radical independence concealing a fragile, wounded core.

Nancy always thought Maya had an indescribable presence that could have made her a star and tried to imagine a younger version of her cast in this role. They needed an American, of course—chess played a cultural role in the Cold War against the communist Soviets—but Maya could have come close enough to move past that objection if she had to. Her eyes burned with a quiet intensity, gleaming like obsidian kissed by moonlight, hinting at untold stories and unshaken resolve. Her round cheeks framed her face with an almost regal elegance, their curves lending her an air of timeless beauty. In Nancy's opinion, she was at least as striking as the show's star. There was a gravity about her, a magnetism that seemed to draw the world's attention whether or not Maya sought it.

There was something in the assertiveness of the chess-playing process itself—the steely look in the eyes, the decisiveness of the movements, the lack of remorse or second-guessing—that reminded Nancy of her daughter. Maya had a confident way of walking that brooked no apology to the world for her presence in it. With a destination in mind, she had a quick swagger that showed she knew exactly where she was headed. At other times, like yesterday when they explored Fifth Avenue, she walked with a slow saunter that clearly claimed the space she was in.

Nancy thought back to a study she'd once read, where psychologists interviewed convicted rapists to understand how they chose their victims. While the subject chilled her to the bone, there was one result that offered her, as a mother, some small comfort: attackers avoided women who walked with the kind of confidence and assertiveness that came naturally to Maya.

The show was compelling in its depiction of the destructive personality traits that stemmed from the orphan's troubled childhood in ways that made Nancy reflect on her own orphaned daughter's demons.

After her recovery, Maya had—*thank God!*—avoided the drugs and alcohol that plagued the show's protagonist. She was far more sexually promiscuous, though. Nancy, with her Victorian tendencies, had struggled to accept this part of her daughter for years. But once Maya reached an age where her choices were her own, and she showed at least an appreciation for safety, Nancy had learned to let go. It was hard to imagine reining in someone like Maya, whose very existence seemed to defy convention.

Hannah, of course, had never faced the same struggles as her mom. She grew up with the typical American mix of ambition and angst, a life built on the foundation of security and opportunity. As far as Nancy could tell, Maya had done everything in her power to shield Hannah from her demons, but in doing so, she had also failed to pass down that unshakable spark, that *fuck-you swagger*, that *nothing-will-get-in-my-way attitude*. Hannah was strong, no doubt, but hers was the cultivated strength of someone consciously using privilege to better herself. Maya, too, had enjoyed privilege for most of her life—Harry and Nancy were well-off and well-connected— but she had never seemed at ease with it.

Maya could never let a good thing ride too long before sabotaging it. She was excited to go to that expensive high school in Ottawa, for example, only to get expelled less than a year later when her aggressive gambling collection led to that #2 pencil ending up in the flesh between Tommy Nielsen's thumb and forefinger of his left hand.

Maybe Maya fled from good situations because it was her way of holding onto that fierce independence that propelled her into Nancy's life in the first place. Or maybe, when she didn't have the right kind of fight in her life, she ran to manufacture that fight-or-flight response she needed to feel deep down inside. Nancy couldn't fully understand it, but she suspected that, for Maya, running wasn't just a reaction. It was a kind of self-protection, a way of keeping control in a world that had once tried to take everything from her.

With a delicacy honed from decades as Harry Bennett's wife and dinner partner to high-ranking government officials, Nancy had tried, ever so gently, to help Maya see this particular demon of hers before she divorced Richard. Nancy had hoped for a moment of self-reflection to prevent her from sabotaging her marriage. Instead, she had been met with a sharp, unrelenting fuck-you response, the kind that reared its head every time the subject came up. As last night had proven, not even a well-curated amuse-bouche of crickets and mezcal under the forgiving skies of the Mexican Caribbean could pierce those defenses.

Nancy blinked at the iPad and turned the volume up, trying to distract herself from the throbbing pain in her temples. This damn headache was unrelenting, like ice picks stabbing at her eyebrows from the inside out, more like the kind of headache you get from eating ice cream too quickly than from drinking too much. She fumbled in her purse for some ibuprofen and popped two tablets, deciding to let the closed captioning go for now so she could rest her eyes.

For years, through the end of Harry's life, it appeared as though marrying Richard and raising Hannah had calmed Maya. A wild beast can never be domesticated, though. She was like the white tiger that casually ignored Siegfried's screams as it dragged Roy off stage by the throat. The cat wasn't vicious about it; it was just instinct.

Nancy frowned at this strange and morbid thought, not comfortable claiming it as hers.

She sighed and closed her eyes, letting her mind drift, unwilling to follow that line of thought any further. She didn't know for sure, and she didn't dare ask, but her assumption had always been the same: Maya had been unfaithful. Promiscuous little slut.

The orphaned chess player seemed to move in fits and bursts, like a marionette controlled by a clumsy puppeteer. Her movement was halting, slow. She had lost her confidence and looked drunk. Or worse, like she had some kind of muscular disorder. She slurred her words. Nancy frowned. There was something wrong with the iPad.

She reached out to adjust it, but the surreal sluggishness seemed to extend beyond the screen. Her arm moved as if submerged in a thick syrup, a slow-motion blur she couldn't quite control. She had to focus to see its outlines and follow its movement through space. She tried to perceive its boundaries, to remember where her own body began and ended. She felt like a viscous liquid sloshing in a vast, cosmic sea.

Her thoughts took on the same fuzzy nature as movement and sound. They were formless, shapeless. She could stare at them but struggled to find words that would inflate them and carry them to the altitude of her consciousness. She winced as the ice pick stabbed her brain again.

Think, dammit!

Last night, they had dinner with Marianne. She asked about their flight. And then her daughter married that man. The hag with the fag.

The ice pick seemed to have pierced some pressurized container of the purest void inside of her, and she felt its contents spilling out like a toxic gas leak in her brain. Her thoughts scattered, inconsistent and fragmented, evaporating into nothingness for spans of time she couldn't measure. She couldn't hold on to anything for long.

Help.

Her wounded sense of identity spoke in a whisper, its voice weak, its focus diffuse.

With monumental effort, she planned the muscle contractions necessary to fumble for the phone. Her mind strained against the simplest of tasks—calculating the angles of her elbow, the flexion of her wrist, the precise extension of her fingers. The phone was right there on the table in front of her, its rectangular outline bathed in light. She tried to focus, to absorb the energy reflecting off its surface, to make sense of its shape.

Her arm lifted slowly, her shoulder dragging it forward as if through an invisible current. Her fingers curled clumsily, dipping into the edges of the phone. For a moment, she thought she'd succeeded, but the light radiating from the screen blurred into indistinct, swimming shapes. It faded, sinking into the table as her grip faltered.

She tried to remember what she was doing as she stared at the phone, but the thought slipped away, dissolved by the stabbing pain in her brain and the strange, prickling sensation creeping up her chest. The sound from her iPad reached her in fragmented bursts, jumbled, alien, and mostly unintelligible. The world around her frayed at the edges, the threads of comprehension unraveling one by one.

Help. Call Maya.

The heart increases its pace, reverberating through
the entire body like a bass drum echoing through
a dark, empty cave, loud, scary, and cold.
The stomach floats on violent waves.

Panic.

The throat clenches.

My body is telling me to panic!

Desperately, she clawed for clarity, trying to piece together the scattered fragments of thought floating in the void. Words slipped away as quickly as they formed, like sand falling through her fingers. She had never felt so lost within the confines of her own body.

Maya needs my help. The chess player needs help. Maya stabbed Tommy with a pencil. Tommy needs help.

That wasn't right. She tried to focus through the pain and the fog of consciousness to find the right thought so she could direct her body to act.

I need help. Call Maya. Open the phone.

Eyes stare at the table. They direct the hand toward the
phone, until the hard rubber case enters their awareness.

Her hand jerked forward, fingers trembling as though each movement required immense effort. She watched, disconnected, as the tendons in her wrist flexed, pulling her index and middle fingers toward the phone's glass surface. The faint echo of muscle contractions seemed louder than the fractured noise coming from the iPad, the distorted piano melody floating like warped waves through her muddled awareness.

Her fingers landed with awkward, stuttering precision, tapping the screen until it finally flared to life. The light was blinding, scattering her thoughts like startled birds. She blinked slowly, trying to focus, her hand twitching as she attempted to swipe up from the bottom of the screen. After a few shaky attempts, she managed it, and the glowing surface responded, merging her movement with its own energy.

The numbers appeared next, but they were foreign to her, blurred, shifting hieroglyphics that refused to resolve into anything familiar. She squinted. The soft piano notes continued to swirl with the indistinct voices from the iPad, a cacophony that felt impossibly dissonant with the beat of her own heart.

Get help. Call Maya. Open the phone… I can't read the numbers…

The eyes open again, although a shade
has been drawn down over one.
They study the shape between the hands.

Use facial recognition!

Her hands, clumsy and trembling, worked in concert to lift the dark rectangle before her. The motion felt surreal, as though she were orchestrating the movements of someone else's body, her awareness rippling through this viscous, dreamlike reality. The phone felt heavier than it should be, its smooth surface slipping slightly between her unsteady fingers. She directed her arm upward, slow and deliberate, until the glowing screen aligned with her face.

Her thumb dipped into the glass, radiating its light like a pulse in the darkness. She swiped upward again, her gaze fixed on the phone as though willing it to act. Her breath caught in her chest as the light paused, the frozen hieroglyphs taunting her. She tilted her head, adjusting her hold, angling the phone so it could see her face. The screen flickered, deliberating, before flashing the unintelligible symbols once more.

Call Maya. But my phone does not recognize me…

Her thoughts wavered between frustration and despair. The phone was blind to this unfamiliar version of herself that even she couldn't recognize. Her reflection, fluid and fragmented, didn't fit the parameters it was trained to see. The device required a coherence she no longer possessed.

The hands open, and the device slips free,
landing with a muted thud on the table. The eyes
register the glow of its light but do not act.

Use Siri.

Both eyes look down at the blurred edges of the
phone on the table and wonder at it impassively.
They regard the device's energy with the
detachment of an outsider, impassive and still.

She stared down like a monk in silent meditation, as the void within her mind grew vast, consuming. The noise of thought receded into nothingness, leaving behind a strange calm.

The diaphragm contracts to pull air into the body,
circulating the invisible forces of the universe through it.

The exhale came slowly, deliberately, dissipating tension with every fraction of breath. In that moment, the urgency dissolved, replaced by an aching presence, vast and encompassing. She sought guidance, action, meaning. Instead, she found a hollow peace that seemed to radiate outward, holding her within its quiet gravity, even as pain throbbed at the edges of her awareness.

It was the voice, when it came, that disturbed this peace.

What am I doing? What am I doing? What am I doing? What am I doing? What am I doing! WHAT AM I DOING!!!

> The question swims down the tingling in the throat, wraps itself around the pleura of the lungs, and sends a challenge deep into the adrenal gland. It grips the heart, makes a fist around it, squeezing it into a faster, frantic rhythm.
> The voice navigates once-familiar physiological pathways to marshall the body's resources into action.

Call Maya. Use Siri to call Maya!
Siri, call Maya, she thought and waited for her vocal cords to respond.

> The muscles around the diaphragm slacken, releasing their hold.

She pushed air up her throat, but the sound that escaped was a coarse, guttural grunt, barely more than a noise, tangled with the distant echo of the chess player's words.

> The mouth sips in a few shallow breaths to prime the pump, but the rhythm falters.
> The tongue curls, uncertain in its purpose.

She hissed out the first letter—*S*—a feeble wisp of sound. She tried to scream, to summon the voice from deep within, but the mechanics of it had unraveled. She had forgotten how.

And even if she could, she realized, no one would hear. She couldn't even hear herself.

> The eyes flutter shut, surrendering to the darkness.
> The diaphragm stumbles in its search
> for breath, its rhythm chaotic.

During the alternating waves of silence, she tried to fish for memories or dreams or words in the ocean of energy descending on her like a dense fog. In the eons in between her panics, the void comforted and seduced her, silenced her, calmed her.

When enough of herself surfaced to panic again, she tried to talk and couldn't, so she tried to listen. A sultry Franch accent said something about chass.

> The heart galumphs and papounds with its
> cannon-like BOOMs, each reverberation rippling
> through the body's cavernous interior.

When the panic came, it grabbed her by the throat and choked her and her inner voice whinged, frustrated by its own senility.

> When the void comes with its peaceful serenity, the
> awareness shifts toward the machinery of the body,
> its stomach rising and falling as the breath connects
> the awareness of the body with that of the flowing
> energy around it, uniting them into a broader gestalt.

It was during one of those moments of panic, choking on the shadow of a scream, that the void reached her right shoulder and bombed like an explanosion, shark waves coresetting through the intercoastal muscles attached to her ribs.

> The smoulder tries to fall, but because it is still
> attacherated, it pulls the head down on its decent
> until the table catches the head and the ears feel the
> Franch words gurgling through the trackle of blood.
> The colors of the show swim through the
> eyes when they can open. They pulse and
> blur, smeared across the field of vision.
> The blood-encrustated ears absorb the waves of the scream
> even as the throat spasms, closing to avoid drowsing.

She didn't think this position would hold long, but she couldn't figure out how to stabitize it, so she once again sent out the massenger signals of panic to the coronaries of her existence.

> *Mom*, the word attached to the thought coming with a
> certain desperation, swimming through the waves of ⬳.

She tried to throw her arm out to see if she could catch the edge of the table and maybe hold herself up.

> *Help.*

Her throw was more of a flop, but it didn't matter.

> *Help.*

A word, a sound, a ball of energy floating in the ether like St. Almo's Fur.

The void bombed the entire world around her right smoulder and the rubble of its ruins now supported her.

Mom. Mom. Mom. Mom.

Mom. Mom.

Mom.

MOM MOM MOM

MOM MOM MOM MOM!!!!

The last thought she could attach to words before the void wrapped its comforting wings around her was, *Oh Maya…*

NARROW IS THE WAY

"You ready, honey?" her dad asked through the bedroom door.

"Just a second!" Madison surveyed the line of shirts draped over the hangers in her closet. "You put my purple blouse in the wrong spot!" He knew she liked her clothes in ROYGBIV order.

"Sorry! Guess I was in a hurry," he said. "Kinda like now."

She lifted the purple blouse and pressed it to her chest to gauge how it looked. She didn't have anything yellow to go with it, but she had her green pants and her orange locket that opened to a picture of her mom. With two colors, going on opposite ends of the color wheel makes sense, but with three colors, breaking it into thirds was better. Triadic harmony—that's what it was called. She wrapped the blouse over her head and pushed her arms through.

She found her dad standing outside when she opened the door a couple of minutes later. "Ready?" she asked. He had a tight, hard face at first, but he softened after her question, lightening his eyes and pulling his lips back into a smile. She reciprocated. She'd learned to imagine pulling her gaze back a little from where it's meant to land to get the right look. She thought of it as her Amused mask.

A light rain coated them as they made their way into her dad's silver Ford F-150. Nirvana blasted out of the speakers when he turned the engine on.

"Do you think he'll remember me?" Madison asked.

"Probably not," her dad said. "He's a pretty busy man, and that was a couple years ago. Not much interaction. Folks like that don't tend to pay too much attention to their contractors."

"I can't believe he's Pastor Lawson's son," she said.

"Yep. Still pretty new at the youth ministry. Don't think he's long out of seminary. Should be fun." He glanced over at her in the passenger seat. "And with those vibrant colors, hard to imagine him not remembering *you* after tonight." He winked at her.

***

The youth room was nothing like the formal sanctuary. Beanbag chairs and casual folding seats replaced the rigid pews, and contemporary Christian posters covered walls painted in bright blues and greens. The faint smell of microwave popcorn lingered from previous gatherings, a stark contrast to the solemn incense of Sunday service.

"Everyone, I'd like to welcome Madison Quinn to our little group." The other teenagers nodded at her. She turned to see some of them behind her and noticed the sign hanging above the door that read:

"JESUS SAID"
COME UNTO ME,
ALL YE THAT LABOUR
AND ARE HEAVY LADEN, AND
I WILL GIVE YOU REST

The placement of the quotation marks didn't make sense. She was still staring at it with a tilted neck when Eli Lawson prompted her. "Would you like to tell us a little about yourself, Madison?"

"Um, sure," she said, turning away from the strange quotation marks to face the group. "I'm Madison Quinn. I'm thirteen years old. I go to Pearce Middle School. I'm in eighth grade. Is that enough information?"

"What brings you to youth ministry?"

"Oh, I want to get baptized so I don't go to hell." A few of the teenagers laughed, and she saw Eli Lawson's cheeks lift into a smile. She followed suit, slipping under her Amused mask until she felt safe to take it off.

"Well, you've come to the right place. We're always looking to welcome new souls into the Kingdom of Heaven. Why don't you join us in prayer, Madison?"

Madison didn't think he looked anything like his father. He lacked the hard edge of Pastor Lawson, with softer, kinder eyes. He wore a black crew neck T-shirt with dark jeans and fancy tennis shoes, giving him a kind of expensive casual appearance. She liked his confidence. He looked like he knew what he was doing.

He caught up with her as she was getting some Chex Mix and a Coke. "Hey Madison, meant to ask. You look super familiar. Have we met before?"

"Yes!" She felt a little warmth in her cheeks. "Your dad sometimes hires my dad for electrical work at the church, and I used to have to come along in the summer."

"Is that right? Small world, huh?" He looked around. "Met any of the other kids yet?"

She shook her head, her mouth closed as she crunched on the Chex Mix trapped inside.

"Well, I don't know if you're as shy as I was, but I know sometimes it can be kinda awkward to meet so many strangers. Do it anyway. You'll meet some amazing young men and women here, and we'll learn something about the Bible along the way." He smiled warmly.

"Okay," she said.

He put his hands gently on each of her shoulders and stared at her kindly. "I'm glad you're here, Madison. I feel privileged you've trusted your time with me."

"Thank you," she said.

She met some of the other kids later that evening as Eli explained the game rules.

"Okay," he said. "This is called 'Stand Out.' There's something on each slide that's off, like this." He flashed a slide up containing a bunch of yellow smiley faces with blushed cheeks and one wide-eyed blue face showing its teeth in a grimace with what looked like ice growing on its chin. "The first person to ring the bell and say what's wrong gets a point for your team. Let's do girls versus boys. Madison and Lily, you go right there. Alex and Justin over there. Ready?"

He flashed up a slide of Lego superheroes. Madison buzzed first.

"Spiderman," she said. "All the others have mouths."

"One point for the girls!" Eli exclaimed, smiling at Madison.

The next slide had a bunch of snowmen. There were some distractions with a few wearing scarves or a hat, but Madison once again buzzed first.

"One of *them* is also missing a mouth, and a carrot nose," she said. "Second row, third from the right."

She was first on the next one, too. "Middle row, close to the right. There's a yellow Pikachu in all the SpongeBobs."

"Seems like you've got a knack for finding things that stand out," Alex said.

Eli called the game at 10-0 for the girls. "Guess I should've made it harder," he said with a self-deprecating laugh that didn't quite reach his eyes. "Dad always says I go too easy." He glanced toward the door reflexively, as if his father might materialize there to critique his performance.

As they dispersed from the game, Madison noticed the shift in the room, the way the others gravitated toward each other, forming a tight circle of whispers and shared glances. Lily hovered at the edge of their group, caught between politeness and the magnetic pull of belonging. Alex made a tapping motion against his temple when he thought Madison wasn't looking, and Justin stifled a laugh. The invisible barrier between them and her was familiar; Madison had seen it form countless times before. She drifted toward the refreshment table alone, methodically arranging her Chex Mix by shape on her napkin.

Pastor Eli appeared across from her, watching her sorting with undisguised fascination. "Impressive work on 'Stand Out,'" he said, his voice warm and inviting.

"Thanks," she said.

"You know," he said, "most people never notice patterns like you do. I bet there's so much more going on in your mind than anyone realizes." He leaned closer, his voice a conspiratorial whisper. "I'd really like to understand how you see things, Madison." She nodded and took a bite of Chex Mix. "Sorry the boys didn't take it well." He had a kind way of looking at her. It made her feel different from how she usually felt around people.

She shrugged. "I'm used to it," she said.

"Hmm," he said, motioning to a pair of chairs nearby. "Mind if we sit for a moment?"

She hesitated before taking a seat, her fingers playing with the fabric of her green pants.

"So," he began, leaning slightly forward, "why don't you tell me about that?"

"Not much to tell. I'm just not much of a people person."

He scratched his chin and looked at her contemplatively. "By choice, or because folks like Alex get a little grumbly?"

"Umm, by choice, mostly. And the boys don't bother me. In fact, I prefer boys. They say exactly what they mean. No gossip, very direct. Girls…" She paused, wrinkling her nose. "They're different. Meaner. Girls use too many words and don't say what they actually think. They expect me to understand things they don't say. It's exhausting to keep track of all the rules they never explain."

"Rules, huh?" He chuckled. "Never thought about it like that. You seem pretty sharp, though. Bet you hold your own."

"Sometimes," she admitted, her lips moving into a faint smile.

"That's what I thought," he said, his own smile widening as he leaned back. "You've got something special, Madison."

The compliment hung in the air between them, and she felt heat rise to her cheeks. She glanced away, her fingers tugging at her hair. "I think a lot of the girls at school have schadenfreude," she said.

Pastor Eli laughed unexpectedly, his eyes crinkling at the corners. "Didn't know you spoke German."

"It's English," she corrected him. "Means taking pleasure from someone else's misfortune. We just borrowed it from German, like 'wanderlust.'"

Some of the other teenagers started a game of cards at one of the tables. Pastor Eli and Madison looked at them.

"I know that one," he said. "The enjoyment of travel. Didn't know it came from German, though. Do you like to travel much, Madison?"

"Not really."

He laughed again at her bluntness. "Well, to each their own. I travel for the church a fair bit and enjoy the occasional vacation overseas. We have our Youth Conclave in Austin coming up this fall, if you have any interest in traveling a little bit and meeting all sorts of Southern Baptist leaders and teenagers like yourself."

"Okay," she said.

"And with a vocabulary like yours, maybe you could help me prepare. I'm supposed to give a talk, and I could use a sharp editor."

She tilted her head, curiosity sparking in her eyes. "Edit what?"

"My speech!" He smiled and opened his palms up. "I wouldn't ask you to write it or anything. But you've got an ear for words, and I could sure use some help polishing it."

Madison studied him for a moment, unsure. He gazed at her without wavering, a soft, steady smile on his face, one that felt meant only for her. It reminded her of something she hadn't felt since her mom died. *Seen.* "Maybe," she said.

"Good," he said, his voice low and encouraging. "You know, don't take this the wrong way, but in some ways, you kind of remind me of my dad. He's got a gift with words. Did you know Governor Callahan hires him as a speechwriter sometimes?"

She blinked. "Really?"

"Yep." A shadow crossed his face, there and gone in an instant. "He can bring a crowd to tears with just the right phrase. Me, I'm still figuring it out." He straightened his shoulders slightly. "But Dad says I connect better with the youth, which is why he gave me this ministry. Words matter, Madison. They can change hearts and minds. I think you'd be good at that."

Madison looked fascinated.

He gave her a lighthearted smile. "But you're way prettier than my dad."

She felt the warmth of the compliment settle over her like a blanket, comforting and a little overwhelming. "Would I have to be baptized?" she asked.

"Oh no," he said, waving the question away. "We believe that salvation is a personal choice, not a birthright. That's why it's pretty rare for someone your age to be baptized. Most people wait until their later teen years so they can be sure they're not just doing what their parents want."

"What if I already know I want to be baptized?"

Pastor Eli studied her, that same kindness still etched onto his face. "Your mom and dad also Baptist?" he asked.

"Dad is, Mom was," she replied.

"What happened to your mom?"

"Died."

The matter-of-fact way in which she said it seemed to take Pastor Eli aback. "Oh! I'm sorry, I had no idea."

"That's okay. She was the real churchgoer. We'd always make a routine of it every Sunday. She'd help me pick out the right dresses so we'd color match."

Pastor Eli stared at her before reaching out with his right hand and delicately lifting her necklace. "Like this beautiful orange locket to match your outfit?" he asked. Madison smiled. She was unused to having grown-ups notice things like that, at least since her mom died. "Tell me about your mom," he said.

"She was the only one who ever *got* me," she said. "With everyone else, I always feel like I have to guess what they're thinking and wear a mask to fit in, but she always accepted me for who I was. I think we were a lot alike; I think she was just better at wearing masks than me."

He nodded. "When did she pass?"

"Two years ago."

Eli's expression softened. "I understand feeling misunderstood." He leaned forward, his voice dropping to a confessional whisper. "Everyone expects me to be just like my father. Sometimes I think nobody sees *me* at all." His hand moved toward hers but stopped midway, hovering awkwardly before retreating. "That's why I notice people like you. The ones who don't quite fit in." He stared at her for a moment before speaking. "The Lord works in mysterious ways sometimes, Madison. I can't imagine how hard the past couple of years have been for you, but I'm so glad you came here and our paths crossed."

"Me too," she said.

MAYAN RUINS

Giant blocks of gray limestone loomed out of the jungle, their weathered edges stretching skyward like ancient sentinels. Less majestically, a patchwork of colorful umbrellas sprouted from tourists' hands, tilting and shifting to shield their heads from the light drizzle falling from the heavens.

The air carried a wet haze that clung to skin and clothes, somewhere between mist and rain, soft yet unrelenting. Above, shades of gray coiled and twisted through clouds that filtered out most of the sunlight, casting the ruins of Chichén Itzá in a muted, dreamlike glow.

Many there seemed to regret their prepaid visit, grumbling as they tiptoed around puddles and mud. The crowds were sparse, at least. Groups darted into the open just long enough to snap selfies with the Temple of Kukulcán in the background, bright raincoats clashing against the subdued palette of the ruins. Then they'd move back to cover to avoid the rain and the mud as they captioned their photos with forced joy on social media.

One couple stood alone in the open field, staring at the temple. Aside from the raincoats they wore, they appeared not to notice the weather much. They also didn't seem to need to talk much. Mostly, they just stood in the rain and looked at the temple, as though it held answers to unspoken questions.

"Where'd you hear about the equinox thing?" the man asked, ending a long bout of silence.

"Dinner. Our waitress mentioned it," the woman responded.

The rain pattered softly against their raincoats and slid in rivulets down the limestone blocks in the distance. Still, the two of them didn't move, their eyes fixed on the temple as though it were the only thing anchoring them to the world.

The man tilted his head to study the laminated pamphlet, sending a miniature cascade spilling from the brim of his chocolate-colored fedora. "Says Kukulcán is related to Quetzalcoatl, the patron god of the Aztec priesthood."

She looked silently at him for a moment before turning her head back to the pyramid. It was a gigantic structure, a series of increasingly smaller square terraces stacked on top of each other, with stairways up each of its four sides.

"Here it is. So I guess we're looking at the north staircase. See where the balustrade comes down to the head of the snake?" She nodded. "When the sun sets on the equinox, it casts diamond shadows on the balustrade. As the sun sets, it's supposed to take on an undulating appearance, like the tail of the snake."

"Huh," she said, somewhat blankly, her gaze steady on the temple. It was nearly the equinox, but neither held out hope of seeing the snake move.

"Ninety-one stairs up each side," he continued, reading from his pamphlet. "When you include the platform on top, that's 365 steps. The Mayans had their own 365-day-a-year calendar called the *Haab'*. It ends with an apostrophe. No idea how to pronounce it. Eighteen months, each with twenty days, with five days at the end they call the 'nameless days.' I think our tour guide mentioned it was the babies born during those nameless days who got turned into coneheads."

"I think I remember that," she said.

"Ever stop to consider just how many ancient cultures independently came up with the idea of crushing baby skulls? Crazy."

She nodded, then furrowed her brow and looked at him again, as if it took her a minute to register her surprise. "Wait, what?"

"Yeah, you've probably seen one of those famous pictures of the tribe in Africa who does it, you know, with the woman whose hairstyle emphasizes her cone-shaped head. Island cultures. Native American cultures like the Mayans. I think the Huns."

She shook her head. "So cruel."

He shrugged. "The gods told them to do it. Thought they were making them smarter."

They stared at the temple some more, the drizzle turning into a light rain that splashed in a pool forming in front of where they stood.

"Didn't think you knew anything about religion."

He folded up the pamphlet and tucked it in a pocket of his raincoat. "Not much, obviously. Tried to read *The Golden Bough* when I was younger."

"What's that?"

"Some study of comparative religion." He shrugged. "It was controversial because it was published around the turn of the century—1900—when you had these dangerous ideas like evolution through natural selection out there, but still an overwhelmingly religious Western population. I mostly just skimmed a condensed version of it—a bit too dense for my tastes."

She gave a perfunctory laugh. "Talk about coneheads in the book?"

"I don't remember, but that's definitely the *kind* of thing that would have been in there. The things that religions tend to have in common. I think that's why it was controversial. People didn't like thinking their religion wasn't so unique after all, especially Christian people."

"Like what?"

He looked at the top of the temple. "Like treating the resurrection of Jesus as just one example alongside rebirth myths in pagan religions didn't exactly win people over."

She nodded. "Yeah, I don't think Mom would have enjoyed that, either." They stood silently again, immobile as the rain picked up and muddy water splashed over their feet, soaking into the corkboard of their flip-flops. "Lots of resurrections in other religions?" she asked.

"I guess," he said. "Born again, rebirth, reincarnation."

"Lot of killing though, too."

"Yeah. That's the part I probably remember best, all the human sacrifices."

"Sexy. Any winners on the method of execution?"

He scratched his chin. "I don't remember all the details, but I think there was a custom that was common to multiple religions where the sacrifice was preceded by deity worship in the individual about to be sacrificed. So you'd get to be king or queen for a day, get whatever you wanted, then walk up those stairs,"—he pointed back to the temple—"and…" He made a slashing motion across his throat and let out a "Fffft" sound to signal the sacrifice.

"Go out with a bang," she said.

"Go out with a *big* bang. Then who knows? Come back as a frog or saint or maybe as the color blue. Depends on the religion." He paused thoughtfully. "I think they saw themselves as sacrificing their own story for the greater good."

She continued to look at the temple. Mist clung to the massive stone blocks, veiling and unveiling them like memories too painful to fully confront. The rain—not quite falling, more like suspending itself around them—created a bubble of isolation that separated them from the other tourists.

"The sacrifice was sacred," he continued. "For that final day, they were no longer mortal, but something divine. Everything they desired was granted: feasts, pleasures, worship. It was as if the community were thanking them for the ultimate gift they were about to give. They believed the sacrifice didn't end a life but transformed it, releasing the spirit to be reborn into something greater. Death was just a doorway."

She watched the rain trace paths down the temple steps like ancient tears, wondering what it might mean to walk toward the edge of your story. "I wonder if they went willingly," she said, her voice almost lost as the rain picked up momentarily.

He turned to look at her. "The chosen ones weren't victims. They were powerful."

Her eyes lifted to the top of the temple, where ancient priests once stood holding obsidian blades. "It's strange," she said, "how something can be both an ending and a beginning." For a moment, the mist parted, and she imagined not ancient priests at the temple's peak but herself, surrounded by flickering torchlight, stripped of pretense, of armor.

A shaft of sun temporarily poked through the swirl of gray in the sky. They stood there silently again. Finally, she turned, wrapped her arms around him, and put her head to his chest. He looked down and smiled sadly, then wrapped his arms around her and held the back of her head against him. "This is too much to ask," she said.

"Nonsense. You know how much I love your mom. We'll get along great."

"It won't be for long."

"You already said that. Don't worry about it."

"It's just, with the breakup…" Her lips started vibrating, and the tears interrupted her talking. It was okay; he already knew. After she broke up with Matt, she moved into a temporary studio apartment.

"I'll take care of it once I get back to the States," she said, after she had composed herself.

"I know." He pulled her into a tighter embrace.

"I don't have anyone else."

"I'm glad you called me. Anything I can do." They both turned to look at the temple again for a long and contemplative silence.

"What does 'ischemic' mean, anyway?" he asked.

"Nope, wrong type. Think of ischemic as like a hose that gets clogged with a clot. She had an aneurysm, which is considered hemorrhagic. The blood vessel weakens and collects blood until it balloons out and bursts. It means the blood escaped the arteries and killed the surrounding neurons."

He nodded. "What's your take on her next steps?"

She looked down at the ground. "Not great. It's like she's not even there, sometimes." She choked on the start of a cry.

He nodded. "With all that lucid dreaming stuff, ever study sleep disorders?" Somewhat miraculously, she'd been able to recognize dreams while inside of them ever since he'd known her. She even claimed to be able to direct them, to an extent.

She shook her head.

"You've heard of somnambulism, though?"

"Sleepwalking?"

"Yeah, except it's broader than that. Sleep talking. Sleep eating. Sleep fucking, even, apparently." He looked up at the sky as the clouds shifted some more, covering up the little sun they had.

"What's that got to do with a stroke?" she asked.

"Oh, probably nothing. I was thinking about how you said it seems like she's not even there sometimes. I always thought somnambulism was kinda fascinating, like it challenged the very notion of what it means to be *you*." He looked at her in that way he used to when he would explore a mystery of the universe through a single clue, like staring at a jigsaw puzzle piece and extrapolating what the final picture must look like. "Think about it. Your body can do a lot more than just breathe and keep you alive without your conscious awareness. It can chew food—hell, prepare it to begin with. It can respond to questions from your partner coherently. It's like the story of you is just a figment of your imagination, a metaphor for something far more advanced than we give it credit for."

She stayed silent for a minute, contemplating this. Finally, she spoke again without looking at him. "I guess it's the same as when we were babies."

He nodded. "Yeah, before your earliest childhood memories."

She stood impassively in the rain, looking at the temple. He stood looking at her, his heart suddenly racing a little, nervous he might have accidentally triggered her childhood defenses.

She showed no emotion. "It does sound pretty anti-religious, that we're all just a story we tell ourselves."

"And just a story to get laid, at that. Just so our genes can keep on keeping on."

They went silent again for some time before he turned, wrapped his hands around the top of her arms, and stared down at her. "Listen, your mom's still there, maybe just not as many of her stories. I'm really looking forward to seeing both of you more."

He had a solid ten inches on her, so she had to strain her neck to look up. "Your fedora's getting soaked," she said.

"Makes me look like Indiana Jones." He pivoted his head, looking around. "Especially here."

∽∾

As they departed, he sat gazing out the airplane window, his head resting against the glass, his fedora in his lap. When the flight attendant asked if there was a doctor on board, he looked at her, and they both looked around the plane—him a little calmer. He smiled softly at her when she reluctantly raised her hand, then shifted to her seat in the middle after she worked around her mom to the aisle. She watched him clasp her mom's hand in both of his and comfort her before she followed the flight attendant to row 28, where a young man wore a wide-eyed look of concern as he tried to console the early-twenties lady wearing a Patrick Mahomes jersey next to him.

"What's your name?" she asked.

"Nick." "Sara." They spoke at the same time. His voice sounded scared; hers was slurred.

"How much have you had to drink, Sara?" she asked.

"Four drinks," Nick said, as Sara slurred her answer simultaneously. "*Pelo de lobo.*"

"Does she speak English?" She looked at Nick.

"Itt'sss the drink!" Sara said.

"Hair of the wolf," Nick shrugged.

"Ah," she said.

The couple looked expectantly at her, nervously awaiting her diagnosis. The flight attendant held her breath.

"Have you had anything other than the alcohol, Sara?" she asked.

"Tyla Nol PM!" Sara said.

Nick shrugged. "She gets flight anxiety." He looked back at Sara, the wrinkles on his forehead making his concern clear. "She okay?"

"Drunk. Probably dehydrated. There's lower humidity up here, and less air pressure, so she's a little hypoxic. Give her water, lay off the sedatives, and if you need to puke,"—she looked at Sara now—"do so before we start landing."

"Hi pox sick?" Sara asked.

"There's a lower supply of oxygen, so it's harder for your tissues to stay nourished."

"I *knew* something was wrong with me!" Sara said. She punched Nick's arm and shot him an ugly look.

THE END OF INNOCENCE

Travis Quinn slumped into the couch, letting the cushion cradle him like a weary traveler finally at rest. He reached for the remote, though he didn't much care what flickered on the screen. All he needed was something to drown out the noise in his head. He took a long swig of his beer, the darkest, meanest brew he'd found at the local grocery store.

He kept a rotation of two frosted glasses in the freezer specifically for nights like this. There was something about the chill of the glass in his hand that made the experience feel deliberate, ritualistic. He enjoyed the frost biting into his palm and how the beer, when poured into such a glass, let its aroma blossom. His old university physics professor used to call this method "putting your nose in it," a phrase that had stuck with Travis long after he'd failed out following Amy's accident.

Tonight, more than ever, he needed to bury his nose in the dark, comforting abyss of that glass. At least he was pretty sure that's where his nose belonged. What he wasn't so sure of anymore was whether it belonged in his daughter's business.

He held the glass up, tilting it slightly to admire the beer's impenetrable opacity. He couldn't see to the bottom of the glass, just the smooth, black surface reflecting the glow of the TV. That's how dark it was, a craft milk stout with a kick. He inhaled deeply, savoring the aroma, then brought it to his lips for another sip, letting it glide over his tongue like cold, liquid velvet.

The TV flickered in front of him, washing the room in a soft, shifting light. He stared at the screen, pretending to follow the program, but his mind was miles away. His thoughts wandered, circling back to the one question he kept avoiding: how involved he should (or even could) be in his daughter's world.

He never used to drink when Amy was around. He'd occasionally indulge with a buddy at the pub, but Amy was a teetotaler who always had a pitcher of sweet tea at the ready. The house had felt different back then. Lighter. Calmer. Less like a puzzle missing its crucial piece.

Jesus, he missed Amy. She had an almost supernatural ability to navigate Madison's moods and quirks, to anticipate her needs in ways he was increasingly sure he'd never master. He could've used some of that magic tonight.

Becoming a single dad to a teenage daughter had been an exercise in humility. Her first period had been a trial by fire, though at least he knew enough to see it coming and made some effort to prepare. Stocking up on supplies was the straightforward part. But when it came to helping her figure out exactly how to use a tampon... that had been uncharted territory. He'd naïvely assumed that girls sort of had some innate sense of insertion protocols for objects that fit into their vaginas. It was only when Madison, frustrated and apparently unembarrassed, turned to him for help that he realized how little he'd ever considered the mechanics of it.

Amy had always been private about her cycles, and she probably hid the emotions that rode the roller coaster of hormonal regulation behind her mask of pain killers. A woman's period was, to his mind until recently, a logistical concern, a few days that might interrupt sex or require adjustments. Only recently had he begun to understand that a period wasn't just a once-a-month inconvenience but the visible crest of a much larger, invisible wave. It was a cycle, a rhythm that left emotional and physical contrails through the entire month.

It was that kind of emotional complexity woven into the very fabric of a teenage girl that left him feeling out of his depth. Amy had made it seem so effortless. And now, staring into the dark swirl of his beer, he couldn't help but feel like he was failing.

He briefly considered the idea that Madison's meltdowns might somehow be tied to the hormonal tides of her cycle, but the timeline didn't add up. Her tantrums predated her periods by years. There, too, Amy always seemed to know what to do. She always seemed to know when to comfort Madison and when to let her simply let it all out and exhaust herself. Travis never felt sure of himself. He felt like he was improvising every time.

He wasn't even forty years old yet, but you wouldn't know it by looking at his reflection. He was hard-pressed to find a single strand of hair on his head that hadn't surrendered to gray. The weight of it all—the responsibility, the uncertainty, the relentless feeling that he was falling short—carved permanent worry lines into his face.

The meltdown tonight—boy, was that a doozy.

He'd been out later than planned, installing one of those video doorbells that required a new circuit. After texting Madison to give her a heads-up, he picked up a pizza on the drive home. He was tired when he came in, but it was the kind of tired that came with a sense of accomplishment. Sergeant Baker, the German Shepherd Amy adopted as a puppy a couple years before her death, greeted him enthusiastically at the door, tail wagging like a metronome. Travis scratched behind the Sergeant's ear and teased him about finding his own food as he lifted the pizza box in his other hand.

Walking into the dining room, he had dropped the box on the table, along with his keys and wallet in the small ceramic tray. Then he crouched to give the Sergeant some proper attention, chuckling at the slobbery licks on his cheek. "Such a good boy," he'd said as the dog barked twice, loud and sharp, in response. Travis replayed the moment in his head; he hadn't exactly crept into the house. His arrival was no stealth operation. Madison was in the living room; she must've heard him.

He thought about the stack of teen mags she kept in her room, some tame, some a little racier, like *Cosmo*. He'd been okay buying them for her, even the saucier ones. They were part of growing up, after all. Maybe it was his clueless-dad attempt to signal that it was okay for her to think about sex, that she didn't need to be afraid to talk to him about it.

She had a way of consuming those magazines, almost studying them, like the way she mimicked TV stars or repeated the dialogue of book characters she admired. He knew she'd picked up on what masturbation was. What she hadn't seemed to pick up on was that it was supposed to be a *private* activity.

"Dinner's ready, hon," he called out, spotting the back of her head over the couch.

"Give me a minute," she said, making no effort to move.

He walked over, still in a good mood and unprepared.

"Woof! Woof!" Sergeant Baker said as they stepped into the living room.

Travis's smile faltered as his vantage point widened. He froze halfway into the room, piecing together the scene. Madison slumped into the couch, her hand inside her panties, breathing slowly and deeply.

"Madison!" he shouted. (Shrieked? Gasped?)

"Give me a minute," she said. Definitely said.

"WHAT ARE YOU DOING?" he yelled, screamed, roared, the pitch of his voice leaping uncontrollably.

"What?" she said, turning her head lazily toward him, her eyes finally opening. Madison didn't startle or try to hide what she was doing. Instead, she looked at him with genuine puzzlement, her expression open and unflinching. "I just need a minute," she repeated, as if he were the one behaving strangely. There was no shame in her posture, no recognition that she had violated a social boundary, only mild confusion about why he was interrupting.

What followed was a cacophony—his panicked yelling, her defensive shouting, Sergeant Baker's confused barking—all of it blurring into a maelstrom of noise and chaos. In the madness, the Sergeant seized the opportunity to nose the pizza box off the dining room table. By the time things quieted, he lay contentedly on his bed by the window, his muzzle glistening with pepperoni grease and tomato sauce, his betrayal unmistakable.

Travis had never felt so lost without Amy. He looked down into his beer, tight creases above his eyes pulling them into a pained expression.

Amy would've known how to talk about sex with their teenage daughter. How to talk about masturbation. How to prepare Madison for her periods.

Even with the pain killers coursing through her system, she'd prepare dinner, go over Madison's homework with her, arrange her doctor's appointments, her playdates. Even with those glassy eyes—maybe, he thought now, *especially* with those glassy eyes—she'd bring her erotic goddess to bed, kinky and playful and always hungry. She would be whatever he needed her to be and open herself up to him in ways he used to think were vulnerable, but he now sees as her way of hiding.

Even when she stayed up late to ensure that Travis slept deeply, she always woke early to prepare breakfast and the needed morning preparations for school and work. Her mask had a smile that hid false contentment and shame, and he let her keep wearing it because he liked the way it looked on her.

Oh God, Amy. I'm so ashamed and I'm so sorry and I need you so much. I don't know what to do.

"Mr. Quinn," the voice on the other end of the line had said when he answered. The call had come from Amy's phone, but it wasn't Amy. It was a man, and he sounded nervous.

"Sir, your wife gave me her phone and asked me to call you. It's a little hard for her to talk, sir. She's been in an accident."

It had all started when the cherry end of that drunk nineteen-year-old's cigarette broke off and tumbled into his lap. He flinched, instinctively jerking the wheel just enough to miss the red light entirely. His rusted-out Chevy Caprice barreled through the intersection and into Amy's sedan, T-boning the driver's side at nearly fifty miles per hour. The steel frame crumpled like foil, and the entire driver's compartment collapsed inward.

The impact hit just behind the front wheel well, a devastating angle that sent all the force straight through Amy's body. Her seatbelt locked instantly, the webbing biting deep into her collarbone and ribs, leaving behind an angry red burn. Her head whipped sideways, and a sharp, sickening pop cracked through her neck, jolting pain straight down her spine.

The driver's door buckled inward, pinning her left leg against the firewall. The dashboard slammed down, crushing her thigh against the seat frame. There was a split-second delay before the femur gave way, a deep, splintering snap that sent shockwaves of agony radiating through her entire body.

Before she could even scream, the airbag detonated. A concussive, searing burst of heat and force punched into her chest, sending shockwaves through her already-battered ribs. One of them snapped outright, another fractured inward, puncturing her lung. A sharp, wet wheeze replaced her breath, and she felt it, that drowning sensation, like inhaling through a straw filled with water.

The windshield exploded. Glass turned to dust, fine razor-like shards embedding into her cheek, neck, and shoulder. The world blurred—blood, light, impact, pressure.

Amy's right hand was still gripping the steering wheel when the force wrenched it violently to the left. She felt the pop in her wrist first, a sharp dislocation as her arm was twisted past its natural range. But the real damage came next.

The steering column collapsed toward her chest, shoving the console straight into her forearm. Bone met steel. Steel won.

Her right arm crumpled under the pressure, still bent at the elbow but now trapped between the crushed console and the folding steering column. Her wrist snapped first, a sickening crunch that barely registered before the next blow came. The pressure mounted, her forearm caught in a tightening vice of metal, plastic, and brute force. The steering column shifted another inch, and then...

A deep, wet crack.

Then another.

The radius and ulna snapped together, their structural integrity shattered by the sheer crushing weight. The pain didn't come right away—her nerves were too overwhelmed, her system too flooded with adrenaline. But when the pressure finally released, the fire came.

A searing, white-hot agony exploded through her arm, a pain so immediate, so suffocating in its intensity that it consumed her entire body. She tried to move, but the limb was foreign now, no longer connected in any functional way. A grotesque, unnatural bend formed just below her elbow, a new joint where none should exist.

The momentum from the impact rolled the car once. Twice. A brutal, chaotic freefall. The third revolution slammed it roof-first into a ditch, crushing what remained of the windshield. Amy dangled from her seatbelt, barely conscious, bleeding, broken.

The kid who hit her?

He was already standing outside, unharmed.

Recovery from an accident like that was necessarily awful. But somehow, Amy had been the cheery one through it all. That goddamn kid had simply walked out of his car with nothing but a few glass cuts from his windshield. Travis had carried his anger like a festering wound. Amy moved on, and, eventually, after months of titanium rods being screwed into bone, skin grafts that burned like fire, and physical therapy sessions that left her trembling and drenched in sweat, she made a more or less complete recovery, at least on the outside.

But the OxyContin had grown roots.

Travis forced himself to stand, to keep from collapsing into himself. He poured another beer into a fresh frosty glass from the freezer, shook his head at the Sergeant's disloyalty, and plopped back onto the couch, pretending to watch TV again.

The Oxy had grown roots, and now here he was, a clueless single dad of a teenage girl with no idea what the fuck he was doing.

This church thing—that was all Amy. It had been part of her bonding with Madison, a sweet little ritual that Travis never quite replicated. Every Sunday, Amy and Madison would carefully coordinate their outfits, blue dresses with orange belts one week, yellow dresses with purple shoes the next. It was their thing.

After service, they'd head to the neighborhood diner for lunch, where Amy always made a point to chat with Lauren, the proprietor and an old childhood friend. It wasn't just about church; it was about creating moments, building something solid and safe for Madison.

Her involvement in the youth ministry had undeniably made an improvement, but Travis wasn't sure what to make of Eli Lawson.

Something about him just felt *off*. Maybe it was the inevitable awkwardness of being the son of someone important, trying to find his footing under the weight of expectations tied to a famous last name.

Travis rolled the beer glass between his palms, trying to make sense of the nagging feeling in his gut whenever he thought of Eli Lawson. Every time he met the young pastor, Eli had been nothing but polite, enthusiastic even, his smile wide and his handshake firm. Yet something in the way Eli's gaze lingered a beat too long on Madison, or how his voice softened specifically when addressing her, left Travis with an inexplicable discomfort.

Still, Travis couldn't deny that Madison had latched onto Pastor Eli. She seemed to be fitting in, by her standards anyway, and Travis couldn't ignore the slight relief that brought.

"He's not like a lot of the teachers at school," she had told him. "They're supposed to be in charge, but don't fix things. Pastor Eli's different, and I like having him in charge."

Travis had asked casually, almost offhandedly, but it was a covert attempt to calibrate his own opinion of Eli. Sure, Travis appreciated the attention Madison was getting. She thrived on structure and direction, but it still felt… odd. And he was still Madison's Papa Bear.

"Does he have any other teenagers help him with his work?" Travis asked one night.

"Yeah. Adam preps a lot of the games. But I do the most," she said, in a matter-of-fact voice that registered no indication of anything interesting down that line of inquiry. "Pastor Eli lets me organize his notes by color and theme. He says my brain sees connections others miss. Last week, I corrected his Bible verse citations. He thanked me in front of everyone and said my memory was a gift." Her expression softened with an unusual hint of pride.

He felt conflicted about letting Madison go to the upcoming Youth Conclave in Austin. It was a big step, spending so much time away from home, and she rarely handled large crowds well. He worried about her getting in over her head and melting down in public, and was still working out exactly where he'd be. It would be nice to stay in Dallas and make up some ground on work with a free schedule, but he didn't think that young Eli was mature enough to handle a meltdown.

For that matter, he thought ruefully as he hovered his nose over his beer and sucked in its aroma, he hadn't exactly shone in that department either.

Maybe it was best if he stayed nearby. Harlan was one of his old high school buddies and had moved to Round Rock; maybe he could pay a visit. Maybe it was best if he stayed in Dallas and let Madison work through it herself.

Maybe he needed to learn how to let his daughter grow up.

Fuck, he thought, putting his nose in his beer and inhaling deeply, before taking a long sip and looking up at the TV to help turn his brain off.

A TRIP DOWN MOMORY LANE

Nancy's speech came back slowly after the craniotomy, accented by the childhood stutter that Richard only now learned had haunted her past. The stutter gave audible shape to the struggle it took her to locate each word, a struggle made visible in her clenched jaw and furrowed brow, so he aimed for patience and kindness in his interactions with her.

They all could see how hard it was for her to summon and release her thoughts into words, so they adapted, speaking to her with slow, measured tones and simple, monosyllabic phrases. Conversations became less about content and more about offering her the space and support to practice, like a toddler learning to navigate language for the first time. The effort drained her. They reorganized their routines to allow Nancy ample time to sleep off the exhaustion that followed even the smallest interactions. In this, too, she was toddler-like.

Richard worked out an agreement with the university to allow for some work-from-home flexibility, and he built an accessibility ramp for the front door. Maya did what she could to adjust her schedule to provide coverage when he was away, and she paid for a caregiver to cover the gaps. She fired the first one, a frumpy fifty-something widow with her hair tied in a bun. Her mom said the way the caretaker always pushed her made her tired.

"Tired means fired," Maya muttered, and Richard stared at her kindly, somehow sensing how her inner voice had adopted the tone of the children's books she'd been reading, how she resented her own tone with its patronizing imitation, resented her own resentment given everything her mom had done for her, and continued her confused internal battles until she broke down in tears.

"Cried means tried," Richard said softly, and she tried again until she found Charlayne, a Black grandmother who was the kindest, most patient cheerleader imaginable when talking to her mom, but who could stare down a grizzly bear when needed, a skill she often employed to navigate busy healthcare workers who labored under the delusion they had the luxury of being distracted.

Maya took over Hannah's old room. Richard assumed she was still paying for her apartment, but he didn't ask any questions when more and more of her clothes filled Hannah's closet. He found an unexpected peace in having her and Nancy around, despite the struggle of the recovery.

When the weather allowed, he'd wheel Nancy out back, start a fire during the Texas chill (which he defined as anything under 90 degrees), and talk to her about old memories. He seemed comfortable enjoying long bouts of silence, just as he seemed comfortable doing all the talking. He seemed to know she needed the connection, and after the struggle of finding and exercising the recently scrambled synaptic connections, he knew she needed the comfort of rest with no pressure. So he would talk slowly to her about Harry and Hannah and Maya and Adam Lewis, laugh about faux pas of yesteryear, celebrate past achievements, and then he'd be silent, giving her time to bathe in these revisited memories, letting her struggle to find those neural trails that had become overgrown by the jungle vines of trauma.

Maya seemed to lack the same comfort, the same patience with her mom. One morning, Richard paused in the doorway, watching as Maya sat behind Nancy on the bed, methodically drawing the brush through her mother's thinning hair. The scene struck him as both tender and strangely detached. Maya's movements were precise, almost ritualistic, her expression focused yet distant, as if performing a necessary task rather than sharing a moment of intimacy. Nancy's eyes were closed, her face relaxed in a way it rarely was these days, seemingly savoring this rare physical connection.

When Nancy's trembling hand reached back to touch Maya's, he saw it, that nearly imperceptible flinch, the slight stiffening of Maya's shoulders before she shifted her position, putting those few extra inches of space between them. Her hands never stopped their work, but her gaze drifted to the window, as if seeking escape while her body remained dutiful. It was the same look he'd seen countless times during their marriage—Maya physically present yet emotionally halfway out the door, already running from the closeness that threatened to tether her.

When Maya joined him and Nancy on the back patio, he dubbed the gatherings *momversations*, a twinkle in his eye as they would laugh about old embarrassments. Charlayne would join them when she was there, and Charles Ruddick and Julia both stopped by from time to time. The momversations and visitors gave him a sense of domestic peace he hadn't felt since Hannah moved out.

He would celebrate those signs of progress that lay hidden for so long beneath the surface, only to burst forth and brighten the room with their positive energy. Like the day Nancy put the puzzle of the US states together by herself. Or the day she read an old copy of *Danny and the Dinosaur* out loud, a book saved over from his own childhood he used to read to Hannah. Nancy stumbled over the word *hour*, so when the dinosaur said, "It's good to take a ho-ho-ho-ho-*whore* or two off… after a hundred million years," they laughed until they were all crying.

Nancy's stories returned even more slowly than her voice, burdened with a kind of psychic stutter that fractured them into jagged glimpses, like flipping through a strobe-lit flipbook with several pages missing. Richard called this *taking a trip down momory lane* and celebrated each trip in its imperfection. Hannah rolled her eyes and told him he was just the worst at Bad Dad Puns, but she smiled easily the night she joined them on the back patio for one such trip.

Charlayne was there, mindlessly darning a pair of socks. Julia brought cookies, and Charles Ruddick brought an ascot and the charm of someone of Nancy's generation, armed with his proper English accent.

"You ka-ka-ka…." Nancy blinked in annoyance and gritted her teeth before trying again. "You ka-ka-ka-cried when I cut your hair!"

Hannah laughed out loud. "Oh my God, I remember that!"

Maya smiled. "That was when your dad and I went to a wedding for one of Richard's old friends and left you with Grandma," she said.

"Hard to imagine the formidable Hannah Russell ever crying over anything so trivial as hair," Charles said, in that way he had of speaking that made you think you were talking to Batman's butler.

Richard added some context for the visitors. "Hannah was, I don't know, eight or nine, and determined to grow her hair down to her knees. We didn't necessarily do Nancy any favors, leaving her to take care of Hannah during the summer. She was like a fish back then, spending all her time in the water, and her tangles were the stuff of legend."

"God, I was a bitch to that poor hair stylist," Hannah said a little sheepishly.

"She was a ba-ba-bitch back!" Nancy said, and everyone laughed.

For the next half hour, as the Texas breeze wrapped them in its warm embrace, they relived the experience of eight-year-old Hannah's act of rebelling against authority and the struggle of separating her from her split ends. Richard and Charlayne always had the keenest awareness of when Nancy had had her fill, and it was Charlayne that night who graciously wheeled Nancy in to get her ready for bed.

When one trip down momory lane led to Maya's graduation from medical school and the mother-daughter trip to Italy that followed, Maya felt inspired to recreate the experience. She spent an entire afternoon making homemade linguini, a glass of wine close at hand as she dusted herself and the kitchen in flour.

"Remember that cute couple outside Florence who gave us a pasta-making lesson?" Maya asked, the wine warming her voice.

"They were ga-ga-gay!" Nancy said with a triumphant nod.

"Right!" Maya grinned. "Retired from the fashion industry. Remember the one who was super into Madonna? And wanted a cow?"

"But the other didn't want to sm-sm-smell a cow!" Nancy said, connecting the dots.

Maya recounted the elegant simplicity of Italian food as she opened the egg into the volcano-like structure of flour she had built on the counter. "Just simple ingredients: pasta, pecorino cheese, black pepper," she said, as her cheeks adopted the color of the wine. "It's the attention to detail that bridges the gap from simple to extraordinary. It's not just pecorino cheese; it's aged pecorino Romano cheese, stamped with the PDO certification," she adopted a singsong Italian accent, "to ensure that every step-ah from breeding to production takes place in Lazio of Sardinia, maturing five to six-ah months, through a tradition dating back to the Romans."

Her mom smiled her half-smile as Maya wiped flour on her apron and drool off her mom's lips.

"And the pasta, too, right, Mom?" she continued, abandoning the accent. "Perfect pasta means a perfect egg. Charles Ruddick was kind enough to give Richard these eggs from his own chicken coop. Powder-fine doppio zero flour. That's what gives this nice stretchy behavior to the gluten." She pressed down again on her ball of dough, pushed the flattened part back over the top, rotated the ball a quarter of a turn, took a sip of wine, and continued kneading.

"What does that do?" Richard asked after she covered the dough in plastic wrap.

"Resting it. That's the magic that gives the pasta its bite," she said, her dark eyes radiating in that unique way of hers. "It lets the gluten bonds relax, so the egg-ah and the flour can form a more perfect union." She kissed him on the cheek.

He was there to console her when the *cacio e pepe* was ready, well after her mom had run out of steam and gone to sleep. He tried to repay the effort embedded in each strand of linguini with his company, knowing how poor a substitute he was for what Maya needed.

"What was that award your dad won?" Richard prompted one evening over the crackle of an entirely unnecessary fire on the patio. Maya, Charlayne, and Nancy sat a little farther back, giving the flames some space.

"It was a humanitarian award, remember, Mom?" Maya said, leaning forward slightly as if the words might nudge Nancy's memory. "The Kuwait constitution talks about justice, freedom, and equality."

Nancy's eyes lit up as she found a path to her ex-husband. "Ka-ka-ka…" She blinked in annoyance. "Ka-ka-compassion!"

"Yes, that's right!" Maya encouraged, smiling at her. "'Coopera-tion and compassion are the bonds between citizens.'"

"He was so proud," Nancy said. She smiled sleepily as she

wrapped herself in the memory, lacking the details through its foggy haze but not its emotional texture.

"Y'all have such a fascinating background," Charlayne said.

Richard noticed the pattern of deep contentment Nancy displayed with memories involving her ex-husband, so he aimed to introduce Harry into momversations from time to time. Maya's details were often enough to trigger some flicker of recognition— the award ceremony in Kuwait City, for instance, or the time Harry and Adam Lewis got so drunk in Ottawa that they ended up pissing in the bushes behind the bar. Nancy had to escort them both to the car, but only one at a time; they struggled to walk with their pants trapped around their ankles.

Charlayne called him the day Nancy broke her hip coming out of PT. He met her and Maya at the hospital and noted the deep bags under Maya's eyes. They had to once again adjust routines and expectations, with the pain medication slowing progress on the momversations. The stress and exhaustion became permanent fixtures on Maya's face. When she curled up her fists to her chest and trembled, he'd wrap his arms around her and hold her head to his chest, calming her with his heartbeat. He didn't try to fix anything. He just held her.

"Don't expect gratitude, Richard," Julia had told him one evening. "Maya's not wired for it, not when she's this vulnerable. She'd rather eat glass than admit she needs someone. Your reward will be those rare moments when she forgets to keep her walls up."

He was half asleep one summer night when Maya opened his bedroom door, silhouetted against the light of Hannah's room down the hall. She wore a silky robe and stood there for a long moment, as if gathering her courage. At last, she stepped inside and untied the robe, letting it fall to the floor. He opened the sheets to invite her to once again share his warmth and his heartbeat.

As Nancy recovered and Maya struggled with the stress and

workload, she would enter his room from time to time at night. She never spoke about it, and he never inquired or tried to initiate.

"You know you get to write your own story," he said one night as they lay in bed together. "All it takes for me to be part of it is for you to want it so." She said nothing in response and was out of the bed long before he woke in the morning.

As they weaned Nancy off the pain medications, the momories came back like a slow drip from a leaky faucet. Fragmented thoughts, disconnected and unpredictable, trickled back like drips from a broken spigot. Each drip seemed to take its time building pressure before falling, isolated and incomplete.

"I walked in on you with that ba-ba-boy," Nancy said one night on the back patio, struggling to remember the boy's name. Maya and Richard sat separately on the two chairs, the firelight reflecting off their faces.

"Ryan Tinsbury," Maya said, a soft, nostalgic smile coming to her lips.

"Ryan," Nancy said, slurring the name as she struggled to wrap her tongue around the phonemes. "Why?"

"You mean, why was I a horny teenager?" Maya asked, her smile widening.

"No," Nancy said, frowning in concentration. "Why… you didn't like him?"

"When did that ever stop me?" Maya quipped, causing both her and Richard to laugh. Nancy looked curious and confused.

"God, he was so scared when you walked in," Maya said, an impish gleam in her eyes. "That's the only time I've ever seen an erection disappear so fast that the condom fell right off."

"You weren't ska-ska-ska-ska-scared," Nancy said, gritting her teeth to get the word out. "You were mad."

Maya chuckled again, but this time it was softer, tinged with something unspoken. "And you were horrified," she said.

"Why were you mad?" Nancy asked.

A shadow fell over Maya's face. She still smiled, but the smile lost its natural support structure and adopted an artificial look. Her eyes looked heavy instead of light and radiating. "It was a long time ago," she said after an extended pause.

"So now you can, can tell me?" Nancy said, her fragmented memory grasping at clarity.

Richard looked over at his ex-wife and saw her inhale deeply through her nose, like she was gathering her response carefully.

"It was the Gulf War. You and Dad tried to talk to me about it, but I was going through some pretty complicated feelings."

Nancy paused, confused, unable to connect the drips into something that made sense. "Harry was… it was important to him." She cocked her head and looked at Maya.

Maya nodded slightly but kept her eyes on the fire, saying nothing.

"His ka-ka-career. It was important to his career."

This was a new story to Richard. He took the old joke about turtles all the way down and applied it to Maya: she was onion all the way down, but if you cut too deeply, you'd end up in tears. He felt uneasy with this trip down momory lane, worried that Nancy and her fragmented memories were close to just such a cut.

"Dad was gone all the time. I guess I was mad at him. Like I said, stupid teenager," Maya said. Richard sensed she was trying to close off the conversation.

Nancy nodded, trying to fold this new page in her flipbook so everything would somehow make sense. "Were you mad at me?"

"I don't remember, Mom." Maya sighed. "That was a long time ago."

Richard weighed his options and decided to engage. He did so with trepidation, not sure it was a wise decision, but his curiosity got the better of him. "That must have been hard on you," he said.

Maya nodded her head but didn't elaborate.

"Why was it hard?" Nancy asked.

When Maya looked up at her, she had that familiar sharp edge in her eyes, her gaze narrowing to something predatory and glinting like a blade drawn in self-defense. The soft curves of her face seemed to harden into angles, her lips pressed into a thin bloodless line while her nostrils flared with barely contained hostility. It was the look that had made journalists retreat, had silenced ex-lovers, had warned Richard countless times she was about to strike. It wasn't anger, but the cold, calculated readiness of someone who had long ago mastered the art of attack as preemptive protection.

"Nancy, what do you say we turn in for the night?" Richard said, standing and walking over to her. She looked confused as she turned to him.

"She's still mad. I don't ga-ga-get it," she said, staring at Richard.

"It's not hard," Maya said coldly. "I was a teenager. Teenagers get mad." Her tone was flat, emotionless.

Richard grabbed the wheelchair's handles and gave them a gentle squeeze. "All right, let's get you ready for bed," he said, his tone light and warm. As he wheeled Nancy toward the house, she kept her head turned, her gaze fixed on Maya, who remained seated by the fire, the flickering light casting long sharp shadows across her face.

The deep cut of the onion came a few weeks later, with Charlayne perched on the loveseat, her knitting needles clacking softly.

"The most pow-pow-powerful thing in the world…" Nancy said, her words halting, her voice laced with sadness. Maya's face went hard, and Richard's turned to stone. "… is a story."

"What's that, honey?" Charlayne asked, still focused on her knitting, oblivious to the shift in the patio's atmosphere.

"Fatima al-Rahbani wrote that," Nancy said, her gaze locking onto her daughter.

"My mom," Maya said, returning Charlayne's cheery-but-confused look with steel and ice.

Charlayne's knitting slowed. She looked at Nancy, then at Maya, trying to piece together a puzzle she didn't know she was solving.

"She wrote a book." Nancy said, her eyes welling with tears. "The most pow-powerful thing in the world is a story."

Charlayne shifted uncomfortably on the couch, her gaze darting between the two women. Richard looked mournfully between them.

He had read and watched everything he could to learn about the enigmatic depths of his ex-wife, but it had always been a forbidden topic with Maya.

Iraq's literary culture fascinated him. Most of it was propaganda, trying to write history as it was being created during the war with Iran. They were attempts to imbue a sense of nationalist pride, a unifying culture to hold back the Persian demons to the east, and the US loved Saddam for it. And later, when Saddam himself wrote the novels as the wars shifted to the West, they depicted the US as raping the ancient purity of Mesopotamia.

But beneath the layers of state-sponsored narratives, there was resistance, an undercurrent of dissent, led by a sayyida descendant of a renowned clerical family. Fatima al-Rahbani developed a formidable reputation as a Shia educator and novelist, urging women to hold on to their faith and culture amid liberalization campaigns designed to curry favor with the West. Saddam favored the Sunni minority and touted women's education and inclusion in the workforce as a weapon to engender Western sympathies. Fatima served as a figurehead for a significant resistance.

There was no evidence that either Fatima or Maya's dad had any role in the attempted assassination that led to the Dujail massacre, but blaming her for the attempt served as a convenient opportunity to remove her influence. Saddam had personally killed her as well as Maya's dad and brother and would have killed Maya if he'd found her.

"Look her up," Maya said, her voice sharp as glass. "Fatima al-Rahbani."

"Wha…?" Charlayne asked, feeling off balance.

Richard looked at Maya, clearly struggling with what to say. Maya stared directly into her mom's eyes, her own eyes narrowing dangerously. Charlayne, aware by this point that she was in over her head, remained silent and still.

After a prolonged silence, Nancy tried to speak again. "She would be… proud."

Maya glared at her mom. "Proud? You think she'd be proud of me?" There was a sharp edge to her words.

"And Harry would be proud."

"I'm glad all my dead parents would be proud."

"You're ma-ma-ma-ma-mad," Nancy said, her stutter emphasizing her fragility.

Richard evaluated his options. He knew trying to wheel Nancy away at this point would end poorly. Charlayne looked equally paralyzed.

"Aren't you proud of them?" Nancy asked, slurring her words.

"Proud?" Maya's voice rose, her eyes burning. "Do you think I look or act anything like an al-Rahbani or a Bennett?"

"I think you be-became a doctor because of her. To help women, like she did. You are straw-straw-strong like them."

"And look what their strength did for them!" Maya's voice snapped like a whip. "The strength to hide behind a veil? The strength to bomb his daughter's people? Is that what I should be proud of?"

"Ba-ba-ba-but Harry. Harry saved you."

"Really? How is he different than Saddam? Saddam killed my family. Dad bombed my people."

"He did everything for you!"

"And you put him on a fucking pedestal."

"You ka-ka-ka…"

"Idolized the man who won a fucking award for compassion while he supported Saddam as he murdered my family—"

"…ka-ka-ka…"

"—and then attacked my people after he changed his mind!"

"…cunt."

"All right, that's enough," Charlayne said, giving Maya her grizzly bear stare. "It's time for bed." She didn't wait for permission to wheel Nancy inside.

When Richard woke after a restless sleep, he heard the silence louder than a scream could ever be, the silence more like a black hole that sucked in the sound around it. All that was left was the hurt and the shame and, for her mom, nothing was left, courtesy of a second aneurysm that happened during the night. He saw her there, her arms wrapped over her mom, her head on her mom's chest, her body heaving. He thought he saw, for the first time since he'd known her, a glimpse of that seven-year-old girl whose story so many people had tried to uncover—lost, scared, confused, uprooted, and alone, unsure of who she was or what to do next.

He stood there by the bed in the guest bedroom, staring down at the lifeless form underneath his ex-wife. The stroke had distorted Nancy's face into something half grotesque and half at peace.

He forced himself to take steady breaths through his nose, letting the adrenaline take its ninety-second shock-and-awe tour through his body, waiting for it to pass so he could steady his pulse. He held his lips together and consciously tried to relax his cheeks and his jawline, feeling his feet planted firmly on the floor. He stood up straighter as he exhaled slowly, measuring his breath, calming himself in the presence of Maya's grief. As she cried and her body trembled, he held his body still, his breath steady. It was only when she stood up, an eternity later, that he wrapped his arms around her and held her head to his chest, giving her the slow, steady rhythm of his own heartbeat to calm the chaos of hers.

IN HELL

The shrill siren of the ambulance cut into her consciousness like sonic waves with their sharp, curved blades that scraped against her skull, oscillating from high-pitched wails to low-pitched moans back to high again, waves of sound that merged dissonantly into the flashing blue and red radiating through the back window.

"Synesthesia," she muttered, her voice a fragile rasp. The harsh, clinical smell of the antiseptics bit her, stung her, and made her eyes water. The ambulance accelerated suddenly, jerking violently to the left.

"Is that your name?" the paramedic asked.

"Madison," Pastor Eli answered, his voice tight, his knuckles white as they gripped the side of the gurney.

The rubber gloves and tubing emitted a caustic, sterile odor. Traces of exhaust seeped through the back door and joined with human sweat to form a noxious fog. The metallic taste of nearby oxygen tanks merged with the bile rising in her throat. Radio static transformed into a series of beeps announcing the muffled voices of medical dispatchers. They spoke in unintelligible codes. The medical equipment around her creaked and rattled. She struggled to breathe and felt wrapped in a cold blanket of fear.

She turned to look at Pastor Eli. "Baptize me," she pleaded. He looked scared. "Baptize me," she repeated, tears streaming down her cheeks.

She felt like she needed to throw up as the ambulance shifted lanes again, collapsing her stomach into the honk of the horn before the siren waves of sound ended unexpectedly, such that only their ghostly shadows swam through her pain. The ambulance took another violent turn, slowed, turned some more, and stopped. The back doors burst open in streams of blue and red and the sound of raindrops splattering on the tin covering. As they lifted the stretcher and moved her, she fainted.

Bright, flickering fluorescent lights assaulted her when she opened her eyes, so she closed them back hard, but the light was too bright and pierced through the thin armor of her eyelids. The wheels ground violently against the vinyl floor. One had a slight wobble that sounded like that shopping cart at the grocery store, and she felt the conflict between the structural wobble and the straight-line effort of the men rolling her bed.

"What's your name?" a woman's voice asked, following her movement.

"Madison," she said, the effort causing her to faint again.

There were four white coats fussing over her when she awoke. She felt them undressing her and the background hum of someone talking to Pastor Eli outside. The telephone rang and took four rings before the nurse answered, his voice tired and bored, a low mutter that swam underneath the blinks and beeps, like radioactive crickets in distress.

"Madison, my name is Dr. Murphy. Can you tell me where the pain is?" a man's voice asked. Other white coats pushed her onto her side and put a bedpan under her. Someone stabbed her in the arm, and she screamed. Sweat drenched her hair, matting it against the uncomfortable pillow. The man held out a hand to the other white coats. "I'm sorry, Madison. We have to draw some blood to help you." A jolt of pain coursed through her right shoulder, and she screamed again. "Madison, can you tell me what happened?"

"Hurts so bad," she said.

"Where does it hurt, Madison?" Dr. Murphy asked.

"My butt. My belly. Right here," she tapped the tip of her right shoulder with her left hand. "Ow!" she screamed as Dr. Murphy pushed down on her right lower abdomen.

Dr. Murphy looked at one of the nurses. "OB/GYN," he said. The nurse scurried out.

The machines whirred and beeped, blanketing the sound of an old man in the room next to hers having a coughing fit. One of the white coats taped down a tube that seemed to run into her vein. She followed its length to see the IV drip it attached to. Tears welled. She rocked her head and tried to clap her hands to her ears but only managed to cover the left one.

"She said she thought it was period cramps," she heard Pastor Eli say outside her curtains.

"It hurts it hurts it hurts it hurts!" she screamed, desperately wanting to stop the noise and the smells and the light and the unbearable pain. She tried to tune out the hustle of people outside and the low mutter of voices talking about her with words she couldn't comprehend.

"Madison, I'm Dr. Maya Russell. I'm here to help you."

She opened her eyes to see a woman in a white coat, with long black hair and coal-dark eyes that seemed to radiate light despite their darkness.

"Are you okay if I take the tampon out?" Dr. Russell said.

She nodded her head and felt the dizziness and the sweat and the awful cumin-like smell of her armpits. And something else, nauseating in its olfactory assault. Infection, perhaps. She felt like she needed to poop so badly.

"Madison, is it possible you're pregnant?"

"I took the pills."

Dr. Maya Russell looked up to stare at her, her lips forming into a thin straight line. Her face, despite its serious look, was the only sign of comfort around her. The pain was worse than anything she'd ever experienced before. She felt like she was swimming in a toxic sea of bright lights and machine beeps and hurried conversation and coughs and telephone rings and more beeps and iodine and cumin. She felt the acid in her throat and waited to see if she would vomit. Dr. Russell was the only person who seemed to see *her*, her pain, her need.

"Madison, I need to do what's called an ultrasound, where we insert a probe into your vagina to see if we can identify what's causing your pain. You may feel cold and wet."

Madison rolled her head to one side and threw up. The chunks sublimated in the open air and their olfactory form swam into her consciousness as the liquid of her sweat and vomit merged into a pool around strands of her hair.

"We got in touch with the dad," a nurse with a gravelly voice said. "He was in Round Rock. He's on his way."

She heard the whirl of the lights above her, almost like they were screaming the light out, yelling to make it brighter, whiter, making her feel like she was constantly under siege. The pain felt like it was in the cavity of her butt, like it would tear her in two. She felt the hum of the air conditioning blow over the sheets, causing them to merge to the sweat of her body, and she fainted again.

She woke to the low *thwoop thwoop thwoop* of a heartbeat echoed through a machine. She turned her head away from the vomit and saw a TV screen showing shades of gray.

"There's a lot of fluid," one of the other white coats said, staring at the screen.

"Beta HCG thirteen oh ninety-nine," someone said through the door.

"Is that the fetus?" Dr. Murphy asked.

"It's in the uterus," Dr. Russell said, looking confused. Madison was burning up. Everything was going black around her. The room spun.

"She's close to going into shock," someone said.

Beep beep beep the machines screamed.

"There!" Dr. Russell said. "At the tubal isthmus. *That's* ectopic. Get the dad on the phone."

"Calling," someone else said.

"Should we consult legal?" the gravelly voice asked, sounding nervous.

"We need to get her into surgery," Dr. Russell said, her gaze sweeping the room like a lighthouse beam, daring anyone to challenge her. "Get the dad on the phone, now!" Madison fainted again.

She woke in an icy heat that reminded her of the light shining out of Dr. Russell's dark eyes. The buzz of a machine cut into her aural canal like a chainsaw, piercing through the coughing fit next door and through the beeps. She tried to breathe through her mouth to block out the awful smells. When she caught herself hyperventilating, she tried to slow her breath down. Pastor Eli was there, looking scared. She looked up at him.

"Baptize the baby," she said, using every bit of strength she could muster to get the words out.

He looked paralyzed, helpless, wearing none of his past authority and confidence. "Baptize the baby!" she croaked. "Baptize the baby!" she screamed. "Baptize the baby!" she choked as the tears merged with the sweat and the vomit.

She saw a blur of red flannel enter her field of vision. Pastor Eli waved his hands in front of him and said something that sounded like "Waaaa!" before Papa Bear's fist collided with his cheek.

She heard the bone underneath crumple from the blow and watched as Pastor Eli's face sagged under the loss of structural support. She heard his scream of agony and the gravelly voice scream at Papa Bear as someone said, "Jesus!" and the phone kept ringing and ringing and the person in the room next to them kept coughing and coughing and Papa Bear screamed vulgarities at Pastor Eli.

"I'm here, baby girl," he said, turning to look at her. "Hang in there. I love you."

The room looked blurry, like she was staring at it through a camera lens that was smeared with oil around its border. She had a weird sensation that she'd been here before, like she was reliving a scene from her past.

"Mom," she said, trying to place where she was.

The butterflies seemed to launch all at once from the crags of pain overlooking the sea of her womb. She felt a tingle that traced their path up to the tip of her right shoulder, and an electrical buzz seemed to hang in the air above it like St. Elmo's Fire. It felt like someone was squeezing her tighter and tighter. People were talking—her dad, Dr. Russell, Pastor Eli, white coats—but their voices were underwater.

Her mom floated above her, her auburn hair flowing down her shoulders. She smiled down at her. *Shhh,* she said, putting her finger to her lips. *There's no need to say anything. I'll always be here for you.* It was the same thing she used to say to her during her meltdowns.

I love you, sweetheart.

I love you too, she tried to say, but couldn't, the link between thought and words broken. She was vaguely aware of the men tackling her dad in the background. The room increased in volume with shouts, but they were unintelligible, garbled.

I'm so scared, she tried to tell her mom.

Is this what your pain felt like? she tried to say, but no words came out.

She opened her eyes as streams of bright light blinded her. Both shoulders now ached. Her legs throbbed. Her arms felt stiff and strained, as if they'd been clenched for hours. Every muscle in her body felt impossibly tight, coiled like a spring that had been wound so much it almost felt bruised.

The muddied voices swelled around her. She was confused, the kind of confusion you get from abruptly waking up from a dream, or from not waking up and staying stuck in it. At the back of her head, she felt a bass drum, its reverberations echoing off the cavern of her skull. She looked through a fog at the white coats around her. There were blue uniforms there now, two of them surrounding her dad with his red flannel, his arms pinned behind his back. He was talking, but she couldn't hear him over the drumming in her brain.

She felt a *whoosh* like wind through a tunnel and stared at where her mom was.

Mom, she tried to say, and once again found herself unable to control her vocal cords.

"Noor awlogy," her mom said, but the word sounded slurred, the way her voice had sounded near the end, when the morphine had consumed her. "Post ictal sea sure," she heard her say, her mom's proximity allowing the words to penetrate her consciousness.

Her mom held her hand and stared down at her kindly. Madison couldn't look away from her coal-like eyes.

"Madison, I'm here," her mom said, but something wasn't right about her hair. "You'll be a little disoriented. Don't worry, I'm here for you."

Another white coat rushed in, and she heard the background whisper of hurried voices. A man came over and said a few unintelligible words before shining a flashlight into her eyes, blinding her. She closed them tightly, trying to hide from the light.

"Madison, Dr. Thomas is just making sure you're responsive. You've had a seizure. Do you know where you are?"

Madison nodded her head.

"Good. You're bleeding inside your uterus, Madison." Her voice was reassuringly calm despite its forceful urgency. "You had two fetuses, but one of them got stuck in your fallopian tube, and when it grew, it poked a hole in your tube. We need to operate to make you feel better, but we might not be able to save the other fetus. Do you understand?"

Can you baptize the babies? she tried to say, but the words turned into tears, causing the room to look like it had through the smeared camera lens earlier. The frustration of not being able to talk became unbearable, so she shook her head violently from side to side.

The lights swam around her as they wheeled her out of the room, away from her dad, from Pastor Eli, from the police officers. The wheels scraped the vinyl like nails on a chalkboard. They burst through double doors, blowing them open like an explosion, as the brightness of the room assaulted her. Another white coat mumbled at her. She tried to close her hands over her ears, but the pain was too intense, so she just screamed and rocked her head some more. Dr. Russell put her hand gently on her good shoulder.

"Madison, Dr. Stanley is going to give you something for the pain, okay?" She shook her head in fear, staring up at Dr. Russell's eyes, trying to plead with her.

They put an oxygen mask on her, its Darth Vader-like inhales and the clicks of the exhale sounding like an air leak in her head.

"We're going to do everything we can to take care of you and your baby," Dr. Maya Russell said, her voice gentle. She looked over at Dr. Stanley, who gave her the nod. "Can you count down from ten?"

She heard the background hum of unfamiliar voices. A machine let out two beeps in rapid succession, paused, then repeated. Another machine sounded almost like the busy signal from a phone. She thought she heard the hiss of gas.

And then her world turned to black.

Her vision blurred from pain as the CPS caseworker asked her questions. Madison couldn't remember the caseworker's name. She'd tried tuning her out, blending her voice into the background cacophony of beeping and chirping and ringing and shuffling and hustling and coughing. *She* couldn't cough or laugh or cry or sit up. It all hurt too much.

"Well, this is lovely. Who gave it to you?" the nameless and form-less apparition of a caseworker asked, her annoying persistence requiring Madison's attention. She was looking at the austere brown shelf along the window. There were no get-well cards, no balloons, no bouquets of flowers, no stuffed animals. The only decoration was a rice bowl, a shiny cerulean sheen that sparkled when the sun caught it. Two gold-filled cracks formed a curvy *X* on the side.

Madison didn't answer. Even if she could remember how to coerce thoughts into words, she had no desire to push those words through the bile coating her throat. In this hazy, dream-like world she'd woken into, where memories and pain-induced hallucinations blended into the present, she thought back to the memory—or the hallucination—of the bowl.

"It's called kintsugi," the doctor had said, after they wheeled her back into her room following the blood transfusion. "I've taken it up recently myself." She went quiet for some time, not trying to rush the conversation. She didn't scold Madison for not clicking her analgesic pump like the nurses did. She didn't lecture her on how important it was for her recovery. She didn't try to cheer Mad-ison up. She didn't ask for details about what happened. She didn't even try to get Madison to talk.

She just stared at the bowl silently. Underneath the brilliant radiance of those coal-black eyes, Madison felt somehow accepted in a way she couldn't put into words.

"It's a Japanese art form," the doctor said when she finally returned her gaze to Madison. "You can see where I broke the bowl here." She traced her index finger over the wavy lines of the X on the side. "I broke this one on purpose, because I wanted to learn, and kintsugi is about taking something broken and celebrating its repair as an act of beauty unto itself rather than something to be hidden."

Madison followed her fingers as she spoke. "You can see where I applied the lacquer to seal the cracks, and where I dusted it with gold. That's what kintsugi means: 'gold joinery.' It's different now from the bowl I bought, but despite my lack of skill, this new bowl has its own kind of beauty too. I'd like you to have it, if that's okay." She put it on the shelf to allow the sunlight to reflect off it.

The caseworker pointed at the wire for the analgesic pump that Madison had stuffed under her pillow to avoid the incessant prodding from medical staff to push the button and let the morphine flood her veins. Madison stared at her blankly and shook her head.

"You're sweating all over, dear. Dr. Russell said you won't take anything other than acetaminophen. Why won't you push the button?" Madison turned her head and could see the doctor outside. She and the caseworker had exchanged a few words before the caseworker entered her room.

The caseworker sighed. "Your dad's bail hearing is today," she said.

Madison turned to look at the TV, mute like her, and saw her own picture plastered on it. It was that stupid school photo where someone thought a sepia filter would do her colors justice. A reporter appeared to be talking about her, but she couldn't read the chyrons because her vision was too blurred.

"Madison, the police officer I spoke to said you wouldn't talk to him. I know this is incredibly hard for you, but I need to know if you feel safe around your dad."

Madison tried to shift in the bed because her butt was hurting. The saline drip and catheter seemed as awkward in their shifting as she felt. Her soaking sheets couldn't quench the fire that consumed her entire body.

The caseworker sighed again and looked at the TV. "Awful situation. I heard the Attorney General's getting involved." She turned back to look at Madison. "So listen. Assuming your dad can make bail, he'll be able to visit you tonight. Are you okay with that?"

Madison blinked and nodded slightly. That seemed to be enough.

The caseworker gave her a solemn look, invaded her hand with touch just like all the tubes and needles, stood up, and walked out.

Madison watched her leave after saying a few more words to the doctor, who stood outside with her back to Madison, her long black hair flowing over her white coat, standing next to a tall man in blue jeans and a short-sleeve shirt wearing a chocolate-colored fedora. Madison followed the doctor's gaze to a large TV hanging on the wall, which featured a picture of the doctor herself in the upper-right corner as two talking heads blabbered at each other.

She turned to her own TV screen and saw a reporter interviewing Governor Callahan. With trembling fingers, she reached for the remote and turned up the volume loud enough to hear over her pain.

"Look," Governor Callahan said. "My medical advisors tell me that there was a viable twin baby. We'll let the investigation play out, but our law is clear, and if we find that doctor provided an illegal abortion, the hospital can't shield her from personally facing the consequences."

"Does that involve prison time?" the reporter asked.

"Once again, our law is clear. It's a criminal offense for any doctor to perform an illegal abortion. Whether you like it or not, our nation was founded on Christian beliefs that hold the sanctity of every life inviolable, which puts abortion on the level of murder. When we signed the law, we knew there would always be difficult scenarios to work through that we couldn't think of up front, and that's why we'll have a vigorous investigation to learn if this doctor abided by the will of the people and the law of the land. If she did, then we can learn how to continue to improve the law. If she didn't, then of course we'll send her to prison."

She turned to look out of her room again. The doctor and the man in the fedora stood side-by-side, facing away from her. Slowly, the doctor held out her arm. Still watching the TV, the man reached out and took her by the hand.

ACT 2:
PLATEAU

A CACKLE OF HYENAS

As Richard navigated the labyrinthine halls of the maternity ward, he thought ruefully about the unreality of the situation, the hospital walls hiding Maya's torment, like a volcano's fury trapped in the sterilized façade of a denuded mountain. The threat of criminal prosecution rattled her, of course, but what really had her off-balance was the thirty seconds it took the media to discover her history, converting an already explosive story into a weapon of mass destruction. It reminded him vaguely of that Hieronymus Bosch painting, in which the bird-like demon sat on a high-backed chair devouring human souls, just to shit them out into the pit below—Maya's endless cycle of hell's torture.

The break room lay tucked in the far corner, separated from the bustle of patients by a nondescript door with a push bar. Zulima, the head nurse, gave him a knowing nod as he passed. Inside, a row of fluorescent lights hummed overhead, washing everything in a thin clinical glow. The décor was minimal, white walls interrupted only by a bulletin board plastered with colorful flyers for upcoming staff events and pinned-up memos about shift changes.

A few mismatched chairs circled around a square table that bore signs of heavy use, decorated with coffee rings, a few pen marks, and a half-finished jigsaw puzzle pushed to one side. Against one wall sat a small kitchenette with a humming refrigerator, a microwave sporting a missing knob, and a coffee maker hissing and gurgling as it dripped lukewarm coffee into a stained pot.

It was between shifts now, so the room was quiet, empty except for the stale scent of leftover takeout in the trash and the low buzz of the ventilation system. Maya sat alone at the table, both palms pressed tight around a paper cup of coffee that she wasn't actually drinking. He walked up to her, rested his hand on her shoulder for a moment, and sat next to her.

"How many?" she asked.

"A lot," he said. "And more coming."

She looked down at her coffee and frowned. "Scavengers. Fucking hyenas," she said.

"You're not dead," he reminded her.

"But they smell blood. You can hear their glee like hyenas laughing. What do you call a pack of hyenas?" She looked at him.

He looked thoughtful for a moment. "Don't know," he said. He pulled his phone out of his pocket and performed the necessary search. "A cackle."

She sniffed out a sardonic laugh. "Figures." He was unaccustomed to this level of bitterness from her. After a moment of silence, she continued. "And now everybody I work with feels obliged to wrap me in their sympathy. Fucking Andy and his fucking… *concern*."

She let go of the coffee cup, giving him an opportunity to rest his hand on top of hers. He gave her a determined look. "I'll be with you the whole time."

"What do I say?"

"Didn't Gordon give you advice?" Gordon was the hospital's general counsel.

"Yeah, no comment. But that's not what I meant."

"Oh," he said. He knew Nancy's stroke-fogged attempt at getting Maya to talk about her past was nothing compared to what lay ahead. *Maya protected those memories from others*, he thought, *to protect herself from those memories*; decades of layering scars upon scars had forged battle-hardened armor. "Say the same things you've always said when the hyenas start cackling. Tell them to go fuck themselves."

Maya gave a weak smile. "Don't think Gordon would approve of that line."

Richard nodded. "Maybe say nothing then."

She took a sip of her coffee and grimaced at the taste. It had gone cold. "It's different this time. I won't be able to simply hang up the phone or tell them to fuck off. It's not going to just blow over."

"No, it's not." He gave her a penetrating look. "Maya… I'll support you whatever you do, but I can only do that if you don't run away from me."

She put her head on his shoulder and held back a tear. They stayed that way for a couple of minutes. Someone opened the door to the break room. Richard and Maya didn't move and couldn't see the door behind them. Whoever it was must have seen who was inside and decided their snack could wait.

After some time, she lifted her head. "You ready?" he asked.

She gave him a tormented look back and nodded. They stood and walked out of the break room.

"*Te queremos mucho. ¡Dales con todo!*" Zulima said as they walked past the nurse station. "Give 'em hell, girl, we love you!"

Maya forced a wan smile, though it felt brittle, like glass on the verge of shattering. Her hand clung to Richard's, her grip tight enough to betray the fear and the anger simmering beneath her composed exterior. The familiar hum of the maternity ward—newborn cries, whispered lullabies, the muted voices of weary mothers—washed over her like a cruel irony.

The elevator ride to the ground floor felt like a descent into the underworld. The air felt stagnant, suffocating, as if the walls were closing in. She felt trapped. But when the doors slid open, the cafeteria's bustle pressed in on her like an unwelcome crowd. Conversations and laughter blurred into an indistinct roar that made her ears hum. Richard took the outside track, holding Maya's hand as she tried to shrink into the walls, but she could still hear the laughter transform into surprised intakes of air, conversation turn into gossiped whispers. The whispers seemed to chase her, unintelligible but menacing.

For the moment, she was the most famous person in the country. Everybody was looking at her.

As they stepped through the hospital doors, the crisp fall air hit her like a slap. The brilliant sunshine mocked her, its warmth a stark contrast to the chill spreading through her chest. The hospital's glass doors closed behind her with a soft *whoosh*, trapping her in the blinding light of this world waiting to devour her.

Through her blurred vision, the parking lot transformed into a grotesque orchard of media equipment, endless rows of vans and cameras planted in precise formation. The boom microphones reached toward her like skeletal branches, their shadows falling sharp and jagged across the pavement. She could hear the hyenas cackling between the metal trees, their laughter echoing off the hospital walls.

Richard's arm tightened protectively around her shoulder as the noise assaulted her and her legs went weak. Cameras clicked and voices barked from every direction like a biblical swarm of locusts. Richard guided her forward, his grip steady, his voice firm, but the chaos churned around them like a storm with no eye.

The attacks came jagged and piercing. *Dujail. Saddam. Fatima. Mayyada. al-Rahbani.* Each shouted name was a claw raking over her psyche, carrying an undertone of ambition to be the first to pierce through her famous armor, each flash of light a predator's tooth glinting in the sun. The voices overlapped and multiplied, becoming a deafening cacophony.

The world spun around her. She wanted to shout, to tell them to mind their own fucking business, to push them on their asses. She wanted to vanish, to outrun the questions that attacked her from every direction. But there were too many of them, and there was no way to escape their gnawing eyes and snapping jaws. Her legs felt heavy, as if the ground beneath her had turned sticky and treacherous.

She grew dizzy. The air grew hotter, clawing at her throat. Through the haze, she heard Richard's voice, calm but commanding, cutting through the din like a machete. He shouted something—she couldn't make out the words—but it created the faintest ripple in the crowd. The *beep* of his car sounded like salvation, and she clung to it.

Her vision blurred as Richard opened the passenger door and helped her inside. She collapsed in the seat, her body trembling, her fingers gripping the cool leather as if it might anchor her to sanity. A sharp, hollow sound against the glass made her flinch as someone tapped on the window. She felt the car shift as Richard climbed into the driver's seat.

Moments later, it was over.

THE HYPOCRITE

John Lawson looked around the outdoor dining area the country club had set up for them and chuckled to himself at what a thousand dollars bought: overly sweet iced tea and fried green tomatoes with a remoulade sauce. The filet mignon, no doubt, would be a worthy meal, but no one here was paying for the food.

He noticed the young Hispanic waiter refilling water glasses, probably no more than twenty, with tired eyes that avoided direct contact. The boy's hands trembled slightly as he reached across the table. Lawson remembered him from the church's ESL program last year; his name was Miguel, and he worked three jobs to support his mother and sisters after his father's deportation.

The pastor had written a character reference for the family's immigration case. Miguel caught his eye now and gave a slight nod of recognition, a flash of gratitude crossing his face before he moved to the next table. Lawson watched him go, aware of the contradiction, fighting for traditional values while quietly helping those the system overlooked.

The boy represented the messy reality of ministry, where the clear lines of rhetoric blurred against the complicated humanity of each soul. These were the moments that kept him humble, reminding him that God's justice and God's mercy somehow had to coexist.

He gave a silent thanks to God. Thirty years ago, he was a largely unknown preacher, but with an unflappable conviction to spread the Word. As he saw it, that meant saying what other preachers were afraid to say, saying what they were too politically correct to say, and so it was his fiery sermons on homosexual marriage during the '90s that first landed him on Fox News. These days, he was the head of a presidential candidate's evangelical advisory board and therefore, arguably, the most influential evangelical leader in the country. God had been good to him.

Wade Callahan wore his smile as neatly as the collar of his expensive white shirt, starched and held in place with magnetic stays above his power red tie. He surveyed his dinner companions—evangelical donors, friendly journalists, staff members.

"Thank you all for coming tonight and showing your support. I know there are a fair few places you could've gotten a cheaper dinner." The crowd let out an encouraging chuckle.

"Before we get to our meals, though, I thought I'd say a few words about what your money tonight supports. When I signed up to be governor of this great state of Texas, I promised to be a fighter, to fight against the leftist relativistic rot trying to infect this country. We're in a battle for the soul of this state and this country from those who would try to corrupt it with their immorality."

John Lawson sat at the table of honor, to the left of the currently vacated seat of the governor. This played to his vanity well, placing Caesar to the right hand of God. He not only knew what was coming; he had written much of the speech and coached the delivery.

"As you all know, I signed the toughest abortion restrictions in the country." The crowd gave the expected polite clap.

"As you *probably* know, my recent announcement of enforcing the law has upset a fair few in the medical community. People keep warning me I'm engaging in political suicide by enforcing the law I signed. Lots of people, in fact. I tell them all the same thing: that's okay." He gave a well-practiced impish smile. "It turns out there are a lot more Christians than gynecologists."

The crowd laughed, as expected.

"Still, it turns out that the gynecologist in question is somewhat famous, and that means this case is getting even more attention than it otherwise might. I'm thankful for that. Don't get me wrong, she's got one heck of a story, even just the little of it we know. I won't hold being Muslim against her, and I applaud her for making something of her life. But"—here he raised his voice to emphasize the point—"if anyone should understand the importance of protecting the lives of those who cannot protect themselves, it should be a child who survived Saddam Hussein's reign of terror!"

The crowd clapped enthusiastically, with a few "Hear, hear!"s thrown in.

"For fifty years, too many in the medical profession wielded the lazy and murderous policies of abortion to ignore their oath." He raised his eyebrow. "Did you know the Hippocratic Oath explicitly bans abortion?"

The crowd looked wide-eyed at the governor, anticipating the next delightful educational morsel about the hypocrisy of the secularists. It was an oratorical technique the pastor had mastered.

"It's true! It says—the Hippocratic Oath, that is—'I will not give a woman a pessary to cause an abortion.' A pessary was a device used in ancient times for gynecological purposes; nowadays it'd talk about pills. But it says nothing about broken bones or parasites or heart attacks, just abortions. The very foundation of our medical profession is built on the principle of 'Do no harm,' a principle that explicitly points out that includes harm to the unborn. So I say unto these doctors who fail to live up to their own oath: the law I signed protects against *exactly* this type of Hippocratic hypocrisy!"

Several members of the audience stood up to applaud. It was a good line, and the pastor was pleased to see it deliver the goods.

The governor looked thoughtful as the applause quieted, and the crowd sat back down to sip their tea. He gave them an extended silence.

"You know where that word comes from, *hypocrite*?" he restarted. "It's a Greek root—*hypokritēs*—which means to interpret from underneath. It referred to the actors of the ancient world. Now Joanne and I—" He pointed to his wife seated at the same table as Pastor Lawson. "—had the privilege of spending one anniversary in that part of the world a few years back. We got to see one of those Roman theaters in Ephesus, a 25,000-seat stadium. The acoustics are absolutely incredible.

"Think for a second what it would mean to be an actor back then in front of 25,000 people, before the days of microphones and cameras and big screens showing you what was happening on stage. What they'd do is hold up a big mask on a pole, say of a man smiling when they wanted to emote happiness or of a sad frown when they wanted to emote sadness. That's what it meant to 'interpret from underneath.' They wore masks to the outside world to pretend to be something they weren't. Hypocrites are mask wearers.

"As you know, Jesus had a few things to say about hypocrites. In his day, it was the scribes and the Pharisees. In our day, the hypocrites wear the white robes denoting the priesthood of medicine, wearing a mask of saving lives while willfully ignoring the lives of the unborn. As long as I'm governor of this state—or, with your blessings and generous contributions, president of this nation—I'll make sure that those white-robed hypocrites face the black-robed justices versed in the rule of law. And if that means sending the Girl from Dujail to a Texas jail, I say welcome to America, the land of laws."

The crowd applauded loudly. Moments later, it turned into a standing ovation.

Other advisors were uncomfortable with that last line, feeling it may have been a bit too aggressive for a polite audience. It was Pastor Lawson who had pushed for it, and he pushed aggressively. He knew the community well. They needed a fighter, he knew, not a second-rate politician who shied away from causing offense. He felt vindicated by the crowd's response.

The steaks took another twenty minutes, giving Wade Callahan plenty of time to showcase his conversational ease rubbing elbows with the movers and shakers in the evangelical community. He patted the pastor's back as he took his seat when the filets arrived.

"Well done, as always. Can't tell you how much I appreciate what you do."

"You keep fighting against liberal immorality, and I'll make sure the evangelical community keeps fighting for you." He genuinely liked the governor, but he always wanted to make sure Callahan knew the relative rankings of Caesar and God, and which side Lawson represented.

"How's your boy?" Callahan started, cutting into his filet with an expensive steak knife.

Pastor Lawson shrugged. "He'll need surgery. The doctor described it as kind of like that punch Michael Corleone took from the cop in *The Godfather*. And he's a bit traumatized by all the attention. It's a bit much for him."

"Arthritis bothering you?" the governor asked, eyeing the awkward way the pastor was cutting the filet.

God's sense of humor, as his late wife used to say, giving a fire-and-brimstone preacher hands that couldn't match his voice. She'd been his counterbalance for thirty-seven years, tempering his righteous anger with gentle mercy until cancer took her. The day after her funeral, a reporter had cornered him, asking how a loving God could allow such suffering.

He'd responded with rehearsed theological comfort, but privately, he'd raged at the Almighty in his empty bedroom that night. The doubt had nearly broken him. Yet he'd risen the next morning and preached anyway, carrying both his certainty and his questions to the pulpit. Faith wasn't the absence of doubt, he'd realized, but the courage to keep walking through it.

Lawson let out a sigh as he settled into the sawing motion. "Must have misplaced my pills, and it was more of a headache than I would've liked to get them refilled."

The governor nodded empathetically until he stilled himself to swallow. "What about the dad?" he asked.

Lawson gave another shrug. "You're prosecutin'; I'm suin'. I hope he burns in hell. Not just for what he did to my son, but for what he let happen with his daughter."

Callahan shook his head sadly. "As far as I'm concerned, Eli saved that little girl's life. He got her to the hospital, stood by her side the whole time. Damn shame. No good deed goes unpunished."

"I appreciate your support with the media on that front. It's not fair what happened to him, and he's having trouble dealing with the whisper campaigns."

"Anything else I can do to help?"

Pastor Lawson chewed his own bite of steak and contemplated the governor's question as he gave his aching joints a rest. He swallowed slowly and took a sip of his sweet tea.

"Keep talking like you did tonight. The entire evangelical community is behind you because they believe you're finally delivering what other politicians failed to deliver for fifty years. But know that they're also watching you because fifty years is a lot of time to learn some healthy skepticism. When the general election begins, you'll be tempted to appease the abortionists by adding nuance. Don't fall for Satan's trap."

The governor sat up at the directness and smiled at the pastor.

He deliberated for a moment, choosing his words carefully. "Pastor, you know I have to ask. Is there any chance that the dad had a reason to punch Eli?"

Pastor Lawson didn't hesitate in his response. He showed neither surprise nor annoyance at the question. "No. And even if there was, my response would be the same."

THE DREAM OF THE SACRIFICIAL GANGBANG-VIRGIN

She listens to the opening saxophone, knowing he wants her to hear the lazy effort of him pushing air through the bamboo and the brass, wants her to feel the rawness of the instrument, its primal nature. He blows out, letting her hear the contrail of sound that follows a natural sax note, letting her feel it raise the hairs on her skin and tickle her. As he shifts to the more polished melodic horn she is used to, it feels as if he is showing her, on the one hand, how those clear notes are practiced and perfected, how the timing of the finger movements, the pressure, the embouchure of the lips, the amount of air blown through them are perfectly calibrated to produce the clarity she is used to, the simplicity of boundaries between notes of the same volume and pressure, of square instead of sine waves, of the pursuit of perfection.

But then he blows those raw notes again, and she realizes he is also telling her that those perfect notes are not natural, and as beautiful as they are, they can never reach her this deeply, they cannot make her feel the animalism of these slow notes, where she can hear the air differentials as he blows slowly, the smaller volume of air at first, the middle of the wave (the only part we usually hear) sustained for a moment or two, then the wave cresting back downward as the air once again thins. She hears all of it. She feels all of it. It crawls over her and arouses her. She feels her skin tingle as the note's texture reaches inside of her. She finds herself hungering for those raw, naked, unpracticed, unhurried notes. Every time he blows a bass note out, it's like bellows to the fire growing inside her as his breath lazily kisses her, tastes her.

It turns her on at that place of deepest desire, the one buried so deep that shame fuels arousal to boiling hot. The bass lifts her, holds her; she wears its fuzziness like a blanket. She feels it more than hears it, feels it in the small of her back, feels her stomach move to its beat, feels herself breathing into it. He lets her know that no matter how sophisticated she becomes, this, too, is part of her—this animal hunger.

She wraps her lips around his, one hand running through his island beard, the other scraping over his scalp. She breathes in the scents of his labor, the steak with its peppercorn, the smoke absorbed into his skin and his beard, the sweetness of the cake with its liquor aftertaste. With the music guiding their movements, she dances her tongue over his, the rhythm the only intermediary to this primal union where thought disappears into the abyss of raw desire. She tastes his art in the kiss, his palette of spice and smoke, his timing and combining and creating.

"Eating your meals is like you making love to me," she tells him through their kiss. She tells him how each bite warms her up slowly, with a slight flushing of the nipples when its heat first signals its presence through her nose, the flush moving to her skin as it absorbs the spice. Of how it explores her tongue tastebud by tastebud and leaves her lips tingling and her tongue buzzing. Of how she wants him in her mouth so he can enjoy the feeling of electricity he has put inside of her. Of how it pleases her until satiety wraps its arms around her like a blanket in the sleepy and contented aftermath.

"Making a meal is like making a song," he kisses her back. It has a

key and therefore a root note, but the other notes give it texture. The way you play them gives them character. Sometimes you play it safe with fourths and fifths—salt and pepper. You make it bright and happy with a major third, like the squeeze of citrus. You make it melancholy with a minor third—the whisper of smoke that evokes the memory of something burnt and charred. With a seventh, you add tension, temporarily unbalancing the listener with the intense bite of a raw onion. You break the rules with a sharp fifth, adding cayenne to something sweet. You work at a fast tempo to show off your virtuoso technique with a knife and vegetables. You add anticipation and sensuality with a slow tempo, like a demi-glace that simmers all day.

But you never play it the same way, never play at just that temperature, with the brass expanded in the heat just so, with the crowd grinding their hips and turning you on until your desire transmutes into music, fat notes and fast notes, breathy ones that will never bounce off the walls quite the same way at that particular humidity ever again.

Even when you simply follow the sheet music, you're improvising with the dynamics. You have to feel it. And so! How can you just follow a recipe? The recipe says nothing about the tempo and the dynamics, the nature of the wood you light the fire with, the seasoning on the iron grill, the ambient temperature.

And the ingredients change every time! They've lived lives of their own and bring their own history. We honor those histories in their sacrifice to make something beautiful.

She turns her head to the side to look at the parsnips and carrots and potatoes. The brilliant blue of the bowl is reflecting the sunlight, but the light seems to swim through the gold wavy X, making it glow and seem to shimmer and move.

The girl is there, sweating her fever through the sheets of her hospital bed. She has her eyes squeezed shut tightly, as if the light is attacking her. She claps her hands over her ears and rocks her head. The girl's pain punctures through the warm cocoon of pleasure she's wrapped herself in.

She doesn't like this, so she turns away.

Her body knows the rhythm—tense muscles from worry that can only unwind through touch or flight, a pattern etched into her nervous system long before she had words for what she was running from. Her body knows the path instinctually, this well-worn escape route she's traveled since her first desperate early fumblings, when running from herself meant running toward another's touch.

The sunlight moving through the gold of the bowl leaves imprints on her vision. The gold wraps around itself and coils into the serpent eating its tail, bathed in the sea of ink that snakes around his hairless, sculpted chest, lines of inscription carved into his abs. He flows over her body like the warm water of a luxurious bath, blanketing her in heat. His breath, too, is warm, like the wind at the Mexican beach with the sun at full glory, where she would bask in its light and the radiant blue it painted the sky. She feels his heat penetrate her, take her from the inside, spread its webby tendrils and radiate from her core to her extremities. She feels her skin flush from this subterranean fire of arousal.

His tongue rolls over her like the slow waves of the ocean—warm, covering her whole body, then crashing over her as she watches the next one building, just a little bigger than the one before it, her anticipation building with it. She breathes in his fullness and feels the heat down her front as she breathes her own fullness back into him.

His tongue somehow knows that it isn't simply there to follow those beautiful sax notes. It dances as part of the ensemble, joining the sax and the bass and the drums as a new instrument on its own.

Its rhythm merges senses, blending sound into texture, taste into pleasure.

Its rests and pauses allow her to look inside herself and feel those invisible vibrations of her own arousal.

Its solos tease her, torment her as he swells the ocean in front of her and lets her see what he will do to her, leaving her paralyzed in anticipation of the impact.

He holds her in complete stillness as the waves crash inside her and move through her body.

She feels the airiness and the tingling and the heat of the orgasm, feels each organ gently buzz as the wave moves from her groin up her chest, until she moans it out with her breath and her eyes roll to the back of her head.

His stillness serves as a mirror, reflecting the frequency of her own body back to her.

She uses it to feel the aftershocks and slight tremors, the muscle spasms, until she's tuned her antennae so precisely that she can still hear the resting vibrations through the deep bass drum of her own heart.

She can sense him building another wave even though she's looking inward, and she feels herself surrender to it.

She stays tuned into her body as she turns her head and wraps her mouth around him. She rolls her tongue over the folds of his member as he hardens inside her, the energy of arousal converted into matter.

She watches her own arousal inside of her. Long, ropy muscles lift her womb up and forward, pulling it taut like a bowstring. She watches as the lift of her womb pulls her cervix out of the way, giving a pleasurable tug at the muscular opening of her sex even as it creates more space inside her.

She sees this now as the invisible complement to the male erection. Whereas his excitement makes him visibly greater, her own arousal makes space for him inside of her. It is the dance of desire, both of their bodies rearranging themselves for each other, one visible, the other internal. It is managed by some physical process below the level of thought and memory, and it is beautiful.

She feels him enter her and feels the tickle of his mustache as he kisses her neck. She sees now how she actually leads him, how the angle of her hips, the rate of her breathing, the way she squeezes her eyes, gives voice to her desire and guides him like invisible strings. No outside observer will see this. This is her hidden power.

This, too, is part of the dance; visibly, he leads, but only because she makes space for him to do so.

She watches his thrusts inside of her. They start shallow, running his shaft up and down between her labia and gently inside before repeating the process. Gradually, slowly, he teases her, each thrust an inch deep, the pressure on her vestibule pulling her labia against his member on the way in, the pressure released on the way out as he glides in her slickness until he moves northward and his glans kisses her own, sending pulses of electricity throughout her body. She feels the heat inside her, and sips in shallow breaths as she begs for him to plumb her depths. He does not, yet, resisting her desire so he may amplify it.

When he pushes in, he does so slowly, deliberately, allowing her to feel his penetration as a form of completion, like two jigsaw puzzle pieces with their empty spaces and protrusions fitting perfectly inside of each other. He holds her in this position, long enough to forget the temporal separation between their separate bodies. And then, slowly, he retracts out of her, once again individuating them, until, slowly, he returns, and her identity dissolves again.

She feels the wave building inside of her as he builds up speed, the desire that tunes out everything else, that speaks only the language of body when allowed to abandon the false pretenses of its ghostly spirit. It is this feeling she craves, to separate from herself, to forget herself, to lose her sense of self. To fall into her body and be nothing more.

She watches inside herself again as the wave crashes into the sea, as it swells and releases, the wave cresting and crashing around him. He holds still to absorb its tremors until she recovers, until she stops squeezing around him, and then he caresses her from inside herself, kisses those most primal parts of her with that most primal part of him.

This is the dance.

Looking through this laparoscope view makes her uncomfortable, so she looks up again for the golden serpent. It is undulating down the staircase of the Mayan temple, formed in the movement of the shadows cast against the balustrade.

"The dream of the sacrificial gangbang-virgin," he says, holding her hand, watching the dance of the sun and the serpent. His hand feels like a welcome blanket and a warm fire on a wintry day.

"Don't ignore the hyphen," he says, and she feels the corner of her lips lift and her eyes lighten at the incoming barrage of pedantic absurdity. "Absent its connective tissue, one might wonder if 'gangbang' is but an internal adjective to the noun at large, putting your lack of purity under doubt. Contrast that with the effect of gangbang hyphen virgin, quite clearly a singular concept, one noun unto itself, leaving no ambiguity as to how broad the scope of the word 'virgin' applies. The hyphen, I'm afraid, is a critical part of your story."

Her cheeks warm from the humor. "Ryan Tinsbury wasn't even the first," she says, turning to him.

He wraps his arms around her, holding her so tightly she can feel his heartbeat. It is calm, inviting. He turns his head toward the pyramid. She follows his gaze, staring through the aperture of her hijab. The girl is there, mute, staring back at her.

"They want her story," she says.

"They want to erase her story," he says, pointing to the man in the olive green uniform and thin black mustache. He stands at the top of the pyramid, knife in hand.

The tears blur the hijab's opening as she tastes the salt of her own fear. The icy wind of it blows inside her and causes her to shiver.

"I'm so afraid," she says.

"I can't do this," she says.

"You write your own story," he says, his arms' embrace comforting her.

She listens to the measured drum of his heart and absorbs the heat of his body. Her own heart pounds against her ribs like a captured bird, and she imagines it plucked from her chest, still beating, offered up so that the sun might rise again, so that something greater than herself might continue.

"I don't know how." Her body trembles.

He turns to hold her hand and stares at the temple.

"I don't know how to help her," she repeats, feeling the icy prick of self-pity. She feels the sudden and familiar urge to run.

"Yes, you do," he says. The girl walks up the stairs of the temple, each step slow and deliberate.

She turns to him, seeing herself in the mirror of his blue eyes.

"I'm afraid," she says.

She turns to look behind her.

She thinks of running.

THE DAD

He held her hand as they walked down the school hallway, his steps fast and purposeful, almost dragging her along. His eyes stayed fixed straight ahead, burning through the space in front of him as he ignored the stares and murmurs of students. His grip on her hand was a contradiction in itself, the gentleness of his thumb pressing down on the top of her hand, the firm grip angling awkwardly over the wrist that conveyed both urgency and made it less socially awkward for a teenage girl to be hauled out by her father. But mostly, his grip conveyed an overwhelming sense of dread.

"Slut," a boy whispered just loud enough to want to be heard, his voice slithering out from behind the row of lockers. Fury burned so hot in his chest that for a split second, his vision narrowed. He had to resist an instinct to race behind the lockers and shake some throats until he identified the guilty party. The rage obliterated every logical thought; he spared no consideration of what would happen if he actually caught the son of a bitch.

Madison hurried alongside him, silent, her shoulders hunched under the weight of the moment. They pushed through the school doors and into the late afternoon sunlight, the cool evening air doing nothing to temper the storm brewing inside him. They moved across the parking lot in sync, his long, angry strides forcing her to match his pace.

When they reached the truck, he yanked the passenger door open, his hand landing on her back to guide her in. His touch was firm and distracted, as if he was in a hurry and somewhere else. She slid into the seat without a word, her movements stiff and automatic. He shut the door with more force than he intended, the sound echoing across the parking lot. He rounded the hood and climbed into the driver's seat. The truck roared to life as he turned the ignition, and before he had even fastened his seatbelt, they were moving.

They said nothing as he drove across town, his foot heavy, his stops and starts rapid. With both windows down, he tried to embrace the wind as it punched him in the face but could not penetrate his scowl. He raced into a parking lot and parked in a wide open space, partially covering the spot next to it with the bed of the truck. He threw the gear into park and opened his door in one motion.

"Stay here," he said, slamming the door behind him. Heart racing, he tore into the lobby of Preston & Sons Funeral Home.

"Travis," Adam said, holding up his hands in surprise.

"I need to speak to him, Adam," Travis said, his voice urgent and uneven, like a taut rope about to snap. Despite playing through multiple scenarios the entire way here, he still had no idea what he would say.

Adam nodded solemnly. "Have a seat. He's with someone now, but I'll tell him you're waiting."

Travis stared dangerously at Adam before walking to the waiting room and taking a seat. He stared up at the TV long enough to see his and Madison's pictures on it. He whipsawed his head, looking for the remote control. Not finding it, he stood up and ripped the plug to the TV from the wall.

Minutes stretched into what felt like hours until finally, a man in a crisp blue suit appeared. His perfectly combed gray hair, starched white shirt, and cross-embossed cufflinks gleamed under the fluorescent lights. He held Travis's gaze as he walked in and sat opposite him. He wore a stern expression across his dignified face.

"Come on, Ted, you can't do this," Travis blurted, more desperately than he had rehearsed in any of the scenarios he had run through in his head. He felt his throat closing up.

"Travis, listen." Ted sighed, his voice slow and deliberate. "My barber is an ex-felon. Stole a car. I can work with a lot of people."

"Then give me a chance," Travis said.

"But I can't work with someone who punches a pastor." Ted closed his lips and stopped talking, letting the finality of his statement sink in. He was the type of man used to providing conversational clarity amid emotional distress.

"Ted, I'm begging you," Travis said, his voice breaking. "Don't do this. I need the business. I'll give you a discount, whatever you need. Ted, I need the business." His cheeks were flushed with some grotesque combination of anger and shame. Sweat drenched his shirt.

Ted shook his head slowly, continuing to hold Travis's gaze.

"Goddammit, Ted! Do it for Amy. Do it for Madison."

"I'm sorry, Travis. I need you to leave before I call the police."

Travis felt the acid in his throat with each breath. He held Ted's stare for a few helpless moments before standing up and walking out of the funeral home and into the cloudy dusk.

"Jesus!" he yelled as he took in the chaos unfolding in the parking lot.

A reporter had a microphone shoved through the open passenger window of his truck. Around them swarmed media vans, cameras, and a tangle of spotlights casting harsh beams that illuminated Madison like an animal trapped in a predator's glare.

"… is it true that you were on the pill?" he heard the reporter say to Madison through the window.

Travis froze for half a second, staring through the windshield at his daughter. Her small, fragile figure looked paralyzed in the spotlight, her face contorted with fear. A deep, molten fury wrapped itself over him like a fiery cloak. His fists clenched as the rage burned through his veins.

"You motherfucker!" he yelled, his voice raw, his mouth in a snarl as he charged toward the reporter. The man stumbled back and started saying something about the First Amendment. Travis turned his eyes sideways to look at Madison. She had clapped her hands over her ears, shut her eyes tight, and shook her head violently. The lights illuminated every wrinkle of her terror, her cries adding audible texture to the discordant sounds of cameras clicking like crickets. He ran to her as she started screaming.

"I know, baby girl, we're going. Get the fuck out of my way. We're going. We'll get out of here and I'll pull over and hold you tight. You people are fucking animals. Cry all you need to, baby. Let's go. Come on."

He jammed the truck in reverse before he'd even fully closed his door. He again waited until he had driven across the parking lot before fastening his own seat belt.

∞

"You did your nails!" Travis said, feigning surprise—he'd given his permission earlier over text. Madison flashed her metallic blues at him. "Been watching TV all day?" he asked.

"No," she said, looking past him to the TV. "Watched some You-Tube, too."

He smiled wistfully down at her. "Glad you lived it up, girl. I'm gonna go chat in the kitchen for a bit, okay?"

She nodded. He gave her a gentle pat on the shoulder before heading downstairs.

"You look like you could use a beer," Richard said as soon as Travis entered the kitchen, offering a cold bottle. Travis accepted it wordlessly. They stood huddled around the island.

An odd thing had happened when Travis called up Harlan, his college buddy in Round Rock. With this morning's court date requiring his physical presence in Austin, Travis had hoped someone nearby could keep an eye on Madison.

She didn't need a babysitter, not really, but he couldn't bear the thought of exposing her to more media attention after her last meltdown. She'd gone completely mute for an entire day after that.

Harlan told him, in no uncertain terms, that they weren't *that* good of friends. Travis wasn't surprised. He'd been losing friends ever since that day in the hospital.

Amy had always been the smart one. Travis had simply hitched onto her network in the SBC and, almost without realizing it, built a business around it. He knew he wasn't as Baptist as most of his customers (he was, after all, drinking beer instead of sweet tea), but he never once thought about that being a problem—at least not until Lauren called.

Lauren, Amy's friend who owned the diner where they often enjoyed their post-church lunches, had always been warm and welcoming. Over the years, Travis figured he'd paid Lauren more money for food than she'd paid him for electrical work, but he was certain she wanted to hurt more than his P&L when she called him to say she would no longer require his services. Ever.

And Lauren begat Ralph, and Ralph begat Andrew, and Andrew begat the coffee shop, and the coffee shop begat the conference center, and the conference center begat the funeral home. He'd built his entire business around the Southern Baptist Convention, and now he couldn't go anywhere near it. It was destroying Madison, and it meant that he had to skip a hotel in Austin and just drive round trip in one day to save the money.

So here he was, drinking a beer with the doctor who saved his daughter's life and her ex-husband. He lied to them about driving back, claiming he'd booked a dog-friendly motel just out of the city. He lied because judgment seemed to follow him everywhere these days, and he couldn't take any more.

They clearly had an interesting relationship, but he was too numb to inquire. The doctor had been the one to reach out and offer help. She had her own legal woes, but they were more complicated and would move more slowly. She was rich, and it was always easier prosecuting someone like him than someone like her.

He tuned out the Saddam stuff. It hurt too much to see all the attention on the doctor instead of sympathy for the victim. He was pretty sure she set this up as a publicity stunt to help her garner sympathy with a jury. He hated himself for not having a better option.

"How'd she do?" Travis asked, his voice low and weary.

"Good, all things considered," Maya said.

"Offered to play some games, but she wanted to watch TV like she's doing now," Richard added. "Took a gamble, thought she might be interested in learning a bit about what you do, so we watched a couple YouTube videos on electricity. Walked her through a couple Wikipedia pages and tried to explain what was going on as best I could. She's smart."

Travis nodded and took a long sip of his beer. He let the silence stretch into a space that bordered on uncomfortable.

"How bad is it?" Richard asked, finally.

Travis's jaw tightened. He had a dark expression as he shook his head slowly, staring at the beer bottle in his hand. "They're throwing the book at me," he said, clearly holding back an unspoken emotional storm.

Richard set his beer down deliberately, studying Travis. "How bad is it?" he asked again, his tone firmer, his gaze sharp and unyielding.

Travis hesitated, took another swig, and swallowed hard. His eyes flicked upward and to the right, as if searching for a way to avoid the words that followed. He blinked quickly, trying to keep a tear from falling.

"They're calling it aggravated assault," he said at last, his voice breaking just slightly. "Twenty years maximum."

Richard stayed silent, holding his gaze steady, giving Travis the space to find his words.

"They're going for the maximum."

Sergeant Baker ambled over and sniffed Richard's butt. Richard softened his gaze, looking down as he scratched behind the dog's ears, letting the moment settle.

"Can we help you find a good lawyer?" Maya asked, her tone careful but direct.

"Got one for you yet?"

"It's easier for me," Maya said.

"All them fancy, expensive lawyers tripping over themselves to take you on pro bono," Travis said.

Maya ignored the pettiness in his voice. "They want to use my story for their purposes."

Travis studied her, his brow furrowed. "Got anyone in mind?"

Maya nodded. "Maybe, but I think it'll take a bit of convincing, and I'm still working out my approach."

"Part of me thinks I deserve the maximum," Travis said, his body slumping. "I hit a fucking preacher in the face in a hospital room full of people trying to save my daughter's life. I put her in danger. What kind of piece of shit am I?"

Maya allowed a sufficient pause to acknowledge the gravity of Travis's comment before continuing. "Travis, I need to talk about Madison for a minute, when you're in the right mindset."

Travis laughed. "I don't expect to be seeing 'right' for a while. How's now work?"

Maya nodded and looked pensive. "I let Madison pick her own nail color. I have a little box of nail polishes and let her go through it to find one." She closed her mouth and stared at Travis, offering a long enough pause in the conversation for him to finish the scene for her.

"She sorted them in rainbow order," he said, putting his beer on the counter. He felt his body tense up in an almost instinctual defensive stance whenever someone talked about his daughter's social awkwardness.

Maya nodded, lips pressed, her gaze locked on Travis. She took a few slow breaths through her nose before continuing. "Have you ever had her tested for autism?"

Travis froze. The words hit him like a gut punch, leaving his muscles slack and his breath unsteady. He grabbed onto the edge of the counter to steady himself, blinking away the sudden dizziness.

"I'm not that kind of doctor," Maya said, her voice gentle. "So I'm not the one to say yes or no. But I noticed her sensory issues in the hospital, and I saw how awful the media experience was for her. They were horrible for showing that, by the way. And for doing it."

Travis stared at her, slack-jawed. Maya let him catch up, maintaining eye contact the entire time.

"I did a little reading," she continued. "Autism looks different in girls than in boys. It's easier to spot with boys because they tend to obsess about something unusual, like train tracks or fan blades, and can't understand the social cues when they talk about it incessantly. Girls are much better at wearing masks to disguise their autism and mimicking other people. And their special interests tend to look a bit more ordinary."

Travis closed his mouth and breathed through his nostrils, unsure if the breath carried anger or hate or surprise or gratitude, only that it flowed through that acid feeling in his throat again.

"Like baptism," he said, his voice sharp. He held the doctor's gaze, dangerously. He wasn't sure if he hated her but was sure that he *wanted* to hate her.

Maya nodded, maintaining the gaze but with a confident softness, empathetic and calm.

Travis took a sip of beer and closed his eyes to calm his heartbeat. This must be his Father of the Year moment. Following up the past few weeks with being recognized for ignoring autism her whole life.

"Anything else?" he asked, still with closed eyes.

"If you talk to someone, mention her seizure and mutism in the hospital. The little bit of reading I did suggested those are more prevalent with autism."

Travis nodded. "Thank you for watching her today," he said, opening his eyes and trying to force himself to be grateful.

They stood through another long stretch of silence, each lost in their own thoughts, the weight of the conversation pressing down on them.

"She say anything about the case?" Travis asked.

Maya and Richard both shook their heads.

"Would you ever let her testify?" Richard asked.

"Never," Travis answered immediately. "Doesn't change my case one bit. I still engaged in criminal activity and endangered my daughter's life. All it does is put her right in the political crossfire with us." He nodded his head toward Maya.

"Speaks to your motive," Richard said.

Another long pause passed, the silence thick with tension. Finally, Maya broke it. "Is there anything I can do to help?"

Travis felt it rise again, that hot, familiar fury burning its way up from his chest to his throat. His jaw tightened as he stared at her, his eyes narrowing with hatred.

"Help?" he spat, shaking with restrained venom. "You saved my daughter's life and did her fucking nails today. That's all the help I need from you. I don't need you diagnosing her with autism after one hospital visit and one goddamn play date." He felt fury's furnace radiate to the surface as his skin grew hot. "You got what you need. You got your fucking day with the victim to parade in front of a jury. Sergeant Baker, let's go. Madison!"

He didn't look back as he grabbed Madison's hand and led her out of the house, the Sergeant trotting behind them. The sound of the door slamming echoed like the finality of a gavel.

At the truck, he opened the passenger door, helping Madison in without a word, his motions clipped and robotic. The Sergeant hopped into the cab backseat. Travis got into the driver's seat, started the engine, and pulled out. It wasn't until he merged onto the highway that he realized his seatbelt was still undone. He yanked it across his chest with a sharp tug, the *click* of the buckle lost under the roar of his truck and the storm of his thoughts.

UNTYING THE KNOT

"I'm coming!" Richard said, flushed with anticipation. He yanked open his closet door, simultaneously kicking off his slippers and pulling his pajama shirt over his head, tossing it to the floor. His fingers fumbled for the drawstring on his pajama pants and pulled.

"Fuck," he whispered.

He frowned at the pants and tried to reverse engineer the unfortunate proto-knot that formed between the two halves of the drawstring. Impatiently, he gambled and pulled both sides under the assumption that it would untangle itself, but that simply tied the knot tighter.

Fuck, fuck, he thought.

"You sure?" Maya asked, her voice tinged with a sultry impatience.

"Be right there!" he assured her.

The knot appeared impenetrable. He lifted it and studied it from multiple angles, searching for an attack vector, but came up empty. In desperation, he tried tugging the pants off anyway, but the taut drawstring held them tight over his hip bones. His erection caused a visible tenting of the crotch area.

Fuck, he thought, not for the first time.

He glared down at the offending drawstring, its faded blue and white stripes mocking him in their snug, twisted configuration. The knot itself was a thing of chaotic artistry, a tangle of intertwined loops and frayed ends, all but fused together in a maddeningly stubborn twist. It was as if the strings had conspired against him, taking on a life of their own, pulling tighter and tighter with each panicked tug. The soft cotton blend drawstring, comfortable at rest, now felt like a noose, tightening its grip with every frantic pull. His fingers fumbled over the knot, growing clumsier with each failed attempt, each attempt increasing the labyrinthine navigational skill necessary to unwind it.

He groaned helplessly as the strength of his erection waned, then looked up to the pocketknife he kept on the shelf with his collar stays. Perhaps, like Alexander the Great and the Gordian knot, his genius could be simple brute force. *No*, he thought, *don't panic*. Instead, he once again scraped his nails against the fabric, searching for leverage, but the knot only seemed to burrow deeper into itself until it became a Möbius strip, an infinity unto itself with no end to grasp, a knotty little fortress against his increasingly desperate assault.

"Everything okay in there?" Maya asked, giving voice to the mocking of the knot against his efforts. Frustration mounted with each passing tick of the clock hanging on the wall outside the closet, her amused chuckles only adding to his sense of urgency. The knot had become the focal point of his world, a stubborn adversary that refused to yield. He yanked at the strings, cursing under his breath as the tangle held fast, growing tighter with every pull. It was just a drawstring, a simple piece of cloth, but at that moment, it was his worst enemy, and it was winning.

He tried to slow his breathing, willing his hands to be steady, but the drawstring seemed to sense his desperation. Every time he thought he had a grip on the right loop, it slipped through his fingers like water, the knot reshaping itself in a more convoluted form. He imagined the knot laughing at him, a tiny devil dancing just out of reach, refusing to be undone.

His fingertips were raw from the repeated effort, each failed attempt only adding fuel to the fire of his growing panic. The harder he worked, the more the knot resisted, becoming a physical embodiment of every minor irritation he'd ever faced, now magnified in this absurd battle. He could hear the clock on the wall ticking, ticking away the seconds, ticking away his erection, ticking away his opportunity. He again resorted to simply pulling the pants down but gave up when he heard the first precursor to a rip.

"Fuck!" he said, this time loud enough to be heard.

"Got something you want to talk about?" she asked.

"Fucking drawstring!" he announced.

"Pajamas?"

"Mmm-hmm."

"Need a hand?"

"No, I got it!" He ran his tongue across his lips and furrowed his brow in concentration. He bounced his cock up and down a couple of times to maintain focus and recommitted to freeing it. He closed his left eye—that was his distance-seeing eye, a heritage of Lasik—and studied the knot intensely. There was almost no separation between the two sides of it. Conjuring up all his patience, he once again pinched the fingers of both hands to pull in opposite directions.

"Fuck!" he screamed at last.

"Sure sounds like you need a hand," she said, her voice more like a laugh.

He sighed and surrendered to the walk of shame to meet her on the bed. She turned the light on and ran a hand over his weakening erection.

"Oh gosh, we better hurry," she said, teasing him. "Yep, you did a real number." She studied the knot attentively. "I think we're gonna need tools for this job." She opened her nail kit and grabbed the tweezers. "Hold still," she said, sitting on the bed as he stood sheepishly beside her.

With surgical precision, she slid the tweezers into the knot, working it loose millimeter by millimeter. He watched as she undid his humiliation, her nimble fingers moving with the patience of someone who knew exactly how much this was tormenting him. Finally, the knot came free, and the pants dropped to the floor.

She leaned back to survey the damage to his ego. In mock disappointment, she slumped her shoulders, curved her spine, drooped her head down, and let her arms fall toward the ground, using her body to mimic his limp member as she looked down upon it.

"Awww," she said, her tone dripping with playful pity. "We're too late."

❦

"Told you it pays not to rush things," she said, as they lay contentedly on their backs, heads tilted slightly until their foreheads bumped to see each other.

"Hmm," he said.

"Hmm?" she asked.

"Let me tell you a story," he said. "It's a story about a kind, patient, loving man. A heroic man, a knight, willing to risk a chaste life to worship his queen."

"Chaste? Does his queen not like sex?" she asked with feigned curiosity. She wore only a thin sheen of sweat reflecting the lamp light off her stomach.

"Oh no, she *loves* sex. And she's good at it, really good, in fact. But she has a particularly sensitive sense of talk…"

"A sense of talk?"

"… and sometimes it's navigating the transition from talk to sex where this knight's heroic qualities really shine, for long ago, he recognized the valor in letting his queen take that transition at her own pace." His limp member curled up in satisfied repose against the inside of his left thigh.

"Sounds like a smart knight."

"When they were young and vibrant," he continued, "this seemed like such a minor sacrifice, for she was full of desire, and the transitions were often so short they were almost perfunctory. But as the months turned into years and the years into decades, the queen's pace slowed, and those transitions took longer and longer. Suddenly, she had more to talk about."

"That's weird," she said in a teasing voice. "Seems like there wouldn't be anything particularly *new* to talk about after being together for so long."

"Indeed. To add to the knight's struggles, his own energy had waned over the years, and to his great dismay, he realized at one point that if he could not successfully manage the transition from talk to sex by a certain point in the night, one that moved earlier and earlier over the years, that there would be no transition at all. This is the risk he took to uphold his vow to his queen."

"I love chivalry in action. Almost more than a bowerbird's bower."

"And it was harder than you think because, remember, he had to nudge the transition invisibly, which meant helping the queen get there on her own."

"A true knight." She clapped her hands together to emphasize the point.

"Well, let me tell you how clever this knight was. He realized that, rather than trying to change the queen's behavior—he knew he could never do that—he could perhaps change the *environment*. So, one day, as they retired to bed, he pulled out his phone and put on some music."

"Technology to the rescue!"

"And it seemed to work, for a bit at least."

"For a bit?"

"For a bit. You know how, when you put an owl statue on the tree or lay down anti-bird spikes on the fence, it slows the squirrels down at first, but they're so smart, within a couple days it just becomes a game to them to flaunt how little difference this new change of environment impacts their ability to chew up your attic."

"So the queen's a rodent now?" She scrunched her eyes and rotated her head more to give him a side-eye.

"Well, no, but you get the general idea. She's smart. Adaptable. Perfectly capable of bringing the environment back to her prior equilibrium without even being aware of it."

"What equilibrium is that?"

"Long transitions from talk to sex, with serious risk of a chaste life for our hero, the knight."

"Hmm. Even with the music?"

"So again, it worked for a bit. But here's the thing. One night, he'd had sufficient indicators of interest that he'd worked up to start kissing her. They were tugging each other's lips, a little tongue action. Then she pulled back and squinted her eyes at him in the way she always does before she sings, and she sang. It was only then—Lil' Kim I believe it was—that he realized how common this behavior had been, and how much time her bouts of singing added to the transition each night."

She shrugged without adjusting her position. "If she likes the music…"

"In fact, it really called into question the idea of a 'transition' as a discrete thing to begin with."

"Why's that?"

"Well, because these lyrical interruptions would occur multiple times in an evening. He had succeeded in, say, pulling in the average time of first kiss, but sometimes he'd have to start all over. Some-times, it would be a brief pause, maybe an epic demonstration of meter and memory in keeping up with Busta Rhymes. He'd offer his appreciation—"

"As a knight should…"

"Absolutely. And maybe then they'd continue this transition, or maybe they'd start a whole new one. But sometimes when, say, a Missy Elliott verse reminded her of an ex-boyfriend—"

"*Boyfriend* seems like such an unnecessarily formal name for this queen's exes…"

"—or when she couldn't remember the artist behind a song and would have to look it up on her phone, there would no longer be an option of *continuing* the transition. He'd have to start a whole new one if he had any hope of getting laid that night."

"Poor guy."

"Maybe, but a clever one, and doughty. He wasn't done chang-ing her environment yet. One day, he realized he could still use music to speed up the transition; he just had to switch to different musical genres than those she'd committed to memory during her formative sexual years. Again, like a squirrel—"

"Which is a type of rodent…"

"—she was only briefly changed by this change of environment."

"How did she chew through it this time?"

"Within a few days, he learned to watch her eyes when they'd start kissing, which again happened quicker with the music. When her eyes would stop looking at him and kind of roll to the upper corner, he knew she was analyzing the lyrics. What did Dave Mat-thews mean by *satellite*? What definition of the word *battery* was Metallica using? She'd start entire conversations based on these puzzles, usually involving her phone to resolve the dilemma so they could put it to rest once and for all. Or maybe she'd notice a pattern in the songs—they all seemed to mention the moon, for instance—and she'd want to talk about the various songs as if they were pictures on a bulletin board and the two of them were detectives pinning the yarn between them. It was worse than just letting her sing."

"Sounds terrible."

"It was, and our knight nearly gave up, until he had one more brilliant insight."

"Oh, what was it?"

"Instrumentals."

"Instrumentals?"

"Yep. Nothing to sing. No lyrics to analyze. It was his best idea yet. He started with some kind of house music because house music is like tofu; it just sort of takes the flavor of whatever you mix it in. But she evidently needed some flavor to get started, so he kept exploring until he landed on playlists that featured erotic jazz instrumentals."

"Sounds sexy."

"Yep. You should see his Spotify recommendations."

"I imagine it's like looking at archaeological layers of sexual manipulation."

"I prefer the term *sexual inspiration*."

"Surely the instrumentals *had* to work for our poor suffering knight?"

"The poor suffering knight thought so too, at first. But it didn't last. One day, she asked if that was a sitar. The knight lifted his ears—ears that had heretofore been trapped between her thighs and therefore unable to really sip the music in—and let her know it was just a slide guitar with some effects before getting back to business. But that was only the start of it. She nearly broke his neck with the realization that she had just figured out what *sitar* meant."

"Hmm," she said.

"Hmm?" he asked.

"You know, I really thought we'd be past this by now," she said.

"*Sitting guitar.* She thought sitar meant *sitting guitar*, and she was so excited by this discovery that she gave him a neck strain that lasted three days."

"I recall you being a little upset."

"Sitar doesn't mean sitting guitar!" Playful frustration colored his voice. "There's no relationship between them!"

She rolled over on her side facing him, lay her head on his chest, and ran her fingers through his greying chest hair. Unlike their still-brown brethren, the white hairs looked thin and long, curlier, with much weaker roots.

"Well, I'm glad our long-suffering knight was able to get lucky on this night, even with its concomitant drawstring and musical challenges," she said, smiling softly.

"Yep. I look for opportunities to use the word *concomitant* in conversation. I love the way it makes my mouth feel. It's like the closest I can get to the Khoisan and Bantu language clicks without being a native speaker. It's way more fun than saying *onomatopoeia,* which always makes me feel like I'm blowing through a vuvuzela."

They rested blissfully in each other's warmth for several minutes. He gently massaged her scalp with his fingernails.

"Still thinking about Elizabeth Lang?" he asked.

She shifted her neck to look up at him. "Having second thoughts?" she asked.

He thought for a moment. "For me, no."

"Go on," she said.

He sighed. "The case against you is weak and performative. Election-year bullshit. Everyone knows that."

"And?"

"And. This could blow over and be forgotten tomorrow, if you wanted it to."

She kept her gaze and said nothing.

"This doesn't have to be your fight."

She nodded thoughtfully.

"And even if you decide that you're in, Lang is pretty much the nuclear option. There's no putting that genie back in the bottle. You could play it out in the courts instead. You've got Carson & McMaster. Or Smith, Thompson, & Young. You're pretty much the best pro bono client a progressive law firm could ever hope for."

"They want me to be the face of their movement and put my name on a famous court ruling."

"I wonder which name they'll pick," he said.

"Yours, I'm sure. I'm still wearing it."

"Lame. Slap your ex-husband's surname on a feminist court ruling. The patriarchy at work."

She sighed as she shifted her neck back to neutral and rested her cheek on his pec. "And Madison?"

"One problem at a time," he said. "All I'm saying is that this is a different environment than your dad's time. It's a lot uglier. Sometimes running away is the right answer."

She ran her fingers through his chest hair some more, contemplating his words.

"You, of all people, should know that."

She bristled at the low blow and sat up abruptly to look at him. "What the fuck is that supposed to mean?"

"I mean, you've been running away from media attention your entire life."

"Oh," she said, deflating a little.

"And I mean that you're the Girl from Dujail. You're literally still alive because you ran when running away was the right option."

"Oh," she said. It was hard to forget these days. The intense media coverage of Maya, and especially of her mysterious escape from Dujail, meant she was recognized everywhere she went.

"So, you didn't mean because I told you that I don't love you hoes, I'm out the door?" she said, converting her momentary anger into a sheepish acknowledgment of her misinterpretation, poetically wrapped up in Snoop Dogg lyrics.

"Funny how you leave me and you get mad at me for not bringing it up," he said.

"Well, I like to keep you on your toes." She crossed her legs to sit more comfortably on the bed. He admired the slight bounce of her breasts as she sat up.

"I don't know," she said after another long pause.

He stared at her quizzically.

"About Lang," she said. "About running away. About Madison. I don't know." She stared at him intently. "But I'm thinking about the nuclear option with Lang, and if I do it, I need to know you're in, because it will be messy."

He nodded thoughtfully and sat up, leaning against the wall to meet her eye level. "Still having lucid dreams?" he asked.

She nodded, her lips curling into a playful, almost mischievous smile.

"Good. Every superhero needs her superpower," he said.

Her smile turned seductive, her gaze locking on his. "Been having some *hot* ones lately."

"I like hot," he said, his grin teasing but his attention sharpening, drawn fully into her orbit.

"I mean, like Joan Jett hot."

His eyebrows lifted, and the corners of his mouth pulled wide in a grin that felt familiar and electric. "Oh, to be that seventeen-year-old boy dancin' there by the record machine," he said, leaning in slightly. "God, I wish I knew what she did with him after she took him home… where they could be alone."

She deepened her smile at the millionth time she'd heard the joke. "I mean, like I've got a hot sexual fantasy."

"I like the sound of this." He noticed a sudden twitch, an

unexpected sign of life in his cock that should be enjoying a deep and, at his age, long slumber after the knightly service it so recently performed.

"I think you'll like it," she teased, her voice low and sultry. "It involves me being queen for a day, and you as one of my loyal knights."

"One of?" he asked, raising an eyebrow.

She nodded slowly, seductively. A strand of her long black hair slipped over her shoulder, brushing the curvature of her breast as she tilted her head ever so slightly. The movement was deliberate, calculated, and devastatingly effective.

"I'm all ears," he said, leaning in, his body and voice tuned perfectly to her rhythm.

"Except…" she added, letting the moment stretch, her smile deepening as she played with him, "maybe not like Joan Jett…"

He chuckled, but she wasn't done. She let the silence linger long enough to keep him on edge. "If you're up for it," she said, her eyes locking onto his, "I think I really want to do it."

There are rare moments in a person's lifetime where time itself dissolves into the urgency of the present—moments where that liminal boundary between body and mind disappears, replaced by a perfect harmony of organic activity focused like a laser beam on just One Thing. Natural selection zigged and zagged for millions of years, adding adaptations and complexity, but it was all for moments like this one, where nothing less than the survival of the gene pool was at stake.

His mind-body reacted with sharpness and efficiency, all parts of his being perfectly cooperating to encourage her to continue. He sat up straighter, lightened his eyes, nodded attentively. Without consciously thinking about it, he let out perfectly timed *mmm*'s and *oh*'s to help her cadence.

"Do you know who yet?" he heard himself ask from a higher

observation point than the ego he was used to navigating the world from. He was firing on all cylinders now, operating at multiple layers of consciousness at the same time, all in perfect harmony to process and rapidly synthesize the information she was giving him so he could transmute her story into their reality.

His body somehow knew she needed to see his acceptance. More. He needed to show his arousal. His erection strained upward from his lap, as if it still belonged to a seventeen-year-old boy. The color in his cheeks complied. The tone of his voice chipped in some assistance.

"So you want to be sacrificed?" he asked her, almost breathless with excitement.

"If I succeed with Lang, I don't see any other option. Queen for a day first, of course."

He let out a small breath through his wide-open smile.

"Of course," he said.

THROUGH A GLASS, DARKLY

The warm water hugged Madison's body like a cocoon. She sat still in the tub, knees pulled to her chest, the waterline just below her chin. Her fingers skimmed the surface, tracing tiny ripples as she stared at the tap, its slow drips of excess water marking time in the quiet of the bathroom. Steam rose lazily, fogging the mirror and blurring her reflection, but she avoided looking at it. Looking down, she saw herself broken by gentle waves into fragments— eyes, mouth, chin, all separated by ripples—like pieces of a faith she couldn't quite reassemble into something whole.

She tilted her head back against the cool porcelain of the tub, letting the droplets from her wet hair slide down her neck. Her hand slipped beneath the water, touching the smooth curve of her stomach, as though she could feel the weight pressing into her skin, and more, as though she could feel the weight of her womb. Slowly, she straightened and leaned forward, letting her palms flatten against the surface of the water.

She whispered, "Upon your profession of faith, I now baptize you in the name of the Father, the Son, and the Holy Spirit. Buried in the likeness of His death…"

She took a deep breath, pinched her nose, and leaned back into the water. The warmth closed over her ears, muffling the world until all she could hear was her own heartbeat. For a moment, she stayed under, holding still, imagining the feeling of being new, of being clean, not just on the outside but in the way that mattered most. She put her hands over her womb and stayed there until she could feel the pressure in her lungs before she broke the surface, gasping.

"… and raised to walk in the newness of life."

But the water didn't feel different. Her chest still felt tight. Her womb felt empty and scarred. She still felt… wrong.

Madison sank back into the tub, the water lapping at her shoulders. No matter how hard she tried, it always felt like she was just outside the circle, looking through a glass, darkly.

She had wanted to reach out to Pastor Eli for advice, but there was a restraining order against her dad, so she had reached out to her online forum instead. At first, she'd been so hopeful, typing carefully, crafting her message. "Can you baptize yourself if no one else will?"

Then the replies had come, fast and sharp as arrows.

"God doesn't work off a checklist…"

"Baptism isn't something you can just do on your own, lol."

"Maybe you should keep your pants on instead of asking dumb questions."

Her profile was under her real name, because she had created her account shortly after her mom died. Back then, the community had helped her through her grief.

"Retard."

She thought back to the clinic, tucked in a nondescript medical complex, a low-rise building with beige stucco walls and mirrored glass windows reflecting the Texas sun. The parking lot had been mostly empty, save for a few sedans and minivans scattered near the entrance. The small blue sign by the door read "Center for Neurodevelopmental Assessment and Support" in understated letters, with a subheading: *"Appointments by Referral Only."*

She remembered how the air smelled faintly of disinfectant and the vinyl flooring gleamed under fluorescent lights. The waiting room had been painted in a soft, calming pale green and cream, with an assortment of simple, functional furniture. There were no loud distractions or harsh lights, just a few neatly arranged chairs, a low coffee table stacked with parenting magazines, and a shelf of picture books and fidget toys for younger patients.

A plexiglass barrier, the edges taped with colorful decals of animals and stars, had shielded the receptionist's desk. Behind it sat a woman in her thirties, her fingers clicking away on a keyboard. On one side of the desk, Madison remembered the corkboard displaying community resources—flyers for therapy groups, notices about sensory-friendly events, and brochures explaining the diagnostic process.

The walls bore framed prints of abstract art (nothing too busy or overstimulating) and a laminated poster listing the clinic's mission statement: "To provide compassionate, comprehensive evaluations for individuals with neurodevelopmental differences."

Madison had entered quietly, her shoulders hunched and her hands gripping the strap of her backpack. She had avoided eye contact with the receptionist and instead focused on the patterned tiles beneath her sneakers, stepping carefully to avoid imaginary cracks. Her dad trailed behind her.

She had walked through a half-open door into a hallway that stretched further into the clinic, leading to private rooms for assessments. On one side, a small playroom was visible, its shelves lined with puzzles and sensory toys, a beanbag chair slumped invitingly in one corner. Beyond that, muted voices had floated through the air, accompanied by the faint hum of computers and the occasional squeak of a chair.

She had noticed everything except the reporter, who she imagined parked discreetly in the parking lot, scribbling notes and taking pictures that later appeared on TV. Notes that, after several generations of synthesis and replay at internet speed, had been distilled down to just one word.

Retard.

After draining the tub completely, she stepped out and wrapped herself in a body towel. A second towel secured her damp hair. Moving to her desk, she plopped down on the chair, lifted the laptop lid, and stared at the screen for several minutes, trying to decide if she was being courageous or cowardly.

Then, she clicked on the capital *M* inside the circle in the upper-right corner of the page, opening her profile. She stared at her name and her picture for a minute, scrolled down, and deleted her account.

THE CUNT

Maya spread her fingers against the color palette, debating whether to stick with winter or leapfrog into spring. She'd once heard that Inuit have sixteen different words for snow, an impressive feat of subtle discrimination until you walk into a nail salon and see dozens of names for shades of pink, but it wasn't the season for any of them yet. She hesitated on coral and sunshine yellow before splitting the difference with the light, metallic gold of champagne.

"This, please," she said.

The gray-haired Vietnamese woman squinted at her nails through smudged readers. "You no like silver?" she asked, lifting Maya's hand with a practiced roughness. The chrome dip still gleamed on her fingertips and kissed her cuticles, perfect and unchipped.

"Time for a change," Maya said, her smile polite.

The woman led her to a seat and turned on the nail lamp. Maya placed her hands under the light, ignoring the furtive glances from other customers who had clearly recognized her. She pretended to pay attention to the home renovation show on the television.

"Relax, please," the woman said. Maya noticed her hand was

trembling slightly. With conscious effort, she inhaled slowly and exhaled even more slowly, stilling her hand. She spent the next several minutes putting her mind to the thrill it must be to take a sledgehammer to the walls of your own house and rebuild it from scratch.

As the manicure neared completion, Maya stared at the almost-finished nails with growing unease. She had mistimed her approach.

"I'm sorry, ma'am, I know you're almost done. Now that I see them, I think I've changed my mind. I'd like a different color after all. Can I pick another color? I'll pay double."

Bemused, the woman agreed. *Cerise*, Maya thought. Weather be damned. It was time for spring, for the renewal of life, for the fucking sledgehammer. With a frown on her face, the manicurist started again.

The bell attached to the door announced the change she was looking for a few minutes later, followed by the sound of audible annoyance from the staff and a sudden uptick in Vietnamese words thrown across the salon. She had been tuning out the phone conversation from the Black woman in the pedicure chair until she heard "Oh, my God." Maya looked up and saw a tall woman wearing sweatpants and a crumpled white T-shirt. Her short dyed-blond pixie cut looked disheveled, as if she hadn't washed or brushed it in several days.

"Vodka cranberry," Elizabeth Lang barked as she reached the bar, in that famous voice a critic once described as sounding like bourbon filtered through gravel, cigarette smoke, and a lifetime of bad decisions. The short man glared at her and said nothing. He poured the drink and handed it to Lang, holding his lips in a thin straight line of disapproval.

"Jesus Christ, Nam, give me the bottle," Lang said, reaching for the bottle of SKYY vodka. Nam instinctively pulled it toward his body, out of reach.

"For fuck's sake, I didn't come here to cure a bladder infection," Lang growled, holding out her cup. Every customer in the salon was now watching the spectacle as Nam reluctantly topped off the drink with another splash of vodka.

Lang took a sip and put the plastic cup down on the bar. She took out her phone.

Maya pulled her hand out of her manicurist's grip. The lady looked quizzically at Maya. "Not done," she protested.

Maya took a hundred-dollar bill out of her pocket and put it on the table between them. Before she could give herself time to think, she stood up and approached the bar. Lang saw her coming out of her peripheral vision and whipped her head to take her in. Maya saw the expected flicker of recognition in Lang's eyes.

"Not interested," Lang said. She tried to dismiss Maya by turning her head to look at the bottles of liquor lined up against the wall, then put her phone down and took a big sip of her drink.

"Free country," Maya said as she took the seat next to Lang. She waved at Nam. "I'll have what she's having, please."

Nam gave Maya an ugly look. He opened his mouth in what Maya assumed was the start of a protest before deciding against it, and poured another drink. He filled it halfway with vodka before topping it off with cranberry juice. She took a sip and recoiled. Her upper lip lifted instinctively in a grimace as she forced herself to swallow.

"This is disgusting," she said.

"Nam!" Lang said, raising her cup for a refill.

The entire salon—staff and customers—watched the scene at the bar. Most attempted some form of surreptitious spying, but a few customers took Nam's approach of openly staring at the two famous women.

"How do you drink this?" Maya asked.

"Nobody's forcing you," Lang said.

"Nobody's forcing you either, but you still seem to manage."

Lang turned her head to stare at Maya, then let her gaze drop to the hand wrapped around her cup. "You need a refund," she said flatly. "Who did your nails?" Maya glanced around until she spotted the diminutive Vietnamese lady and nodded her head in that direction. "Never get an older woman to do your nails. They can't see. You need young eyes."

Maya examined her own nails. "Guess that means neither of us has a future in cosmetology."

Lang shrugged. "Thank God we're both already rich and happy."

Maya attempted another sip, wrinkled her nose, and set the cup back down. "So, listen—"

"No," Lang interrupted. She downed the rest of her drink. "*Garçon!*" she called, raising the empty cup.

Nam continued to glare silently at her as he filled her cup with vodka and cranberry juice.

"*Garçon* is French," Maya noted.

"They should *be* French if de Gaulle hadn't lost his nerve," Lang said.

"Don't like Vietnamese people?"

"Can't stand the way they talk. Sounds like nails on a chalkboard." Lang turned her attention to Nam. "Say something," she commanded.

Nam's lips seemed to disappear beneath a baleful stare.

"Sounds like they have a cold and are trying to hawk a loogie," Lang said, turning back to Maya.

"It's awfully magnanimous of you to spend so much time with them."

"I do what I can for the little person," Lang said, taking another sip. "But I draw the line with Shia sluts." She turned, fixing Maya with a stare so sharp it could shatter glass.

Maya met the gaze and smiled organically, her dark eyes shining.

"Sorry, just thinking how much my best friend would have appreciated that bit of redirection. She used to be a professional dominatrix."

"Told you you're a slut." Lang glared at her. Part of it, she knew, was pettiness for having her insult waved away so casually.

"She told me that the trick is to always send your attention outward, forcing your clients to look inward. She said that the best way to respond to a challenge is to challenge them back, keeping them on their heels."

Lang showed her teeth in what was either a smile or a snarl.

Maya smiled ruefully. "Well, since we're on the subject of piss and vinegar, I guess it's time for me to catch up." Reluctantly, she lifted her cup, stared at it for a long moment so she could gather her courage, and drained it.

Once she regained control of her facial muscles, she smiled sweetly at Nam and held out her cup. He tried and failed to hide the sneer on his face before reaching for the vodka.

The two women sat in silence for several awkward moments. Lang picked up her phone again, pretending to scroll through the news. Maya broke the silence. "Ever think about directing that bark at something other than Nam and his shitty vodka?" she asked.

Lang put down her phone and stared at Maya. "Says here you signed up with Smith, Thompson, & Young." She nodded down at the newsfeed on her phone.

"I did."

"Yet you're still so desperate for counsel that you got your nails painted two different colors just so you could flirt with me over drinks?"

Maya paused, taking the measure of her drinking companion. Lang had bags under her eyes and evidence of mascara she hadn't washed off all the way. Her nose and cheeks glowed red from inflamed skin and busted capillaries.

"Counsel, yes, but not *only* legal counsel," Maya said at last.

Lang relaxed her prepared attack, like a tightened coil gently relaxing. She twirled her hand in a loose, impatient circle at her wrist, a theatrical gesture dripping with annoyance, silently urging Maya to get on with it.

"But that's where it gets weird," Maya said. She took a sip, grimaced, and continued. "I need attorney-client privilege before I can talk about the nonlegal counsel."

The attack drained out of Elizabeth Lang as she laughed out loud. She actually snorted before her smoker's cough kicked in. "You know, you're not as dumb as you look," she said after recovering, with what almost sounded like genuine admiration. "You know what a soft spot I have for the creative tapestry an unscrupulous media organization can weave with nothing but an anonymous leak. Too bad I don't do pro bono."

"Oh, I'll pay you."

Lang looked quizzically at Maya, interested in this riddle in spite of herself. She took out her pack of cigarettes and started tamping the box. "You know the AG will file a motion to disqualify me."

"I know," Maya said. "Lucky for you, I know some good lawyers willing to bend over backwards to keep me as a client, and they have an hourly rate of zero."

Lang scratched her forehead, picked up her drink and downed it. For the first time, she seemed unsure of herself. "Tell me one reason I should say yes," she said.

Maya hesitated and looked down at her cup. She stared at it contemplatively, lifted it, studied it, took another sip, and closed her eyes as the spirits assaulted her senses. She kept them closed for a long minute before opening them and staring directly at Lang.

"Because I think you're afraid of becoming irrelevant."

Lang's eyes darkened, her pupils shrinking into pinpricks as her lips curled into a thin venomous line. "You're a real cunt, you know," she hissed.

Maya paused, then smiled sadly. "No, I have my sharp edges, but I'm definitely not a cunt. In fact, that's kind of why I'm here." She leaned forward. "I'm in the market for a good cunt."

⚬⚯⚬

Assistant Attorney General Tom Henshaw approached the witness box, the lighter hue of its oak contrasting with the rich, dark mahogany of the bench, reflecting the soft lighting of the courtroom with its deep sheen.

"Ms. Lang, can you tell the court about your most recent legal filing?" The soft, rhythmic tapping of keys from the court recorder added background texture to his question.

"Objection, irrelevant." The AAG turned his head to look at the defense bench, filled with dark navy pinstriped suits made from high-quality wool, crisp white shirts with French cuffs, burgundy silk ties, and tailored black pantsuits.

"It speaks to the character and fitness examination," the AAG said.

"Overruled," the judge said, his face framed in silver glasses underneath a thinning palette of white on top of his head that contrasted with the folds of his traditional black robe. He wore a stern expression of authority.

Elizabeth Lang seemed unfazed. Her pixie cut looked regal. She wore an elegant emerald-colored dress of wool and silk, her rosacea buried beneath layers of primer and foundation. "I filed a complaint against Nail Heaven," she said calmly.

"Can you tell the court the nature of your complaint?" Henshaw said.

"They tried to deny me booze," Lang said.

Henshaw widened his eyes in mock surprise. "With your pedicure? Or did you try to purchase the alcohol separately?"

Lang looked at Henshaw, then beyond his bench. Given the amount of publicity surrounding the case, Judge Harper had restricted electronic devices in the courtroom to minimize distractions and prevent recording. Journalists seated in the courtroom scribbled in their notebooks, trying to capture just the right quote, the right look, weaving their tapestries out of nothing more than a simple sigh or momentary exasperation. They were snakes. She was a snake charmer, but she knew to be careful; everyone who dances with snakes gets bitten from time to time.

"They tried to deny me *free* booze," Lang clarified.

Henshaw allowed for a pregnant pause before continuing. "Can you elaborate on why you sued a nail salon because they refused you free alcohol?"

"Because the TABC—"

"The TABC?"

"Because the Texas Alcohol Beverage Commission mandates that salons that have liquor without a license must not deny any adult who enters the venue and requests it. And they must not accept money for the liquor, not even a tip." Lang spoke emotionlessly, betraying neither embarrassment nor hurry.

Henshaw nodded his head slowly. "So, let me get this straight. You, with all your wealth, sued a bunch of poor Vietnamese people to serve you their alcohol for free on their premises?" he asked.

"Objection."

"Overruled."

"Guess I needed a fight," Lang said.

Henshaw adjusted his jacket and looked at the defense before turning back toward the witness box. "Ms. Lang, even without your involvement, Dr. Maya Russell has highly competent legal counsel," he said, waving his left arm toward the sea of Italian fabrics behind the defense table. "But you have a particular history with Governor Callahan, is that right?"

"Objection," interjected a voice draped in a meticulously tailored pinstriped suit. "The state OAG is the plaintiff, not the governor."

"Your Honor, as you no doubt know, Governor Callahan has been quite vocal about the case. It speaks to bias," Henshaw said.

The judge hesitated for a moment, looking thoughtful. "I'll allow this line of questioning for now," he said. "Make your point."

"Yes," Lang said, smoothing the dress out over her thighs. She'd clearly been expecting this question.

Henshaw nodded. "Is it true that both you and Governor Callahan co-wrote an article that was guest published in *USA Today* last year?"

"Yes," Lang said, staring directly at Henshaw, almost as if daring him to continue his own line of questioning.

Henshaw walked back to his bench and grabbed a sheet of paper. "Can you verify that this is a copy of that article?" he asked, handing it to Lang.

Lang scanned it with squinted eyes and pursed lips. "Yes," she said, willing her heart to slow down.

"Thank you. Can you read the highlighted section for the court, please?"

Lang put her thumb to her temple, closed her eyes, and slowly ran the pad of her index finger across her forehead before opening her eyes. Let the snakes have a field day.

"For years, the Left has been trying to invent new ways to divide us, slowly eroding the system of values that has held our great society together. Gay marriage wasn't enough for them. Now they want to destroy the concept of gender altogether, to let boys be girls and girls be boys, and both be *theys and zirs*. Their moral corruption knows no bounds. We're proud that the state of Texas, under the leadership of Governor Callahan, has adopted the toughest transgender restrictions in the country."

A thick silence hung over the courtroom. All the journalists stopped scribbling on their notepads, eyeing Lang with curiosity and anticipation, not wanting to miss this weave in their tapestry. Judge Harper looked curiously through his glasses between Lang and Henshaw. The AAG allowed the silence to last for a few awkward moments before continuing.

"Ms. Lang, can you tell the court why you resigned from the United States Senate?"

Lang silenced the objection before filing, holding up her right hand toward the defense bench without looking at it. She had a primal look as she stared Henshaw directly in the eyes, like an animal about to strike.

"Because I killed my daughter," she said. There was an audible gasp from the audience at the directness of her answer.

Henshaw softened his voice to show empathy, more on his back foot than he expected to be. "I'm sorry, Ms. Lang. I know this is hard, but I need you to be more specific."

"My daughter had gender dysphoria. I knew that when I wrote the article. I did it anyway because it was good for fundraising. She slit her wrists while I was accepting donations on the back of that article," Lang said, her look ferocious.

Henshaw inhaled deeply and sighed. "Ms. Lang, as you know, this trial, and the motions leading up to it during an election year, will be a media circus. Why would you want to subject yourself to it?"

Lang's nostrils flared as she inhaled with deliberate slowness. The air seemed to fuel a fire building behind her piercing eyes. Her lips curled upward into a predator's grin, exposing teeth that seemed ready to tear into her prey. The intensity of her gaze sharpened, unyielding, and Henshaw visibly faltered under its weight.

"Because pretty soon you'll be done asking questions…" she said, her voice dripping with quiet malice, each word slicing through the air like a blade.

"… and then it'll be my turn."

THE ITALIAN, PART 1

She stands in the house of mirrors, each reflection a different age of Hannah, all asking questions at once.

The youngest Hannah, gap-toothed and earnest, tugs at her sleeve. "How did you come to Canada?" It is snowing. The parliament looms before them.

"Granddaddy brought me on a silver bird that flew through the clouds."

Seven-year-old Hannah holds a globe, her finger pressed against Iraq. "Is this where you're from? Can we visit?"

"It's not safe." Her voice echoes off glass that suddenly feels too close.

Nine-year-old Hannah appears in another panel, clutching a school project. "I need to draw my family tree. What were my other grandparents' names?"

The mirrors begin to spin. She reaches for the walls, but they're slick, offering no grip. "Use Grandpa Harry and Grandma Nancy."

"But what about your real parents?"

The mirrors crack but don't break, multiplying the Hannahs into dozens, hundreds. Their voices overlap:

"Do you still speak Arabic?"

"What type of food did you eat?"

"How did you escape?"

"What was your mom like?"

"Can we visit?"

"Why won't you teach me Arabic?"

"Did you see them die?"

She presses her palms against her temples. The room tilts. Teenage Hannah leans against the counter in their old kitchen, no longer asking with innocence but with the surgical precision of adolescent angst.

"You know I can Google Dujail, right?"

Her hands shake as she chops the vegetables. The knife moves faster. "There's nothing to Google."

"1982. You were seven."

The knife slips. Blood wells on her finger, but in the mirror it spreads like water, staining everything.

"Mom, I'm seventeen. I deserve—"

"You deserve nothing!" The words explode from her like shrapnel. In the mirrors, she sees herself transforming. She sees her hands and her words become weapons—shoving journalists, stabbing Tommy Nielsen with a pencil after he teased about her past, screaming at her mom struggling through stroke and stutter, building walls of cruelty like armor.

"That skirt's too short."

"Is that acne?"

"You've been eating a lot lately, everything okay?"

"Who's that boy? He looks too old for you."

"You know, crop tops aren't for everyone…"

Each deflection bounces between the mirrors, amplifying. Hannah's hurt multiplies, but so does her determination.

"I hired a tutor," Hannah announces. "I'm learning Arabic."

"Why?" she whispers through a parched throat.

"Ana sayyida," Hannah says, her pronunciation careful but clear. "I am a sayyida. Like you. Like your mom."

The mirrors ahead stretch ominously like date palms reaching for the sky, their shadows overwhelming her. She runs. Her legs burn. The hallway tilts, spins. She can hear them all, questions and accusations shouted through every panel like footsteps chasing her. The mirrors shatter one by one as she passes, glass flying at her like gold-flecked daggers shooting out of hazel-colored eyes.

She runs blindly, arms protecting her face, searching for any escape. The corridor branches and branches again, each path narrower than the last, until she's pushing through spaces barely wide enough for her body, the mirror shards catching at her clothes, her skin. She falls, shards of glass bloodying her knees and hands. She feels wet tears roll down her cheeks as she regains her footing.

There is nowhere to go, the mirror in front of her blocking her path, her own image reflecting back at her. She bursts through, tumbling into a Texas evening that wraps around her like absolution. She doesn't pack, doesn't plan, just drives until she finds herself at a hotel, then walking, then sitting at a patio where the air doesn't ask questions.

"Prego," he says, pulling out a chair, smiling at her.

⌘

"That him?" Richard asked, tilting the iPad slightly as he looked up at the Facebook profile.

She nodded, her lips curling into a faint, secretive smile.

"That's quite the 'stache," he said, his voice tinged with mock judgment.

She bit her bottom lip.

"Looks like he's still single," he added, scrolling slowly, his tone laced with curiosity.

"Lucky for me," she replied, her voice light and teasing.

The memory of Leo sent a current of electricity through her body, awakening nerves she thought had long forgotten his touch. She could almost taste the remnants of that Chianti on her tongue, feel the weight of that summer night's humidity on her skin.

It was strange how certain memories lived in the body, dormant until summoned, only to rush back with such vivid intensity that time itself seemed to yield.

She stretched out languidly like a cat and tugged on the top sheet, teasing her skin with its velvety texture as her nipples hardened against the soft fabric and goosebumps spread across her flesh. Her smile deepened as she saw him put the iPad on the nightstand.

His lips found her neck, soft at first, then more insistent, his kisses trailing over her skin. She arched her neck, tilting her head to give him more space, inviting his touch.

"So." He breathed warmth against her neck as he bent down to kiss the delicate curve just below her ear. "Tell me about him."

Her lips parted in a smile, soft and teasing. "What do you want to know?"

His fingers traced invisible patterns on her skin, leaving trails of heat that lingered long after he moved on. She watched his face as he touched her, fascinated by the way his pupils dilated when she responded to his caress, the slight parting of his lips when her breath caught. There was something intoxicating about his curiosity, about the way he wanted to map the topography of her past as thoroughly as he'd mapped her body.

He drew the top sheet up to her shoulders. The sheet became a cocoon of warmth, its gentle weight settling over her like a protective embrace. He slowly slid his hand on top of the sheet until it found the fullness of her right breast, his palm settling over the soft fabric like it belonged there. "How'd you meet?" His voice was a mix of curiosity and mischief.

"Mmmm," she sighed. "I think it was when you were in Geneva. I went out one night for Italian when Hannah and I were fighting. He was my server."

He lifted himself so that he could kiss her. For a few moments, they simply explored each other's lips and stared at each other.

They were really going to do this.

His pulse quickened.

It was as if Maya needed to burn away certain parts of herself before stepping into the conflagration that was coming. Elizabeth Lang had shocked the political establishment by emerging from her self-imposed exile to champion Maya's cause, a conservative attack dog now baring her teeth at her former allies. The punditry couldn't make sense of it. Lang, once the darling of traditional values voters, was now publicly eviscerating the state's case against The Girl from Dujail. Each time she appeared on cable news, public interest in Maya increased. The gambit was audacious, its endgame known only to Maya, Richard, and Lang.

It would either liberate Maya or destroy her completely.

She needed this act of abandon. It was preparation, a rehearsal for vulnerability, one last glorious "Fuck You" to the world before the real sacrifice began.

She smiled dreamily. "I went to one of those Italian restaurants with patio seating and ordered a glass of wine. Leo had this amazing Italian accent, and I couldn't stop talking to him."

As she spoke, his fingers wandered under the sheet, tracing the delicate edge of her panties where soft, warm skin met silky fabric.

"*Prego,*"—her voice adopted that singsong lilt she loved to imitate—"he kept saying. And he kept calling me *lady*. He 'splained me about the meal. *Let me 'splain you,* he kept saying when I asked questions. So I asked a lot of questions. I think he *'splained* every meal on the menu."

"Slow night at the restaurant?" he asked as his palm pressed gently against the soft curve of her panties, his fingers on the outside, caressing her inner thighs. His fingers spread out, tracing the edges of the delicate material with his index and ring fingers, gliding up both sides of her panty line simultaneously, like an artist framing his canvas.

Her gaze unfocused as her mind drifted back. "I don't remember. Maybe he sensed my hunger."

"Who made the first move?" he asked. He moved under the sheets. His lips brushed against her skin as he kissed his way down her stomach.

Her eyelids fluttered closed, and she let herself sink into the fog of the memory. "I don't remember," she admitted, her voice becoming softer, tinged with a faintly teasing edge. "It was kind of a dance. I said I was staying at the hotel next door and looking for something to do. He said he got off work at ten." She exhaled slowly, her lips curling into a subtle smile. "None of it was awkward or forced. It just… happened."

He crawled between her legs, the weight of his body pressing into the bed as the air shifted around him. His tongue replaced the path his fingers had traced earlier, gliding along the delicate edge where fabric met skin. The satin of her panties felt cool and smooth against his lips, a contrast to the warmth radiating from her body, only to be reflected back by the top sheet above them. His breath lingered against her, a soft tease of warmth that seemed to amplify every sensation.

"And…?" he said, his voice low and rough, the vibration of his words brushing against her skin.

The interplay of silk, breath, and skin melted her, making thought difficult. She closed her eyes and smiled. "And he fucked me like a stallion."

"What'd he do?" She felt the question as much as heard it.

She frowned slightly and creased her brow. "I don't remember the details like that. I'm not kinky like you."

His lips brushed lightly over the fabric as he spoke. "Can you remember *any* of it?" he asked, his tone a mixture of challenge and flirtation.

She lifted the sheet so she could look at him. "Yeah," she said, her voice dipping into a husky timbre. "Every time he opened his mouth and words fell out of it, I got wet. *Especially* when he got mad."

He let his right hand glide slowly down her left panty line, the pads of his fingers brushing lightly against her skin, warm and inviting beneath the silky barrier. With a slow, teasing motion, he gathered the fabric and gently bunched it to the side, pulling it toward her right thigh crease. The movement caused the panties to press snugly into her, exposing the radiant heat between her thighs.

"He had this… intensity about him." Her eyes grew distant with memory. "Not just in bed. Once, he noticed me eyeing this old man at another table who was dining alone. Leo whispered to me that the man had been coming every Tuesday for ten years, always ordering the same dish his late wife had loved on their first date."

He ran his tongue along the crease of her thigh.

"Umm, do you have any words for what happened in the *bedroom?*" he asked, his voice tinged with a trace of desperation.

She tilted her head, her face twisting in concentration. "Oh. I remember he liked it when I sat on his face," she said finally.

He froze before lifting his head to stare at her. "You sat on his face?" The words landed somewhere between a question and an accusation.

"Yeah," she smirked at him. "Guess he's like you in that regard. And I was hungry."

He blinked, still processing, searching for words.

She laughed, reaching down to pat his head. "Aww… I know sometimes you wish you could be a deep-sea anglerfish."

He frowned dramatically, his lips pulling into a petulant pout that made her laugh even harder.

"Besides," she said, letting the word hang as she traced her fingers lazily through his hair.

"Besides what?" he asked, his tone edging into mock impatience.

"Well…" she teased, drawing out the moment just enough to make him squirm.

"Well, what?" His voice rose a notch, and she could tell he was fighting a smile.

"It's just…" She grinned wickedly. "Well. You saw the 'stache."

He lifted into a knee-down plank position, lifting the sheet off her as she held it up. "You're telling me all I had to do was grow a mustache all these years?"

She looked surprised. "What? No! He had an Italian accent, too."

"What's the accent got to do with sex?" he asked, his voice filled with theatrical indignation.

"I don't know," she said, a little defensively. "I like to just fall into my body. I'm not good at putting words to it like you are."

He sighed heavily, the exaggerated sound of frustration a mix of humor and arousal.

"I can put on sitar music if you want, though," she added with a cheeky grin.

His sigh deepened, long and drawn out, its warmth caressing her down the length of her labia.

Then he put his tongue to a use other than speech.

⁂

The next morning, he sat on the back patio bundled in his thick fleece robe, a blanket draped over his legs to ward off the winter chill that bit at the air despite the weak sunlight filtering through the bare branches above. Faint steam rose from the coffee mug and mingled with his visible breath as he caught up on the news. The distant sound of a neighbor's dog barking and the faint hum of traffic were the only interruptions to the crisp, quiet morning.

He spotted her through the glass of the sliding door. She moved with an almost absent grace, her thick robe clinging to her frame as she poured herself a cup of coffee. She slid the door open and shuffled over to him.

With a deep sigh, she fell into the loveseat and rested her head on his shoulder, her warmth a stark contrast to the cold air. The scent of her coffee mixed with the winter morning, creating an oddly comforting blend of familiarity.

"He said no," she said, her voice quiet but carrying the weight of disappointment.

He turned his head to look at her, his breath momentarily caught. "No?" he repeated, disbelief and hope wrestling in his tone.

She nodded against his shoulder without lifting her head. "It was probably something like 'No-a,' but it was definitely a no." She bit her lip, then gave a dramatic grimace, her expression half-playful, half-pained.

He sighed in sympathy, his breath visible in the air as it joined hers in a moment of shared defeat. They sat together in silence, their coffee cooling under the weight of her words.

Finally, he broke the silence. "Honey?"

She tilted her head up to meet his gaze, her brows slightly furrowed, her lips pursed in question.

"Do you think…" He hesitated. "Do you think we might be in over our heads?"

THE GIRL FROM DALLAS

Madison scrolled through her TikTok feed as they waited. Her dad sat next to her on the lime green bench, opting for it over the teal-colored barrel chairs that looked uncomfortable. Several kid drawings framed the baby blue wall behind her. She'd been to the child advocacy center several times since her hospital visit, but this was the first time since her diagnosis.

Through her AirPods, a Black ex-pastor filled her ears with a voice thick with indignation. "I literally believed that there was a *God* who had inspired men—only men—to write its words in a book, and that every word in this book was true, real, unchallenged, and there were no contradictions in the entire book." His expression twisted, incredulous and sharp. "It was the word of God. By the way, every religion has a book inspired by *their* God. What does that say about *this* book and *that* God?" He pointed upward. "Or that God?" He pointed downward. "Or that God?" He gestured sideways.

Madison scrolled up.

A twenty-something woman with shoulder-length hair and perfect makeup addressed the camera with an unnerving certainty.

"Do you know that people who deconstruct have abandoned the authority of God and made themselves their own authority, essentially becoming their own God? They lean on their own understanding rather than trusting God. Here's the truth about deconstructed Christians…"

She scrolled up.

A white man with sun-bleached hair and a beard talked about his personal journey, how he had to abandon his family to separate from the church.

"Madison," the woman called, opening the door to usher her in. Madison's stomach clenched as she took the AirPods out of her ears, their absence making the world around her uncomfortably loud. She slid them into their container with trembling fingers and stood up. Her dad reached for her hand, gently squeezing it.

"Remember, they're here to help," he said, his smile falling short of its intended reassurance. "Just tell them everything you know, and it will be okay."

She nodded and started walking back. As she stepped forward, her legs felt shaky beneath her. She tried to breathe steadily, but the air felt too thin, as if the walls were closing in around her. Through the door, the hallway stretched in front of her like something out of a nightmare, narrowing with every step. It felt like the opening scene of a horror movie, where the director manipulates the frame to funnel all attention into a single, ominous point. Her heart pounded harder, the beats echoing in her ears like a distant drumbeat.

She intentionally turned her head to break the effect. Ms. Lang looked up from her phone to catch Madison's look, gave her a soft smile, and nodded at her, as if willing her along. Ms. Lang was a curious woman.

Madison turned back toward the hallway, taking deep breaths to calm her beating heart as she navigated it, following someone into the interview room. That's not what they called it, but Madison knew that's what it was. She knew that there were law enforcement observers she couldn't see listening in, and that the entire setup was meant to make her feel more comfortable. She hated it.

The room felt painfully sterile, the chair facing her loveseat, like a forced confrontation. A thirty-something woman with blonde hair tied into a small bun sat down in the chair, dropped her bag next to her, and beckoned for Madison to take the loveseat.

"Hello, Madison," Mrs. Greer said. "I hear I owe you a happy birthday."

"Thanks," Madison said.

"Doing anything fun?" Mrs. Greer asked, as if willing Madison to meet her enthusiasm halfway.

Madison shrugged.

Mrs. Greer responded with a small, bouncing shrug of her own, her smile widening as if trying to mirror Madison into engagement. "Well, thank you for coming. How are you feeling?"

Madison's mind felt like a storm cloud with no rain—heavy and oppressive, but empty at the same time. She searched for a word to give voice to the churn inside her, but found none. Empty? Acid-y? Stormy? All of them seemed wrong and right at the same time. The weight of unnamable burdens made her shrug again; the motion felt heavy and hollow. She felt like she had lost all her masks—naked in a way no one else could see.

"That's okay," Mrs. Greer said gently, as though Madison's silence was just another piece of the puzzle she was eager to solve. "I understand you have an amazing vocabulary. Do you know what *alexithymia* is?"

Madison shook her head.

"Alexithymia describes someone who has trouble identifying

and naming emotions. It's pretty common with people on the spectrum." Mrs. Greer twisted open the cap of her water bottle. The crack of the plastic seemed unnaturally loud in the quiet room. She took a long sip before reaching into her bag and pulling out a laminated circle with several colors emanating as wedges from the center.

"This is called a Feelings Wheel," she said, holding it up like a puzzle piece. "It's kind of like a color wheel, but for emotions. The Feelings Wheel is a way to help you put words to feelings." She handed the wheel to Madison, who looked down to study it.

"Rather than trying to isolate a single word, can you just pick one of the colors we can explore together?" Mrs. Greer continued. "Let's start with the middle circle, which defines the primary emotion. Do you identify with any of those primary emotions?"

Madison stared at the center of the wheel. It was easy to rule out the orange (happy), green (surprised), and brown (disgusted) wedges. After studying it for a moment, she pointed to pink.

Mrs. Greer nodded. "Fearful. I can understand that. And it's okay to be afraid."

Madison tugged at the hem of her too-short grey hoodie to cover the hem of her sweatpants. She'd gained quite a bit of weight since her recovery and had to buy new clothes from Walmart. She avoided the mirror whenever she could; her reflection didn't look like her anymore. Everything felt heavier now—her clothes, her body, her thoughts.

"What scares you the most?" Mrs. Greer's voice was calm.

Madison looked down at her feet. "Dad says I may have to go into the foster care system if he goes to prison." Her voice was almost a whisper.

Mrs. Greer didn't flinch. She simply nodded, her face neutral. Madison hated that expression, the way it showed no surprise, no concern, just professional patience. It felt cold.

Madison shifted her weight in the chair and glanced at the colorful wheel in her lap. It looked garish and absurd against the washed-out tones of her hoodie, a splash of misplaced cheer that only made her feel worse.

"Nobody at church will talk to me anymore." The betrayal stung worse than she'd ever admit. These were people who'd hugged her every Sunday, who'd brought casseroles when Mom died, who'd promised they were her family, too. Now they couldn't even look at her. "Dad asked my mom's friend Lauren if she'd take care of me and she said no."

"Is there anyone else?" Mrs. Greer asked, her voice even, betraying no urgency.

Madison shook her head slowly, her movements small and trembling, like she was trying to stay invisible. Tears slid down her cheeks, soft and relentless. "Dad was raised by a single mom who died of cancer. Mom's parents died a few years back. And all their friends are part of the church and the church hates both of us."

Her voice broke on the word *hates*, and the tears came faster. They felt hot against her cold skin, dripping onto the wheel she still held in her lap. Mrs. Greer sat back in her chair, unmoving, her face as neutral as ever. Madison could feel her watching, studying her, waiting for her to unravel completely. She hated her for that. She hated this room, this wheel, this entire process. She hated feeling like an experiment under a magnifying glass.

The tears slowed, and her chest tightened with a new emotion, one she recognized—anger. It burned quietly in her core, warming the icy edges of her despair. Her hatred steadied her, held her back from the meltdown that had been clawing at her throat. Slowly, she inhaled through her nose, willing herself to regain control. Her fingers tightened around the wheel, her knuckles white. She lifted her head slightly, the tears drying on her cheeks, leaving faint tracks behind.

"Being able to name the emotions doesn't make them go away, but it helps others understand how you're feeling and it can help you deal with them," Mrs. Greer said finally, with a gentle voice.

Madison's breathing hitched as she tried to form words, her chest rising and falling in erratic bursts. "I feel all of these," she finally sobbed, her voice breaking. "Worthless… insignificant… overwhelmed…" Each word escaped her lips like a shard of glass. When the dam inside her finally burst, her words dissolved into gasps and hiccupping sobs as her body convulsed under the weight of it all.

Her throat clenched tight, choking her voice into a strangled whimper. Tears streamed down her face in hot, endless rivers, mixing with the mucus as she tried to breathe through it all. Fragments of thoughts crashed together in her mind, the words spinning faster and louder until they blurred into a deafening roar that drowned everything else.

Prison. Alone. Foster care. Eli. God. Retard. Slut. Broken. Worthless.

Her hands shot up over her head, clutching at the air as if she could pull it down to steady herself. Her body rocked back and forth, a desperate rhythm she couldn't control, the only thing keeping her from falling apart completely.

The loveseat shifted slightly underneath her, her movements like a caged animal searching for an escape. Her fingers clawed at her scalp, tangling in her hair, as her sobs grew louder, more guttural. The emotions tore through her like a storm she couldn't outrun. Each wave crashed harder than the last. Her chest heaved with the effort to keep breathing.

Mrs. Greer sat still across from her, watching the storm unfold, her expression calm but watchful. Madison hated the calmness, hated the distance in it, hated the way it made her feel small and wild and out of control. She wanted to scream at her, to lash out, but the sobs kept stealing her breath, leaving her powerless in the eye of her own hurricane.

It took several tissues and ragged breaths before Madison could finally clear her nose enough to breathe through it again. Her fingers gripped the crumpled tissues tightly, her knuckles pale against the damp, wrinkled paper. "Where do you want me to put these?" she asked in a flat, lifeless voice, devoid of any mask she usually wore. Her face was pale, her eyes glassy and red-rimmed.

Mrs. Greer moved with practiced calm, standing up and bringing over a small trash can. She placed it gently in front of Madison, meeting her eyes for just a moment before sitting back down.

"Madison, I expect anyone would feel overwhelmed in your position," Mrs. Greer said, her voice low and even, like she was trying to soothe a skittish animal. "I want you to know that, even though it may not feel like it to you, you are neither worthless nor insignificant. You're a victim. You didn't cause this."

Madison felt the familiar swooshing sound of reality closing in on her. Everything blurred into a single, claustrophobic point, and she felt like she was being swallowed whole.

"Do you remember what we talked about last time? How disorienting it is for so many people who lose the foundation of their relationship with their church?"

Madison stared at the laminated Feelings Wheel in her lap. "Deconstructionism," she murmured, her voice flat, almost detached.

"That's right," Mrs. Greer said, leaning forward slightly. "A lot of people describe it as losing the 'plausibility structures' that allow them to make sense of the world. It's like the scaffolding you've always leaned on is suddenly gone. Is it possible you're not sure who or what to trust anymore?"

Madison's jaw tightened. "I know everyone at church has abandoned me. I know my dad's going to prison and I'm going to go into foster care. I know everyone's attacking me. I know they're calling me 'a retard' on the news."

Ms. Lang had told Madison that it was almost certainly a private detective—not a reporter—who had taken pictures outside the diagnostic center, and that it was almost certainly Pastor Lawson who paid the bills. Madison refused to believe that a pastor would do such a thing.

She'd spent years organizing her world into precise categories and predictable patterns: color-coordinated clothes, organized markers, lined-up shoes. The church had been another system with clear rules and boundaries. Now everything was scrambled, its pieces scattered and unfamiliar. She couldn't sort through the chaos to make sense of anything anymore. The rules she'd relied on had changed without warning.

Mrs. Greer watched the new meltdown patiently, moving to sit next to Madison on the loveseat as she cried and rocked, close enough to offer her presence without crowding Madison. She waited silently until Madison could blow her nose and speak again.

"I heard former Senator Lang is in the waiting room. Is that right?" Mrs. Greer asked softly.

Madison nodded, her face still puffy and red.

"Have you seen *her* on the news?"

Madison nodded again.

"Powerful stuff," Mrs. Greer said, her tone warm and measured. "You've got a real supporter, someone who knows how to push back on that nonsense."

Madison sniffed. "She says she thinks Dad won't have to do more than a year, but some dominoes have to fall into place first."

"What dominoes?" Mrs. Greer asked, trying to hide the fascination in her voice, conscious she was being watched from behind the two-way glass.

Madison lifted her shoulders on an inhale and dropped them on the exhale. "She says they're calling me 'retarded' and 'a slut' to discredit me, that it's a whisper campaign."

Mrs. Greer smiled wistfully. "Madison, lots of people have

autism. Some of the smartest people alive have it. It's only called a disorder because it's less common, but autism gives you a unique advantage in several areas, like your ability to focus on a single thing over time. The attacks don't matter. It's just people who are scared or confused. A lot of people have lost their plausibility structures over time, and a lot of people lash out when that happens to them."

"Why?" Madison asked, turning her tear-streaked face toward Mrs. Greer.

"Why are they scared?" Mrs. Greer asked.

"No. Why did they lose their plausibility structures? Did the church kick them out?"

Mrs. Greer took another deep inhale and looked contemplative. "No, not usually. And it's not just with the church. We're just going through weird times." She thought for a moment but gave up coming up with anything better. "It's just weird times, and a lot of people are confused. Some of them get angry and start name-calling."

Madison allowed herself to drift back into memory. She remembered her dad's irritation during that first conversation with Ms. Lang.

"Why are you here?" he had asked, his voice clipped, barely concealing his frustration. He stood at the table in the kitchenette. Madison remembered the unwashed pots from their lunch of macaroni and cheese on the small stovetop and the dirty dishes in the sink. She also remembered the way Ms. Lang looked directly at both of them. The intensity of the stare struck her, like she could somehow focus all her attention on you like a laser beam.

Ms. Lang leaned back in the chair at the Residence Inn and chewed at her lip as she thought about her answer. Madison's dad was in the final stages of selling their house, so the Residence Inn had become their new home. Madison remembered how he'd cried when he told her that with the civil lawsuit and the business he'd lost, he'd run out of money and had no other options. She wasn't used to Papa Bear being the one to have a meltdown, especially about something as stupid as money. Besides, Ms. Lang had been clear that she wasn't charging him.

"Is it about that fucking doctor?" he demanded, his voice rising. Sergeant Baker lifted his head as if deciding whether he needed to intervene.

Ms. Lang didn't flinch. She didn't rush to answer, didn't even seem fazed by the challenge. Instead, she sat with an infuriating calm, tapping her fingers lightly on the armrest of her chair. Her silence only seemed to fuel her dad's anger.

"People like you don't help people like me," he said, his voice tight with resentment.

"You're right," Ms. Lang said, finally, like she had been waiting for this acknowledgment before starting. "People like me *use* people like you, and when we're done, we *discard* people like you."

She remembered how her dad had looked away from the stare.

"Unfortunately for you, there are a lot of people like me who want nothing more than for you and Madison to simply disappear. And the only thing between you and them is that fucking doctor."

Her dad's glare darkened, his jaw tightening as the muscles in his neck visibly strained. "She just wants Madison as a prop," he spat. "She'll parade her around to gain sympathy with the jury when it's her turn to face trial."

Ms. Lang took out a cigarette, pressed the butt into the table, and slid her fingers from top to bottom. When her fingers hit the table, she flipped the cigarette over and repeated the process. "Maya will never see a jury," she said, her voice steady, matter-of-fact. "I guarantee you, Callahan and his advisors are already scheming how to drop the case before the general election without losing Lawson and the evangelical vote. He can't afford a trial."

That broke something in her dad. Madison could see the energy drain from his body as he slumped into the chair across from Lang. He reached down to scratch Sergeant Baker behind the ears, his fingers moving absently, his eyes heavy with exhaustion. "Then what *does* she want?" he asked, his voice quieter now, almost fragile.

Lang leaned forward, her eyes narrowing. "Maybe she doesn't want to be collateral damage. What does it matter?"

Madison blinked and pulled herself back to the moment, sitting across from Mrs. Greer. She folded her hands tightly in her lap.

"She—Ms. Lang—talks to me like an adult," Madison said.

"Any part of her conversations you want to talk about?" Mrs. Greer asked, her curiosity carefully concealed beneath a mask of professionalism.

"She said I need to tell you everything I remember to the best of my ability."

Mrs. Greer stood slowly, crossing the small room with measured steps. She settled back into the opposing chair and fixed Madison with a steady, serious gaze. "Madison," she said gently, "no matter how it happened, as a minor, you were victimized. What can you tell me about the father?"

The question hit her like a physical blow, as if the words themselves had weight and purpose, aimed directly at her core. Madison's chest tightened, her throat constricting as though the answer itself was coiling around her neck, choking her. Her mouth opened, but no words came. They were buried, suffocating her beneath the storm.

Instead, a violent gasp broke free, ripping through her like a storm. Her entire body trembled, the quake starting deep in her chest and radiating outward until even her fingertips shook. The air in the room grew suffocatingly heavy.

"I don't remember!" she screamed, her voice jagged and raw.

The sound reverberated in the small room, filling every corner with her anguish. And then, as though the force of the eruption had shattered something deep within her, her body convulsed, folding in on itself. Her hands flew to her head, gripping her temples as she rocked violently, her sobs merging with the tremors that seemed to tear her apart from the inside out.

The world around her blurred—the sterile room, the Feelings Wheel, Mrs. Greer's calm demeanor. All of it dissolved into a haze of overwhelming emotion. She was drowning in it, a sea of colors she couldn't name, unable to find the surface.

THE CHEF

Julia settled into one of the patio chairs, her gaze thoughtful. "They took a sample of the fetus, right? Can they compel DNA evidence without Madison pointing her finger at him?"

On the loveseat, Maya rested her head on Richard's shoulder. A fire crackled nearby, its warmth a counter to the wintry gray atmosphere.

"According to Elizabeth, sometimes, but not this time," Maya said. "Lawson is suing Travis for defamation and putting a sea of lawyers around his son, so it complicates the decision-making for the judge."

"Doesn't help that the judge is the governor's lapdog," Richard added.

Julia stared into the fire pit, her voice subdued. "What does that mean for Madison's dad?"

Richard scratched his chin before answering. "He's going to prison, no matter what. But he'll spend a lot less time there if there's a threat of a sympathetic jury seeing him as protecting his daughter from an abusive pastor."

The fire crackled, filling the reflective silence that followed.

Julia took a sip of chardonnay. "I can't imagine what it must be like for her," she said. "It's like her entire world is turning upside down."

"She's tough and super smart," Richard said.

"I know this is way worse than before," Julia said, giving Maya a concerned look. "How are you handling all the attention?"

Maya shrugged, her cheeks shifting into a faint, tired smile. "I'm pretty used to telling journalists to fuck off, and I guess I've come to some kind of truce with everyone at work. It's the everyday stuff that gets to me, like going to the grocery store and having some grandma recognize me and try to sympathize with my childhood. That's the hard part."

Julia regarded Maya with a somber expression. "I imagine you, of all people, can relate to what Madison's going through."

Maya sighed, glancing down at her own glass of chardonnay. "Took a few years, but thank Allah I turned out to be a God-fearing atheist," she said.

Julia's expression softened behind a short laugh. She smiled impishly, her eyes gleaming. "A pretty hedonistic God-fearing atheist at that."

Maya's lips curved into a self-conscious smile as a faint blush crept up her cheeks. Richard wrapped his arm around her, pulling her into his chest with a grin.

"Are you *really* okay with this?" Maya asked.

Julia leaned forward, her midnight-black hair falling loose from its bun as she fixed Maya with an intense, knowing stare. "Girl, please. I can't think of anything I'd rather be doing than helping you plan your gangbang. God knows no one deserves it more. I'm honored, seriously."

There was a fluid confidence in how Julia occupied space, her posture both relaxed and alert, a woman comfortable with both power and vulnerability. Where Maya built walls, Julia created doors. Even now, she could defuse Maya's tension with a well-placed eyebrow raise or inside joke, references to adventures only they shared: the midnight swim that had nearly gotten them expelled, the weekend in New Orleans they'd sworn never to discuss, *The Canterbury Tales.*

Their friendship had weathered Maya's impulsive relationships and equally abrupt departures, Julia's career controversies, and the geographic distances that had sometimes separated them, sustained by an unwavering certainty that when everything else failed, they would remain each other's constant.

Maya first met Julia during her second month at Harvard, when a persistent student reporter from *The Crimson* kept ambushing Maya outside classes, desperate for an exposé on The Girl from Dujail. After days of harassment, Julia, a fellow freshman Maya had never spoken to, intervened spectacularly, snatching the student's recorder and threatening to "recreate scenes from *The Exorcist* with it" if he didn't back the fuck off.

That night, Julia appeared at Maya's dorm room with a bottle of tequila and two shot glasses. As they worked through the bottle on the roof of Weld Hall, they discovered they'd both slept with Professor Harrison from Comparative Literature, Maya during orientation week and Julia the previous weekend. When Julia described his distinctive habit of quoting Chaucer at climactic moments, they dissolved into hysterical laughter that cemented an immediate, unshakable bond, two women who recognized in each other a similar capacity for both intense recklessness and fierce loyalty.

While Maya was drowning in anatomy textbooks and caffeine at medical school, Julia found her unlikely calling on Boston's underground scene.

It started as a joke, answering an ad seeking "stern women with commanding presence" to settle a long-standing bet with Maya about who could land the strangest job. But something clicked when she first stepped into the converted warehouse in Southie, introducing herself as "Mistress Veritas"—an ironic nod to Harvard's motto that became her professional signature. What started as three clients in a rented studio with improvised equipment evolved into a discreet brownstone operation by the time Maya graduated.

Julia discovered she had a natural talent for reading desires people couldn't articulate themselves, for creating scenes that went beyond physical sensation to psychological catharsis. In that brief interlude after university, she learned more about human vulnerability and motivation than any textbook could teach.

When Maya disclosed her plans with Elizabeth Lang, Julia held Maya's hands, looked her dead in the eyes, and promised to be with her every step of the way, even as she struggled to hold back the flood of tears that threatened to overwhelm her.

When Maya then transitioned to what she euphemistically called "the project," Julia had simply raised an eyebrow and reminded her that orchestrating complex scenarios involving multiple participants' desires was quite literally her professional expertise.

Richard broke into a wide grin as Maya buried her face into his chest, her laughter muffled against him.

Julia's expression softened, and she glanced at Richard approvingly. "You know, I think it's amazing that you're both working through this together. For what it's worth, I think you're an incredible partner."

Richard chuckled. "Well, you know what they say—if you can't change 'em, join 'em."

Everyone laughed, the sound spilling out into the chilly air as the fire crackled softly in the background. Maya shifted slightly, snuggling deeper into Richard's embrace. Her voice was soft, almost contemplative, as she shrugged her shoulders. "Looking back on my life, I'm pretty sure running and fucking have been my primary coping strategies during stress."

"Don't forget fighting," Julia said. "Fuck, fight, or flee—and don't pretend you don't like to fight, bitch."

The patio fire pit cast dancing shadows across their faces, the flames occasionally hissing when droplets from the misty air found their way in.

"First things first," Julia said, a radiant smile wrapped around her face. "What's your timeline?"

"March," Richard said, the answer clearly predetermined.

Julia raised an eyebrow. "Not much time," she said.

Maya took a rueful sip of wine. "I have to shit or get off the pot by May with Elizabeth. So it's working backwards from then. Plus, that's one year after my mom's stroke, right around the equinox."

"Did we tell you about the dancing snake?" Richard asked.

Julia ignored him, regarding Maya as if she was already working through the trade-offs of the scene's logistics. "Budget?" she asked.

"Unlimited," Maya said, giving Julia a fierce look that reflected three decades of friendship.

Julia clapped her hands and leaned forward in her chair, her eyes sparkling. "Oh my God, this is the hottest thing that's *ever* happened to me in my entire life."

"And scariest," Richard said, looking suddenly nervous.

"Fuck that," Julia said, waving her hand at Richard. "Let's get to the *who*."

"Well…" Maya said. "Right now, the only one who's agreed is this Brazilian I met down in Mexico the day my mom had a stroke. His name is Rafa. I'm still working on Leo."

What's this next one's name?"

"Michael," Maya said, her voice soft and lingering, as if savoring the memory. "Always Michael, never Mike." She stared into the fire, lost in thought.

"I call them the Ninja Turtles," Richard said. "She's just one Donatello short."

"And… where'd you meet?" Julia pressed, nudging her along with palpable excitement.

"Oh, I met him when I went to stay with Kate and Shyam on the island. Remember," she poked Richard, "when I helped them for a few weeks after she went back to work?"

Richard nodded, a faint smile playing on his lips. "Right after Indira, yeah. You and Hannah needed that period of détente, as I recall."

"Yeah. I usually had nights to myself, so I went dancing." Maya's lips curled into a sly smile. "That's where I saw him. He was the sax player."

Julia gasped theatrically. "Oh, God, girl! Another musician? Tell me he wasn't a slob like Matt."

Maya burst into laughter. "No, complete opposite. The sax was his way of unwinding, and I just caught him on a night off. He was a chef. Still is, according to Facebook, which makes sense because oh my God, he was good. I'd eaten at his restaurant before I saw him playing the sax, and told him how awesome it was after the show."

Julia sat up straighter, her eyes gleaming. "Oooh, what else happened after the show?"

Maya's voice took on a mischievous lilt. "We had sex in his apartment—"

"Sax sex," Richard quipped, chuckling at his own joke.

"—and he agreed to come over to Kate's for dinner the next night."

Julia's jaw dropped. "Girl! You invited him to your *friend's house!*"

Maya shrugged. "It worked out. I invited another friend too, so it wasn't completely reckless. I told everyone I'd cook dinner."

Richard furrowed his brow, wondering how the conversation had moved on so rapidly from the whole point of the conversation. "Wait. Was the sex good?"

Maya shot him an exasperated look. "I'm *getting* to that," she said.

She closed her eyes for a few moments, then opened them again and smiled, looking away from him. "I made that fish stew I've made for you a few times." Richard, following Maya's adjusted eyes, noticed that the *you* in her words seemed to point toward Julia.

Julia clapped her hands and looked right at Maya. "Oooh! Did he like it?"

"He said he *loved* it,"—Maya's eyes lit up at the word *loved*—"but that it needed a bit more salt. I said *I knew it!*" She sighed theatrically before continuing. *"Kate has hypertension!"* Both women laughed, their cheeks flushed as they fed off each other's energy. The scent of wet earth and wood smoke mingled with the fruity notes of their wine, creating an olfactory backdrop as complex as their conversation.

Richard glanced between them, confused. "What does this have to do with sex?"

Julia waved him off impatiently. "Shh! Let her talk!"

Maya smirked and continued. "I also made cake. He's Jamaican, and I had his black cake at his restaurant. I didn't trust myself to make that, so I made the chocolate espresso cake I used to bake for Hannah's birthdays. I brought it to him at work. We didn't have time to eat it then, but that's okay. I told him I knew it couldn't match his own cakes, but he might enjoy someone else baking one for him from time to time."

Julia leaned forward, enthralled. "Did he like it?"

Maya's voice softened, her expression turning almost dreamy. "He visited me during his break the next day. 'I ate your cake,' he said." Maya attempted to imitate his deep Jamaican accent.

"And?" Julia urged, practically vibrating with excitement.

Maya sighed contentedly, closing her eyes for a moment. "'It was very good,' he said. But Julia, then he reached into his bag,"— Richard felt oddly like he was becoming increasingly irrelevant in the conversation—"and he pulled out a jar of currants he had been soaking in rum for a long time and handed it to me. 'Would you make one with these, please?' he asked."

Julia's hands flew to her face. "Stop. He *did not!*"

"He did," Maya said with a grin, sinking into Richard's shoulder as if the memory itself were a warm embrace.

Richard cleared his throat politely. "Um," he said, raising his eyebrows and curling his lips in a look of genuine confusion. Both women looked at him. "So… what does any of this have to do with sex?"

Maya straightened up indignantly, pulling away from his shoulder. "Oh my God," she said.

Julia rolled her eyes at him. "You're disgusting."

Richard glanced between the two women, realizing too late that the energy had shifted. The flush on their cheeks had faded, replaced by looks of disappointment and exasperation.

An awkward silence settled over the patio before Julia tried to rekindle the mood. "So… what was *his* food like?" she asked, her tone carefully light.

Maya's face lit up again as she leaned toward Julia. "Oh, Julia, you have no idea. He was like a magician in the kitchen and grill. A few nights later, he made me a private meal, jerk chicken with a papaya salad."

Julia clasped her hands together, leaning in closer. "Tell me *everything.*"

Maya closed her eyes, savoring the memory. "Everything about it was perfect. Allspice, thyme, scotch bonnet peppers, a hint of sweet cinnamon, smoke, acid…"

She looked dreamy before giving Richard a playful elbow in the ribs. "… sex," she said with a wicked smile.

"Oh God, he sounds amazing," Julia said, leaning back in her chair. She took a slow sip of her wine, savoring both the drink and the story. "You plan out your approach yet?"

"Not really," Maya admitted, shifting on the loveseat. "That's part of why I need your help."

Julia raised her eyebrow. "What'd you do with the Italian?"

"Leo?" Maya said, running a hand absently along the stem of her glass. "I messaged him on Facebook and arranged a phone call after Richard went to sleep."

"What'd you say?" Julia asked. Beyond the protective awning, a light drizzle started, creating a gentle percussive soundtrack and glistening diamonds on the nearby foliage.

"Well," Maya hesitated. "I said it'd been a long time, and I'd been thinking about him. Then I asked if he was up for catching up over the phone. When we talked, he said he'd seen me in the news a lot lately."

Julia gave a knowing nod. "Mmm-hmm, it's important to address that point."

"Well… maybe that's another area I need your help," Maya admitted, frowning. "I tried to move past that as quickly as possible."

"Oh, girl," Julia groaned, her voice dripping with mock exasperation. Her voice softened to that intimate timbre that always made people lean in closer, as if she were sharing sacred knowledge. "There's no getting past that point. In fact, that *is* the point. This isn't just a booty call. You're enlisting soldiers in an epic battle of good versus evil. You need to appeal to their hero instinct."

Maya looked sheepish. "I rushed it?"

Julia sighed dramatically and leaned back in her chair. "Sounds like it. But don't worry," she said with a wink. "We'll role-play it out a few times before you reach out to Michael-not-Mike. What'd you say after you moved on from your most recent brush with fame?"

"Umm, I told him how I'd been thinking a lot about our time together, and that I had a proposition for him."

Julia froze, her hand flying up to her mouth in mock horror. "Oh, Maya! *No!* I'm glad you called me. Sounds like you *really* need my help."

"What?" Maya asked, confused.

Julia leaned forward, her tone taking on the patient cadence of a teacher. "Think about what you're doing. You're asking a man you cheated on your husband with years ago to come fuck you with your ex-husband and other strangers to distract yourself from a news cycle."

A neighborhood cat perched silently on the garden wall, its reflective eyes occasionally catching the firelight as it observed the human drama with detached curiosity.

"Yeah, I suppose that is kind of awkward," Richard said after a long silence.

Maya groaned. "So what should I do?"

Julia leaned closer, her voice dripping into a conspiratorial whisper. "Flirt! You know how some things seem really weird, but when you're turned on, they seem really hot?"

Maya lifted her head, her cheeks flushing slightly. "Well, yeah…"

Julia gave her a triumphant smile. "You gotta build up the temperature, but slowly and artfully. You can't lead off with 'a *proposition*.'" She put air quotes around the word. "You don't give away the game on the first phone call. Anticipation is your best weapon—build up to it!"

"How do I do that?" Maya asked, her tone equal parts curious and desperate.

"Men love to feel desired," Julia said, her voice slowing as if sharing a great secret. "And they love to feel like they're good at pleasing us. Start with a walk down memory lane. Remind him how hot it was. Let him know how rarely you've felt so satisfied—sorry, Richard." She flashed a quick grin in his direction before continuing. "Just say all this attention and stress has you reflecting on those moments in your life where you felt truly happy, and you want him to know that you shared some of those moments with him. Thank him. Then text him random flirts."

"What about me?" Richard asked, his brows furrowing slightly. "How do we get past the awkwardness of me being part of the scene?"

"Yeah, you're gonna have to address that," Julia said, nodding thoughtfully. "Say you and your ex are getting back together, but you're talking about opening up the relationship, or are excited to explore, or are chasing a fantasy, or whatever. And don't be shy talking about what's going on in your life. Admit that you're scared. Let him be your courage. Make him your hero."

Maya visibly slumped on the loveseat. "I definitely rushed it with Leo," she said, a distressed look on her face.

"That's okay. We'll nail it with Michael. We're going to practice and practice, and then when you get him to 'yes,' you just hand him over to me, and I'll take care of it from there. Girl, I'm gonna make sure you have the time of your fucking *life*!"

⸙

She took a sip of her water and smiled softly as her eyes lingered on the text glowing on her phone. Her cheeks carried a rosy flush, and her coal-black eyes sparkled with a light that had been dormant too long. She let her thumb hover over the keyboard for a moment, savoring the growing anticipation, then typed her response with deliberate care.

The screen flickered, and the three familiar dots appeared. Her breath quickened, as if syncing to the rhythm of her beating heart. Her lips curved upward, and when the dots finally gave way to words, a soft laugh escaped her before she could catch herself. She quickly brought her hand to her mouth, trying to smother her reaction.

"What's so funny?" Dr. Mercer asked, raising an eyebrow from across the table.

She shook her head, still smiling, as she lowered her hand. "Sorry, nothing. Just an old friend."

Her phone buzzed again. She glanced down, her eyes sparkling with renewed energy, her composure slipping slightly as she read his latest reply. This time, she bit her lower lip, struggling to keep her smile from growing too wide.

"You realize your cheeks are still laughing," Dr. Mercer teased.

Maya's audible laugh escaped her attempts to constrain it, her voice light and free. "I'm sorry," she said. "I need to step out for a few minutes. I'll… I'll be back."

Phone in hand, she navigated the halls of the building, her steps quick and purposeful. When she reached the exit, she pushed through the door and walked to the side, far from prying eyes and accidental encounters.

Finally alone, she looked down at her phone. Her smile, no longer restrained, blossomed fully, and she laughed softly, the sound almost musical in the crisp air. She exhaled slowly, gathering herself, then tapped his name on the screen and pressed the call button.

"Hello," the booming voice answered on the first ring.

Her breath caught for a moment, and then she spoke, her voice warm and glowing with an excitement she hadn't felt in years. "Hello, Michael. It's Maya."

THE RUDDER

The elder Lawson's eyes swept over the room, landing with deliberate weight on his son. Eli sat stiffly, an annoyed scowl etched into his face, his slightly sunken right cheekbone casting a shadow that made his irritation even more pronounced.

"Ron," Lawson said finally, his gaze fixed on Eli, as if daring him to meet it. Eli, however, kept his eyes glued to his phone, pretending its contents were more compelling than the meeting at hand.

"Yes, sir," Ron said promptly, his voice clear and eager. Not yet thirty years old, Ron wore black pleated slacks and a crisp white shirt with a starched collar held down with magnetic stays. *A sign of respect*, Lawson thought. *Something his son needed to learn.*

Lawson's words turned formal, imbued with a sense of gravity. "While I appreciate the work Eli has done for the youth ministry," he said, letting the weight of his words settle, "I've decided that his talents are needed full-time with the political arm of our efforts."

Eli's jaw visibly tightened, but he didn't look up.

Ron's face lit up with a knowing grin. "Taking back the ship?" he asked.

Lawson led the so-called pirates of the SBC, those determined to storm the ship and steer the Convention away from heathen liberalism. The moniker had recently made the news, highlighting the internal power struggles of the SBC against those who took a more lax view of morality and invited secular oversight.

They sat in high-backed leather chairs around a large, polished mahogany table that stretched the length of the room. A heavy, ornate cross adorned the wall behind Lawson's seat. A large painting of a shepherd leading a flock hung prominently opposite the cross.

The elder Lawson forced himself to smile and turned his gaze to Ron, his voice measured. "Ron, are you familiar with how James described the human tongue in his epistle?"

Ron's eyes widened, eager to please. He straightened in his chair. "I believe so, sir. He likens the human tongue to a small rudder that directs a massive ship."

Lawson nodded, his approval subtle but deliberate. "And the tongue is a fire, a world of iniquity," he said, quoting Scripture. "So is the tongue among our members, that it defileth the whole body, and setteth on fire the course of nature; and it is set on fire of hell."

Ron's grin faded into solemn reverence. He nodded, his wonder almost childlike. Lawson let the moment stretch, his steely gaze driving home the unspoken sermon: steer the ship, or let it burn.

"Yes, sir," Ron said at last, his voice hushed. "And I thank you both for steering the ship in these dangerous times with your own rudders."

Deacon Martin, Lawson's stalwart right hand, leaned forward. "We need you to take the helm of the youth ministry, Ron," Martin said, his voice a low rumble of authority. Ex-military and known for his no-nonsense demeanor, Martin's words carried weight.

Ron's eyes lit up like a child's. "Yes, sir!"

The group spent the next few minutes discussing transition

details, Ron's enthusiasm brimming as he left the room with a spring in his step, the door clicking shut behind him.

A long silence hung like a cloud in the room after the door shut.

"Speak," Lawson said to his son.

Eli finally looked up, his eyes hard. "You're trying to hide me," he said, his voice infused with a rebellious petulance.

Lawson nodded slowly. "You want to continue to lead the youth ministry?"

"I want to feel like you're not undercutting the hard-earned trust I've had to build—and rebuild—with all the parents," Eli said. A slight waver textured his voice as he pushed the words through the lump in his throat, a common occurrence when he over-rehearsed his argument with his father. "It's like all of a sudden you're afraid of what those scumbags in the media say."

Lawson waved his hand dismissively. With the governor's help, he made sure the right messages got out to the press. Despite his disdain for the Fourth Estate, he had sat down for various interviews, creating sympathy for Eli's trauma and, more importantly, for the cause he had fought so hard for over the course of so many decades.

"Nobody's saying anything, not worth listening to," he said. "Say what's really bothering you."

Eli took a sharp breath, trying to steady his heartbeat. He hated how small he felt in this room, in the shadow of his father's carefully cultivated authority. "You call it 'the political operation,' but you're not having me do *anything*," he said.

"Have patience," Lawson said.

Eli laughed and looked at the bookshelf full of leather-bound religious texts clearly meant to be admired but not read.

"Did you know that Elizabeth Lang has been asking several of the kids about you?" Lawson asked, his tone deceptively calm.

Eli froze, visibly taken aback. It was as if a verbal slap had wiped the petulance and confusion off his face.

"What does she want?" he stammered at last, his voice uneven, betraying the faintest tremor.

"What do you think she wants?" Lawson asked, his gaze unflinching, the steady intensity forcing Eli to confront the implications.

Eli's eyes darted between Martin and his father, his thoughts visibly racing. "So this is what I get for taking Madison Quinn to the hospital?" he asked, his voice climbing an octave with frustration. "Getting punched in the face *and* kicked in the balls?"

"Control yourself," Martin said.

Lawson had perfected the technique of speaking through closed lips, his gaze like a mirror, reflecting the inner voice of whomever he stared at until their thoughts poured out.

Eli's chest rose and fell quickly as he gestured wildly, his panic leaking out. "Why can't everyone see that, if I had *anything* to do with her situation, she would have said so by now?" he said, his voice strained, his words spilling out in a rushed tumble. His eyes were wide, frantic, his palms lifting in a helpless gesture as if pleading for some unseen jury to understand his plight.

"The other kids say she was known as a… promiscuous harlot anyway," he added, the phrase awkward and bitter, the word *harlot* tasting sour even as he spat it out.

"Probably part of her… mental disorder," he said after a pause, his voice quieter now, tinged with a faint disgust that pulled his lip back involuntarily.

"I can't believe I ever tried to help her." His words trembled with indignation.

At length, his energy seemed to drain away, and he slumped slightly, his shoulders sagging. "Who is Lang talking to?" he asked, his voice resigned now.

"Just some of the other kids," Lawson said evenly. "It's a fishing expedition, nothing more."

Eli exhaled sharply through his nose, staring down at the polished table as if its surface might hold answers. He shook his head slowly, his thoughts spiraling.

"The Quinn family will receive no succor from our community," Lawson said, his voice low but resolute. "And I will not tolerate secular interference in our evangelism. But," he added, his tone hard and menacing, "I'm not willing to fan the flames."

Eli wore a mean look on his face as he nodded. "So that's that, then," he said. He knew better than to make it a question.

"So that's that," Lawson confirmed, his tone carrying the finality of a gavel.

Eli grabbed his papers, looked at the cross for a few moments, and stormed out.

A thick silence settled over the room, broken only by the faint crackle of the fire in the hearth. Lawson remained seated, his fingers lightly drumming against the polished mahogany as he stared at the empty chair his son had vacated. His expression betrayed nothing, but a fleeting shadow lingered in his eyes, a faint sadness as he processed Eli's reaction to learning about Lang.

"Have you talked to Tom Demaro?" Lawson asked at length.

"I have," Martin replied. "Sounds like the idea is mainly Barbara's."

Lawson nodded slowly, his gaze shifting from the table to the cross. His fingers stopped drumming, his hands folding together as he leaned slightly forward. "They willing to meet?"

"Thursday morning," Martin said. "Already got it on your calendar."

"Thank you," Lawson said.

This was hard business, but moral defeats happened by degrees. It was like boiling the proverbial frog, with those earlier warm temperatures easy to rationalize, losing sight of the fact that they were simply waystations on the journey to hell fire.

"Tom, good to see you." Lawson extended a firm handshake. "Barbara, thanks so much for coming." He flashed a generous smile. Tom's grey hair and bushy eyebrows were outdone only by the wisps of white hair Barbara wore. After exchanging pleasantries, they sat down in the plush leather chairs set aside for them, only slightly less expensive than Lawson's high-backed chair. A side table held up a King James Bible. A large cross hung on the wall behind Lawson, with several verses of Scripture written in calligraphy on other walls.

"Thanks again for agreeing to see us, Pastor. We've been praying on what the right thing to do is," Tom said. Barbara nodded her head solemnly.

Pastor Lawson looked pensive, nodding himself. "I appreciate you being willing to invite me into your counsel," he said, his drawl slow and measured, like the deliberate strokes of a steady oar cutting through turbulent water.

Tom leaned forward, his voice earnest. "Listen, I just want to say up front that I understand—we *both* understand," he glanced at Barbara for emphasis, "—that what the dad did is beyond reproach. And I know you're personally affected by it, what with what happened to your son."

Lawson allowed a brief, reflective pause before responding. "I assure you that my counsel will have nothing to do with any personal grudges I bear," he said. "I, too, have been doing some praying."

"Thank you for saying that," Tom said, exhaling as though a weight had been lifted. He reached out and held Barbara's hand.

Barbara looked up from her hand to Lawson. "It's just that poor girl, you know. She doesn't deserve this."

"Oh?" Lawson asked, raising an eyebrow.

Barbara looked a little flustered by his response. "Well, she's sure suffered a lot already."

Lawson scratched his chin and looked out the window. Most of the light in the room was natural. He had it designed to capture the rays of the sun in the morning to enhance the spiritual aura.

"That she has, surely," Lawson said, nodding his head with a mournful slowness.

"And if not us, then who?" Barbara asked.

Lawson let one of his practiced pregnant pauses linger in the air before speaking. "Are you familiar with the story of Dinah and Shechem?"

Both Tom and Barbara shook their heads, their expressions a mixture of curiosity and unease, as if sensing that his question carried more weight than it appeared.

Lawson picked up the Bible and opened it to Genesis. He flipped through a few pages until he found what he was looking for, then handed the open book to Tom, who pulled his glasses out of his shirt pocket and started reading. Barbara looked down her bifocals, scooting closer to see.

"Shechem violated Dinah, the daughter of Jacob," Lawson began in his hickory drawl, summarizing as they read the Scripture. "You can read what happened: conflict and bloodshed between Jacob's family and Shechem's people."

Tom took off his readers after he finished, handing the Bible to his wife, who used her finger to find her spot and continued a few moments more. At length, both looked up at Lawson, the Bible still open on Barbara's lap.

Barbara hesitated, looking nervous. "Do you think Madison was raped?"

"No, I don't," Lawson said. "Not by force anyway, even if the law calls it rape due to her age. If she was, I imagine we would've heard about it by now. But even if I'm wrong, as you just read, as God tells us in the Good Book, these sins have widespread consequences."

Tom shifted uncomfortably in his chair, exchanging a puzzled glance with Barbara. "What are you saying, Pastor?" he asked.

Lawson leaned back, as if weighing his words carefully. "I'm saying that while your compassion is commendable, you must ask yourselves if this is truly God's path for you. Taking Madison into your home would mean inviting those consequences into your household. Are you prepared for the strife it may bring?"

Tom let out a self-deprecating chuckle. "I'll be honest with you, Pastor. I expected you to talk about our age."

Lawson smiled wistfully. "Well, of course there's that. Travis Quinn may go to prison for several years. I hope he does, which would put you in charge of his daughter into adulthood. But my counsel would be the same, regardless."

Barbara ran her hand over the Bible. "But doesn't she deserve a chance?" she asked.

Lawson nodded, his expression solemn. "She does. And I pray she takes it. But that's between her and God." He looked down at the Bible in Barbara's lap. "You might want to flip to the Book of Hebrews, Barbara."

She hadn't remembered the order of books in the Old Testament; she looked a little flustered until she found it.

"I'd start with chapter 12," Lawson said patiently. "The Word tells us that, as hard as holding a moral line is, such is the only path to righteousness."

Barbara read silently. Tom put his readers back on and looked over her shoulder.

"Sounds like God's version of 'tough love,'" Tom said, his voice tinged with sadness.

"'Render therefore unto Caesar the things which are Caesar's, and unto God the things that are God's.'" His gaze softened as it met theirs, reflecting the sadness that lingered in their eyes. "This is a hard thing. A sad thing, and it's natural to feel the weight of it."

Barbara's lips trembled as she looked to her husband, then back to Lawson. The pastor leaned forward slightly, his hands resting gently on the polished wood of the table, his tone steady and calming. "But we must trust in His plan. Caesar already has a system in place for teenagers who lose their parents," he said, his voice tinged with the faintest trace of regret. "And we know God has a system in place for teenagers who lose their way. It's not ours to question, nor ours to carry burdens that were never meant for us."

Barbara dabbed at her eyes with the edge of her sleeve, her hands trembling. Tom exhaled slowly, his shoulders slumping as if the room itself were pressing down on him.

"I see your hearts full of compassion and love, and I respect you both deeply for it," Lawson continued, his voice low. "But sometimes, even the best intentions can stray into paths that are not ours to walk. In this instance, I fear you'd only be getting in God's way."

Tom and Barbara exchanged a fleeting glance, the kind shared by those who sense the ship has turned and realize they are no longer at the helm.

"Thank you, Pastor," she said, her voice trembling. "We'll pray for her, we surely will. But we thank you for your wisdom."

⚬⟋⟍⚬

Eli Lawson ordered a cappuccino. "Anything for you?" he asked.

Kim beamed. "Oh, a vanilla latte, please. Large. Half decaf. Two pumps of caramel, oat milk, and... um, four Splenda." She tapped her ruby-red nails on the counter as if the rhythm might help the barista keep track of her order. She wore large hoop earrings, an oversized sweatshirt, and sneakers that gleamed unnaturally white.

They took their coffees to one of the wooden bench seats in the coffee shop. The crowd was sparse—a couple of individuals huddled over their laptops and an elderly couple enjoying a breakfast of pastries.

"How goes the…"—Eli made air quotes with his fingers—"*influencing?*"

Kim let out a high-pitched laugh, flipping her hair over one shoulder. "Hah! I prefer to call it 'digital marketing.'"

"How many followers do you have now?" Eli asked.

"Well, way more than you," she teased. Her social media image was a distinct blend of scenic Bible verses, Gen Z memes, and pop-culture references aimed at engaging the flock's younger members. She viewed herself as a bridge between the digital-savvy younger generation and the wisdom of the Bible.

Eli took a sip of his cappuccino and wiped the foam from his mouth. "I wonder what Jesus would think about 21st century evangelism," he said, more a tease than a point of serious reflection.

"Oh, I think our Savior would've slayed at it," Kim said, her eyes glowing. "I mean, imagine the Sermon on the Mount but with hashtag-blessed."

Eli chuckled. "You think so?"

"Well, yeah! I mean, Jesus was all about reaching the people where they were, right? Instagram would be, like, perfect for Him." She took a dainty sip of her latte, her lipstick leaving a crimson mark on the lid.

"You know," Eli said, a bit more seriously. "As much as I personally get out of what you do, and I know I'm not alone in that, I do sometimes worry about how social media is kinda like just giving a loudspeaker to the Devil."

Kim nodded eagerly. "Oh, most def," she said. "I try to not look too much at what's out there, but you know, in my line of work, I still have to check. And there's some real Devil's work out there."

A family walked in—a mom pushing a red stroller, a dad holding the hand of a bouncy toddler who pointed eagerly at the art on the walls.

"There's some real good out there, too," Eli said, smiling faintly.

"Thank God!" Kim said. "I'd be out of a job if there wasn't!" Her phone buzzed. She pulled it out of her purse, tapping at it with her manicured fingers dancing across the screen. She smiled and put her phone down on the table.

"Everything okay?" Eli asked.

"Yep! Just some comments."

"On your Corinthians post?"

Kim's cheeks flushed and she nodded her head, looking a little nervous.

"Can I see?"

Kim's phone buzzed again as another comment came in. She glanced at it before handing her phone to Eli.

Kim had posted a picture of the famous line about sexual immorality: "All other sins a person commits are outside the body, but whoever sins sexually, sins against their own body." Underneath the quote was a caricature of a teenage girl holding hands with two boys walking into the sunset.

To prevent accusations of targeting a specific person, the artist stylized the caricature, but to Eli, it looked like Madison Quinn all the same.

"join my new ig group..." the new comment said. "it's called 'everyone-but-madison.'"

Eli smiled a little sadly. "What do you do with comments like this one?" he asked.

"Just like you said. I let them be. The Lord works in mysterious ways," Kim said.

"You ever join any of those groups?"

"I mean, this is my job, so *of course* I have to look from time to time."

"What do they say?"

Kim's phone buzzed again. She looked at it before putting it back down on the table and sipping her drink. "Oh, you know," she said. "Sometimes girls can be real bitchy, but they're just letting off steam."

Eli nodded. "I talked to my dad about it, too," he said.

"Oh?" Kim said, looking at her phone. "What'd he say?"

"Something about cutting off cancer to save the patient," Eli said.

The family, after an extended negotiation at the counter, took their seats at the table next to Eli and Kim.

"Awww, she's gorgeous!" Kim said, looking at the baby girl in the stroller.

"Thank you!" the mom said with pride.

"I'm gorgeous, too!" the toddler boy said.

Everyone laughed at the interjection. *Life can be beautiful*, Eli thought to himself.

⁓

"How's the arthritis?" Governor Callahan asked as he settled into one of the leather chairs near the side table holding the King James Bible.

Lawson clenched and unclenched his hand, the movement deliberate, like testing the gears of an old machine. "Getting better," he said. "Still gets to me when it's cold outside."

Callahan nodded and picked up the Bible, flipping through a few pages with casual reverence. "I hear Lang's been snooping around these parts," he said.

"Got any idea what she's up to?" Lawson asked.

"The case with the dad, I imagine."

Lawson nodded slowly, allowing a thoughtful pause. "I mean, got any idea why she's involved with the case at all?"

Callahan shook his head and looked thoughtful. "God only knows. Redemption, maybe. Or maybe she's planning on running for office again. Wish I knew, though."

"I'm afraid if it's redemption she's after, she's going about it the wrong way," Lawson said.

"Yep," Callahan agreed.

"Been pretty loud with the media, too," Lawson continued. "And not just about Quinn. About that Muslim doctor, too."

Callahan nodded. "I'm sure that's part of the answer. The doctor can't talk to the media, not while her case is ongoing. Probably not ever, given the way she's treated journalists her whole life. She needed someone to represent her in the court of public opinion."

"Still awfully strange that Lang, of all people, would say yes to being a Muslim's attack dog."

"I've been thinking the same thing. Like I said, wish I knew."

"Think she's behind some of these false prophets talking about us pirates in the SBC?" Lawson asked. While it hadn't hit the mainstream press yet, there were rumors of the pirates protecting sexually predatory behavior amongst members of the Executive Council.

Callahan shrugged. "Wouldn't surprise me. Welcome to the snake pit."

Lawson let out a measured sigh, letting the weight of the moment hang between them. "What'd you think of the sermon this morning?"

The governor's face broke into a wide grin. "I thank you for fighting the good fight, Pastor. And, if you'll pardon my French, I think the best thing that could happen to both of us would be for them sons of bitches in the IRS to try and come after you."

Lawson smiled faintly, his expression measured. This morning's sermon had been a calculated risk; he'd wanted to acknowledge it before he steered the conversation toward his request.

The Johnson Amendment was a provision in the tax code that prevented a nonprofit from putting its thumb on the scales of an election through political endorsements. Lawson and others in the evangelical community had been tempting fate for years. This morning, Lawson gave a fiery sermon opposing liberal immorality and explicitly endorsing Callahan for president. He virtually taunted the federal government to respond, since the recorded sermon would be rebroadcast on his network and replayed in political ads.

"I might need a bit of your help to push back on this noise about us pirates," Lawson said.

"You know I can't get involved in that," Callahan said, his voice suddenly stern, sensing a trap.

"Oh, I don't mean you personally," Lawson said, waving his hand dismissively, his stare direct. "But if we're already in the snake pit with these vipers, I could use your help getting our story into the right hands to drown out the rumors from those false prophets."

Callahan looked back at Lawson, his expression unreadable but his tone light. "Like I said, I can't get involved." He paused, then added with a faint smile, "But maybe I've got a friend who can make a few calls."

"Thank you, Caesar," Lawson said.

THE BAPTISM

Sergeant Baker lifted his head and instinctively peeled back his ears. Alert now, he listened to the familiar sound of the TV and the cars in the parking lot and the voices through the hotel walls and the peaceful sound of running water he had dozed off to several minutes earlier. He took in the slightly stale smell of the furniture and the mostly empty beer cans on the side of the bed and the empty bag of Doritos he had helpfully cleaned of crumbs before his nap. The bedside lamp was on, and the TV flashed artificial light in a room that had otherwise faded into the night with the shades pulled down.

And something else, too, a sour edge that prickled the air, the musty scent of anxiety, as if the air itself was holding its breath. He sniffed and tasted the whisper of something sharp and tangy, something of copper and iron, like a set of rusted keys. He whined and wagged his tail nervously, looking at Travis expectantly, but Travis showed no signs of waking.

The Sergeant walked around the bed, toward the bathroom and the sound of the running water. There, through the crack in the door, he saw light. And water. It slowly streamed out from under the door in a way he'd never seen it do before. He wet his paws as he padded through it on the carpet. He stared at the door and barked.

When nothing happened, he barked again, louder this time, and kept barking, pausing to sniff for the shadow of the girl who would open the door from the inside. He growled at the invisible threat on the other side of the door and whimpered and whined and barked again. With a series of leaps, he attacked the door, standing on his hind legs and repeatedly scratching it with his paws until the paint tore off and his front paws were raw. He no longer cared if someone yelled at him or swatted his nose. He needed to get through that door.

He heard voices down the hall yelling at him. He barked louder until he heard the annoyance in their yells and barked a few more times for good measure.

He ran back to the bed and licked Travis, barking inches from his face. Travis moved slowly, trying to push him away. Someone started banging on the door. Travis got up groggily and ran his hand through his hair, trying to clear his mind. The Sergeant barked again, looking up at him, wagging his tail excitedly.

"Jesus Christ, calm down," Travis slurred, getting to his feet. He walked to the hotel door to see who was banging on it.

Sergeant Baker gently bit Travis's hand and tugged, pulling him toward the sound of the water. "What the hell is wrong with you?" Travis asked, giving the Sergeant an evil look as he ripped his hand free. The phone rang, presumably the hotel staff trying to calm the commotion.

Sergeant Baker ran in front of Travis and barked loudly. He ran toward the sound of the water and turned to see if Travis was following him.

"Are your paws wet?" Travis asked, confused, following the paw marks the dog left on the carpeted floor. Sergeant Baker barked.

Someone kept banging on the door. "Shut that damn dog up!" they yelled through it. The phone kept ringing like a buzzsaw ripping through Travis's grogginess.

But Travis was looking at Sergeant Baker oddly now. Ignoring the banging at the door and the ringing of the phone, he followed the dog to the bathroom door. His heart sank when he opened it and saw the pills in the sink and on the floor and the empty bottle of ibuprofen on the counter. He ran into the back recess of the bathroom, the part that housed the toilet and the running bathtub. The air surrounding him suddenly felt like a hot, viscous fluid, slowing his movement and his reality.

"Oh, God!" he yelled. "Oh God oh God oh God oh God." His voice became weaker, trembling in the same way his body trembled.

Bloodied water spilled over the edge of the tub.

"Oh God," Papa Bear said as he fell into the tub, lifting his baby girl as Sergeant Baker whined and wagged his tail nervously.

THE MIRROR

They say the eyes are the windows into the soul, but in that brief, passing glance, Maya saw more of a malevolent mirror. It was a look that exploded like a bullet in her brain, ricocheting off the back of her skull, its debris scattered inside her until she could recoil from its metallic taste, until it knotted up her intestines, until it made her dizzy and nauseated and weak. They were the kind of eyes that looked into the soul of their owner as much as to the world outside, and shone hate and loathing in both directions.

Elizabeth Lang did not deign to hold the glance or to slow her pace or even bother with a flicker of recognition as she walked past Maya. A look of tortured disgust contorted her face as she pulled her cheeks taut and pressed her lips together. It was but a momentary burst of baleful radiation through the exit wounds of her inflamed eye sockets, and Maya was collateral damage.

Lang's walk and body language screamed at everything and everybody she passed, her yellow pixie cut and angry face juxtaposed against the austere white walls of the psych ward with shadows cast by the glaring fluorescent lights. She left a mushroom cloud of emotional destruction in her wake, like the contrails of the Enola Gay as it flew from Hiroshima. Maya knew she wouldn't stop walking until she exited the hospital doors and found a corner to hide from the vultures in the media outside so she could calm the boiling of her blood with nicotine and isolation and self-loathing.

There was no turning back now, Maya thought ruefully. *She was committed.*

Travis didn't make eye contact. Instead, he slumped in the stiff hospital chair, his body folded into itself as if trying to implode like a black hole under its own gravity, to disappear and suck all light with him. His hair stood up in uneven tufts, fingers having passed through it too many times, tugging with the weight of every sob he stifled. His unshaven face was gaunt and hollow, his skin drained of all color, leaving him pale and clammy. He looked like a grotesque caricature of an apparition.

His eyes, bloodshot and sunken, floated above dark circles that seemed seared into him by a branding iron. A crumpled, sweat-stained shirt hung half-tucked on him; his pants looked as if they were pulling him down. Maya could see the shame etched into him. His entire body seemed to tremble and vibrate.

He sat there for what felt like an eternity, the silence bearing down on the room like a heavy fog. And then, without warning, he lurched forward. Pushing off the back of the chair, his legs wobbled beneath him, barely supporting his weight as he staggered to the bathroom. His cheeks puffed out, his face twisting as nausea overtook him.

Maya heard the retch before he made it all the way to the toilet. The sound of him vomiting tore through the stillness, raw and violent, a guttural expulsion of everything he couldn't say. The echo filled the sterile room, and for a moment, Maya felt like she could taste the bile herself, bitter, acrid, burning the back of her throat. She stared at the bathroom door, frozen, as the sound of his heaving slowed, each wave weaker than the one before.

When he finally emerged, he looked even smaller, as if the act of purging had taken the last of whatever he had left. He didn't speak, didn't meet her eyes, just sank back into the chair, folding in on himself again, a man crumbling under the weight of his own devastation.

❧

Elizabeth Lang sat alone at her long walnut dining room table, its polished surface gleaming faintly under the soft glow of the chandelier above. Opposite her hung the ornate mullioned mirror, an expensive relic of a life curated for appearances. She stared at the woman in the mirror and contemplated her sobriety. The rosacea she had spent years concealing with green-tinted primers and layers of foundation had faded, leaving behind a patchwork of faint veins, like roads leading nowhere.

She traced the rim of her glass with her finger, watching as condensation beads formed on the surface. No lime, no garnish, no effort to make it palatable. She wanted the gin bitter and sharp, as unyielding as the thoughts that gnawed at her. *Gin*, she thought, *is a spirit that demands confrontation.* Just like the reflection staring back at her.

Her eyes drifted to the photo on the credenza beneath the mirror. Olivia. Eleven years old. Shoulder-length hair. The version of her daughter Elizabeth had clung to, had paraded to constituents. Olivia's wide smile radiated confidence, her light caught in a moment Elizabeth now realized she'd never fully understood. Jack stood beside her in the picture, his arm draped across her shoulders.

They had been the perfect portrait: a smiling mother, a supportive father, a beaming child, all of it staged to scream motherhood and apple pie.

Jack had left her after Olivia's suicide. Fuck him.

Her gaze lingered on Olivia's face. Even in a photo, the light in her daughter's eyes felt like an accusation, cutting sharper than any spirit ever could. Olivia had looked up to her once, back when the world was simpler, before puberty etched lines of confusion and pain into her daughter's features. A bit of a tomboy, maybe, but Elizabeth had dismissed it then as a phase she'd outgrow.

But phases don't end in funerals.

She gripped the tumbler tighter, her knuckles whitening around it. The scent of juniper stung her nose as she raised the glass to her lips, letting the alcohol sear her tongue without swallowing, the vapors sanitizing the hurt inside of her. *Easier than a lobotomy*, she mused.

Elizabeth stared back at the mirror, her reflection fractured by the ghost of Olivia in the photograph beneath it. Her media resurrection had demanded the retelling of her daughter's death, a narrative reshaped for public consumption, sterilized and gutted of its truth. Madison had undoubtedly watched, a girl teetering on the same razor's edge of rejection her daughter had once walked.

Olivia had slit her wrists in a bathtub. Elizabeth was sure Madison had paid attention to that detail.

She stood up and spat out the venom violently. The gin blossomed into spidery veins on the mirror over her own reflection like broken, ghostly capillaries.

She picked up the nearly full bottle and stared at Olivia's face through blurred vision, a cruel reminder of everything she had failed to protect. "You deserved better," she whispered, her voice cracking under the strain.

With a guttural snarl, she hurled the bottle across the room. It struck her reflection with a shattering crash, exploding into shards of glass and streaks of liquid that splattered the photo. Elizabeth stared at the destruction, her chest heaving, her hands trembling at her sides. Somewhere deep in her chest a sob rose, but she swallowed it back, choking on the bitterness. There would be no absolution tonight. She turned away, her eyes burning as she left the room, leaving the broken glass and the memories to drown in their shared silence.

❧

Maya listened to the audible crackle of the wood wicker as the candlelight flickered and shadows danced on the wall. She examined her own nakedness stretched out before her, the way her labia floated on the water like fronds in a pond, as beautiful and contradictory as a Zen koan. Not normally a bath person, she tried to embrace the stillness of the heat surrounding her like a fragile cocoon. She closed her eyes to focus on the feeling of warmth, but her beating heart would not let her embrace the calm she hoped it would bring. She listened to the ticking of the clock and looked over to see the second hand bouncing one hop at a time through distinct numbered boundaries.

History doesn't repeat itself, but it rhymes.

With her eyes closed, she kept her attention to the sound of time's regularity, the *click, click, click* of each second pushing the present into the past. She thought back to the grandfather clock that hung on the wall in Dr. Abdelhossein's office in Ottawa. Her own clock was too regular, each *click* indistinguishable from the next, but Dr. Abdelhossein's grandfather clock had more character.

Thump. Thwack! Thump. Thwack!

Every other second seemed to jump out and exclaim its tinny presence, until some secondary gear engaged, and she could hear the background metallic slide of one cog resetting against another.

Maybe there'd be two muted, bass-filled *thumps* before an excited *thwack!* and the pattern would reset. Dr. Abdelhossein taught her the meaning of the Roman *Xs* and *Is* and *Vs* on the clock. Everywhere else, she could read the numbers, just not the language, with its funny letters written left to right.

"How are you feeling today, Mayyada?" he would ask, speaking Arabic even though it was snowing outside, and she was surrounded by people she could neither talk to nor understand. Some days he wore round circles for glasses and some nights he wore horns and claws and chased her as she screamed and hid in the date orchard.

Her new dad gave her a golden watch. If she held it up to her ear, she could hear the mechanical regularity of the *tick tick tick*. He spoke Arabic to her, too, but then he would disappear for long stretches of time and leave her with a mom she didn't know and who spoke gibberish and who'd try to treat Maya like a toddler half her age, and so she ran.

They hired Layla Hassan to help her with the transition. She was a young Iraqi refugee from the Iran war who Maya's new dad had helped find refuge in Canada. She braided Maya's long hair and volunteered at the local immigration support organization. Layla was instrumental in helping Maya learn English and would calm Maya down after shouting insults in Arabic at her new mom. When Maya would run away, Layla would help find her.

"Are you getting enough sleep, Mayyada?" Dr. Abdelhossein would ask through his round glasses, and when she slept, she would run from him as he chased her like a shadowy jinn, whispering her voice in the dark, looking for her hiding spot in the date orchard. It was Qiyamah, the Day of Judgment when all souls were to be judged, and a fire was consuming the earth.

Hal anti bikhayr?

Are you okay?

She was not okay. She couldn't even discern reality from nightmare anymore. Nothing made sense. So, when forced to sit still and stop running, she would listen to the battle of the *thumps* and the *thwacks!* in Dr. Abdelhossein's office, and when her new mom and the kids at school started speaking gibberish to her, she would lift her watch up to her ear to listen to the *tick tick ticks* and close her eyes.

Her new dad enrolled her in a madrasa, with its strong scent of wood and faint traces of attar. Sunlight spilled through its arched windows, casting patterns on latticework, but as the sunlight dimmed and the shadows stretched long, the walls seemed to tighten, the calligraphy curling and twisting and writhing like serpents, so she ran. He enrolled her in an Islamic school where she could speak Arabic, but when the shadows formed, spilling across the floor like black ink, and when she turned to her teacher for help only to find his features smearing like wet ink across a page, she ran. She ran through the labyrinth of halls and through the labyrinth of streets until Layla found her.

"Your mom wrote many books," Dr. Abdelhossein told her once as he reached for a loose sheet of paper and started scribbling on it. "It was she who said, 'The most powerful thing in the world is a story.' Did she teach you to read?" He folded the paper and handed it to her. She refused to look at it until that night, in her bed or in her dreams.

يمكنكِ الهرب من الجميع إلا من نفسكِ. في يومٍ ما ستضطرين إلى مواجهة ماضيكِ.

She remembered screaming at this unwelcome invasion. In the distance, she saw Imam Mahdi in the graveyard, wearing Dr. Abdelhossein's round glasses. She called out to him, but her voice turned to ash as the graves split open and the dead raised up from the ground. "You have forgotten us," Mahdi told her. "You do not belong." He turned away, his light faded. In the distance, she saw the Bridge of Sirat that all souls must cross to reach Paradise. It was as she had been told—narrow, sharper than a sword, thinner than a strand of hair, stretching over an abyss filled with fire and screams. She looked up as the sky ripped apart; she heard the aftershocks of the crumbling mountains and the shaking earth. So she ran.

Dr. Abdelhossein described it as a psychotic break. Nothing made sense. Her environment, her family, her language, her religion. The safety of cruelty replaced by the cruelty of safety.

She ran with the frantic energy of someone trying to outrun her own shadow. She ran from the flames that rose from the ground. She ran across the cracked sidewalk with the alien houses and their pointed roofs. She ran through the shadows of the date palms as Dr. Abdelhossein chased her with his olive-green uniform, pistol in hand. She ran out the school doors into the snow outside. The local police had rescued her so many times that they were on a first-name basis with Layla and her new parents.

It would be a few years yet before she'd find escape wrapped around another body, so she used the *ticks* and the *thumps* and the *thwacks!* to ground her. She habituated questioning reality so much that the habit infiltrated her dreams, where she learned that neither Roman numbers nor Arabic ones could penetrate, where *ticks* and *thumps* and *thwacks!* lacked mechanical regularity. She learned she could separate reality from nightmare by the blurriness of time itself.

She opened her eyes and flipped her right forearm over, as she had done so many times when she was young. She traced the bluish vein up her arm and imagined letting the poison of her bloodline out. For she was birthed from the womb of a sayyida, a distant descendant of Husayn, and therefore of the prophet Muhammad, and this bloodline caused her family to be murdered.

And now even her new mom was dead. The last emotion she felt before the hemorrhage took her life was Maya running away from her, all for pulling off the scab of this scar Maya had worked so hard to bury.

She thought about what Dr. Abdelhossein had written her all those years ago:

You can run from everyone but yourself. Someday you will have to face your past.

A tear streamed down her cheek. She didn't bother to stop it. Instead, she let her belly heave, surrendering control. Her cry became audible, and she let the tears and the snot and the fear out of her body and into the warm water, just as Madison had done with her blood.

FAMILY TIES

The flickering TV cast shifting pools of blue light across Hannah's apartment, a cramped Georgetown walk-up she'd somehow made feel expansive through careful curation. Moroccan tapestries draped the walls, their geometric patterns echoing the Arabic calligraphy framed above the kitchenette. Books sprawled across every surface: dog-eared Arabic poetry collections, international relations textbooks stacked atop copies of *Vogue Arabia*.

The space felt like Hannah herself: deliberately cosmopolitan, defiantly intellectual, just messy enough to suggest a rugged authenticity. Outside, a bus sighed on Wisconsin; inside, the old radiator ticked like a wind-up metronome to combat the winter chill.

Hannah sat cross-legged on the white couch she'd scored from a neighborhood listserv and rehabilitated with throws from the Eastern Market, one hand on the remote, the other draped over Tarsha's waist. Tarsha sprawled across the cushions, her head in Hannah's lap, dark curls spilling over Hannah's thighs. She wore one of Hannah's Georgetown hoodies, the sleeves rolled up to reveal the delicate astronomy tattoo that wrapped around her fore-arm—constellations Hannah had traced with her fingers more times than she'd admit.

"Are we really watching the news again?" Tarsha teased without looking up. "You, daughter of chaos, watching cable news like some retiree?"

Hannah's fingers found their way into Tarsha's hair, an absent gesture that felt comforting. "They're doing a mini documentary about my grandmother after the talking heads."

Elizabeth Lang's voice cut through the apartment's intimate quiet like a blade as Hannah adjusted the volume. "… state's case is performative and cruel," Lang said. "Madison Quinn was in sepsis. Dr. Maya Russell, under time pressure, made a decision that saved her life. End of story."

Lang's pixie cut caught the studio lights as she leaned forward, a predator sensing weakness. Her opponent, a gray-haired white man with an aquiline nose, leaned in aggressively. "Dr. Russell isn't God," he said, reciting a common refrain from Callahan's attack dogs. "She doesn't get to decide who lives and who dies."

"Actually, she does," Lang spat, her eyes narrowing to slits. "That's literally her job."

The man's face reddened, clearly annoyed. "Governor Callahan is protecting the sanctity of life. Something Dr. Russell clearly doesn't understand."

"Protecting?" Lang's laugh was sharp. "By criminalizing medical care? By turning doctors into fugitives?"

"Christ, she's good," Tarsha said. "I'd hate to be on the other side of that stare."

Hannah shifted uncomfortably. "I don't trust her."

Tarsha rolled her head up to study Hannah's face. "I don't blame you. Opportunists make terrible saints. But sometimes they make useful swords."

On screen, the gray-haired man pressed on: "Governor Callahan has a mandate from the people of Texas—"

"To what?" Lang interrupted. "To let teenage girls die to protect their rapists?"

"Callahan's *protecting* minors. This isn't politics; it's accountability."

Hannah let out a breath she didn't know she was holding. "Dad calls people like that 'deep-sea anglerfish.'" She muted the TV.

"Who?" Tarsha looked up again.

Hannah nodded, her fingers still moving through Tarsha's hair, needing the grounding sensation. "The people who blindly follow a bright lure and a big mouth. That authoritarian instinct to simply attach yourself to a leader and outsource all your thinking to them."

Her cheeks flushed with a sudden heat. The memory surfaced unbidden—her dad, attempting to explain sexual dynamics through elaborate animal metaphors.

Her *dad...*

She shook her head, both happy and sad at the memory, at her naïvety. God, that wasn't even a year ago. A shadow crossed her face, the same expression Tarsha had learned to look for since Hannah had returned from Austin—shattered, furious, and feeling like her whole world had tilted off its axis.

Tarsha sat up with the fluid grace of someone who'd studied dance before switching to public policy, pressing her forehead into Hannah's. "You okay?"

Hannah wanted to say yes. She wanted to be the composed diplomat-in-training, the one who could navigate complex international crises. Instead, she couldn't even navigate the minefield of her own heritage. She felt the familiar sting of tears, the weight of everything she'd discovered crushing down.

Tarsha had been there the night when Hannah returned from Austin, had held her while she sobbed, had made her tea at 3 a.m.

while she worked through the anger, the bitterness, and the resentment towards her mom—and that complicated thread of grudging admiration.

"Hey," Tarsha said. She kissed Hannah's forehead tenderly.

"It's just… weird," Hannah said. "Mom spent her whole life running from cameras, and now she's everywhere." A tear slid hot and uninvited down her cheek. "I'm scared, and I know she is too."

They breathed together for a few seconds, the radiator's tick marking time.

On-screen, bold letters announced the mini documentary: *Daughter of Revolution: The Woman Who Defied Saddam Hussein.*

Hannah fumbled for the remote and turned the volume up. The documentary opened with a black-and-white still, a woman in a dark hijab, half-visible, addressing a crowd, her posture commanding despite her obvious frailty. Hannah's breath caught. Even through decades and poor photography, Hannah recognized that defiant chin, those coal-dark eyes that could burn through steel. That same defiance lived in her mother's face; sometimes she revered it, sometimes it terrified her.

The narrator, his voice BBC crisp, came in over a soft string pad. "Fatima al-Rahbani came from one of Iraq's most influential clerical families…"

"God, she looks like you," Tarsha whispered, studying the grainy image. "That jawline."

Photographs: annotated pages, a living room dense with patterned abayas, a borrowed samovar steaming. Elderly women laughed without showing teeth; girls leaned forward, notebooks open.

"They called her collected essays the *Sayyida Letters,*" the narrator said. "In Baghdad, Najaf, Karbala, young women passed dog-eared copies hand to hand."

"I mailed Mom those books," Hannah said, her voice tight. "Can you believe she'd never read them?"

"Is she reading them now?" Tarsha asked.

"She's trying. Her Arabic is rusty." Hannah swallowed. "Mine's better than hers. That feels… fucked up."

The screen shifted to footage of crowds and protests. The narrator's voice took on a darker tone as he described the 1979 Arba'een pilgrimage ban.

"Karbala," Hannah said, almost to herself. "Mom never told me about any of this growing up. I learned about Husayn's martyrdom in my Arabic classes, not from her."

"Maybe it hurt too much," Tarsha offered.

"Or maybe she wanted me to be an atheist American." The bitterness in Hannah's voice surprised them both. "Clean slate. No baggage."

The documentary continued, describing the massacre at Karbala—protestors shot, thousands arrested.

"But protest is easy to see," the narrator continued over close-ups of fabric and thread. "Al-Rahbani's insight was to encode resistance where men refused to look. The hijab and abaya became both covering and signal. Through sewing circles framed as charity, she and her students built what came to be known as the *Fabric Codes,* a secret code for civil disobedience that formed a network of safe houses en route to Karbala and supported dissidents."

Animations showed various stitching patterns. Five tight, three long: meet on the fifth day at the third hour after noon. A hidden blue thread: avoid arriving as a group.

"Prayer rugs hid maps of safe houses in their border knots. Bridal chests were modified with false bottoms to ferry letters to the hawza and cash to detainees' families. No male checkpoint dared paw through a bride's linens."

"Your grandmother was a fucking genius," Tarsha said.

Hannah smiled. "I was able to get one of those abayas with the special stitches."

Tarsha looked at her, open-mouthed. "How?"

"There were *thousands* of them. My grandmother had real influence. I connected with some of the refugees over the years. When one of them realized who I was, she mailed me her abaya with a note about how much my grandmother meant to her."

"You *have* to show me," Tarsha said.

The documentary's tone shifted. The color drained from the image; institutional green bled into gray. A camera tracked down a corridor to a metal door. Hannah's body went quiet and rigid, the way a violin goes still right before a bow strikes the string.

"They came for Fatima al-Rahbani after evening prayer," the narrator said. "No warrant. Just boots and a list with her name on it. At intake, they removed her scarf and confiscated her rings. They set a confession form in front of her, denouncing her teachings and her influence, the signature line waiting. She placed her hands behind her back and stared at them in a way they mistook for negotiable."

The bulb's hum in the interrogation room seemed to leak into Hannah's apartment, as if the TV had bent the air. A drain on the screen split the concrete floor like a scar.

"The first method was simple, the kind that leaves no signature on the face. *Falaqa*, a standard of the regime. They bound al-Rahbani to a table, her legs elevated, the soles of her feet exposed and lashed with braided cables until pain blossomed like fire. They brought a bucket filled with salt water, not for mercy but to teach the nerve endings to remember. A guard recorded the number of strokes. Another kept time. They did not touch her head. They will need her eyes."

"Jesus," Tarsha muttered, burying her face against Hannah's shoulder. Tarsha's hand found Hannah's, fingers interlacing with practiced ease. The touch grounded Hannah even as she felt herself fragmenting, watching this clinical dissection of her family's tragedy, trying, as always, to understand her mom. And herself.

But it got worse. Next, they rolled the truck tire in and folded her grandmother into it, knees to chest, arms pulled through. The narrator explained how the technique kept the blows efficient; the body cannot curl away. "The cable landed on hip and thigh and back until the skin became a single bruised thought. Between sets, they poured more salt water to wake the nerve endings."

Tarsha felt Hannah squeeze her hand tighter.

"On the second night, they took her to the bathtub, but not to clean her. They laid her down and placed a folded towel over her mouth. They poured until the towel turned to ocean and her body rowed against itself. When consciousness failed, they lifted the towel, stealing death from her until she woke so they could continue. They talked to her as to a child. 'All this can stop.' All they needed from her was to sign the confession and renounce her teachings."

The narrator's voice softened, sounding mournful. "On the third night, they brought in her father, the Ayatollah."

A weathered photograph appeared, an elderly cleric with kind eyes. Hannah's great-grandfather.

The documentary didn't show the torture, but the narrator's clinical description was somehow worse. Suspension from the ceiling, his wrists bearing his entire weight until his bones separated. Beating the soles of his feet until the ability to stand became a distant memory. Electric cables pressed against his temples. Cigarette burns mapping his face. Fingers broken one by one. For three days, they made Fatima watch, chained to a chair as they systematically destroyed her father.

Hannah's breath shortened. Tarsha folded herself closer, as if to make a harbor.

"On the fourth day, they brought in a young Shia cleric, barely more than a boy, and gave both the Ayatollah and his daughter a choice: renounce Fatima's influence, or watch this innocent die.

When they refused, they shot the young man in front of them both. Then another. By the sixth day, seven young clerics had died. Each one blessed the Ayatollah with their last breath, each one telling Fatima to stay strong."

As they brought the Ayatollah to the courtyard in front of an assembly of forced witnesses, they read a list of his "crimes": spreading Persian influence, corrupting Iraqi women with religious extremism, conspiracy against the state. He was given one final chance to denounce his daughter's influence. His last words, according to the witness testimonies that emerged years later, were "My daughter writes with the pen of truth. Truth cannot be killed, only martyred."

"The execution was patient and methodical," the narrator continued. "They made Fatima watch this, too."

Tarsha was crying now too, her tears soaking through Hannah's shirt.

The documentary described the remaining five weeks—the shaving of Fatima's head, the mock trials where they forced her to stand naked before panels of men. The sleep deprivation. The recordings of her father's screams on loop in her cell.

After a long, mournful pause, the narrator continued. "The specific horrors of what happened in those cells—the sexual degradation, the psychological torture—would only fully come to light during Saddam's trial decades later. What we know is that they tried to film her breaking, to record her renunciation of her beliefs to broadcast to the Shia population at large."

The music swelled a half-step.

"And that she never gave them the satisfaction. When they finally released Fatima al-Rahbani, she could barely walk. Everyone expected her to disappear. She didn't. Within days, she stood in front of a gathered crowd—head covered, voice hoarse—and spoke. Of her father's martyrdom. Of the boys who would not recant. Of Husayn's martyrdom. Of duty and piety. The regime meant to make an example of her. They succeeded, but not in the way they intended. The woman who emerged from Abu Ghraib was no longer just a writer and a teacher. She had been transformed into something the regime could never kill—a symbol. She said the regime may be able to kill her body, but they could never kill her story."

Hannah wiped at her cheeks, angry at the tears and at what they admitted. Tarsha's arm wrapped across her, palm flat over Hannah's racing heartbeat.

The narrator's voice grew quiet again. "A little over one year later, she was dead, executed alongside her family in Dujail, but it was too late. The voice they tried to silence had become immortal."

The screen froze on a final photograph: Fatima smiling despite her trauma, those coal-dark eyes shining at the camera.

Hannah's body heaved. Tarsha gathered her in, cheek to Hannah's temple. For a moment, the room was only the hush of two people crying and the small domestic noises of a city apartment—the radiator's tick, the hum of the fridge, a car door thudding in the street.

HAIL CAESAR!

"Elizabeth, can't say how damn happy I am to see you here again. Looking mighty fine, too, if you don't mind an old dog like me complimenting you."

Elizabeth Lang offered a perfunctory smile as she sat down in the high-backed chair. The office smelled of leather and power, the kind of calculated scent that neither impressed nor offended, but subtly reinforced that everything here was expensive and controlled.

"Well, shit. This calls for a drink," Callahan said, standing up to walk to his crystal whiskey decanter on the credenza. He moved with the deliberate ease of a man accustomed to every room reshaping itself around his presence.

Lang grimaced momentarily before responding, "Just water for me, Gov'nor."

"You sure?" He raised an eyebrow to give her a moment to reconsider. "Well, suit yourself." He poured himself a small glass of whiskey, stoppered the decanter, and filled a glass with ice water from the crystal pitcher on the credenza. The glasses bore no fingerprints, meticulously hand dried and arranged by gloved staff,

Callahan's touch the first mark on their pristine surfaces. He walked over to her chair behind his desk and handed the glass of water to her. "Cheers," he said. They clinked glasses and, with a friendly smile on his face, he strutted back behind his desk and took a seat.

Lang placed her water glass directly on the gleaming surface of his desk, deliberately missing the coaster that sat inches away. A small pool of condensation formed around the base, threatening the immaculate finish of the wood. She noticed the subtle wrinkling around Callahan's practiced smile, and behind the mask, she saw the effort it took for him to dominate his eyes, preventing them from acknowledging this small act of territorial defiance. As the ring of moisture slowly expanded on his pristine desk, his refusal to address it became its own form of power play, a message that her small provocations were beneath his notice.

After that bullshit about the whiskey, she had to test him.

Callahan rested his chin between the thumb and forefinger of his left hand and stared at Lang. "All bullshitting aside, it really is great to see you looking healthy again, Elizabeth. I can only imagine the hell you've gone through."

Lang nodded. "Guess I needed your help to get my head out of my ass after all," she said, offering a wan smile.

"Hah! Well, in that case, you're welcome!" When Callahan laughed, the sound contained echoes of countless political victories and private jokes shared over decades. It was also the laugh of someone who had navigated treacherous waters for so long that he'd forgotten the possibility of drowning. "One hell of a shock, though, I gotta admit."

Lang took in the governor's office. Carefully selected photographs of Callahan with various dignitaries adorned its walls, forming a visual timeline of allegiances formed and broken. She noticed her own absence from this curated history, though there had been plenty of such moments worth framing. She lingered for a few moments on the large painting of Callahan above the credenza. "Needed something to do, I guess," she said at last.

They spoke like old friends, though each word carried undercurrents as they gently probed each other's defenses.

"You know what I regret most, Elizabeth?" Callahan said, his voice dropping to a near whisper as he leaned forward. "Not reaching out when you stepped away. Politics aside, we've known each other too damn long for that." He met her eyes with practiced sincerity, hedging personal admission with a lack of personal exposure. Lang recognized the gambit immediately. It was designed to elicit a vulnerable response, to make her feel valued while revealing her current attachments and anxieties.

"That's kind of you to say," she replied with a teasing smile. "Guess I found my own way to reach out."

Callahan leaned back in his chair good-naturedly. "Elizabeth, if all I had to do to get you healthy again was take a few bumps and bruises in the media, and maybe lose the election as a result, I want you to know I think it was worth it."

She let out a perfunctory proto laugh through her nostrils. "I wasn't the dumb shit who took on a major abortion case in an election year."

Callahan smiled amiably and took a sip of whiskey. "No, I suppose you weren't."

"Especially one involving a doctor who survived an attack by Saddam Hussein and saved the life of a raped thirteen-year-old girl."

"Yeah, that was an unfortunate setup," Callahan said. "Still, I'm not ready to concede the abortion was medically necessary to save her life just yet."

"Oh bullshit," Lang said, waving her hand dismissively. "I'm not here as a lawyer, Wade. Madison Quinn was hemostatically unstable and in shock. Not to mention the sepsis."

Callahan gave her a long look. "Why'd you get involved, Elizabeth?"

Lang shrugged. Outside the governor's window, the grounds stretched green and manicured, a cultivated wilderness that reminded Lang of their political relationship—wild by nature but trimmed into something presentable, something that appeared more civilized than it truly was.

"Like I said, I needed something to do to crawl out of the bottom of a bottle."

"Now who's the one speaking bullshit?" Another gambit, designed to send her off balance.

"The truth is, I'm not entirely sure myself. Maybe I'm just a media whore and this opportunity fell into my lap."

"Is it true she approached you at a nail salon?"

"Mmm-hmm."

"Why you?" Callahan studied her, probing for information.

Lang returned his stare with casual indifference. "When was the last time you saw *her* talk to the media?"

"Never."

"Then I'll circle back to me being a media whore. Seems I have a reputation."

Callahan swirled his whiskey, frowning thoughtfully. "The thing is, Elizabeth, there are plenty of media whores who don't require a nail-salon intervention. Some of them even specialize in this shit."

"You mean abortion shit?"

"That's the shit I mean."

Lang nodded thoughtfully. "Think any of them could've given you all those bumps and bruises you just appreciated me for?"

Callahan laughed. "No, I suppose not. Damn, it's good to just talk to you again."

His fingers drummed a slow, deliberate rhythm on the armrest of his chair, like a general timing the approach of reinforcements the enemy couldn't see. His eyes flicked briefly to the family photo on his desk, positioned to be visible to visitors without dominating the conversation. It was a deliberate calculation, but Lang knew that the devoted family man preserved in the frame and the ruthless politician sitting in the chair were performances that never quite merged.

"How's the girl?"

Lang gave a soft shrug. "Hurting. Don't know if you heard, but the doctor offered to take care of her if Travis Quinn goes to prison."

"Well, that's mighty big of her." He paused, looking thoughtful. "I know it's not my place to ask, but should I be worried about a publicity stunt?"

"From the doctor?"

Callahan nodded, measuring Lang's reaction carefully.

"When was the last time you saw her talk to the media?"

"Never."

Lang let the silence be her response. She didn't even express enough interest in the questioning to bother holding his gaze. The portrait of Callahan above the credenza caught the light differently now, the artist's brushstrokes somehow capturing both the man's charm and ruthlessness in oil and canvas. Lang wondered if the painting had been commissioned before he'd learned to hide the latter quality better.

"I'll say this," Callahan offered. "I think it's mighty big of you, too, to support Madison Quinn. I never wanted her brought into all of this, and I was sick when I heard about what happened."

Lang turned back to look at him. "How's your relationship with Everett Sinclair coming along?"

Callahan smiled, and his eyes lightened. "Well, you know. Building relationships is what I do."

Sinclair was on the Executive Council for the SBC and was well-connected in the evangelical community. He was very clear that he was *not* a pirate and did not hold the SBC to be immune from ethical lapses or secular scrutiny. As a result, Lawson hated Sinclair, a power struggle that threatened a schism inside the SBC.

Lang raised an eyebrow. "Got your exit ramp from this case with the doctor sorted out yet?"

Callahan laughed and slapped his thigh. "Why Elizabeth, I thought you weren't here as a lawyer!"

"A player's gonna play," she said.

"You calling me a player?"

"Takes one to spot one."

"All right, player to player, tell me what you would do in my shoes, then."

Lang took a sip of her water. Callahan briefly looked down at his phone as she replaced the glass on the wood of his table. "Well, it's like LBJ said when it comes to building a coalition. You can either have them inside the tent pissing out, or outside the tent pissing in. If I were you, I'd want the evangelical community inside my tent. But I'd make damn sure they weren't standing in a puddle with a line of dicks outside pissing on their shiny church shoes."

"Go on…"

"You can't drop the case without losing Lawson, so I imagine I'd do exactly what you're doing. Cozy up to Sinclair, spread rumors about Lawson being a sexual predator in the '90s, and look for an opportunity to throw him under the bus. Make the investigation seem fair and disciplined and drop it before the general election so it doesn't look political."

"Between us, Elizabeth," Callahan said, lowering his voice as if sharing a confession, "this Lawson situation has kept me up nights. When you've been in this business as long as we have, you start to see the patterns, and I'm worried about where this ends." He dropped his gaze to his glass, a masterful display of constructed intimacy that had loosened countless tongues over the years, all (in this case) without having to reveal which *Lawson* he had in mind.

Lang tilted her head slightly. "I understand completely," she said, allowing a carefully measured sigh to escape. "Since getting sober, sleep isn't what it used to be for me, either."

Callahan took a small sip of whiskey and leaned back. "Remember what Senator Ashland told us that night at the Capitol? 'Politics makes strange bedfellows, but the truly dangerous ones are those who've shared the same foxhole.'"

Lang nodded and smiled amiably. They'd been young staffers then, witnessing their first major political scandal unfold. "Ashland was right," she said. "Nobody knows your weaknesses like someone who's seen you under fire."

"Did you know the son of a bitch Lawson is trying to get me to show up in public with his son?"

Lang laughed, legitimately caught off guard. "That's… clumsy."

"Yeah, that was my reaction, too."

"He wants you in the same foxhole with Eli Lawson to protect him from my attempts to get a DNA collection warrant. Which, by the way, you've done a mighty fine job of so far, you bastard."

"Now Elizabeth, you know I believe in the separation of powers. You'll have to take that up with Judge Beaufort."

"Uh-huh."

"God, I've missed talking to you, Elizabeth."

Lang contemplated for a moment before speaking. "What are your plans with the doctor? When you drop the case, I mean?"

Callahan shrugged. "She's kinda tricky, isn't she? Like you said, not much of a talker, but she's got one hell of a story. Got a recommendation?"

"Thank her publicly." Lang narrowed her eyes. "Anonymously, burn her to the ground."

Callahan shifted to a more serious look as he sipped his whiskey and pondered her unexpected response. "Not a fan?"

Lang shook her head and flashed a look of disgust across her face. "Got me back in the saddle, but she's a righteous bitch."

The grandfather clock's persistent ticking filled their silence, each second a reminder of political mortality. Lang had always thought of Callahan as having perfect timing—the handshakes, the policy announcements, the strategic retreats—but now she wondered if even he could hear the countdown bearing down on them both.

Three seconds stretched to seven. Ten. Callahan ran his finger along the rim of his whiskey glass, his expression thoughtful but unconcerned. He settled more comfortably in his chair. Fifteen seconds now. Twenty. The grandfather clock seemed to grow louder with each tick, marking the battle of wills unfolding in the quiet room.

After thirty-five seconds, Callahan sniffed out a gracious laugh of defeat. "Mind saying that one of these days when the cameras are rollin'?"

"Seriously," Lang said, giving Callahan a fierce look. "You ever get a whiff that bitch wants to get in your way, give me a call. I can tell you some stories."

They locked eyes for a long moment. Lang broke it this time, softening her face into a smile. "As soon as you drop the case, I mean. So she's no longer my client. Separation of powers, and all."

Callahan laughed and gazed out the window. "I hear you've been getting some of your political operation back together."

"Leaving my options open."

"Thinking about your old seat?" After Lang had resigned, Callahan fulfilled the governor's responsibility of assigning a temporary senator, who had cruised through the primary and was expected to sail through the general election this year.

Lang shrugged. "Maybe governor. I hear there may be an opening soon."

Callahan laughed. "I sure hope so."

"Well, anyway, keep me in mind when you rule the world."

"You're impossible to ignore, Elizabeth," Callahan said. "And for what it's worth, I'd much rather have you inside my tent than outside it."

He took another sip of whiskey. It was a calculated move. He had poured himself a small amount and made small sips designed to look friendly and dignified and thoughtful, never enough to dull his wits. But he welcomed the warm sensation that coursed through him, calming him against whatever attack lurked beneath the doublespeak. He knew, better than anyone, that Elizabeth Lang was not one to be underestimated.

"What do you want, Elizabeth?" Callahan asked finally.

"A trade," she said.

Callahan nodded. "I see. What are you selling?"

The leather of Lang's chair creaked as she shifted her weight, the sound cutting through their calculated silence like a warning shot. Neither of them had ever been good at staying still when there was ground to be gained.

"Someone who will testify that John Lawson molested her in the '90s when she was a teenager."

Callahan's eyes widened in shock. "Jesus."

"She wants it handled inside the SBC, to encourage some soul-searching."

"So it's true?"

"Yep, and I have the goods."

Callahan tried to take another sip of whiskey before realizing his glass was empty. Absent-mindedly, he stood and poured more whiskey into his glass. He stood frozen with his hand on the stopper of the decanter.

"Who else knows?"

"No one but me. Some good ol' fashioned legal investigative prowess. You're welcome."

"Jesus." He finally let go of the stopper and took a sip of whiskey. "This is fucking good news, Elizabeth. Fucking good news."

"What can I say? Christmas came early this year."

Callahan strolled back to his chair and slumped into it. He spun around, doing a slow 360. "This would bring down the pirates with him," he said.

"Yep."

Callahan scratched his chin and looked at Lang for a long time before speaking.

"Okay. Now will you tell me what you actually want?"

Lang smiled, her victory wrapped in silk but edged with steel. "Oh, I suppose a single strand of hair should do the trick."

Eli Lawson paced the length of his living room, his feet moving faster than his thoughts could untangle themselves. His brain seemed immersed in some toxic combination of fear, anxiety, confusion, and despair.

Remote in hand, he turned the volume up and read the chyrons. He continued to pace, his brisk steps not keeping up with his heartbeat.

"… why would she wait thirty years to say anything about it?" his dad's famous voice barked through the TV speakers. The camera lingered on the elder Lawson, his jaw clenched as he waved off the reporter's microphone, before cutting to the newsroom panel.

"I'll tell you this," a Black woman on the panel said fiercely. "I don't care *how* long it takes. What Rachel Phillips did took *courage*." She slammed her hand on the table and showed her passion with a mean look on her face.

Rachel Phillips. Brooke Phillips. He saw the thread Lang must've pulled on. Brooke had always been a gossip. She wasn't in his youth ministry, but she and Kim were best friends. Lang must have connected the dots through Kim. Either Rachel was making up the whole thing and had gone through the trouble of telling her daughter, or his father was the biggest fucking hypocrite he'd ever known.

"How do you think this will play out in the case against Travis Quinn?" one panelist asked. "Remember, he punched Lawson's son after his thirteen-year-old daughter nearly died from a pregnancy while under his care."

"Hang on," one of the panelists said, touching the earpiece that connected him to his producer. "We're getting reports that Governor Callahan and Everett Sinclair from the SBC are issuing a live statement."

Eli jumped and dropped the remote as the doorbell rang.

His heart beat like a bass drum when he stared out through the peephole and saw the blue uniforms, but he couldn't think through the panic and the lump in his throat and the tunnel vision. Almost mechanically, as if the entire world had slowed down, he opened the door.

"Eli Lawson?" the officer asked.

"Yes," he squeaked.

"We have a search warrant." The officer held out a sheet of paper. "I'm going to need you to come with us, sir."

THE UNIVERSAL LAW OF ATTRACTION

"Why?" Madison asked, scratching behind Sergeant Baker's ear, her brow furrowed in curiosity.

"Yeah, it's all a bit weird, isn't it?" Richard said, twirling his fedora around in his hands as he looked thoughtful, searching for the right explanation. "I think it's helpful, sometimes, to think of the whole universe as nothing more than a bunch of tiny particles bouncing off each other. And certain types of particles have *charges*, which means they either attract or repel other types of particles."

"Or even their own type," Charles Ruddick added, leaning forward slightly.

"Like atoms?" Madison asked.

Richard smiled. "Even smaller than that. Think electrons—they have an electrical charge that pulls them toward protons, but they'll push other electrons away." He pointed at the two magnets Madison had just finished playing with. "That's more or less what you're feeling when you try to push the same poles together and feel the resistance."

"What other types of charges are there?" Madison asked, looking down at the magnets.

"Well," Richard began, "there's something called a *color charge* that pulls even smaller particles together in groups of three, so tightly it's almost impossible to break them apart."

"Like… they're attracted to different colors?" Madison asked, her head tilting slightly.

Charles fielded this question. "Since everything's so small that we can't see it, we just use the word *color* as a metaphor."

"A metaphor?" Madison asked.

"Yep," Richard started. "A metaphor is—"

Madison rolled her eyes. "I *know* what a metaphor is."

Charles snorted, his grin spreading wide as he gave her an admiring look of camaraderie, almost like a high-five without the slap. "Well…" he said, dragging out the word in mock dignity, before switching into a comically exaggerated American accent for "*anyway…*" Madison laughed.

"The '*metaphor*'"—he put the word in air quotes—"lets us use what we *do* know as a bridge to those things we *can't* know."

"So they're not like, attracted to purple then," Madison said, frowning.

Charles's smile widened, genuine and warm. "Think of it like this," he said. "Maybe they're attracted to a type of purple we can never see, but we know exists."

"And that's kinda the point," Richard continued. "It's like metaphors give us an impoverished sixth sense. It will never be as sharp as our other five, but when all of them fail, metaphors are all we have. Without them, we miss the truth entirely." He smiled at Madison, his expression gentle. "With a good metaphor, maybe we discover the truth that there's something beyond our senses."

"How?"

"Math!" Charles exclaimed, holding up his finger for emphasis. "Math is the best tool we have for bridging realities."

"How does math help you tell which colors a particle is attracted to?" Madison asked.

"Young lady, that's an absolutely *fantastic* question," Charles said, his enthusiasm palpable. "We use giant magnets—"

"*Ginormous* magnets," Richard interjected with a smirk.

"—to speed up particles to even more ginormous speeds and have them crash into each other, and then, if we're clever enough, we can use some maths to help us figure out what happened, and some metaphors to try to explain it, kind of like a detective mystery."

"But you can't use magnets to crash stars into each other, can you?" Madison asked.

Charles chuckled warmly. "You don't let much slip past you, do you, Madison?" he said, his admiration evident.

Richard smiled and flipped his hat onto his head with a touch of flair. "There's one charge that's kinda different from all the others."

An expectant silence hung in the library before Richard, an impish smile on his face, could no longer stand the tension that he himself had built and blurted out the answer.

"Gravity."

"Gravity's a charge?"

"Well, we used to think of it like a charge that attracted mass to mass. But then Einstein came along and came up with a different metaphor, where everything in the universe falls because gravity curves the very fabric of spacetime itself."

Madison looked at both men curiously. "But stars don't fall, do they?"

"Hah!" Charles said. "You're doing exactly what we all do, the first time we figure this out—"

"And for the rest of our lives," Richard interjected.

"—trying to explain things in a way that makes sense to us." He paused, passing a sympathetic smile to Madison.

He tore off a sheet of paper from a legal pad on the desk and held it out to Madison. "Would you mind holding those two ends for me, dear?" he asked. "That's it, hold it level. Now, Richard, if you'll do us the honor."

Richard picked up a steel marble, part of a collection on his bookshelf, and gently placed it in the middle of the paper, held up by Charles and Madison. The paper sagged under its weight, forming a smooth, curved indentation.

"So, you remember how *color* was just a metaphor that helped us think about something we can describe with math?" Charles asked.

Madison nodded, her eyes fixed on the bulging paper.

"This is more or less the same idea," Charles explained. "Let's imagine this sheet of paper represents the entire universe. Of course, paper is just a flat, two-dimensional surface. But we can't visualize a four-dimensional fabric—three for space and one for time. So, we cheat. We pretend, because if our metaphor helps us make sense of something in two dimensions, then the same math works in four dimensions."

Madison stared at the paper for several seconds, watching the marble create the depression. "So, this paper is supposed to be 4-D?"

Charles smiled. "Physicists talk about the *spacetime fabric*, which is just one of those metaphors like a color charge. It helps us think about it, and then we can test our thought with math in four dimensions to see if our metaphor was close or not."

"And this marble is a star?" Madison asked.

"Exactly!" Charles said, grinning.

"It's not really falling," Madison said.

"Like I said, young lady, not much slips past you. Richard, would you do us the honor again?"

Richard, clearly enjoying himself, grabbed another steel marble from his collection. With deliberate care, he placed it on the paper, some distance from the first marble. As soon as he released it, the second marble rolled down the paper's curve and collided with the first.

"That one fell," Madison observed.

"Indeed!" Charles said. "Bartender, hit me!"

With a theatrical flourish, Richard grabbed another marble and dropped it onto the paper. It immediately slid toward the others, adding its weight to the growing sag in the paper.

"That's gravity?" Madison asked.

"Gravity's like that bulge in the paper under the weight of the marbles," Charles said.

Madison furrowed her brow, her eyes fixed on the marbles. "Mom always told me to be careful of stories about invisible stuff we can't see making things happen." She cocked her neck to study the bulge under the paper.

After Richard grabbed the marbles, Charles put the paper on the desk and smiled at Madison. "Think of 'invisible stuff we can't see' as just a metaphor that lets us use some math. As long as the predictions from that math keep coming to pass, we keep using the metaphor. It's like a story we tell ourselves that helps us make sense of the world." He rubbed his left wrist unconsciously, where a faded scar stretched across his skin. Few knew the story behind it: a laboratory accident from his early research days, when an equipment malfunction had nearly cost him his hand. It was perhaps why he approached physics with such reverence, speaking of mathematical models with the gentle awe that others reserved for religious texts. He had touched the raw power that his equations described and learned that understanding didn't equal mastery.

"Hey," Charles continued, "you know what weighs a *lot*?"

"A star," Madison said.

"Exactly!"

"Here's where things get weird," Richard said with a wry smile.

"Um, things have been weird the whole time," Madison said.

Richard laughed gently. "Yeah, I suppose they have. But here's where things get *really* weird."

"Richard's right, Madison," Charles said, his tone conspiratorial. "When *really* heavy stuff curves the fabric of our universe, some *really* weird stuff happens. Are you sure you're ready for this?"

Madison nodded, her eyes wide open.

"Well, let's think about it for a second," Charles continued, as they took their seats again. "Where did that second and third marble want to fall?"

"Toward the bottom."

"But what was in its way?"

Madison thought for a moment before answering. "The first marble was blocking it," she said.

"Exactly!" Charles slapped his thigh for effect. "So now let's imagine something—let's say some gas molecules—keeps falling into the group of marbles."

"Umm…"

"Maybe think of what happens after a million pounds of gas molecules fall into the marbles," Richard said.

"A million pounds?"

"Yeah, good point," Richard said, smirking. "Let's say a zillion pounds."

Madison laughed.

"So now," Charles jumped in, his tone patient but his excitement palpable, "you have a zillion pounds of gaseous mass that's all trying to fall into a zillion, zillion, zillion pounds of solid mass, which is heaviest at the center."

"I guess it still keeps trying to fall toward the center," Madison said. "But I guess the solid stops it."

Charles shook his head and exhaled in obvious awe of Madison's intellect. Richard's smile widened and his eyes brightened.

"Just like this floor stops us from falling toward the center of the earth," Charles said. "But we're only one or two hundred pounds. What if we're a zillion pounds?"

Madison looked down at the floor, then back up at Charles. "Um, the floor breaks?"

Charles nodded his head solemnly. "Could happen," he said. "Remember those tiny little electrons?"

"So tiny we can't even see them," Richard said.

Madison nodded.

"Well," Charles continued, his voice taking a dramatic turn, "as they get squeezed into tinier and tinier spaces, they start bouncing around faster and faster—"

"Their wavelength decreases," Richard said.

"Yes!" Charles's voice lifted with excitement. "When they're that small, we often think of them as waves, which is just a metaphor that lets us use some math. As they get squeezed tighter, the wave gets more excited. That pressure of it pushes back against those zillion pounds of mass trying to collapse inward."

Richard adopted a comically mournful face. "Better hope you don't end up as a white dwarf," he said.

Madison was absent-mindedly petting Sergeant Baker, her attention rapt on the conversation. "That's a weird name," she said, cocking her neck. "Why is being a white dwarf bad?"

"Because…" Charles started.

"… it's cold and dead…" Richard added.

"… forever!" both men said together, adopting an ominous tone tinged with mock drama.

"Oh." Madison frowned. The concept of forever wasn't new to her, but this was a stark contrast to the fiery hell she'd associated with it. "Can a star avoid turning into a white dwarf?"

"Yep!" Charles said. "So it turns out that when we say a zillion, zillion, zillion pounds, we really mean about one and a half times as massive as our sun. But if you get heavier than that…" He paused, his voice dropping theatrically.

"… the gravitational squeeze keeps going," Richard finished for him, his voice low, adding to the dramatic build.

"Sometimes," Charles continued, "it's so heavy that it bursts through the electron bubble wrap and it bursts through the stronger neutron bubble wrap and it keeps going, so that bulge in the paper keeps getting bigger and bigger and bigger…"

"And then what happens?"

"A black hole," Richard said, the words rolling out with a sense of triumphant satisfaction.

"A black hole?"

Charles laughed warmly. "Oh Madison, you should've seen the reaction from those uptight French when physicists decided to name them 'black holes.'"

"Especially when Wheeler said that 'a black hole has no hair,'" Richard added, his grin widening mischievously.

Madison furrowed her brow, looking between them. "Why?"

Charles leaned in conspiratorially, lowering his voice as if letting her in on a secret. "Well, Madison. I'm not sure I should tell you. You promise you won't get me in trouble with your dad?"

Madison's eyes widened slightly at the thrill of being let in on something forbidden. "I promise."

Charles hesitated dramatically, glancing at Richard, who gave an encouraging nod. "Okay, well, here's the thing. The term is what we call a *double entendre*. Do you know what that means?"

"It means… oh!" Madison said, her face lighting up. Her expression shifted to one of sudden understanding, her cheeks flushing slightly as a shocked but delighted grin spread across her face.

Everyone let out a laugh. Sergeant Baker stood up, stretched lazily, made three counterclockwise circles on the rug, and plopped down again with an exaggerated groan. He let out a slow and lazy fart.

"So, here's where things get *really, really* weird, Madison," Charles said, after the air cleared. "You know how that electron and neutron pressure got stronger and stronger the more gravity squeezed the star?"

Madison nodded.

"Well, that pressure keeps increasing as all that mass squeezes into an increasingly small circumference, until it gets so small that at some point, God has no other option but to show us what happens when he divides by zero."

"What happens?" Madison asked. Sergeant Baker lifted his head, alert to the sound of urgency in her voice.

Richard curled the fingertips of his two hands together and spread them apart, mimicking a bomb with his motion and making an explosion sound.

"No one really knows," Charles shrugged. "But one theory suggests it makes a bigger explosion than you could ever imagine."

"A Big Bang," Richard said.

Charles narrowed his eyes as if letting Madison in on a secret. "Except it seems to explode backwards in time."

Madison tilted her head, her eyes wide with wonder. "How does time move backwards?"

"Oh, it's just math again," Charles said, waving his hand. "We really have no idea, but the math works."

"It rips open a whole new reality." Richard said.

"A new beginning," Charles said.

"That's *really* weird."

"Told you," Richard said.

"And we're not done yet," Charles said.

"Yeah, now we're gonna get really, really, *really* weird," Richard said.

"Are you ready?" Charles asked.

Travis sat slumped in the patio chair, his eyes wandering over the neatly trimmed Japanese yews lining the backyard. He raised his hand to his face, thumb and forefinger spread wide and rubbed his eyes like he was trying to erase the exhaustion etched into them.

"So, you took a class from Charles at UT?" Maya asked, breaking the silence.

Travis nodded. "Small world. Failed it, though. That was the year Amy got hit. I failed out of school." He shrugged. "Never went back."

"What was he like as a teacher?"

Travis shook his head. "Kooky. Brilliant."

"Sounds like what he's like outside the classroom, too," Maya said, smiling softly.

Travis returned the smile briefly, but then looked away, his face clouding over. "Amy was always the smart one. I just rode her coattails as long as I could. I've been so lost without her." His voice broke slightly as he blinked hard, trying to hold back the tears.

"She graduated from UT?"

"UT Dallas," Travis said. "After I failed out, we moved into her family's house in Garland." His voice carried a weight of regret.

Maya took a deep breath, steadying herself. "So, what do I need to know?"

"About Madison?" Travis gestured toward the two suitcases sitting by the door. Most of the clothes inside, he'd said, were colors she hadn't worn since the hospital, replaced by the sweatpants and hoodie she currently wore.

Maya nodded.

Travis thought for a minute, scratching his chin. "Do you really think *I* know the answer to that question?" He looked miserable.

"Yes," Maya answered without hesitation. She held her gaze steady, trying to lift Travis out of his imploding depression.

Travis took a shaky breath. "Just…" His voice cracked as he choked back tears. "Just take care of her." His lips trembled, and he swiped at his eyes with the back of his hand.

"I will," Maya said, her voice gentle but resolute.

"She needs a fresh start," he managed. "A different environment. Something to fill the void."

Maya nodded.

"She likes pizza," Travis said. "And pineapples." He laughed to relieve the pressure.

Maya smiled. "We'll get her enrolled in a school around here, and Richard will help. We'll make sure she has a fresh start. And it's just six months."

"Yeah," Travis said, nodding slowly. "Lang said Governor Callahan really didn't want me going to trial. Apparently, having a minor daughter with autism, who was sexually abused by Eli Lawson and then tried to kill herself, isn't exactly great for his electoral chances." His tone was bitter, his lips pressed into a thin line. The prosecution had been quick to offer a revised plea bargain, which Travis accepted.

Maya let the silence stretch between them for a few moments before continuing. "Elizabeth said the civil suit fell apart, too?"

Travis nodded.

"Has Madison spoken to you about it?" Maya asked.

Travis shook his head, the anger visible in his jaw as he began aggressively sucking on his lips. "Says she still can't remember. But… not in a date-rapey kind of way, I don't think."

Maya inhaled deeply. "It's more like she's afraid to face herself," she said.

Travis turned to her, his eyes hollow, a tortured expression carved into his face. "Why did the son of a bitch give her arthritis pills?" His voice cracked with desperation, his words dripping with both rage and anguish.

Maya held his gaze, steady and unwavering, her eyes soft but unflinching. "Methotrexate," she said. "We use it to treat ectopic pregnancies because it interferes with the folic acid and stops cells from dividing. It's usually paired with misoprostol for abortions, but the arthritis pills were all he had access to. He must have read just enough to assume that if she was pregnant, the pills would solve the problem for him."

Travis shook his head, his lips curling in disgust. "Must've hated his dad, though, to admit all that."

Maya nodded thoughtfully. "At the very least, he must've been tired of trying to live in the story his dad wrote for him."

"What does that mean?"

Maya paused, drawing in a slow, deep breath. She searched for the right words, her gaze drifting to a red-bellied robin pecking near a bush. "Something Richard told me once, when my mom was recovering from her stroke. That I get to write my own story."

Travis studied her, his brow furrowing slightly.

She continued, her voice softer now, as if sharing a quiet confession. "I haven't always been comfortable depending on other people. I have a bad habit of running away from the people who try to help me. He knows that."

Travis's gaze was a storm of conflicting emotions. "Is that why you're doing this?" he asked, his voice low.

"Taking care of Madison?"

"No." His tone was sharper now, almost accusing. Travis's look was some combination of hatred and wariness. Maya met it and let the silence linger before offering a faint, tired smile.

"Ah." She nodded her head slowly without releasing her gaze. "Yes, in part."

Travis leaned forward, his cheeks reddening slightly. "I'm serious when I say I don't want Madison anywhere near the shit show."

Maya's expression didn't change. She nodded again, maintaining eye contact. "I'll do what I can, but it's going to be messy."

"Then why the hell are you doing it?"

Maya turned her face away, blinking quickly, but the tear slipped down her cheek before she could stop it. There was no point in hiding it now. She turned back to him, her jaw set, her eyes steady. "Because," she said, her voice trembling ever so slightly, "as much as I try to hide it, I know—fucking better than *anyone*—that sometimes we all need a little saving from time to time."

Travis held the stare, a hurricane of contradictory emotions swirling through his eyes.

Maya and Travis walked side by side down the hall toward Richard's library. They seemed at first curious, then amused by the sound coming through the walls. They heard what sounded like Richard making the impression of the crack of a whip. Sergeant Baker let out an energetic bark.

"Step roigh' up! Step roigh' up!" Charles called out, like a Cockney carnival barker. "Where not e'en 'Eisenberg could go. I tell ya! Ge' a gander at wha' we go' 'ere, ladies an' gents!"

The Queen's English Charles had cultivated over decades lay like a thick veneer over his East End roots. He'd grown up the son of a postman and a seamstress, his path to Cambridge paved by scholarship exams taken by candlelight when the electricity had been cut off. Those rare occasions when his hard-earned mask dropped filled Maya with a profound sense of kinship.

But the most amazing sound came from Madison, a sound that pulled every ounce of air from Travis's lungs.

She was laughing.

"Uh-oh," Maya said in mock horror as they rounded the corner and caught a glimpse of the scene inside.

Richard, balancing precariously on a chair, had his fedora tilted at a rakish angle, his right hand swiping through the air in a clumsy imitation of Indiana Jones cracking a whip. Sergeant Baker squatted as if ready to pounce, wagging his tail excitedly as he looked up at Richard. Charles stood in the corner, his hands cupped over his mouth in a makeshift bullhorn, amplifying the absurdity.

Madison sat cross-legged on the carpet, her face lit with an energy Travis hadn't seen in months. Her eyes sparkled as she turned to look at him.

"Dad!" she called out, her smile impossibly wide. "I never knew you were an electron tamer!"

For a moment, Travis couldn't move. He couldn't even blink. The warmth in her voice, the light in her eyes—it all crashed into him like a tidal wave, overwhelming and impossible to contain. He felt the hormones wash over the floodplains of his brain like a warm, dizzying flush until his vision blurred.

For that moment, he forgot to breathe.

Charles straightened his ascot with an air of mock dignity and turned to address Travis. "Young man," he began, his tone playful but his eyes kind, his Queen's English back in command. "If you have any interest in moving to Austin when you get out of the clinker, I could put in a good word for you at the university. We always have a need for talented electron tamers."

"Would you teach me, Dad?" Madison asked, her earnestness reflecting in her gaze.

His lips quivered as he tried to speak, but the words wouldn't come, lost in the fog of shame and self-doubt he'd been wearing like wet clothes for so long. He blinked hard against the wetness clouding his eyes, his throat tight as he swallowed back the storm of emotion threatening to break free.

"Yes," he croaked, his voice breaking under the strain of the moment. "Yes, of course, honey."

THE ITALIAN, PART 2

Lines of rain slashed through the headlight beams and disappeared into the blacktop. The windshield wipers of the unremarkable Toyota Camry whipped back and forth, straining to keep up with the downpour. It moved down the residential street slowly, its driver clearly scanning for an address in the poor visibility. Soon, it paused for verification before it slowly turned into a driveway of a modest, one-story ranch-style house.

The engine cut off, the lights blinked out, and the driver emerged—a figure cloaked in a yellow raincoat with a large hood, who half-ran in a crouch to the covered porch before ringing the doorbell.

The homeowner opened the door wearing a button-up seersucker shirt and dress pants, having only recently come home from work himself.

"My *Gawwd*," he said, his voice singing that rich, rolling melody.

He glanced past her to the car in the driveway, his mustache twitching with irritation. "*Ees thaht—ahhh yoouurrrs?*" The words came out like a rollercoaster, soaring sharply on *thaht*, before plummeting into a long, indulgent drawl on *ahhh yoouurrrs*, every syllable stretching like caramel.

"Rental," Maya said, glancing over her shoulder to hide her smile. There was something about his accent dipped in indignation that was better than foreplay. "Not mine, either. My best friend's, the one I told you about."

She read the next words out of his mouth in their lilting audible font: "My *Gawwd*, GET *eee-na*, quick, before anyone *seeeeeess!*"

The way his voice leapt on *Gawdd*, like a cymbal crash, then tumbled downward through the stretched-out *eee-na* and finally unraveled into the syrupy *seeeeeess*, sent a shiver straight through her.

She was pretty certain that the rain wasn't the *only* reason for the intense wetness she felt.

He stepped aside with an exaggerated flourish, letting her in the foyer, before closing the door with the precision of someone locking away a scandal. He darted off to fetch a towel and a basket for her raincoat, muttering something unintelligible but delicious under his breath.

"You're sure-ah no one saw you?" he asked, his brow furrowed.

"I could barely see myself, even with lights and the windshield wipers at full blast," she said, trying not to grin as his mustache twitched with concern. When he still looked unconvinced, she touched his shoulder and smiled. "Relax," she said. "I'm not *that* famous."

That seemed to drain the tension from his shoulders. "Sorry," he said, his words slipping into their signature cadence. "I just don't want to be caught up in it, you know-ah." His voice lingered on the *know-ah* like an unspoken apology, curling gently in the air between them.

"Trust me, I get it," she said, her tone warm, reassuring. "Neither do I."

His lips curved into a soft smile, his mustache twitching with the movement. "It's so good-ah to see you, Maya," his voice wrapping around her name like a caress.

Maya's grin widened. "It's so *gouda* to see you too, Leo."

He let out a soft chuckle. "Ah, yes, well. Come in, please." He motioned her inside and led the way to his living room. The space was modest with a low ceiling and a fireplace. A simple fabric couch sat alongside a low wooden coffee table and a well-worn recliner. Beyond the small bar, the oven hood peeked out from the kitchen like a quiet sentinel.

"Vino?" he called from the kitchen.

"Sure, I'll have a glass," Maya said, settling into the couch.

Moments later, Leo returned, balancing two glasses of red wine in his hands. He handed her one with a small appreciative smile. "*Cin cin*," he said.

"*Cin cin*," she echoed, their glasses meeting with a soft *clink*.

He lowered himself onto the couch beside her, resting his left arm along the back of it, his body angled toward hers.

There was a pregnant pause before Leo spoke again. "Why-ah… didn't you tell me about your… story? Before?" His words wavered slightly, the accent adding a soft rhythm, as if he was navigating a fragile bridge between curiosity and caution.

Maya shrugged. "Same reason I haven't told *anyone* my story. I've spent four decades trying to forget it. Being reminded of it pissed me off."

Leo watched her carefully. "It still pisses you off?"

She sighed and took a slow sip of wine, letting the warmth settle in her chest. "I'm working on it."

Leo studied her, his brow furrowing slightly as he swirled the wine in his glass. He sniffed out a laugh. "And thees… *theees* is how-ah you deal with it?"

Maya tilted her head, her lips curling into a knowing smile. "You know I've got a bit of a rebel streak." Her voice carried that familiar undercurrent of mischief.

Leo chuckled, shaking his head. "Ah, *si*. I noticed. Thees"—he waved his arm in front of him, vaguely indicating everything he barely understood: the case, the media, the trauma, and the fear of what came next—"must be hard for you to handle." He understood their relationship had always been an escape valve for her, and she was asking for that again.

She leaned back, her fingers trailing lazily around the rim of her glass. "Everyone's got a plan for me. Cry on TV. Play the martyr. Be a hero." She let the words linger, then exhaled a slow, defiant breath. "Somewhere along the way, I realized…" Her voice dropped just enough to draw him in, her eyes gleaming with something dark and electric. "I don't have to play by their rules."

Leo took another slow sip of wine, his dark eyes studying her with something between admiration and wary amusement. He'd always known Maya had a fire in her, but seeing it now, unapologetic, untamed, made him suddenly aware that he was sitting across from a woman who had stopped asking the world for permission.

He exhaled, shaking his head with a small chuckle, then lifted his glass in a half-toast. "You know-ahhh that I *steeell* don' wanna be caught up in any-a thees."

Maya's lips curled into a teasing smile. "Oh, that's the easy part," she said, swirling her wine with a little flourish, like a magician about to unveil her next trick. She let the anticipation build for a beat, savoring the moment before setting her glass down and leaning in as if she were revealing state secrets.

"You take a separate bus from Cancun to Tulum," she began, her tone full of theatrical intrigue, "until you meet my friend Julia." She lifted a brow, giving Julia's name a mysterious halo. "That's her car rental in your driveway. She takes your phone, like she takes everyone else's. It's yours if you need it, just not near the rest of us."

Leo raised an eyebrow. "I should-a be taking notes?" he asked.

Maya let out a soft laugh, her eyes shining as she met his gaze.

Leo leaned back, giving her an exaggeratedly skeptical look. "Julia sounds like a good-*ah* friend," he said, stretching out the last words with playful suspicion.

Maya gave him a mischievous grin. "The best. Thirty years of friendship, and she's still the only person who calls me on my bullshit without making me feel like I need to run." She took a thoughtful sip of wine. "This whole experience… it's partly for me, but it's also because she helped me see I was telling myself the wrong story all along." She held his gaze, savoring the moment. "So, now she's my gangbang planner. It's like a wedding planner, but for gangbangs."

Leo let out a sharp laugh, short and surprised, but the moment it escaped, he pressed his lips together, his mustache bristling like it was trying to shield him from the sheer audacity of Maya's words. *"Madonna mia,"* he muttered, before taking a slow deliberate sip of wine.

Maya leaned in slightly, her voice dripping with playful mischief. "She and Richard—that's my ex-husband—have scoped out a *private* resort," she said, smiling through the *private* just enough to make his ears twitch. "Totally secluded. No one around but us. A whole week." She paused, watching him, letting the weight of the offer settle. "All on me, if you say yes."

Leo smiled and shook his head, like a man trying to process something both absurd and undeniably fascinating. "You're *crazy*, you know?" He gestured vaguely with his wine glass. "Having *sehx-ah* in front of your *ex*-husband." His voice caught a little on *sehx*, like it was debating whether it should be involved in this conversation at all.

Maya grinned, unbothered, and waved a dismissive hand. "Yeah, that part's a little weird. But we'll have Viagra, and one of the other guys lives in Playa del Carmen; he's agreed to bring some pot to take the edge off. Everyone gets tested ahead of time, and I take care of the birth control." She listed it out so practically, it might as well have been a grocery run.

Leo blinked. "And he's, uh… *okay* with this?"

Maya smirked "One hundred percent. Turns him on, actually." She raised her eyebrows and leaned in slightly, as if confessing a scandal. "He *loves* it when I tell him about my… other experiences."

Leo shifted uncomfortably in his seat. "He likes… *words?*" The way he said it, with a skeptical squint and a hint of disbelief, made it sound like the most degenerate kink he'd ever encountered.

Maya sighed theatrically, setting her glass down on the coffee table with exaggerated patience. "I know; it's perverted. But he's a good guy."

Leo narrowed his eyes. "This has *gotta* be the stupidest fucking idea I ever heard." He punctuated the statement with a sip of wine, as if the drink might somehow cleanse him of even entertaining the thought.

Maya leaned forward, her eyes sparkling, her excitement barely contained. "*I know!*" she said, her voice bubbling with energy. "And I think it might be kinda awesome, too."

Leo shifted in his seat. "You knooow I don' wanna play-ah with another man, *si?*" His voice dipped lower, as if he was confessing a sin in church.

"I promise the only time you'll have to touch another man is when you high-five each other at the end."

Leo laughed, sat back, and turned his body to face the TV. "What I don't understand," he said, "is why-ah it's so important to you."

Maya's smile lingered for a beat before it softened, her fingers absently tracing the rim of her glass. "My life is about to get a lot more complicated," she said, her voice measured, like she was testing the weight of the words before fully committing to them.

"Ahhh, so this is a *before* thing, *si*?"

Maya gave a smile that was the daughter of mischief and mis-givings.

Leo studied her. "This *thing* sounds like a *big* thing."

Her sparkling eyes dared him to admit his intrigue.

Leo shook his head. "I don't know-ah. This is soooo awkward."

Maya smiled. "And a once in a lifetime opportunity. This is the stuff of legend."

"And you're the hero?"

"No, *you're* the hero. I'm the queen."

"The queen?"

Maya took a seductive sip of wine. "Richard always talks about knights needing a good challenging quest so the queen can see their heroism, and they can bask in her appreciation."

"Richard… seems to have a way-ah with words."

"I know. He's perverted like that."

REFLECTIONS

"How's Ottawa?"

"Warming up. There are definitely times I wonder why I didn't follow Harry to Phoenix."

Maya walked alongside Adam Lewis, their steps crunching softly against the forest trail. Sunlight filtered through the canopy, dappling the ground in shifting patches of gold. Adam slowed his pace, pausing to study a cluster of trees, his gaze thoughtful.

"Whatcha thinking?" Maya asked.

Adam shook his head, a small smile playing at the corners of his lips. "Just noticing." He gestured toward a towering oak, its thick trunk stretching high above them, breaching the canopy with effortless majesty.

"Looks like a tree to me," Maya said, her hands in her pockets.

Adam nodded, his white hair matching the wispiness of his voice. "A good, solid, dependable tree. One that never struggled to find the sun. One that will never understand the struggle of those who had to bend and warp their way into the sun's rays."

Maya watched him, patient, letting him take his time.

"Not like this tree." He pointed to a smaller tree, its trunk listing at an uneasy angle, roots half-exposed and gnarled, clutching at the earth like desperate fingers refusing to let go. "And look at that one right there," he added, motioning toward another, its trunk twisted into a sinuous, sideways-*S*, its entire form a testament to years of struggle, bending and contorting just to catch the sun's fleeting kiss. He sighed, pulling off his glasses to rub his eyes.

"You're getting awfully poetic in your old age."

"Hah! Maybe so." He turned to Maya, slipping his glasses back on, his gaze settling on the towering tree above them. "I'm like this one," he said, gesturing toward the massive trunk rising unwavering into the canopy, its branches sprawling with effortless dominance. "Harry was, too. And the governor."

Maya smiled, tilting her head as she gestured toward the contorted tree. "And this is more my scene," she said, her fingers tracing the air along its twisted path, a silent acknowledgment of its resilience.

Adam drew in a deep breath, letting the crisp scent of earth and leaves fill his lungs. "Those trees in the shadows… they bend or they die." His voice carried the weight of years. He exhaled slowly, his gaze drifting upward toward the unyielding canopy. "And we upright oaks, we judge the survivors for bending."

"This is starting to sound like a Rush song."

Adam chuckled. "Just thinking this is an unexpected way to spend your newfound freedom," he mused, glancing at her with something between admiration and trepidation.

Maya smirked but said nothing for a minute. The state had officially dropped the case against her after an "extended and thorough investigation," acknowledging that Madison Quinn was on death's bed, and Dr. Maya Russell had made a life-saving decision to abort the viable fetus to save her life. Governor Callahan, standing next to Everett Sinclair of the SBC in front of the cameras, thanked Maya for her rapid decision-making under stress.

"You think I'm making a mistake?"

Adam gave a slow, wistful smile and nodded his head. "Maybe I do. Harry always said your greatest strength and weakness was your willingness to burn everything down when cornered. I can see that look in your eyes again. But what happens to Hannah if this goes sideways? To Madison?"

Maya nodded, tilting her head to see her reflection in the tree. "Depends on if I make it to the canopy or not." She let out a slow sigh. "But I'm done running, Adam."

"I can't even imagine how hard this must be for you," Adam said, gazing at her intently. "I wish Harry and Nancy could see you now, like I see you." He paused, his voice steady but full of quiet conviction. "And I think you should know, I'm your biggest supporter."

Maya hesitated. "Adam, there will be some things that come out about me…"

"Fuck them," Adam cut her off with a sharp wave of his hand, his voice thick with emotion. His eyes glistened, his lips trembling as he pressed forward. "None of that matters to me. You're here. The only thing you need to know about me is that… I *see* you. And I don't give one shit about those bends you had to take to get here."

Maya didn't fight the tears that slipped down her cheeks. She stepped forward and wrapped her arms around Adam, gripping him as tightly as she had at her dad's funeral years ago and her mom's funeral months ago. He pulled her in without hesitation, his embrace steady, his cheek resting against the top of her head.

"Just please tell me you won't let Lang control the narrative."

"You don't trust her?"

Adam thought for a moment. "No. Liz Lang doesn't just burn down her enemies; she burns down everyone around her. Promise me you'll keep your distance when the match gets lit."

"I promise."

"And it doesn't even matter if I'm wrong. Once she starts speaking for you, it's hard to take back your voice."

"Thank you for coming," she sniffed. "I can't tell you how much it means to me."

"I wouldn't miss it for the world."

They stayed in that embrace, unhurried, letting time settle around them like leaves on the forest floor. Harry's best friend—the Canadian ambassador to the US, the man who had helped move Harry and Nancy to Phoenix. And she, the rebellious girl who had once made their lives a whirlwind of heartburn and headaches, now about to give a taste of that rebellious spirit to dangerous people.

Maya slowly pulled back, slipping her hand into Adam's as they started walking again.

"Oh! What's this?" Adam teased, looking down at their joined hands.

"Turning over a new leaf," Maya said, her grip firm but playful. "Learning to depend on other people from time to time."

"Interesting!" Adam said, squeezing her hand with mock skepticism. "Just so long as you don't lose that famous fuck-you swagger."

"Oh no, I'm keeping that."

He let out a laugh. "You know, I just remembered, Harry and I had a bit too much bourbon one evening. You must have been in your twenties, told both of us off, and stormed away, shoulders back, head high, walking like you owned the goddamn world. I still remember how he looked as he watched you walking away, smiling from ear to ear, shaking his head." He turned to look at her. "Then he turned to me and said, '*That's* what Mayyada means.'"

Maya laughed, the warmth of the memory spreading through her like sunlight breaking through the canopy. "Pretty close," she said, swinging his hand, her face wrapped in a smile.

Oh Harry, Adam thought. *I wish you could see her now.*

Choosing the right metaphor to wear was an epic battle between fabric and color. Madison helped Maya sort her options into a perfect ROYGBIV order, but finding the right dress was an extended journey of self-discovery.

Maya stood before the mirror in deep emerald green, a crisp white blazer draped over her shoulders. She studied the reflection.

"Forest after a storm," she mused. "Fresh, alive, but… a little too clean."

"Too clean?" Madison asked, arching an eyebrow as she sat cross-legged on the bed, watching the selection process with the scrutiny of an art critic.

"I need something with more… *story*." Maya winked at her, flashing a wicked grin.

Maya slipped into a deep burgundy gown, its plush fabric caressing her skin as it draped elegantly over her form. She turned to the mirror, the rich hue accentuating her complexion.

"The last sip of stolen wine," she declared with a playful grin. "Rich, with a dark history, but maybe a little *too* indulgent."

Madison studied her carefully, her fingers tracing patterns on the bedspread. She shrugged her shoulders, unimpressed.

Maya tossed the dress into the rejection pile.

She tried again, slipping into a dress of deep indigo satin that blended its way to lapis lazuli as it flowed down her. It clung in places, fluid in others, shifting like ink spilled across the skin.

"A bruise," she judged. "Right before it fades. Healing, but still tender."

Madison shook her head, so it went into the rejection pile.

At some point, Madison began her own journey. She wriggled into a butter-yellow dress with a ruffled hem and twirled in front of the full-length mirror, the skirt fanning out around her.

"Yellow circle!" she exclaimed. "Like the sun."

She tried again. A deep maroon that pooled at her feet. "Autumn leaves," she said, shifting to watch the fabric catch the light. "But not crispy. Not quite dead yet."

Maya took her turn at the mirror, wearing a seductive crimson dress with a plunging neckline, the silk clinging in all the obvious ways. She turned to Madison and smirked. "Red hot sin," she said.

Madison frowned. "But those boobies…"

Maya sighed. "All sex; I'd never be taken seriously." She yanked it off and threw it in the rejection pile.

Next, she pulled on a high-necked black gown, the kind that was sleek and elegant but swallowed her whole. She studied herself in the mirror and frowned. "Widow at a funeral."

"No sex!" Madison laughed.

Maya smiled and shrugged. "I'd never be noticed."

Madison flopped onto the bed, watching Maya with sharp, expectant eyes. "What *should* your metaphor be?"

Maya raised an eyebrow. "Ohhh, I never thought of *starting* with the metaphor and working my way to the dress…" She narrowed her eyes and scratched her chin. "Got a suggestion?"

Madison sat up, wide-eyed. "I think you should be *The Big Bang*."

Maya laughed. "Have you been talking to Richard?"

"Sometimes the only way to start over is to rip open a new reality."

Maya froze, staring at Madison with a stunned look.

"And besides," Madison added with a shrug, as if what she was saying was just so obvious, "if you don't keep growing, you end up cold and dead *forever*." She rolled her eyes at *forever*.

Maya straightened. "Get your shoes on," she said, her eyes sparkling. "We're going *shopping*."

They hit three boutiques before Maya found something that made her stop and really look. The dress was a molten shade of copper-red, with a metallic sheen that shifted between fire and rust depending on the light. She held it against herself and arched an eyebrow.

"Supernova."

Madison rolled her eyes. "You mean a dying star?"

Maya hesitated. "That's not... no, that's..." She squinted at the dress. "*Really?*"

"Supernovas are explosions that leave black holes behind," Madison said, her voice matter-of-fact. "Are you saying you're going to collapse in on yourself and become an infinitely dense point of nothingness?"

Maya burst out laughing. "Okay, I'm definitely putting this one back."

Madison wandered off and returned with a bright electric blue dress for herself. She pressed it against her body, tilting her head in thought. "This is like... static electricity."

Maya smirked. "That must be why it's making my hair stand on end." She winked at Madison. "Keep looking."

At the salon, they poured over nail polish swatches. Maya quickly gravitated toward a fiery gold. Madison lined up five shades of pink, whispering under her breath as she ranked them from 'barely pink' to 'hyper pink.' She turned to Maya.

"Which is more *salmon?*"

Maya blinked. "Salmon?"

"They swim against the current."

Maya smiled and studied the shades with her. "This one's pinker, but this one's closer to the actual fish." She pointed to a muted coral.

From the salon, they wandered into a boutique shoe store, where glossy heels and shimmering flats perched on mirrored shelves. The scent of leather and new fabric hung in the air.

Madison, barefoot in the middle of the aisle, studied the lineup of heels like they were puzzle pieces. "What do these do?" she asked, slipping on a pair of silver stilettos, gripping Maya's arm for balance. She wobbled experimentally, her heels hovering a fraction too long above the ground before settling.

Maya's eyes glowed. "They make you taller. And more dangerous."

Later, Madison stepped out of a dressing room wearing the color of ripe plums, the fabric thick and velvety. She smoothed her hands down the sides, feeling the texture.

"Fig skins," she announced. "Not the inside. Just the outside. Soft but not squishy." She spun once, testing the way the skirt moved. "Not a spinning dress," she noted. "More like a…" She paused, searching, then brightened. "A melted candle!"

Maya laughed. "A melted fig candle. Very poetic!"

Madison tried on a pale blue dress next. The fabric was soft, flowing in gentle waves, but the fit was slightly off. The waist sat a little too high; the sleeves were a little too long. She shifted her weight, fidgeting with the cuffs. She glanced at herself in the mirror. "It's… almost right," she said slowly.

By the end of that third night, they stood before the mirror to admire Madison's final choice: a sleek, cerulean dress that caught the light just enough to shimmer but not enough to overwhelm, coral nails, and simple silver heels.

"A wave outside the sea," Maya said, nodding appreciatively, her eyes shining.

They stood in contemplative silence for a few moments, admiring their own reflections.

Finally, Madison looked up at her. "You're gonna do great, you know."

Maya smiled and reached out to hold Madison's hand. With her other hand, she smoothed down the fabric of her dress—midnight blue, streaked with crackling veins of gold—the first sparks of energy bursting through the dark.

Like the first moment something becomes *everything*.

THE BIG BANG

Hannah leaned forward, a mischievous glint in her eye. "Remember the time that reporter tried to interview Mom when they hung Saddam?"

Richard let out a hearty laugh. "*Al Jazeera*. You were still pretty young."

"I remember she emptied her glass of water on him!" Hannah exclaimed, her vibrant floral dress swaying as she gestured animatedly.

The group chuckled in unison.

"Can't even recall how many 'never call me again's and 'go fuck yourself's I heard her say into the phone over the years," Richard (in the sport jacket that matched his eyes) said, shaking his head with a nostalgic smirk.

Elizabeth Lang, draped in an impeccably tailored navy pantsuit with a crisp white blouse, crossed her legs and smiled knowingly, the kind of smile that made journalists sweat under their own studio lights.

Julia, dressed in an emerald-green A-line skirt paired with a sleek black blouse and heels sharp enough to draw blood, caught Maya's eyes. "They fucked with the wrong bitch," she said, her voice laced with amusement.

"My favorite," Adam Lewis said, adjusting the cuffs of his crisp white shirt beneath the soft navy of his tailored sports jacket, "has to be The Cappuccino Confrontation."

"Legendary," Richard said, grinning.

Maya reached over and gave him a playful shove. "You weren't even there!" she teased.

Richard shrugged, unfazed. "But I heard about it every Christmas." He turned toward Adam with a conspiratorial smirk. "I don't think this crew has ever heard the full story of The Cappuccino Confrontation."

Adam chuckled, shaking his head at the memory. "Happened with Harry—Maya's ambassador dad." Through the mirror, he caught Maya's eyes, a playful glint in his own. "They were seated outside one of those coffee shops. This reporter who'd been hounding Maya for weeks just walked up and sat down at their table, uninvited. Didn't say hi, didn't even hesitate, just parked himself there like he belonged."

He paused for effect, smiling at how Madison was leaning in.

"Maya didn't even miss a beat," Adam continued. "She reached across the table, grabbed the guy's cappuccino, took a slow sip, looked him dead in the eyes with her foam mustache, and said—" he dropped his voice into an exaggerated imitation of Maya's deadpan delivery—"'*Tastes desperate.*'"

The room held its breath, hanging on his words.

"Then she dumped the rest of it on the sidewalk and walked away, all fuck-you swagger and zero regrets."

The room burst into laughter. Julia was the first to recover. "Bad. Ass. Bitch."

Adam caught Maya's eyes in the mirror again. "*Mayyada,*" he said, winking at her.

Maya grinned back, unapologetic.

"A true fiery spirit," Charles Ruddick said, wearing his wrinkled blue dress shirt and a magenta ascot. "Not just reporters, if memory serves. Who was that poor boy you stabbed in the hand with a pencil?"

Adam let out a deep, knowing laugh. "I remember that!"

Madison's eyes went wide. "You *stabbed* someone?"

Maya, unfazed, watched her reflection as a studio stylist worked through her hair. "Well," she said breezily, "he was delinquent in his gambling debt."

Madison blinked. "What was he gambling?"

"Oh, just flipping coins, heads and tails. He just had a bad run of it, and I only did it once."

The makeup artist stepped back, examining Maya's face. "Look at me," she instructed, then proceeded to blot and powder Maya's skin.

"What does that do?" Madison asked.

"Keeps her face from appearing too shiny in front of the cameras," Lang said.

Adam shook his head, sighing. "I still remember that *Globe and Mail* reporter who tried to grab Maya during her high school graduation. She literally pushed him off the sidewalk. He fell back on his ass and landed in a mud puddle."

The hairdresser—Felicity "Flick" Turner—was a vivacious stylist in her late forties. She glanced up with a playful smile. "Should I warn Annie to be careful?"

Everyone laughed. Hannah chimed in, "Probably not her usual type of guest."

Flick smiled and turned Maya's chair toward the mirror. "Looks good," Maya said.

"Ten minutes," Flick said. "We'll send someone in. If you all want to follow me, I can take you to the green room."

"The green room?" Madison asked.

"Oh, that's just what we call it," Flick explained. "There'll be snacks and beverages. You can watch a live feed, but it's sound-proofed to avoid interfering with the set itself."

Lang touched Maya on the shoulder. "Remember," she said softly, "the goal is to simply make a good first impression. You won't get into the messy stuff; that comes later. This is just the first step on a long journey."

Dangling Maya as a bargaining chip, Lang had redlined all over the show's standard contract, ensuring that certain topics remained off-limits. Privately, she told Maya it was in her interests to reserve some negotiating leverage.

Maya touched Lang's hand, her smile reflecting sincere gratitude. "Thank you," she said warmly.

"Can I have a few more minutes with her?" Richard asked, getting an affirming nod in response.

"Maya Russell!" Charles said, standing upright in a mock salute. "In the immortal words of Teddy Roosevelt, I want you to know how much we all admire you for being the man in the arena."

"The *woman* in the arena," Julia corrected.

Hannah was the last one out, closing the door behind her. The bubble of animated conversation faded down the hallway until only the soft hum of the studio lights and Maya's measured breathing remained.

Richard moved behind Maya, resting a reassuring hand on her shoulder.

"Scared?" he asked gently.

"Terrified," she admitted, her voice barely above a whisper.

"Here, stand up."

Maya rose from the chair, her movements slow and deliber-ate, as if the air had thickened around her. She stepped around to face Richard. He showed her the time on his Apple Watch, then enveloped her in a firm embrace, pressing her against his chest. The steady rhythm of his heartbeat pulsed against her, a stark contrast to her own racing pulse. Gradually, the frantic drumming within her synchronized with his calm, steady beat.

After a few moments, she pulled back slightly, holding his hands tightly in hers. She looked up at him.

"I love you," she said, her voice tinged with vulnerability.

He returned her smile, his eyes warm. "I love you, too."

"You're the man of my dreams, you know."

Just then, the door creaked open, and a man with a plaid shirt peeked inside. "Annie's ready for you," he announced.

She looked back at Richard.

"Showtime," she said.

Seated across from Annie Hampton, Maya felt the intensity of the surrounding lights and cameras. She focused on breathing slowly through her nose to steady herself. Annie, dressed elegantly in a yellow dress complemented by yellow-rimmed glasses, leaned forward with a welcoming smile.

"Welcome to *60 Minutes*," Annie began. "And, boy, do we have a story for you tonight. I'd like to welcome—for the first time in front of the cameras, voluntarily, at least—the famous Girl from Dujail, Dr. Maya Russell."

"Thank you," Maya replied, her throat dry, her voice barely above a whisper.

Annie turned to a camera, her tone measured but electric with anticipation. "Before we dive in, let's lay this out, because I know a lot of our viewers are trying to wrap their heads around how we got here. Nothing quite like this has ever happened."

She turned slightly, as if addressing both Maya and the audience at once. "When Elizabeth Lang resigned from the US Senate, Governor Wade Callahan had the power to appoint a temporary replacement. He chose, of course, then Lieutenant Governor Bill DeWitt. That appointment only lasts until the voters get their say during this election cycle."

Maya nodded, smoothing her hands over her dress. "That's right."

"Now, the deadline to file for the Republican or Democratic primaries passed back in December, and most assumed it didn't matter. DeWitt looked like a lock to keep the seat. It was all but decided." Annie paused, letting the weight of the statement settle. "And then you happened."

Maya let out a small, measured breath. "Here I am." She forced a smile.

Annie didn't miss a beat. "Even before your announcement, Texas was already poised to play an outsized role in this year's elections. Governor Callahan is polling as an early favorite for the White House. But here's the twist: if you run as an independent, you don't have to file until May."

She let the moment hang, her eyes locking onto Maya's. "The Attorney General has dropped the case against you. And in one of the biggest political curveballs in modern history, you're not just here—you're running for office!"

Maya inhaled, her fingers tightening subtly against her lap.

"Not just running for Senator Lang's old seat," Annie continued, "but with Elizabeth Lang herself backing your campaign." She leaned forward slightly, her expression unreadable. "What made you decide to run?"

Maya parted her lips, then hesitated, her fingers tightening against her dress. Her eyes flicked toward the clock on the wall.

This is real.

In the green room, Madison leaned forward, gripping the armrests of her chair. Richard's hand found Hannah's in a silent squeeze.

Lang's expression remained carved from stone, but her knuckles whitened around her glass of water. Julia held her breath. All of them could see what the cameras captured in that moment, the split second when terror and resolve battled across Maya's face.

That moment kicked off what would become the most replayed interview in *60 Minutes* history.

It was, perhaps, Edward Kruger of the *Washington Post* who best captured that brief moment in his opinion piece that ran the morning after the interview aired. Her words were adequate, he said—nervous and halting at times, always authentic, occasionally bold—guided by the gentle guardrails of a seasoned professional who expertly navigated this historic interview. But in that brief moment of hesitation, Kruger saw what he called an intense portrait of humanity.

Why is it, he asked, that hurricanes with female names kill more people than those with male names? The conventional wisdom is that we hunker down for those formidably named ones and ignore the feminine-sounding ones. And how is it, in a political season dominated by ambitious men clamoring for power, that Dr. Maya Russell Bennett al-Rahbani had shifted the course of history with an unexpected, unstoppable, gale force, simply by paying the impossibly high price of inviting the public to get to know her story?

(Her trail of destruction, he noted, almost certainly includes the presidential ambitions of a certain governor from Texas.)

She didn't even have to win the race to change the entire political landscape. She simply had to have the unexpected courage to show up and proclaim that she mattered, knowing the mud that desperate men would sling against this sayyida daughter of a martyred cleric, this rebellious ambassador's daughter, this little girl who had been discarded and saved, this woman who saved the discarded.

And in that moment of hesitation, Kruger wrote, we glimpsed

the terror that exists inside the eye of this hurricane. For what could someone who had outrun one abuse of state power and outmaneuvered a second possibly fear more than her own story?

It was the kind of moment, he wrote, in which heroes are born and tyrants are toppled.

ACT 3:
ORGASM

THE SACRIFICE

The crow's four-toed steps danced down the fronds of the palm tree, bending each finger as though tuning the strings of a divine instrument. Each hop seemed to hold a rhythm, an unspoken cadence that pulsed in harmony with the breeze. She watched the fronds bow under its weight, springing up in gentle arcs, their tips trembling like the quivering strings of an ancient oud—that pear-shaped stringed instrument her Arab dad used to play. The crow paused at the end of a frond, tilting its head as if listening for the resonance of its work. She closed her eyes and felt the vibrations of this primordial music ripple through her.

"It's time," Julia said.

"Are you ready?" Richard asked.

She looked up at him and smiled. "I'm ready," she said. Her face glowed almost as much as her eyes.

He took her hand in his, the warmth of his touch steadying her as they approached the base of the small temple. It was a scaled replica of the temple at Chichén Itzá, crafted with painstaking attention to detail and shimmering under the moonlit sky. Richard and Julia had had it constructed at great expense, the culmination of weeks of covert planning and whispered promises.

Maya, who had always lived with an instinctual wariness of capitalistic indulgence, had allowed herself this one, glorious, extravagant, act. Julia had navigated the labyrinthine negotiations, clearing the resort's reservations and securing agreement for the "art installation" on the condition that it be dismantled the next day. This temple would be as ephemeral as the moment it represented.

Richard had planned the ceremony down to the last detail, or so he thought. Maya stood at the base of the small temple, facing the semicircle of supplicants. The moonlight spilled over the white sand behind them and glinted off emerald waves, casting a soft glow on the gathering. Behind her, the temple rose in all its glory. The silken robe she wore rippled in the ocean breeze, the fabric teasing her bare skin beneath. The belt around her waist was tied just loosely enough to suggest the ritual's inevitable unveiling.

Julia stood at one end of the semicircle, her white cover draped over her bikini, her sharp eyes taking in everything. All the men were shirtless, their physiques reflecting varying degrees of gym dedication. The firelight played over their skin, lending a sense of primal reverence to the moment.

Richard approached Maya with deliberate care, holding the props in his hands as if they were sacred artifacts. She slipped on the old wedding ring, the metal cold against her skin, followed by the watch her father had given her years ago in Ottawa. Then came the golden hijab, which Richard tied with the utmost gentleness, his fingertips brushing against her temples as he worked. He took a moment to hold her hand, steadying himself, before addressing the semicircle.

Richard cleared his throat and pulled an index card from his pocket. "I'd like to read now from *Song of Myself*, by Walt Whitman," he announced, his voice filled with what he hoped was gravitas but might have sounded more like nervous enthusiasm. Leo squinted at him, his mustache twitching as he tilted his head in mild confusion.

Richard straightened, reading with exaggerated seriousness. "The past and present wilt—I have fill'd them, emptied them." He looked up, gauging the audience's reactions. Julia raised an eyebrow; Leo deepened his brow's furrow.

"And proceed to fill my next fold of the future. Listener up there! what have you to…" He hesitated, squinting at the card. "… uh, confide to me?" He frowned and scratched his head. "I'm gonna skip forward a little."

"Practice hard for that one?" Julia asked, frowning.

Richard blushed. "Thought it'd be better as the whole chapter," he said, a tone of defensiveness creeping into his voice. His lips seemed to keep moving as he read his index card silently.

"What are ya even talkin' about?" Leo asked, looking confused and mildly annoyed.

"Well," Richard stumbled. "I thought this one would be good because it's full of sexual innuendo."

"Yeees, is *very* erotic," Rafa said.

Michael looked at Rafa, confusion written on his face. "Wait, is 'fold of the future' supposed to mean the pussy?"

"Umm," Richard said, studying the index card. "No, I don't think so…" He sounded a little deflated. His voice faded away, as if hoping that everyone would stop looking at him if he just spoke a little more softly.

"They kick-ed him out of government because he write-ed sex poems," Rafa said.

Richard turned to look at him, as if relieved by the unexpected support. "Exactly!"

"You sure they didn't kick him out of government because he never learned how to rhyme?" Julia asked.

Maya smiled, her own flush deepening. "Can we have the pot now?" she asked.

"Great fucking idea," Julia said, continuing to frown at Richard before shifting her gaze to Rafa. "Got the goods?"

"Yeees," he said, reaching into his pocket and pulling out a vape pen. "Here you go. Just a puff or two, no more."

Maya closed her eyes and took a puff, blowing it out slowly through her mouth, before handing the pen to Richard. He inhaled deeply, looked to the heavens as he let the vapor fill his spirit, and then coughed violently, handing the pen to Julia as he bent over in agony. Julia immediately passed it to Michael without drawing a puff herself. Each of the men settled their nerves with the pen before it made its way back to Rafa, who pocketed it after a long puff.

All eyes turned to Richard, watching him get his cough under control. When he finally stood up, his eyes were still watering.

"Now, Richard," Maya said, her smile reaching her eyes. "What were you saying?" She felt the wetness between her legs. She had shared the details of her cycle with Julia, who had made the most of that information in the scheduling.

"Oh, yes," Richard said, pocketing the index card and looking at Maya. "Do-I-contradict-myself?" He shrugged. "Very-well-then-I -contradict-myself. I-am-large, I-contain-multitudes." He blurted it all quickly, eager to be done with this part of the ceremony.

Maya and Rafa nodded, Maya's smile still shining through her eyes. Michael squinted at Richard.

"How is that-a *erotic*?" Leo asked.

Richard turned to catch Leo's stare and shrugged. "I don't know. I just thought it kinda described Maya."

"It sounds like you're calling her fat," Michael's voice boomed.

"No, is deep," Rafa said, nodding his head up and down. "She wears many masks."

"Masks?" Michael asked, throwing Rafa a genuinely confused look.

"How do you say," Rafa said. "She wears many faces."

"Maya?" Julia said with a frown on her face. "Your call. I promise it's okay if you want to call the whole thing off after that performance from Indiana Jones over there."

Maya, smiling from ear to ear, turned to Richard and kissed him on the lips. "Thank you," she said. She felt her nipples tingling.

"Well, thank God that's settled," Julia said.

"I love you," Maya whispered to Richard.

Richard blushed even deeper. "Well, we should probably get up there," he said, looking at the top of the pyramid.

The structure stood proud against the backdrop of the night, its steps illuminated by soft torchlight. White, diaphanous curtains draped the custom, oversized bed at the summit, swaying gently in the breeze. Richard had engineered the feat to get the bed up there: eye bolts, a winch, and large sheets of plywood meticulously angled up the steps. This was his Taj Mahal, his bowerbird's construction. Instead of blue trinkets, he dressed the bed in blue sheets.

Maya nodded, her coal-dark eyes shimmering like embers in the night. He reached for her hand, marveling at the way their fingers intertwined so naturally, the spaces between them filled with a warmth that felt eternal. Their hands moved together, a slow, deliberate rhythm, fingers sliding in and out, brushing lightly as if rediscovering the simple, profound magic of touch. Time seemed to pause, the world narrowing to just the two of them.

Richard lifted his chin, his chest expanding with a breath that tasted of salt and moonlight. Reverently, he turned and led her up the temple stairs. The warm ocean breeze teased his calves and his back as he took one step at a time, each step deliberate. He imagined how the same breeze was caressing Maya, the fabric of her silken robe shifting delicately against her bare skin. She matched his pace, their ascent a slow, ritualistic march, as if they were walking into a sacred moment together.

He caught the toe of his flip-flop on the edge of the penultimate step. He stumbled forward, arms flailing, barely catching himself before his nose could collide with the platform.

"Easy, cowboy," Julia said.

He steadied himself, finding his footing again as they reached the summit. The oversized bed loomed before them, its white curtains billowing like a temple veil in the night breeze. Richard reached into the folds and withdrew an emerald green ceramic bowl, its surface marred by three jagged cracks, each repaired with shimmering gold. He admired the way the moonlight kissed the kintsugi lines, as if breaking the bowl had made it yet more beautiful.

Maya turned to face the gathering below, her movements regal, deliberate. The crowd, now barely more than a sea of silhouettes in the moonlight, seemed to hum with expectation. Richard stood beside her and inhaled deeply, as if summoning the courage of a stoned prophet.

"Maya Russell," he boomed, his voice surprising even himself with its resonance. "Your story no longer belongs to you." He stared at her profile to connect with the gravity of his words. "Tonight, we sacrifice it for the greater good."

She turned to face him and held out her hand. He reached for it, marveling at the silken curve of her fingers against his. The golden wedding band caught the light as he slid it from her finger. Reverently, he let it fall into the bowl with a soft *clang*. For the first time, he saw how Maya's eyes caught the moonlight.

They glowed as she looked at him, her cheeks flush with desire. He met her gaze and smiled softly. This was the secret part of the ceremony, their own private agreement, sealed with a stare and a smile.

After tonight, no more running.

"Maya Bennett," he continued, puffing his chest like a modern-day oracle addressing the masses. "Tonight, you will be reborn, washed clean of your past."

As she extended her wrist toward him, he trailed his fingers over it with the kind of deliberate care that felt both sensual and surreal. Was her wrist always this elegant? This slender? He brushed the underside of her forearm, his fingers searching for the watch clasp, mesmerized by the softness of her skin. When he finally freed the watch, he dropped it next to the wedding band in the bowl with a dull thud. They locked eyes again, and he smiled at her.

After tonight, no more hiding.

"Mayyada al-Rahbani," he intoned, his voice dropping into a reverent baritone, "child of the great Sayyida Fatima al-Rahbani. Soon you will become immortal, one with the gods."

He held out his hands in front of him and spread his fingers, smiling as he shifted his gaze between them, wondering at the video game-like quality of his vision. With impossible gentleness of movement, he caressed the pads of his fingertips against her cheeks, tucking his fingertips inside the edges of her golden hijab.

The air seemed to hold its breath. He bent forward to kiss her, tenderly, and slowly, giving himself time to untie the cloth. She closed her eyes and met his kiss with a soft moan, like the opening note of a symphony. He felt his bathing suit push away from him with an almost unearthly force at the strength of his erection.

When he finished untying the hijab, he pulled back and placed it in the bowl before reverently kneeling and putting the bowl on the platform. He stayed that way for several seconds, looking up at her, before standing. She seemed like an angel from heaven, full of heat and light and desire. He tried to take a mental picture of the way she was looking at him so he could remember it forever.

After tonight, everything *changes.*

He put his hands on her hips and gently twisted them in a

clockwise fashion. She followed his lead, turning to face the bed. His bathing suit reached out through the distance between them and traced lines up and down across the top of her butt and her lower back. He looked down at this unexpected vigor and smiled even more deeply.

Reaching into the bowl, he pulled out a blindfold. He took a baby step forward, pushing his member up her back, angled upward, reaching for the heavens, and gently tied the blindfold around her eyes. He traced his fingers down her cheeks, down her neck, and over the silky collar of her robe. His fingers continued their unhurried march over her breasts and down the valleys on the other side. Her body trembled as they reached her stomach and outlined her vulva.

"Are you ready to get naked?" he asked.

She nodded.

Carefully, he pulled the ends of the belt apart and released the knot. The robe fell to the platform.

THE VIRGIN

"Maya?" Annie Hampton asked, her voice gentle.

"Because-I-think-I-can-make-a-difference!" Maya shouted through one hurried breath. After refilling her lungs, she closed her lips and snorted air out slowly through her nostrils, like a rodeo bull waiting for the gate to lift. Her eyes narrowed into a fiercely determined expression, their gaze focused like a laser beam on something that seemed to be about one mote directly behind the centroid of Annie's left cornea. She looked like a feral animal, as if something had just been ripped off her and she didn't yet know whether to defend or attack.

"Oh, I think we can all agree with that." Annie held up her hands in surrender. It was the kind of moment that made her one of the best in the business, almost as if her hands and her facial expression lifted to deflect an attack borne of panic. It was her instinct for disarming, self-effacing humor that made her the clear choice for this once-in-a-generation interview, an instinct that somehow released the tension on set before anyone's heart rate even had a chance to accelerate.

Even Maya felt the tension crack like an egg. She seemed to feel the relief most acutely where the yolk of her chin fell downward and pulled her face into a deeper oval, causing her mouth to open into a lazy circle and her eyes to widen like tunnels into dark, empty coal mines.

"Maya?" Annie said, tilting her head seventeen degrees to the right, smiling broadly, as if her eyes cast a soft, warm light on everything they landed upon because she was too relaxed to focus their radiant energy on any *one* thing in any kind of way that could possibly be construed as judgmental. She lifted her shoulders up in a slight shrug and vibrated her body softly side to side, almost imperceptibly, like the short-wave buzz teenage girls might give off when engaging in secret gossip they only want their friend to see, not everyone else around them.

"Th-thank you," Maya said, her focus seeming to ride the bumpy tracks of the coal mine trolley cars toward the sunlight.

"You're welcome," Annie laughed lightheartedly. "And, thank *me*? My goodness! I just want to say, I've been in this business for a long time. Like everyone else in my industry who knows a story when we see one, I've been wanting to know something, *anything…*"— she balanced the *anything* on a short golly-gosh laugh—"… and holy cow!" She opened her eyes wide and broadened her smile. "You announce your candidacy and I get the great privilege of sharing in your journey tonight. Thank *you*!" Her smile shifted into a kindly closed-lipped shape, her eyes soft and light, her head nodding slightly at a little off-center angle.

Maya nodded, biting her lip slightly.

"Do you need some water?" Annie asked in an almost nurse-like tone.

Beneath the empathy, there was a quietly hard edge to her voice, audible only to those in the studio. But for those who worked with her every day in this crazy, adrenaline-surged industry, that hard edge was an urgent cue that 1) some shit was about to go down, 2) she wasn't sure she could contain it, and 3) their only hope of avoiding catastrophe depended on rowing together as a goddamn team as if their lives depended on it. The camera operators straightened visibly. The production assistant's eyes narrowed, looking for any angle for rescue.

Of course, everyone at the studio knew that something like this was a possibility and had done everything they could to prepare for it. They had run through what Dinah, the executive producer now hidden in the control room, called the "Russian scenario," which evoked the time Annie interviewed a Russian political activist.

He was clearly worried about the unusual habit, common amongst Putin's enemies, of suicide by defenestration. It was, understandably, a rough start to the interview, as his voice cracked through the stress of airing his resistance through so public a bullhorn as *60 Minutes*. At multiple points throughout the interview, Annie offered him breaks so he could splash water on his face. Ironically, this made Laura, the makeup artist, a celebrated hero inside the studio when the interview aired and no one was the wiser.

There was also the cute teenager who won *American Idol*, but had attempted to calm his nerves for the interview by taking a couple of gummies beforehand, which made him so paranoid throughout that Annie had to perform magic with her facial muscles and the relaxation of her stare to encourage the boy's bug eyes to retreat into something moderately presentable on TV.

"Mmm-hmm," Maya said, puffing her lips slightly. Her cheeks had adopted a slightly dark hue under the glare of the camera lights, the powder from the makeup artist absorbing their rays, illuminating her face without reflecting the light back to the viewer.

"Okay… okay… here, look, here you go!" Annie took the bottle of water from the tall, gangly PA in corduroy pants and black button-up shirt. Annie and Maya were in open chairs, facing each other, placed on the outer edges of an elegant, rustic circular rug. Annie leaned over, handed Maya the water, and made direct eye contact, seeming to will Maya out of her stupor.

(Madison, in the thousands of times she would rewatch this scene well into her adult years, would eventually collect that look as her Calm the Fuck Down mask. She would have to suppress a slight giggle every time she wore it.)

Maya nodded her appreciation and lifted the bottle with both hands, trembling slightly, as if lifting it to her mouth was a great struggle. She bent her head down slightly and delicately sipped the water like a grandmother testing soup. She dropped the bottle before realizing she had nowhere but the floor to place it upon. It thudded against the rug and splashed the water onto Annie's shoes.

Annie jerked back with a desperately disarming laugh. "Oh gosh, don't worry about it," she said, brushing the entire episode aside as if it were nothing but an endearing bit of silly stage fright.

"Oh God, I'm sorry," Maya said, partially standing up and holding out her right arm, as if her brain had calculated that it was this very move that would somehow allow her to catch the bottle and prevent its spill, despite being five seconds too late.

"No, no, no need to get up." Annie giggled. "Look… Jeremy… yes… thank you, Jeremy. See, look, it's like it never happened." She scooted her chair back in a friendly gesture of solidarity, beaming at Maya.

"You all right?" Annie asked, her voice wrapped in an encouraging laugh.

Maya nodded and sat down. "My God, this rug…"

"It's a beautiful rug, isn't it?" Annie asked, looking down.

"Persian," Jeremy said.

"But it's just water," Annie said, waving her hand dismissively.

"… and your shoes," Maya said.

Annie beamed at Maya. "Do you like them?" Annie wore stylish red wedges. She laughed lightheartedly. "So let's start there, yeah?" she asked, crooking her neck slightly and lifting her eyes up at Maya conspiratorially. "Although we don't know many details, we all know how long your journey has been. But what if, instead of talking about your past or your future, we start with the right now? How do you feel right now?"

Maya's eyes widened.

"Take your time…"

Maya's cheeks widened.

Annie flashed a panicked look at Jeremy.

Maya jerked up suddenly, knocking the chair out from under her. She bent over in agony as if something was being rent out of her with great violence. She opened her mouth and vomited all over the Persian rug and Annie Hampton's elegant red wedges.

Richard pressed pause on the remote control. The scene on the TV turned into a still picture: Maya leaning forward, a look of horror on her face, as her watery effluvia spread its tendrils down Annie's ankle.

Hannah was bent over, clutching her belly, tears streaming out of her eyes. She gave Madison a soft elbow nudge next to her on the couch. Madison looked entirely unable to escape the silly giggling fit that had consumed her since the start of the recording.

Richard held the remote in the air theatrically, like a wand. Combined with the fedora, he looked something like a cross between Indiana Jones and Harry Potter. "But wait," he said, teasingly, "the best part's yet to come!"

"Oh, my God!" Julia said, her cheeks glowing. "Girl!" She leaned over and gave Maya a teasing pat on her knee. The edges of Maya's lips lifted into her ears in a sheepish grin. Combined with her reddened cheeks and the sparkle of her eyes, she had a radiant, light appearance.

"That was truly, fucking, tragic," Elizabeth Lang said, shaking her head ruefully. "We *practiced*, bitch."

"And that… snooty… old…" Charles Ruddick started, in what was by now a familiar phrase of his. Madison looked over the couch to see Charles standing next to Adam Lewis at the back of the room.

Madison picked it up before Charles could finish. She signaled her intention to finish by shaking her head side to side so much that it required a little contribution from her shoulders, like the anticipation of what was about to happen was almost unbearable. "… Edward Kruger of the *Washington Post*…" she said, ending in a high pitch—her invitation for someone else to pick up where she left off.

Charles held out his fist. Adam followed through with a fist bump. Both men wore smiles that spoke of a deep, restful contentment.

"Like *seriously!*" Julia said. "What the hell was he smoking?"

"'Her words were adequate,'" Elizabeth said in a mocking voice, quoting the editorial.

"She couldn't even get any words out!" Hannah laughed, then gasped for air.

"Because-I-think-I-can-make-a-difference!" Madison snorted through snot bubbles filled with laughter.

"She verbally hyphenated them!" Hannah shouted, red-faced.

"But the best part…" Richard teased, still suspending the remote awkwardly in the air. His voice trailed off, waiting for someone else to finish his sentence.

"… is yet to come!" Hannah and Madison shouted at the same time.

"Are you ready?" Richard asked in a mysteriously dramatic tone. Everybody got quiet.

"Oh, just get it over with," Maya said, waving her arm dismissively, her cheeks red.

"One…" Richard said, eyeing everybody to make sure they were paying attention.

"Two…" Madison held her breath. Her whole body seemed to vibrate with anticipation.

"Three!" He pressed play on the remote.

"FUCK!" they all yelled in unison with Annie Hampton of *60 Minutes* as she jumped backward, lost her balance in the motion's suddenness, and fell over her own chair. As her legs lifted over her head, gravity pulled the folds of her yellow dress over her head, exposing her nude-colored Spanx underneath. The force of the fall caused one of her puke-covered shoes to fly off her foot.

Maya fell to her hands and knees and let out another round of vomit all over the Persian rug.

100,000 STEPS THROUGH THE DARKNESS

The orchard stretches before her, endless rows of date palms that sway unnaturally in the moonlight. Their shadows fall sharp and jagged across the ground, weaving a pattern that seems to shift as she moves. The air is heavy with the sweet, fermenting scent of overripe dates, cloying and oppressive.

She can't remember why she is running, but her fear pushes her on. Every step falls harder than the last, the ground beneath her softening like tar, sticky and relentless, pulling her down. She looks over her shoulder and sees only date palms, but the feeling of pursuit is suffocating, pressing against her chest, forcing her breaths to come quick and shallow. The air pushes back against her, trapping her. Unintelligible, dark, and dangerous whispers fill the air as the leaves rustle overhead. The orchard seems to stretch infinitely in all directions. The trees lean in, their fronds brushing against her skin like accusatory fingers.

The air grows hotter, suffocating, clawing at her throat and stinging her eyes with the acrid scent of smoke. A fog descends upon her, electric, acidic. Her legs refuse to move, her body locked in place. She feels the fear rise from the core of her being, making her hairs stand on edge and her heart beat faster.

The ground turns to quicksand and she feels herself sinking. Run! she tells herself, and tries clawing her way back to the surface, but the ground keeps swallowing her up, plunging her into a darkness so deep it feels alive. The void pulses with faint echoes of screams. She flails about blindly, searching for something solid. She claws at the roots of the date palm, her fingers bloodying, desperately lifting herself up—and she runs.

The date palms loom larger, their trunks twisting grotesquely. Fronds brush against her skin, but they feel sharp, like blades, slicing across her arms as she pushes forward. The whispers turn into cries, then into screams, overlapping and deafening.

Mayyada, run!

She hears the urgency in the voice, the desperation, and she feels the sweat tickle her skin as her body overheats and she feels herself beginning to faint.

The date palms morph into headstones, their inscriptions written in Arabic. The calligraphy shifts, blurs, as if the dream refuses to let her read them. A figure stands at the edge of the graveyard. The ground beneath her splits open, graves yawning wide as skeletal hands claw their way out, grasping at her ankles.

She struggles to pull free, to run again, but her limbs feel heavy, weighted by decades of buried pain.

The figure walks toward her slowly, his olive-green uniform causing her to scream.

He raises the pistol and points it at her.

She hears the explosion as he pulls the trigger.

He caught her as she jerked up suddenly, her eyes wide open in fear, her breath hurried. "Shhh," he said, and pulled her into his chest so she could share his measured heartbeat. She looked down at the Apple Watch he wore to bed to monitor his own sleep. The colon blinked softly, fading from white to gray and back again, separating the 4 and the 13. She wrapped her arms around him and fell into his tight embrace. She stayed there, not moving, until her own heart slowed to match his.

"Get anywhere?" he asked.

She shook her head, still nestled between his neck and shoulder. "Can't get past the nightmares."

"A hundred thousand steps through the darkness," he said, and held her tight.

⌗

He spent the unusually warm winter morning on the patio, coffee in hand, his iPad resting on his knee as he scrolled through a journal article. He glanced up and saw her in the kitchen, still in her night-gown, her movements sluggish. Even through the glass, he could see the weight of the exhaustion in her eyes. She poured herself a cup of coffee, cradling it in both hands as she walked outside and sat next to him on the loveseat. Without a word, she rested her head on his shoulder, and he slid an arm around her.

"You all right?" he asked softly.

She nodded, but the silence between them felt heavier than usual. He set his iPad aside, moving carefully so as not to disturb her, and took a sip of coffee. For a while, they sat together, letting the morning sounds fill the space between them, listening to the rustling of leaves and the chase of squirrels.

Finally, she broke the silence. "What did you mean when you said a hundred thousand steps?"

"Oh, that's a Gilgamesh reference," he replied.

"Gilgamesh?"

"Yep. That's the OG piece of literature; we've never found an older work of fiction. It was found on clay tablets in modern-day Iraq."

"Never read it."

He shrugged. "You wouldn't talk to me about your past, so I read everything I could over the years. Gilgamesh was the king of Uruk, but after he lost someone close to him, he went on a journey searching for immortality. That led him to his hundred thousand steps through a tunnel so dark he couldn't see where he was going. He had to feel his way through, every step a confrontation with himself."

"What was on the other end?"

"Forgiveness."

She smiled and sipped her coffee.

"Tell me again how you started with the lucid dreams."

She sighed, her voice soft. "I was… adjusting," she said. "The first year or so after Kuwait was a whirlwind, and none of it made sense to me."

"It must've been like being abducted by aliens," he said.

She pulled away slightly and took a sip of coffee, her brows furrowing. "I guess I started questioning everything, all the time. It was a survival mechanism, I think. My parents had me see a psychologist, this bald Arab guy with a round face. I hated him. Told him he wasn't real just to piss him off."

He chuckled. "That sounds right."

"He said I had a psychotic break." Her voice was matter-of-fact, but her eyes were distant.

He nodded, waiting.

"I think I blamed my mom, my new one," she said. "For everything. I looked for ways to hurt her."

"Ryan Tinsbury?"

She nodded. "I think that's how it started, the sex, only I was a lot younger than that time with Ryan. She had such a Victorian view of sex, I knew it would hurt her. Oh God, I wish I could tell her that."

"I think she understood," he said.

She looked up at him and reached out to touch his hand. "But it became about something else." Her lips curved slightly, more a sad acknowledgment than a smile. "I think it felt… safe. Cherished and accepted without having to be seen. I'm not sure I can explain it."

After a moment, he asked, "And the lucid dreams?"

She took another sip of coffee. "It was that habit of questioning reality that got me there. That's where the watch comes in. The habit of looking at it follows me into the dream, just not the numbers. That's how I learned to recognize a dream while I was still in it."

"Can I ask you a question without you running away from me?"

"I think you've earned that."

"Who was Hannah's biological father?"

The question landed like a thunderclap. Her hand froze midair, coffee halfway to her lips. Slowly, she set it down and turned to him, her eyes wide. "You knew?"

He nodded, his face calm. "I've always known, at least since Hannah was little."

"Oh God, Richard. I'm so sorry. I—" She held her hand to her mouth, a look of horror etched onto her face.

"Why?" he interrupted gently. "I knew what I was getting into when I met you. You warned me you'd run."

She stared at him, frozen, gathering her thoughts. "How…?"

He took a measured sip of coffee and offered a soft smile, one meant to steady her. "It's in her eyes. My blue eyes mean I have two recessive alleles, so we know what I would've given her. And I've seen the pictures of your mom and dad. Assuming *he's* your biological dad—and your mom doesn't strike me as the kind to fool around with the postman—then you'd have two purely dark alleles, which doesn't leave any pathways to hazel."

Her head dropped into her hands. "Oh God," she whispered. "Why did you stay?"

He set his coffee down and turned toward her. "The answer doesn't reflect too well on me," he said, taking a long pause. "I knew, as long as she was around… I knew even when you ran, you'd come back, eventually."

Tears welled up in her eyes. "So… why do you stay now, when all my shit is about to blow up and Hannah's at Georgetown?"

His thumb brushed across her knuckles, grounding her. "Have you ever heard of Plato's Cave?"

She shook her head, a tear slipping free.

"It's an old story," he said. "Imagine people chained inside a cave their entire lives. All they've ever seen are shadows on the wall cast by the fire behind them. Shapes, flickers, echoes—that's their whole world. Then one day, one of them escapes. And outside… there's light. Color. Depth. He realizes the shadows were just projections of some higher-dimensional reality. But when he goes back to tell the others, they think he's crazy."

Her expression softened. She wiped her cheek and almost smiled. "You really are the nerdiest man I know." She took a slow sip of coffee. "I'm afraid to ask, but… what does that have to do with me?"

He returned her almost-smile. "Maya, you've given me a glimpse of what's outside the cave. You break all the rules, transcend every reality I've ever known, but you've always done small things because you've been afraid to be seen outside the shadows. What you're doing now terrifies me, and I've never wanted to be with you more."

She stayed silent for a moment, thinking. "I can't even remember the color of his eyes. Brown, I think. Would that work?"

Richard nodded. "Remember his name?"

She shook her head. "I wasn't with him long; I just got… careless. We were getting too close, you and me. I was planning my escape. And then I got pregnant, and I decided to keep her. I didn't know whose child she was… oh God, I'm so sorry."

He bent down to kiss her on the forehead again. "We need to tell her."

She lifted up and looked at him through blurry eyes.

"You're on TV a lot these days, and it's about to get worse. You think I'm the only one who knows my way around a Punnett square? Better she hears it from us first."

"Oh, God." Her face paled as the truth sank in.

He reached for her hand, grounding her. "Remember what we agreed to when you first started talking about Lang? You're not doing this alone. I'll be there every step of the way."

She looked down at his watch. It was 8:42.

⁓

"You washed the sheets?" she asked as she climbed underneath them.

He nodded. "You had them pretty soaked."

She let out a mournful sigh. "God, I hope this works."

"It will. Give it time, and take a break when you need it. Can you wake yourself up in a nightmare?"

"Yes."

He looked at her. "But then you'll never see what's on the other side."

She nodded. "Only about ninety-nine thousand more steps to go," she said.

He rolled over and kissed her forehead. "Remember, you don't have to do this by yourself, but it has to be your choice."

She read the time on his watch. It was 10:27.

THE EXHIBITIONIST

Maya stared at her reflection in the dressing room mirror. Flick's masterful styling had transformed her hair into waves of obsidian, framing her face with calculated elegance. But beneath the washroom's unforgiving lights, she could see the fault lines where the careful construction threatened to fracture. Her eyes, those coal-black pools that Richard claimed could swallow stars, betrayed her now.

The golden veins in her dress seemed to mirror the kintsugi cracks in her psyche, damage repaired but never hidden, transformed into something beautiful and terrible. She watched her hands tremble against the cool porcelain sink and wondered if this was what sacrifice felt like: not the dramatic blade at the top of a temple, but the quiet terror of finally standing still, of allowing yourself to be seen. She turned the tap on and splashed some water on her face.

She looked at the notification on her phone, a text from Richard, the latest in a string of support texts from the green room.

"Remember, you're not the shadows; you're what casts them. Go be you."

Well, the worst was over, she thought, not entirely convinced that was true. It was embarrassing, but she had decided long ago that a little embarrassment was a small price to pay for the opportunity to make a difference. What had Charles called her—the man in the arena? He had gifted her a wooden plaque with the full Teddy Roosevelt quote and had brought it up repeatedly leading to this moment. She played with the adjustments she'd have to make when she talked to him again.

It is not the critic who counts; not the person who points out how the poor bitch dropped her bottle of water on national television. The credit belongs to the bitch who is actually in the arena, whose face is marred by panic and vomit...

If anyone was comfortable with a little *embarrassment*, Charles Ruddick and his ascots fit the bill. She saw a soft smile in her reflection and felt her mood lightening.

Richard's words echoed in her mind: "The most important story is the one you tell yourself."

The irony wasn't lost on her. Lang had prepped her for days, rehearsing polished answers and political pivots. "The moment they sense a weakness," Lang had warned her, "the moment they smell blood, they'll try to destroy you."

"Take your time," Laura, the makeup artist, said. "Let me know when you're ready for me."

Maya let out a friendly laugh and dried her face with a hand towel. "How's Annie?"

"Oh, she's fine," Laura said. "Trust me, she's seen much worse. We thought something like this might happen."

Maya took Laura in. She was in her early thirties, blonde with a perfectly tied ponytail. "You thought I'd vomit all over your Persian rug and Annie's shoes?"

Laura laughed. "Well, we thought something *like* this would happen, but maybe not *exactly* like this..."

She shifted her weight between feet, dropping her voice low enough that Maya had to focus to hear. "I probably shouldn't say this, but what happened out there…" She nervously tucked a loose strand of hair behind her ear. "It's just… we get so many people in that chair trying so hard to seem important, you know? All rehearsed answers and practiced smiles."

She glanced over her shoulder to make sure no one was coming into the washroom. "God, sorry, that came out weird. I'm not trying to make fun of you… just… it's good to see I'm not the only one who gets scared by that chair sometimes. It's kinda inspiring in its own way, that you do it despite the fear. Anyway." She reddened as she busied herself arranging her makeup brushes. "Let me know when you're ready."

A half hour later, Maya was back in the glare of the studio lights, her face re-powdered and her dignity somewhat restored. Annie greeted her with an easy smile. "How ya feelin'?" she asked.

"A little embarrassed," Maya admitted. "How're your shoes?"

"Good as new," Annie replied, twisting her foot to show off the gleaming wedges.

"And the rug?"

"Almost done. It wasn't nearly as bad as you think." Annie offered a smile and a wink. "Don't worry—we're pretty good at editing."

Maya's eyes flicked to the Persian rug hanging up to dry after its bath of white vinegar and baking soda. Two fans were blowing at full speed on it; a dehumidifier hummed beneath it.

Annie followed her gaze. "Clean as new," she said. "And almost dry."

As the crew hustled to reset the scene, Maya took a moment to take in the full expanse of the studio. Overhead, an intricate web of lighting instruments gleamed like a constellation, their precise angles a testament to the gaffer's skill. Cameras loomed on pedestals, their operators adjusting them with quiet focus.

Dinah, the executive producer, had stepped out of the control room still wearing her headset, her voice quiet but firm as she gave instructions to the crew before inspecting the rug. She nodded at Jeremy.

Jeremy and one of the other PAs delicately took the Persian rug down and repositioned it. They put the chairs back on the outer edges of the rug, taking instructions from Dinah, who was apparently double-checking their work through her headset with the control room.

"And… we're set!" Annie exclaimed. "Ready to give it another shot?"

Maya smiled and nodded. Annie gestured with her hand for Maya to sit and took her own seat opposite Maya as Dinah walked back into the control room. Jeremy adjusted the boom microphone with its fur-covered windscreen. The set fell into a hush, leaving only the two women on camera and the weight of Maya's untold story.

Maya saw the center camera operator give a light nod. Annie Hampton seemed to shift subtly in her chair and smiled at Maya. Elizabeth had told her that was how it went on a pre-recorded set like *60 Minutes*. No dramatic countdowns like you see on TV for live productions, everything designed to minimize distractions and reduce the intimidation factor, careful editing to curate the best possible viewing experience.

"So, let's try this again, shall we?" Annie said, her voice warm and inviting. "This has been quite the journey for you. What made you decide to run?"

Maya smiled faintly. "Well, the truth of it is, I've been running my entire life—running *away*," she began, her voice steady but reflective. "And my instincts were to run away from this… this scrutiny, this job, these choices. The impossible decisions where every path hurts someone. The compromises that leave no one fully satisfied."

"It's a hard job," Annie agreed.

"But one that's become too caricatured, compromises waved away as weak. It seems to me that some of those who hold office currently want it too much, are too happy to sacrifice nuance for the comfortable simplicity of tribalism and media sound bites."

"You think you can change that?" Annie asked.

Maya pondered the question. "I'm not that arrogant," she said. "I think people change themselves. I think what I can do is…" She shifted uncomfortably in her chair. "My dad was in politics. I saw some of the impossible compromises he made, and at times, I hated him for them."

"What's an example?" Annie asked before Maya could move on.

Maya let out a soft sigh. "Look, my dad was an ambassador, and I know how easy it is to throw stones at ambassadors." She hesitated a moment, as if gathering her thoughts. "It was the US ambassador to Iraq who effectively greenlit the invasion of Kuwait by telling Saddam Hussein that the US wouldn't get involved in Arab disputes. I was young at the time, and more than a little broken, but when Canada joined the UN forces, I hated my dad for the hypocrisy. It was a miscommunication that had a long tail, when American bombs later destroyed what was left of my home country."

"I imagine that must have felt very confusing to you," Annie said.

Maya nodded. "But hating is easy. I think what I can do is invite the voters to know me as a whole person: messy, deeply flawed, and all too familiar with where tribalism ends."

"That's powerful," Annie said, her mind racing on how to handle the unexpected (and contractually prohibited) invitation to probe into Maya's past. She heard Dinah whisper through her earpiece: "Keep it on her candidacy."

Maya's mind raced to Lang's carefully crafted responses, the words they'd rehearsed until they flowed like pearls on a string. Her lips parted, the scripted answer poised on her tongue like a mask she'd worn so many times before. But as she drew breath to speak, something stopped her, a tightness in her chest that wasn't just anxiety, but recognition.

This was the moment, wasn't it?

"I want to stop running away," Maya continued, preempting the next question. She had decided to call an audible, deciding that her prearranged plan of making a good first impression had already fallen apart. What if, instead of trying to rebuild it, she embraced the rubble? What if, as Laura had hinted, her weakness became her strength?

"Before anyone thinks of voting for me, I want them to see me as I am. Which means… I'd like to make an offer, if you'll accept it." The words felt strange, dangerous even, like stepping onto a frozen lake, not knowing if the ice would hold.

"An offer? What do you have in mind?" Annie asked, legitimately caught off guard.

Maya smiled. "As we just discussed a few minutes ago, when you release this interview, you'll edit it—"

"We do that with all interviews, according to journalistic standards," Annie cut in.

"And to curate the best viewing experience…"

"To keep the focus on the story."

"Yes, but in this case, *I am the story*. So, here's my offer: release the unedited version, so viewers can see the panic attack I just had. Let the voters see all of me."

Annie sucked in a deep inhale. "Jesus," Dinah whispered in her ear. There was an extended pause as both women took this in, the seasoned interviewer across from Maya, the seasoned producer in the control room.

Annie stood and paced. A door opened and Dinah walked out onto the set, looking keenly at Maya as she walked over.

"Look, I respect what you're trying to do," Dinah said. "I really do. But raw footage can contain off-the-record remarks. We don't just edit to curate the viewing experience. We do so to avoid misinterpretations and unnecessary legal exposure."

Maya, feeling awkward as the only one sitting, stood and looked over at Annie, offering a soft smile. "Bleep out what you need to bleep out. Blur out what you need to blur out."

"I'm sorry, that's not how it works," Dinah said, her expression stern.

"And in return, I'll tell you everything."

Both Annie and Dinah stared intently at Maya, dumbfounded.

"Get Liam on the line," Dinah said into her headset, walking away.

"We're checking with general counsel," Annie said.

"Smart," Maya said. "Can you ask Elizabeth to join us as well? Sounds like we've got some *negotiatin'* to do."

THE REBIRTH

Her body is wrapped in nothing but the night. The sheets are impossibly soft beneath her, some divine combination of satin and butter. She wears a blindfold, but she can still see the shadows cast by the stars outside its cavernous embrace. The darkness is alive, a canvas of sensory exploration, amplifying every touch whispered across her body. She can hear the gentle crash of the waves meeting the shore, their rhythm unbroken, as if the ocean itself is breathing. Behind her, the jungle moans in anticipation.

The sheets slide against her body as she shifts, their coolness contrasting with the warmth of the night, the fabric kissing her curves and dancing up her spine. She feels exposed and strangely vulnerable. She is a queen on her throne, the bed's four posters framing her like columns in an ancient temple. Stretching above her head, she feels the pull of muscles, skin tightening subtly, and gravity's gentle weight pulling her deeper into the mattress.

She can feel the light of the stars, their warmth a hint at the world outside her blindfold, soft and inviting, grazing her body like the faintest touch. Her lips part as she inhales the salt-tinged air, the breeze mixing ocean and jungle, carrying with it the faintest hint of something floral, something green, something wild.

Every sound becomes part of the symphony. The rustling of the jungle is a tuba, its breathy moans swelling with anticipation. The ocean plays percussion, its deep resonant timbre and steady rhythm grounding her. Like a cathedral organ, the breeze reverberates in the cavern of her mind, its sonorous tones chasing shadows cast by stars she's yet to see. She has lived in their reflected glow, blind to the firmament, but the melody now teases her toward the light.

Somewhere, the faint creak of wood reminds her of the structure beneath her, the bed's platform perched high atop the pyramid, suspended between sea and sky. She runs her fingertips over the sheets, their smooth surface tinged with a faint charge, a hint of electricity that travels from her hand to her chest, to her stomach, to the core of her being. Her thighs shift against each other, the friction of the sheets and her own skin igniting sparks. Her breath quickens, shallow and uneven, as the anticipation grows.

She is no longer in control. That is the essence of the sacrifice. She surrenders to the earth, the ocean, the breeze, and the hands and the lips that will shape her anew, devouring her and remaking her as their own, each in their own way, no longer bound by the fractures of her past.

The bed seems to pulse beneath her, its frame in resonance with the beating of her heart. She feels the world narrowing, focusing, the stars and the ocean and the jungle all pulling toward her, all converging into the hot arc of desire coursing through her body. She arches her back, surrendering to the pull, the sensation of being utterly open. Of being naked.

And then she hears them: footsteps, soft and deliberate, coming from every direction, making their reverent ascent up the pyramid to join her in heaven's embrace. The steps blend into the orchestra, a drumbeat that grows louder and more urgent, closer, until it surrounds her. Shadows swim outside the thin bed curtains. The jungle quiets, the ocean holds its breath, charged with the presence of something unseen.

Their breath surrounds her now, a symphony of desire in different keys. Richard's comes in measured draws, controlled yet quickening, the familiar cadence of his restraint. Michael's breath is deeper, resonant, almost predatory in its hunger. Leo's catches in his throat, ragged with anticipation, while Rafa's flows like warm honey, sensual and unhurried. The chorus of their exhalations creates invisible currents that caress her skin, raising goosebumps along her arms and thighs. Her body responds to each subtle shift in their breathing, her pulse synchronizing, then racing ahead, her own breath shallow and quick. Heat radiates from her core, liquid arousal gathering between her thighs, her nipples tightening to aching points. She feels herself opening like a flower at dawn, muscles softening and tensing in waves of preparation. The bed becomes her altar, her body the offering, suspended in that exquisite moment between yearning and fulfillment, her mind surrendering to the animal need coursing through her veins.

As she hears the curtains open, she glides her thighs apart on the satin sheets and hitches her breath, preparing to be devoured…

⌒⌒⌒

She closed her eyes beneath the blindfold's hug, shutting out the world and sharpening her other senses, letting the warm ocean breeze wash over her. When she chose to, she could pick out the distinct rhythm of footsteps climbing the pyramid stairs. Three sets, deliberate and uneven. *The Ninja Turtles,* she thought, suppressing a smile that threatened to bubble into premature laughter.

The sheets beneath her felt decadent, exactly as she'd dreamed, smooth as satin, soft as whispers. Richard had made sure of that. By agreement, Julia would remain below, hearing but not seeing, intervening only if summoned. *Yellow*—slow down; I need a minute. *Red*—stop. The safe words from her days as Mistress Veritas. If someone wanted to check in on her: *Green*—keep going.

She focused on the sounds around her. Richard's breathing was familiar, steady but tinged with excitement. Soon, more breaths joined his, mingling with the gentle crashing of waves. There were whispers, conspiratorial, like secrets carried in the wind: "Should I go first?… wait, not yet… left or right?… can I…"

"Sure," she heard Richard say, breaking the spell.

"Julia!" he called suddenly, his voice louder than the night. "Can you bring up another Viagra for Leo?"

"Shhh!" She heard Leo's mortified hiss.

"Where'd you put them?" Julia shouted back from below, utterly unbothered.

"Inside, next to my iPad."

"This stuff really works," Michael chimed in, a little too loudly, a grin audible in his voice. "I might need a new bathing suit after this."

"Yeesss," Rafa purred, like a cat luxuriating in the sun.

Maya bit her lip to keep from laughing. A tiny snort escaped.

She heard Julia's brisk footsteps on her ascent. "Here you… oh… my," she said, clearly taking in the scene. "Well, here you go." Maya heard her descend again. The pop of a pill packet broke the silence. More whispers.

Moments later: "Julia!" Richard again, louder this time.

"Shhh!" Leo hissed, even more insistent.

"What?" Julia, from below, mildly exasperated.

"We forgot the water. Can you bring it?"

A long, theatrical sigh. "Ugh, coming." More footsteps. The *clink* of water bottles placed down.

"Wow," she heard Julia say. "Michael…" The wind carried away what came next. Something about talents.

As she listened to the sound of Julia's descent and of the men getting water, Maya pressed her lips together, her chest quaking with barely contained laughter.

"Oh, *no*!" She heard Leo exhort in horror, followed by the soft crunch of someone's flip-flop stepping on what sounded like a pill.

Richard's voice. "Um, I think you just crushed Leo's dreams." Leo moaned in frustration. A moment later: "Julia!"

"*What?*"

"Can you bring up another Viagra? Michael just stepped on Leo's."

"Shhh!" Leo almost shouted.

"Oh, my God!" She heard Julia's sigh carried up the steps of the pyramid, followed, a few moments later, by her steps, and finally, her winded voice. "Next time… you're coming down."

The sound of Julia's descent. A pill pushed through its wrapper and swallowed properly this time. Maya trapped the laughter inside. She felt it roll down her naked body in waves, as if her whole body were smiling.

More whispers, footsteps scattering, a choreography of anticipation. She felt their presence as the bed curtains shifted, their movements rustling like jungle leaves. The oversized mattress dipped beneath their weight as other footsteps pressed into the wood of the pyramid.

The tension in the air crystallized, impossibly dense.

A universe of possibility balanced on the head of a pin.

And then: a loud rip, the curtain tearing. Someone falling. More ripping. The crash of multiple bodies hitting the wooden platform. Leo's voice, part exclamation, part despair: "*Fuck!*"

Laughter burst out of her like a dam giving way, a force of nature unleashed. It started as a small ripple, the faintest tremor in her chest that escaped in gasps and hiccups, but soon it grew. It rose like a tidal wave, surging higher and louder, spilling over the edges of her self-control until it became an unstoppable tsunami. Her cheeks burned with the rush of it, her eyes streamed, and her chest heaved as her entire body was consumed by this primal, joyous quake. It wasn't a polite laugh; it was the kind that had her clutching her stomach and squeezing her legs, shaking the bed beneath her.

Richard was the first casualty, caught by her delight like an ember setting dry tinder aflame. He doubled over, his own laughter roaring out of him, his hand slapping the side of the mattress in surrender. One by one, the Ninja Turtles followed—Rafa's breathless wheeze, Leo's hearty guffaws, Michael's deep, rolling chuckles—all blending together in an orchestra of mirth.

It spilled down the wooden steps, tumbling like a waterfall, until Julia, too, surrendered to it, her laughter rising in high-pitched bursts that ricocheted off the surrounding jungle. The trees seemed to catch the sound and fling it back, amplifying the echo until the whole scene felt alive with the unfiltered glee of the moment. It rippled outward like concentric circles on water, each wave pulling everyone deeper into its vortex, until the entire group was helpless against its contagion. Every time one of them tried to catch their breath, another would let out a snort or a howl, and the cycle would start anew.

It was laughter so profound it hurt, a joyous ache in her ribs, a tickle that left her gasping, light-headed, and utterly alive. It was a kind of madness, a beautiful, shared surrender to the absurdity of it all, where words became impossible and the only language was the sound of their unabashed delight.

It bounced off the wood, the sand, the sea, filling the night air with echoes that carried into the jungle, as though the world itself were laughing along. And still, it went on, as if the universe had demanded this moment of pure, unadulterated release. Her head tipped back, her blindfolded eyes seeing nothing but the hint of the heavens above. She felt untethered, alive. In this fleeting moment of chaos and hilarity, she was something more—a phoenix soaring above the ashes of her past, flames of joy trailing behind her like sparks in the jungle night.

THE BITCH

The common room was a rectangular space with a scuffed linoleum floor, its glossy surface dulled by years of use. Fluorescent lights buzzed overhead, casting a stark, shadowless brightness over everything. Along the far wall, a mounted flat-screen television hung in a metal cage, its edges dented from years of God-knows-what mishaps. The volume was low enough that the chatter often drowned it out; subtitles crawled across the bottom of the screen like an afterthought.

Rows of plastic chairs, bolted together in clusters of three or four, were arranged haphazardly around the room. Inmates in orange jumpsuits occupied some of them, leaning back with their arms crossed or perched forward, elbows on knees. A few chatted in low tones, their voices blending with the background hum of the TV and the occasional clatter of a mop bucket in the hallway outside. Others sat silently, staring at the screen or into the distance, lost in thought.

In the corner, a worn vending machine glowed faintly, stocked with off-brand snacks and sodas that cost more than they would on the outside. Next to it stood a small bookshelf, its paperbacks dog-eared and yellowed, mostly thrillers with missing covers. The air smelled faintly of bleach, industrial cleaning products, and the ever-present musk of too many bodies in one place. The sound of keys jingling and boots on the linoleum echoed from time to time as guards made their rounds, their presence noted but largely ignored.

Travis sat in a chair near the front, close enough to hear most of the interview, attentive to the subtitles to make sure he followed the rest. His brow was furrowed, his hands clasped tightly in his lap. He shifted every few moments, the hard plastic seat doing little to accommodate comfort. Around him, a handful of other inmates seemed mildly curious about the *60 Minutes* segment, though none seemed as invested as he was.

He was furious.

"What was it like in the ER with Madison Quinn?" Annie Hampton asked.

He felt his heart pounding against his chest.

The camera shifted to focus on Maya's facial expression as she adopted a made-for-TV look of resigned sadness. "Look, I'm a doctor," she started. "We… she was in a bad state, and we all did everything we could to stabilize her. But it was clear her recovery wasn't a given even without the baby."

"So you made a decision?" Annie prompted.

Maya nodded slowly. Travis had told her he didn't want Madison anywhere near her little project. What had she said? It'll be messy, but she'd *try*? How could he have been so naïve?

"She was in shock," Maya said. "My job was to save her life. The state's guidelines nearly prevented me from doing that, and if I had paused long enough to try to parse them, she would've died."

Travis sat up and clenched his jaw. It chewed him up inside that she was scoring political points off his daughter.

Annie cocked her head at Maya. "You're taking care of Madison Quinn while her father serves time for punching Eli Lawson. Why did you decide to do that?"

And there it was, he wanted to scream. *Her fucking plan all along.*

Maya took a theatrical pause before answering. "Paying it forward," she said.

"Paying it forward?"

"Yes," Maya continued. "I was pretty awful to my adoptive parents, right to the end. They bore the brunt of me trying to push the world away." She looked sad for a moment. "They're both too dead for me to apologize to them, but I can pay it forward to the next generation."

"Paying it forward—is that what your candidacy is about, too?"

"Yes." Maya nodded her head.

"Why now?" Annie asked. "After decades of privacy, why expose yourself to this?"

Maya opened her mouth to answer, but no words came. She tried again, but her breath caught. For several excruciating seconds, the camera captured her struggle, a woman visibly fighting for control and losing.

"I'm sorry," she finally managed, her voice cracking. "I had a prepared answer for this, I promise. But… the truth?" She exhaled slowly. "I'm doing this because I'm tired of pretending to be fearless when I'm terrified. Of pretending to not be broken." She gave a small, self-deprecating laugh. "Elizabeth is going to kill me for saying this."

Annie stared at her silently, her eyes willing Maya on, unwilling to interrupt.

"I've spent my life helping women while failing to save myself." Her voice strengthened, finding its rhythm. "But Madison Quinn almost died because people like me stayed silent. We didn't feel we could be both seen and accepted at the same time, so we stayed small. We left the hard conversations to someone else."

The camera caught a tear tracking down her cheek. She didn't wipe it away.

"My birth mother once wrote that when we surrender our stories, when we let them exist outside ourselves, they can transform not just us but others, too. So, that's why now. I'm here to share my story, and in doing so, I hope to represent those too scared to speak their own. Tonight, I'm here to be seen."

The open visitation room was a cavernous space with polished concrete floors. The hum of air conditioning mixed with the soft murmur of dozens of quiet conversations, punctuated occasionally by the clink of chairs against the floor or the faint buzz of a distant PA announcement. Rows of sturdy bolted-down tables, each with matching plastic chairs, filled the room in a grid-like arrangement. The walls were painted in muted beige tones, functional but unremarkable, designed more for durability than comfort.

At one end of the room, a corrections officer stood near a desk, monitoring the visitors and inmates as they interacted. A glass wall separated this area from the main hallway, providing a view of the controlled chaos within. Some tables had children coloring in small notebooks or playing with toys brought by their families, their laughter providing brief flashes of humanity in an otherwise sterile environment.

Richard, Hannah, and Maya sat at a table near the edge of the room, close enough to observe Madison without intruding on her private conversation with her dad. Madison's table was closer to the center, where she leaned forward slightly, her hands on the table, her emotion visible in the tremor of her body. Travis, in his standard-issue beige jumpsuit, nodded encouragingly as he listened to her, holding her hand, a look of deep concern etched on his face.

Richard leaned back in his chair, crossing his arms as he glanced around the room. He noticed the wall-mounted security cameras positioned discreetly in the corners, their presence a constant reminder of the rules governing this shared space.

"She holding up okay?" Hannah asked, nodding toward Madison.

"She's tougher than she looks," Maya replied.

"A bit like you," Richard said, smiling at Hannah.

A small tear formed in the corner of Hannah's eye as she met her dad's smile. She held out her hand, like Madison, to let her dad wrap it with his own.

Maya watched the intimacy of the moment, and a shadow fell over her face.

They had told Hannah before winter gave way to spring, when Dr. Maya Russell was a public riddle that everyone wanted to solve, not a candidate who had changed the entire conversation up and down the ticket.

Hannah sat motionless at the kitchen island, her hazel eyes—the eyes that had suddenly become the center of this revelation—wide and unblinking. Her chestnut hair, pulled back in a loose, practical ponytail, framed a face that seemed to be aging years in seconds. The diplomatic composure she'd cultivated through her studies crumbled visibly; her lips parted and closed several times before she managed to find her voice.

"So that's why you left Dad?" she finally whispered, her fingers curling around the edge of the marble countertop, knuckles whitening. "Because I... because I wasn't..." She couldn't finish the sentence, the implication too painful to articulate.

"No, honey, no," Maya reached across the island, but Hannah pulled back sharply, knocking over her water glass. Neither of them moved to clean the spreading puddle. Richard stood by the refrigerator, his presence solid but unobtrusive, giving them space while remaining available. Hannah's breathing quickened, her shoulders rising and falling in rapid succession as the shock morphed into something hotter, more volatile.

She pushed herself up from the stool. The metal feet scraped harshly against the floor as she began pacing, her hands gesturing wildly in the air. The oversized Georgetown sweatshirt she wore seemed to hang differently on her frame, as if the weight of this new knowledge had physically altered her.

"*Limadha al'an?*" Hannah suddenly shouted, switching to Arabic, her fluency now weaponized to inflict a deep wound. "*Limadha takhbirini alan? Hal huwa bisabab 'annahum jamieuhum yataha-dathun ean madik?*" ("Why now? Why tell me now? Is it because they're all talking about your past?") Tears streamed down her face, leaving glistening trails that caught the kitchen light. Her whole body trembled with the force of her anger, raw and unfiltered. She slammed her palm against the counter, a sharp crack that made both Maya and Richard flinch.

"*Ya sharmouta mal'ouna!*"

You cursed whore. The phrase was even more taboo in Arabic than it was in English, especially when directed at a family member. The *mal'ouna* carried the connotation of being cursed by God. It was an unspeakably disrespectful thing to say in Arabic-speaking cultures.

From one sayyida to another, Hannah knew that.

Maya stepped around the island, moving slowly as if approaching a wounded animal. She deliberately chose to respond in Arabic, her voice halting and imperfect. "*Ana asifa, ya habibti. Ana khayifa.*" ("I'm sorry, my love. I was afraid.") The words felt foreign on her tongue, yet somehow right for this moment.

She reached out and touched Hannah's trembling shoulder, and when Hannah didn't pull away, Maya gathered her daughter into her arms. Hannah collapsed against her, anger giving way to deep, heaving sobs that shook them both. Richard moved closer now, placing one hand on Hannah's back and the other on Maya's shoulder, forming a circle of connection that transcended biology. Hannah mumbled something against Maya's shoulder, her words muffled but her meaning clear, a wounded acceptance beginning to take root, the first fragile step toward forgiveness.

Now in the prison's visitation center, Hannah seemed to detect the mood shift in her mom and wrapped her free arm around Maya, leaning her head into her shoulder. "I love you," she said.

Madison sniffled, stood up, and hugged Travis in the distance. She walked back to their table, her face covered in tears and snot.

"I got this," Hannah said, freeing her hands and reaching into the clear ziplock bag she had gotten past security to pull out some Kleenex.

Maya kissed her on the cheek and stood. She smiled at Madison and helped her sit before walking over to Travis. He had a pained look on his face as Maya sat down across from him. They sat in silence for a full minute or two, Travis eyeing Madison from afar, watching her fall into Hannah's embrace.

"I read you wrong," Travis said at last.

"You had your reasons," Maya said.

Travis lifted his gaze to Maya. "She told me everything," he said.

"About what?" Maya asked, confused.

"About Eli," Travis said, his voice flat.

Maya put her hand to her mouth. After a stunned moment, she glanced behind her to see Madison still collapsed in Hannah's comforting embrace.

"Told her it was God's will," he said. "But she admitted she wanted it, too."

Maya shook her head, trying to take this in.

"He must've felt scared after his carelessness. Told her the pills would make sure she wouldn't get pregnant."

"That was a big step for her," Maya said finally.

Travis stared intently at Maya, his face tense. "She did it because of you," he said. Maya offered another stunned look. "I watched your interview," he said.

Maya stayed quiet, off balance.

"So did Madison," Travis continued, giving his daughter an extended look before returning his pained gaze to Maya. "You did that knowing what it would cost you. Knowing the vultures would circle. Knowing people like me would hate you for it." He shook his head slowly, turning to look at her. "And you did it anyway."

His eyes teared up as he reached his hand toward Maya, palm up. She stared at it wide-eyed, then met it with her own hand. He placed his other hand on top and stared directly at her, not trying to hide the tears streaming down his cheeks.

"For the record," he said, a soft smile curving the outside of his lips, "I still think you're a bitch."

THROUGH THE LOOKING GLASS

He sat up on the bed, watching. Her face, usually so composed, contorted in silent agony as her body twisted and murmured through the storm of her nightmare. The sheets clung to her damp skin, a physical testament to the battle waging beneath her eyelids. She looked trapped, her breaths shallow and sharp, each exhale punctuated by small, involuntary whimpers that seemed to cut through the room like a whispered plea.

He had seen this before, the gasps, the restless movements. But tonight, there was something more. The atmosphere felt heavier, charged with a strange energy, as though her nightmare were bleeding into reality. He leaned forward, bracing for what he knew was coming.

"Maya," he whispered, leaning forward. His hand hovered just above her arm.

She reacted as if struck, her head snapping to the side. Her legs kicked, tangling in the sheets, and she let out a choked gasp that made his heart lurch. Her face twisted in a mask of terror, her lips forming words that never fully escaped.

And then it happened—that cruel moment where the liminal boundary between nightmare and reality disappears abruptly, like a string pulled taut and then snapped. Her entire body bolted upright as if yanked by unseen hands.

The scream that tore from her throat didn't sound human. It was raw, guttural, primal.

It struck him like a blow, reverberating through his chest and temporarily making his heart race. For a fleeting moment, her wide, unseeing eyes stared straight ahead, as if she were looking through him into something he hated to imagine. Her chest heaved as if she'd just surfaced from drowning. He caught her instinctively, wrapping his arms around her trembling frame.

"It's me," he whispered into her hair, his voice steady and grounding. "You're safe."

She blinked, her eyes locking onto his, her breathing slowing just slightly. He tilted his wrist, letting the soft glow of his Apple Watch catch her attention. "See? It's 5:09. You're here. You're safe."

Her gaze fixed on the numbers, and he could see the faintest flicker of recognition behind her terror. She swallowed hard, a single tear tracing down her cheek.

"You're here," she said, her voice cracked and trembling.

"I'm here," he said, pulling her into his arms. She trembled against him, her breaths shaky as she clung to his shirt. He stroked her hair, his chin resting on top of her head. "I've got you. You're okay now."

Her body quaked in his arms. Moments later, she was crying.

◦◦~◦◦

The afternoon sun streamed through the windows, painting the living room in soft, golden hues. Richard paused in the hallway, his gaze falling on Maya seated cross-legged on the rug, surrounded by an unruly pile of books. Their spines, embossed with flowing

Arabic script, seemed to shimmer faintly in the light, their titles as foreign to him as the little girl flipping through them.

She looked up as he entered, her dark eyes flickering with a mix of concentration and hesitation. A loose strand of hair fell across her cheek. She tucked it behind her ear, distracted. "Hey," she said softly.

"Hey yourself," he replied, setting his bag down. "What's all this?"

She rested her hands on the open pages of the book in her lap, the faint scent of old paper wafting up. "They're my mom's," she said, her voice quieter now, tinged with a melancholy sadness. "Hannah had them."

"Hannah?"

"Yeah." She smiled at him. "Turns out all those stories about Arabic studies to become a diplomat like my dad were kinda bullshit."

He smiled at her. "What a bitch," he said.

She shrugged. "Chip off the old block."

"She read them?" he asked.

"Multiple times, evidently."

He crouched beside her, picking up a slender volume with a worn cover. The Arabic script flowed like a river across the spine. He flipped through the pages until he found a verse underlined.

"What's this?" he asked, showing the page to Maya.

"Hannah must've underlined it." She smiled as she read. "Says, 'to raise a daughter with an unbroken spirit is itself an act of revolution.'"

Richard shut the book and put it back in the pile. "You ever read them before?"

She shook her head, a melancholy smile pulling at the corners of her lips. "I'm more the running type, myself."

He studied her for a moment, his gaze soft. "Trying to get closer?"

She nodded. He thought he detected a tear forming in her eye.

"Want to talk about last night?" he asked.

She stiffened slightly without looking up. She flipped a page, her movements deliberate, as though turning the conversation over in her mind. "It's the same one," she said at last. "It always ends the same way."

"With a gunshot?" he guessed.

She looked at him. He returned her gaze with those kind, blue eyes, his face twisted with the choice in front of him.

"You know Saddam traveled with a photographer at Dujail," he said. He paused, his own heart beating faster than he was comfortable with. "They used the video evidence at his trial."

She stared at him, lines of terror sculpted into her expression. "You've… seen it?"

He nodded slowly. "Didn't take long for those hyenas to find it, which means you're just about the only person who hasn't seen it. But I found it long ago." He spread his hand in front of the pile of books. "I might have read translations of some of these, too."

She looked down at her mother's book in her hands, as if looking for guidance. He weighed his options, knowing he could lose her if he continued. He decided to risk it.

"Do you want to see what everyone else has seen?" he asked her, as gently as he could.

She nodded, then shook her head from side to side as the tears started to fall and blur the ink on the page.

She stood up and started to walk past him, to run, her heart beating out of her chest. He grabbed her arm and pulled her into his embrace, both of their hearts beating erratically.

"Look," he said, showing her the time. It was 6:14.

They sat shoulder to shoulder at his desk, a pause button frozen on the screen before them. The grainy footage showed Saddam Hussein in his military fatigues and a beret, flanked by armed guards, his imposing figure casting a long shadow over a group of terrified villagers.

"Ready?" he asked, eyeing her carefully.

Her breath came shallow and fast, her body taut with the tension of what she was about to confront. A muscle near her left eye flickered, her fingers clenched and unclenched rhythmically, and her bare foot tapped against the hardwood floor as if she were trying to dispel the energy building inside of her. He reached to hold one of her hands. Her fingers tightened around him like a vice.

> The memory strikes without warning, the smell of dates fermenting in the orchard, sweet and cloying. She is small, her legs shorter than they should be, too weak to carry her quickly enough. Someone is screaming. The echoes bounce between the trees, distorting the sound until it becomes something inhuman.

"I'll stop the second you want me to. Just say the word."

She nodded once, inhaling deeply through her nose and exhaling slowly to calm herself down. "Okay," she said. "Do it."

He hesitated for a moment before turning back to the screen. His finger hovered over the keyboard, worry etched into his face. He hoped he wasn't making a mistake.

> Her mother's voice cuts through the chaos—urgent, terrified. Her words are thick with desperation. She feels hands pushing her toward the shadows.
>
> *Run, Mayyada!*

She closed her eyes briefly. When she opened them, they were dark and resolute.

He hit play.

The video flickered to life. They had previously watched the clips of Saddam's speech after the assassination attempt. The shots had been fired from the date orchard at his car (or, if you believed his later prosecutors, into the air). Now the villagers stood in a terrified row, their faces hidden by the camera angle but their bodies rigid. Saddam scratched his chin as he questioned one villager.

"Sir, I'm fasting," the villager said nervously. Subtitles decorated the bottom of the video.

"Oh, Khomeini fasts, too," Saddam shot back. The initial confidence in the early days of the war—an attempt to capitalize on Iran's post-revolution instability—had faded once Iran regrouped under the Ayatollah's leadership and mounted successful counterattacks.

"Please sir. Ask about me and my people. I am from Samarra," another man pleaded.

"Take them, each by himself, for interrogation," Saddam ordered his security.

Maya's nails dug into Richard's hand as three figures were forcibly dragged into view and made to kneel before the dictator. The man had dark eyes, a wrinkled face, and a full beard. The prepubescent boy had a round face wrapped in a mask of pure terror.

"Qasim…" Maya whispered, her voice breaking.

She hitched her breath as she stared at the woman, her alabaster skin and rounded cheeks framed in a dark hijab.

> She crawls on her belly beneath the lowest branches,
> scraping her knees raw on rough earth. Her heart is
> a trapped bird beating against her ribs. Men's voices
> grow louder, hard, angry sounds, making her press

> herself flatter to the ground. She holds her breath
> until stars explode behind her eyelids. The smell of
> gunpowder mingles with the fermenting dates.

Maya started trembling.

"The girl?" Saddam said, looking at his guards. The microphone didn't capture the answer.

Richard paused the video again.

"Look," he said, showing her his watch. It was 6:34.

He leaned over to hold her, letting her gather herself, letting her see her family for the last time, again. She cried softly, resting her head on his shoulder.

> The sound shatters her world. She bites her own hand
> to keep silent, tasting copper and dirt. Her shoulders
> shake with silent sobs. She claws her way up and
> starts running again, her vision blinded with tears.

"I'm ready," she said a few minutes later, her voice shaky. Richard moved back over and held her hand again. Hating himself, he pressed play.

Saddam drew his pistol, the metallic sound of it sliding free from its holster echoing in the terrified silence of the villagers. He held it casually, almost like a toy, as he paced around the kneeling family.

"Friends of Khomeini are traitors," he spat. He stopped behind Maya's father, raised the pistol, and fired.

The sound of the gunshot cracked through the computer speakers, echoing in the small room like a physical blow. Maya flinched violently, her body jerking backward, her hand flying to her mouth. Her eyes remained glued to the screen. Tears spilled freely down her cheeks.

Richard's hand hovered over the keyboard. "Maya…"

"Don't," she choked, her voice raw.

Saddam moved next to the crying boy. Another bullet, another fallen body. Maya's knees went weak. Her vision blurred.

> The gunshot steals something from her she'll never get back. The ground beneath her seems to vanish. She collapses, skinning her knee even more as it scrapes against the bark. Choking in fear, she stands up, and once again, she runs, through the blood and the tears and the terror.

Saddam circled her mother like a predator. "Traitor," he hissed, the word dripping with venom. "And your daughter? Hiding in the shadows? A coward like you?"

The famous Fatima al-Rahbani—who would go down in history as the only woman Saddam Hussein ever feared—looked directly up at him through her coal-dark eyes. Her voice cut through the air like a blade.

"She will bury you."

> Something explodes inside her chest. The world fractures into jagged pieces. Behind her, men shout.

The final shot brought Maya to her knees. She vomited, the sound mingling with her sobs as the room seemed to echo with the weight of her grief.

Richard cradled her, showing her his watch. It was 6:40. "It's over," he whispered, his voice thick with emotion. "It's over."

THE SLUT

Her heart pounding, Maya rang the doorbell.

A few moments later, a man answered, his head framed with digni-fied gray on top and a silver goatee below. He was broad-shouldered with keen brown eyes, wearing a long-sleeved buttoned shirt with the sleeves rolled up, showing off his muscular forearms. For a moment, they looked as if they were taking the measure of each other. Then he stepped aside and opened the door wider, offering her entrance. She walked inside and he closed the door behind them.

"Coffee?" he asked. "I just put a pot to brew."

"No, thank you," she said, taking in the staircase that zig-zagged to the second story at the end of the entryway. She followed him to the kitchen, past the open-concept living room with the high ceiling overlooking the second-story hallway balcony.

"Water?"

"That'd be great."

He grabbed a glass, pushed it into the dispenser paddle on the refrigerator to drop some ice in, then shifted it over to fill it with water.

"Thanks," she said, as he poured himself a cup of coffee out of the coffee pot.

"Shall we?" he asked, motioning to the breakfast area table by the bay window. They sat down across from each other and looked out to the backyard.

"Your roses are blooming," she said.

"Seems you are, too."

She smiled at him, her cheeks as rosy as the flowers outside. "Thank you. And *thank you*."

He shook his head with a smile, dismissing the compliment with Southern grace. "This is a treat. It's good to see you in person."

"Again," she said, giving him a sly look.

He smiled. "It's good to see you, *again*. God, you have the most beautiful eyes."

She blushed, making her eyes shine even brighter. "Might be because you're so easy to look at."

He laughed freely before taking a sip of coffee and staring out the window. "How long has it been?"

"Twenty-two, no, twenty-three years."

"Remember the last time?" he asked.

Maya shook her head.

"Well, lucky for you, I do." He offered her a wink and a broad smile.

"Oooh, I must've made an impression," she said in a teasing voice.

"You're impossible to forget," he smiled, and looked out the window again. He paused, looking thoughtful, before taking a sip of coffee. "I cooked for you, remember? Duck breast with bourbon-orange glaze. A side of stone-ground grits with white cheddar and chives, some sautéed collard greens with pancetta and garlic."

"You're making my mouth water."

"And for dessert, I made you a bourbon-pecan tart with sea salt and dark chocolate."

"I hope I made it up to you with my own dessert," she teased.

He laughed. "Like I said, you're impossible to forget."

They sat in silence for a few moments, basking in the reminiscing, looking at spring's renewal in his beautiful backyard. At length, he looked at her and broke the silence. "How's Hannah?"

She took in a deep breath, keeping her view out the bay window. "You know. A chip off the old block."

"Hopefully not as thick as these old blocks," he said, eyeing his left shoulder and flexing for effect.

"Hah!" she laughed, turning to look at him and admiring his good cheer.

"Remind me where we met," he said.

"Shaking our asses on the dance floor," she said, standing up and wiggling her hips in tune to the memory. "You grinding up behind me, pushing that boner into me."

He smiled, looking up at her. "Sounds like a good night."

She sat back down, grinning at him. "Good enough for me to come back for seconds."

They shared another moment of silence. He sighed, took a sip of coffee, and looked out his bay window. "I planted that for Hannah," he said, his voice low.

Maya followed his gaze to the backyard. Amidst the fresh green of the lawn and the budding branches of a live oak, a Mexican redbud tree stood in full bloom. Its delicate magenta flowers were clustered like small bursts of fireworks, its branches reaching skyward as if yearning for something out of reach. Beneath it, a bed of bluebonnets formed a soft carpet, their bright indigo petals swaying gently in the breeze. A weathered stone bench rested under the tree, its edges softened by moss and time, as if inviting someone to sit and reflect.

"She would've been about two; that's when I found out," he continued, his eyes not leaving the tree. "The redbud was small, barely a sapling back then. I thought, when she grew up, maybe she'd have a place to sit, a bit of shade, somewhere just hers, you know?"

Maya stared at the tree, the petals trembling in the breeze like a thousand tiny hearts. "It's beautiful," she said. A tear fell slowly down her cheek. He reached across the table and caught it on the tip of his finger.

"Hope you'll forgive this old man one sentimental indulgence," he said, delicately sucking the tear off his finger.

⁓⁓⁓

Elizabeth Lang carried the picture frame to the couch. She had taken the picture inside the night she had shown how cool a mom she was by playing *Cards Against Humanity* with Olivia and her friends over Christmas break. It was a rare moment of détente in their relationship, helped along by a bottle of 18-year Macallan.

It was the last time she had seen Olivia laugh.

"No, it's just something in the air," Elizabeth said to Olivia, setting her down gently against the couch cushion and taking the spot next to her.

"Must be the pollen," she said. "Walking in, those fucking trees came all over me like it's a bukkake party." She blinked and cleared her eyes. The large LCD hanging on the wall showed Annie Hampton and Maya Russell frozen, sitting apart from each other across a circular Persian rug.

"Want to watch together? I thought you might like this part..." She reached for the remote and pressed play.

Annie Hampton shifted in her seat. It was an almost imperceptible body language transition to the discomfort Elizabeth knew was coming.

"You know running for office will open you up to personal attacks?" Annie asked.

"Yes…" Maya said, looking a little uncomfortable.

"Are you prepared to fight like a politician?"

Maya thought for a moment. "I guess I'd say… I'm prepared to fight like a woman."

"Her line, not mine," Elizabeth said to her daughter as Annie offered an almost sad smile.

"Let's be specific, shall we? I'm sure you've heard the rumors about your infidelities. How would you fight back against that narrative?"

Maya gave an indifferent shrug. "I guess I'd say I don't kiss and tell."

"Hah!" Elizabeth said, looking down at Olivia on her left while slapping the couch cushion on her right.

"So you aren't concerned about people discounting your message because of your perceived promiscuity?"

Maya shook her head softly. "I don't see what my message and my sex life have to do with each other."

Annie gave a brief pause but kept her gaze intently on Maya. "You've said you want voters to know you as a human, warts and all. What do you say to voters who hesitate voting for you because they see your sex life as a character flaw?"

"Character flaw!" Elizabeth spat disgustedly.

Maya offered a soft smile. "I'd say that you don't get perfect choices in politics; that's pretty much the core of my message, actually. You'll have to decide for yourself whether you think a woman having sex without your permission is worse than putting a woman's life in danger for being pregnant without *her* permission, which is the state's current position. I guess you'll have to prioritize your values."

"Fair enough," Annie said. "But just to be clear—you don't deny the accusations?"

Maya held out her hands, palms up. "Accusations are easy," she said. "I don't deny that I've lived a complicated life, but that doesn't mean you should believe everything you've heard."

Annie let out a pregnant pause. "What about Clayton Redding?"

"Ooooooh," Elizabeth cooed, smiling down at Olivia.

Maya inhaled deeply. Her eyes narrowed dangerously. "Clay?"

"Is Clayton Redding your daughter's biological father?" Annie kept her face serious, her focus intense, letting the gravity of the question settle.

"Gotcha!" Elizabeth snapped.

Maya reflected Annie's gaze with a fierce look shining out of her coal-dark eyes. "Richard is the most amazing man I've ever met. He's the best father Hannah could've asked for, even if he's not her biological father. I've already mentioned that I don't kiss and tell, but no, Clay is not Hannah's biological father, either."

"This is *exciting*," Elizabeth said, wrapping her arm around Olivia's picture frame.

Annie's eyes narrowed. "We don't report on rumors, but we do our homework. We talked to Clayton. He confirmed that he had unprotected sex with you after meeting you at a club. The timeline tracks."

"Sorry to disappoint you, but I've never had sex with Clay." Maya spoke simply, as if she was unbothered by the accusation.

Annie leaned forward, her voice lowering. "Clayton told us about your history. He even showed us a memorial he put together for your daughter in his backyard. Are you saying he lied?"

Maya nodded. "A Mexican redbud. It's beautiful. I saw it when I met him in March. For the first time."

Annie cocked her head, nonplussed. "For the first time?"

"Hah!" Elizabeth said, taking obvious glee in the moment.

Maya wore a fierce look. "That's right. We talked on the phone to come up with our story before I met him. Wonderful person. Promised to confirm every detail if reporters ever came a-knocking."

"I don't understand…" Annie said.

"Elizabeth Lang leaked our story, but only to one person in confidence, so we'd be able to pinpoint exactly where the rumor started if it leaked to the press. Clay was a honeypot. And if you'd like to go a-knocking again, both he and Elizabeth would be willing to say so under a lie detector."

"Boom!" Elizabeth shouted.

"In fact," Maya continued, ice in her voice, "if you check with Dinah, you should be getting video confirmation of our plan right about now from Elizabeth."

"Wha…?" Annie stammered. She was unused to being on her back foot in her own interviews, and Elizabeth was certain, had never been on that back foot *this* many times in one interview. "Who did Elizabeth Lang leak the story to?"

"Who do you think?" Maya asked.

Annie paused. "You know I can't answer that," she said.

"Like I said," Maya responded, "you'll have to decide for yourself whether my complicated sex life is worse than the governor being so insecure he's willing to spread rumors about it."

"Are you accusing Wade Callahan of leaking the Clayton Redding story?"

"Perhaps you should ask him to put his denial under a lie detector too, just for good measure."

Annie's lips parted, but no words came. Elizabeth knew she was off-balance enough that she needed Dinah to whisper in her ear that it was time for a break.

Maya leaned forward, raw fury shining through her eyes. "I've spent my entire career studying pussies," she said. "I know how to recognize one when I see one."

Elizabeth pressed pause on the remote and looked down at her daughter with a wicked grin plastered over her face. "Honey, we plowed that ass like a Nebraska corn farmer."

"No, no, it's just the pollen," she responded to her daughter's reaction, the laughter shining through those beautiful eyes looking up at her.

With a trembling finger, she wiped the tears off her cheek.

THE RAPTURE

The mouths and hands consumed her like a sacred pyre, spreading heat from all sides of her existence.

The soft tickle of a mustache brushed against her upper lip, the first embers of a growing promise. Blindfolded, the sensation became magnified, the faint prickles of each hair against her sensitive skin igniting sparks that spread like a slow burn through her body. Lips followed, warm and deliberate, deepening the kiss with a tenderness that felt both familiar and electric, as if he were mapping every curve of her mouth with intention.

The next lips landed just above her ankle, soft and featherlight, sending a frisson down her spine. A moment later: a third kiss, brushing the outside of her other leg with the faint scrape of a beard, its coarse texture a thrilling contrast to the smooth heat of his lips. As the lips ascended, alternating between legs, each kiss seemed to awaken the skin beneath, leaving a trail of warmth and anticipation that climbed higher with every deliberate pause, every grazing touch of hair and lips.

Two lips descended over the curvature of her breast as if from a balloon slowly inflating, the tongue between them circling her areola. She moaned through her own kiss as teeth gently pinched her nipple and tugged upward.

Hands glided over her skin like the strokes of a master artist, layering her in textures of sensation and desire. Some brushed across her like whispers of wind, delicate and fleeting, awakening nerve endings with their ghostly caress. Others moved like waves, heavy and enveloping, grounding her in their warmth as they pressed into her curves. Each touch worked in harmony, dissolving the edges of thought and pulling her out of her mind, until she existed only in the vivid immediacy of her body, alive with sensation and utterly present.

The scene unfolded like a Baroque fugue, each sensation a voice weaving into the greater composition, sometimes blending into perfect harmony, sometimes shifting into unexpected dissonance before resolving again. Leo's baritone mustache brushed against her skin like a bowed bass string, grounding her in its steady, resonant presence, while the tenor of Richard's lips pressed hot and soft against the sensitive curve of her neck, a melody both familiar and thrilling.

The alto voice came as sparks, lips and tongues and hands that waltzed over her legs unpredictably. The ocean breeze joined in as the whispering soprano, warm and teasing, lifting the hairs on her body and leaving behind the faint, salty kiss of the sea. Beneath it all, the percussion of waves crashing against the shore provided the relentless rhythm, a deep, primal heartbeat echoing in her ears and through her chest, tethering her to the earth even as her senses seemed to soar beyond it. Each touch, each kiss, each sigh of breath intertwined, swelling and ebbing like the tide itself, creating a symphony of connection that was as chaotic as it was beautiful.

It was a choreography of voices, both human and elemental, building anticipation, until her body became the instrument and the players brought her to the edge of crescendo, their movements both deliberate and improvisational, as if following the ancient chords written in the sheet music of her deepest desire. Hands and lips danced over her in playful counterpoint. It was a masterpiece of desire, where even the dissonances resolved into something sublime.

It was only the startle of the ensemble shifting that brought back conscious awareness, its movement captured by the contours and ripples of the oversized mattress, like a wave supporting her from underneath. The kiss and the tickle of the mustache continued, and more hands than she could count—her sense of precision overwhelmed by the moment—warmed her body.

She felt two hands, connected to the same body, holding each ankle. When she felt the warmth of the breath caress her inner thighs, her hips arched upward in an almost involuntary moan of anticipation. She turned to catch the hot breath on her neck as soon as she felt it, to taste it, to connect with it until the connection turned into a kiss, Michael's beard on her chin as she tugged his lips, the counterpoint of Leo's mustache on the back of her neck. The hands on her ankles moved up and up some more until one snaked under her thigh and resurfaced on top of her stomach. The breath traced the delicate curves of each inner thigh separately.

She surrendered her neck to the gentle scratch of the beard as the lips gently caressed her earlobe and found Leo's kiss waiting for her as she turned, his hair brushing her upper lip. The breath between her legs whispered up each crease, staying always a fraction of an inch above her hips' attempt to find lips.

Three fingers met the hand on her stomach, mirroring it, before floating softly down toward the slow breath descending upon her, a heat gradient between the warmth of the ocean's exhales and the fiery heat radiating from the furnace of her arousal. The fingers floated over the line of pubic hair, hair by hair, plucking them like the strings of a harpsichord. He spread two fingers wide and outlined the spandrel of hair between the arches of her hips with the reverence of a votary tracing sacred carvings in the walls of a cathedral.

Leo's mustache moved to her shoulder, and the arc of her own wave had her pressing the back of her head into the mattress, sensing the silhouette behind her as fingertips danced across her scalp in soothing, rhythmic strokes. The mustache traced its way down as Leo continued to kiss her, and she felt the melodic echo of Michael's beard as he worked his way up her breast to suck on her nipple.

Moaning, her blindfold enhancing her other senses, she arched her neck more to meet Richard's upside-down kiss. The angle made the connection feel deeper, more intimate, as though they were defying gravity together, here on this temple trapped between sea and sky and jungle. His breath mingled with hers, the kiss both grounding and electrifying, while his fingers moved in rhythmic, soothing circles, as if coaxing secrets from her scalp. Each touch felt like it carried a current of electricity, a silent charge shared in their inverted embrace.

When the extended pinky and forefinger of Rafa's right hand reached the bottom of her vulva, the middle two fingers lifted, plucking each tiny hair note by note on their patient ascent. Moving his left hand closer, he pulled back, stretching the skin between his hands, and no matter how energetic the undulations of the wave in her hips, he kept his touch always just above skin level.

She wrapped her hands into Richard's hair, pulling him into her as he wrapped her lower lip between his own lips, and when the wave of her neck crested and he lifted up, she spread her arms wide. Her left hand caught Michael's bald head and pressed him tighter against her breast, enjoying the feeling of his beard dancing across her skin like delicate arpeggios against the smooth legato of her soft curves. He moved with the rhythm of the ocean crashing beneath them. Her right hand glided down Leo's face, through the brush of his mustache. She traced her fingers down his neck and, as he pulled away to give her access, through the hairs of his chest.

When the fingers on Rafa's two hands finally met, her body vibrating desperately beneath them, he flipped his right hand over and started moving his fingers down again. The fingernails of his index and ring fingers now touched skin, barely, descending both labia as the fingernail on his elevated middle finger electrified her pubic hair before warming her sex with an almost unbearable anticipation.

She tried to push up into it, each disturbance of each pubic hair a suspended note yearning for the resolution that only the tonic of touch could provide, but he moved his hand in rhythm with her hips, always staying at the same elevation above her.

She rolled her neck slowly in a circular motion, surrendering to the delicious scrape of fingernails against her scalp, and continued until she had her neck arched up in anticipation. Richard's lips met her summoning smile upside-down.

They had spent a lifetime together, but they had never, until now, kissed like this. It was a delicious novelty, a rediscovery of their bodies in a way that felt adventurous yet deeply familiar. Her lips parted as he found hers, the angle shifting the sensation into something uncharted, awakening nerves as though they were being kissed for the very first time. This playful inversion stirred something profound, a testament to the infinite ways they could still surprise and delight each other.

Michael had one nipple between two fingers and the other nipple between two rows of teeth. One nipple he twisted; the other he tugged, and when he released the tension, he shifted the angle of his chin to rub his beard down the slope of her breast, licked the echoes of teeth marks off her nipple, and gently sucked again.

When he teased her, she could feel the voltage between her nipples, and when the wave crested, his hand and mouth comforted her, heavy and warm like a blanket.

Leo moaned and pushed his hips out as she traced down his body in time with the patient rhythm set by Rafa. She felt the wave beneath her, the shifting weights on the mattress, as Leo shifted forward and the other men made space for him. Her hand reached his belly button and continued its descent until she felt the soft hair below.

She leaned slightly over and switched hands for leverage, then massaged his pubic hair as Richard had previously massaged her scalp. He continued to scoot up until his groin was inches in front of her. She traced semicircles from his belly button to where his legs met as he lay on his side, but she touched the center of the semicircle with only her breath.

She gave an off-beat inhale as Rafa snaked his other arm under her and parked his upper lip where the mons gave way to labia. She felt the saliva he delicately deposited follow her curves and folds like a slow-moving river. With disciplined patience, like the curtain dropping at a theater, he floated his tongue, broad and soft, on top of the wet trail he had made, such that it seemed not to touch her even as it surrounded her entire vulva.

With his lip anchored and maintaining the same pressure throughout, nothing other than his jaw moved, stretching his tongue long on its slow journey down, curved inward until it felt like he could swallow her but chose instead to tease her by floating on top of the trail of saliva that separated them. Both tongue and vulva seemed to vibrate with hot intensity. He was like the conductor holding the orchestra in suspended silence, the note poised on the edge of release.

She felt hot breath on the back of her neck as she angled up a bit more to tease Leo, her movements deliberate and slow, inviting.

A tongue licked her softly from the part of her neck near her scalp down to the base, the sensation sending shivers cascading through her body. Her breath hitched as the warmth of a mouth lingered there, his presence intoxicating. Michael's bearded kisses traced down her side, each touch deliberate, leaving a trail of tingling warmth in their wake. The coarse texture of his beard against her smooth skin heightened every sensation, an electric friction that made her arch slightly.

When she again reached the gap between Leo's thighs, she spread her fingers wide and glided them up. He moaned again as she caressed up his balls and kept going until she felt the muscle spasms, as if he was trying to summon an erection through some combination of willpower and calisthenics. She spread her index and thumb apart so that they could trace down the top and bottom of his shaft from base to tip and back to base again, enjoying its softness.

Rafa moved his hands with deliberate care, clearing a path for Michael's kisses to descend toward her trembling stomach. The anticipation grew as Michael's fingers danced along her skin, pausing to gently twist her nipple, first in one direction, then in the other. Michael's beard scraped lightly across her navel, the rough texture contrasting with the softness of his lips. He gave a reverent pause before beginning his slow ascent up the side of her body again, his breath warm against her skin, igniting a trail of heat that left her arching toward him.

She teased Leo a few moments more, her lips brushing against him lightly, her breath warm against him, before parting her mouth and inviting him inside. A knowing smile spread across her face, hidden beneath the blindfold but unmistakable in the lilt of her head and in the deliberate way she moved.

She knew he had delayed the pharmaceutical assistance for her sake, a gesture that deepened her appreciation for him in ways words could never express. Leo was the only man she'd ever been with whose ego didn't intrude upon the intimacy of giving her the space to explore the unhurried rhythms of her desire. She began with delicate strokes of her tongue, savoring the folds and textures of his flaccid member like an artist acquainting herself with the raw materials of a masterpiece. Each movement was deliberate, her tongue tracing every contour, every nuance, coaxing him to strength slowly and sensually, drawing pleasure not just from his response but from the act of discovery itself.

Richard's fingers brushed against her temple, deliberate and reverent, as if he were unwrapping a relic too sacred to rush. The soft fabric of the blindfold glided over her skin and hair like a lover's whisper, its departure leaving her bare to the starlight. As he lifted it away, the world shifted, no longer a shadowed play on the walls of her mind but a radiant expanse unfurling before her.

She blinked, and the heavens blinked back at her, infinite and shimmering.

When Rafa finally curved the tip of his tongue and curled his way up through her vestibule and into her inner sanctum, she felt the tension build in her muscles as if they were the strings of her desire, each note plucked to maximize anticipation, weaving together into a harmony that was sublime in its complexity.

She felt her trembling form suspended in the dissonance between ecstasy and surrender, between harmony and chaos. She was Bach's clavier, tempered by the hands that played her, each vibration a testament to the exquisite torment of being both an instrument and the medium through which the music itself was made manifest. Her cries of release echoed in the night, each one a note in the celestial fugue, vibrating in harmony with the earth's rhythm.

As the wave crashed against the cathedral of her body, the nave of her spine curved in invitation, while the transept of her arms spread wide to welcome the union of mouths and hands that traversed her curves. It was as if the architecture of her being was designed for exaltation and this was her moment of rapture.

In the symphony of their bodies, she felt herself ascending, the ancient temple beneath her having fulfilled its purpose, carrying her spirit skyward like smoke from sacred offerings.

MULTITUDES

"Are you ready to talk about Dujail?"

Annie Hampton's voice resonated through the vast dining hall, amplified by the cavernous acoustics and accompanied only by the staccato rhythm of Maya's heels against the marbled floor. The sound echoed, deliberate and steady, like the ticking of a metronome counting down to something monumental.

She walked alone down the center aisle, her gown a masterpiece of deep emerald silk that caught the light with every step. The strapless bodice was adorned with intricate gold embroidery, highlighting her shoulders and collarbone. The dress hugged her form before flaring into a graceful, flowing skirt that whispered against the floor. A delicate gold chain belt cinched her waist, complementing the metallic accents of her elegant stilettos. She wore her dark hair in a sleek chignon, leaving her neck exposed—a quiet vulnerability balanced by the strength radiating from her every determined movement.

It was, she thought, for moments like this that her mom had

named her *Mayyada,* a poetic term in Arabic that conjured images of beauty in motion.

The dining hall stretched out on either side of her, its long rows of round tables draped in crisp white linens. Napkins folded into perfect triangles perched beside pristine glassware, while fine china gleamed like polished mirrors under the glow of overhead chandeliers. The chairs, arranged with meticulous symmetry, waited silently for their occupants. It was a space made for celebration, for speeches and applause, but now it felt like a temple awaiting its goddess.

Ahead of her loomed the giant screen, her image frozen—her face, her eyes, paused in that tentative moment following Annie's question. The two parallel bars of the pause symbol seemed to hang in judgment, holding her suspended between her past and her future. Her frozen expression stared back at her like a mirror she could no longer avoid.

She kept her eyes fixed on that image, walking toward it as if toward an altar. The director had instructed her to make it solemn, deliberate, but the gravity of the moment was real. Each step was a heartbeat, each heartbeat an echo of the sacrifices that had brought her to this point. When the strain in her neck became impossible to ignore, she lowered her gaze to the single chair that awaited her at the front.

It was stark and simple, its black leather contrasting with the white expanse of the tables it faced. She felt small within its confines, dwarfed by the image above her. Straight-backed, hands resting lightly on the armrests, she faced the empty sea of chairs, her back to the screen.

The guests began to arrive.

First a trickle, then a flood, they filled the space with quiet murmurs and the faint rustling of elegant fabrics. Women in tailored suits and dresses walked with heads held high, their movements precise, as if conscious of their roles in history. Some wore hijabs, their eyes searching for the daughter of the only woman Saddam Hussein ever feared. Others donned pink pussy hats and "My Body, My Choice" shirts, their gazes fierce with the urgency of their cause.

There were older couples in formal evening attire, their hands clutching donation envelopes, their faces bearing the weight of battles fought in earlier decades. Younger activists moved through the crowd with the restless energy of grassroots hope, their pins and protest buttons creating small galaxies of color against black fabric. A group of medical professionals clustered near the back, their white coats traded for evening wear but their solidarity unmistakable in the way they stood shoulder to shoulder, having traveled from hospitals across the state to witness one of their own make history.

Tech entrepreneurs in designer jeans sat beside union organizers in pressed khakis. Suburban mothers who had driven hours clutched programs like sacred texts, while college students livestreamed on platforms their parents barely understood.

A delegation of Iraqi refugees occupied an entire table, their presence both tribute and testament to the girl who had survived what their families had not. Conservative women whispered nervously to liberal firebrands who had never imagined they'd share common ground.

Camera operators shifted silently around the room, their lenses capturing the scene from every angle. One focused on Maya's profile, the elegance of her features bathed in the warm glow of the chandeliers. Another panned across the diverse crowd, highlighting faces filled with anticipation. Overhead, a crane-mounted camera descended slowly, framing Maya from above, her solitary figure surrounded by the sea of now-filled tables.

The director gave a silent cue. Maya exhaled deeply, closing her eyes. For a moment, the entire room seemed to hold its breath with her.

When she opened them again, the camera zoomed in. Her gaze was steady and unflinching, her dark eyes glinting like obsidian lit from within. She stared directly into the lens, and through it, into herself. The screen behind her flickered to life, her own voice reverberating through the speakers.

"Yes."

The single word rang through the hall like a bell, its echoes rippling through the air like waves breaking against the edges of a long-forgotten cavern. It touched every person in the audience, settling into an expectant, charged silence. She turned her focus away from herself, shadows of her past flickering on the back of her skull, and looked out toward the crowd.

⚬⚬⚬

The darkness wraps around her like a shroud, heavy and suffocating, broken only by the sharp snap of a twig beneath her feet. She doesn't know where she is running, only that she has to keep moving. Her breath comes in shallow gasps, her lungs burning as the air grows thin and hot. Shadows claw at her, stretching long and jagged under the pale light of a crescent moon that hangs precariously in the sky like the blade of a guillotine. The ground shifts beneath her, crumbling like ash, as though the earth is conspiring to betray her.

She turns her head, just for a second, but it is enough to feel the dread swelling behind her: a presence, indistinct but unyielding, closing in. Her legs grow leaden, her steps faltering as the shifting earth turns slick and sticky beneath her feet, clinging to her ankles like tar. The skeletal branches of trees above stretch downward, their bony fingers scraping at the sky and whispering words she can't decipher, a cacophony of accusations, warnings, and commands. The air grows thick with the scent of burning—acrid, and suffocating.

Run, Mayyada!

The voice is distant but familiar. It pierces through her panic like a jagged knife, steadying her steps even as her body aches with exhaustion. She stumbles but doesn't fall, her feet finding a rhythm that defies the treacherous ground.

Ahead, the landscape twists and stretches into endless rows of date palms, their trunks unnaturally tall, their fronds lost in the void above. The orchard looms like a labyrinth, its rows narrowing with every step she takes. The shadows close in, leaning toward her, their ghostly fingers grazing her skin. Her heartbeat pounds in her ears, a relentless drumbeat of terror, driving her forward even as her body screams for rest.

A faint light flickers in the distance, like a lantern swaying in a storm. She runs toward it, her feet splashing through puddles of dark, viscous liquid that cling to her like blood. The light grows brighter, yet the darkness thickens around her, as if the night is a living thing, desperate to devour her.

The voice is louder now, urgent, commanding. She stops in her tracks, her chest heaving, and turns toward the sound. The light dims, and there, standing at the edge of her vision, she sees her. For a moment, she forgets to breathe.

Bathed in an unearthly glow, her features are impossibly sharp, her eyes filled with something between sorrow and defiance. She reaches out her hand, her movements slow, deliberate, like wading through deep water. Maya's lips part, but no sound escapes. She is rooted to the ground, her feet frozen as if the earth holds her captive.

Her mother shakes her head softly, a warning clear in her expression.
Run, Mayyada!

The command is resolute, her voice unwavering even as shadows swirl around her like a gathering storm. A man steps out of the darkness behind her mother, his figure draped in olive-green fatigues. His face is obscured, but the glint of steel in his hand catches the dim light. Her mother does not flinch, standing tall as if daring the darkness to consume her. Maya's feet move before her mind does, her mother's words compelling her forward.

She hears the gunshots.

She runs, her body trembling, her vision blurred by tears. The orchard shifts and closes in, the date palms twisting and clawing at her as though alive. Her pursuers' voices grow louder, circling her like predators. Their footsteps rustle through the undergrowth. The darkness tightens around her like a noose. There is no escape. Every direction is blocked. Silhouettes close in on every turn. Her breath comes in shallow gasps. Her legs feel ready to give out. A figure looms in her path.

A soldier.

His presence is overwhelming. She tries to dodge past him. He catches her. Pulls her into an iron grip. Her heartbeat thunders in her chest. The panic threatens to consume her. She struggles, but something stops her.

A glint of light. Square and faint.

It is strapped around his wrist.

She stares at it, blinking through the haze of her terror, this square of blurry, formless light strapped to the black band on his wrist.

She looks up at him, and the shadows begin to shift.

Kind, blue eyes shine down at her, steady and grounding.

"You came for me," she whispers, her voice trembling. She presses against him to use his heartbeat to calm her own.

"You let me in," he says, holding her tight in his embrace.

⤳⤳

Maya wiped away a tear, breathed in, and let out a slow exhale through her nose.

"Do you need a break?" Annie asked, her tone as soft as her gaze.

Maya shook her head.

"What can you tell us about him?" Annie prompted, careful not to push too hard.

Maya's eyes flickered back to the camera. "He was part of Saddam's personal security force." Her voice was steady, but her words seemed to weigh heavily in the air.

"And he found you in the date orchard?" Annie asked.

Maya nodded slowly. "He knew who I was. He'd seen Saddam kill my fam…" Her lips trembled, and she moved her hand to her mouth. She gathered herself with visible effort, taking another slow breath. "… and didn't agree with Saddam killing Qasim."

Annie gave her an empathetic nod, leaning in slightly, her expression a silent encouragement. She was too much of a professional to open her mouth to fill the silence. This was Maya's story to tell.

Maya stared blankly at the Persian rug. "He told me my parents had to die, my mom especially, but he didn't think Saddam should have killed my brother. And he didn't think I needed to die. I wasn't a threat." Her voice wavered, and she paused for an extended moment before looking back up at Annie. "His daughter had been wasting away in Abu Ghraib. I think… I think he had a complicated life."

Annie tilted her head slightly, her brow furrowing. "What happened after he found you?"

Maya blinked, as if pulling herself back from the edge of her memories. "He carried me," she said, her voice quieter now, almost a whisper. "I had scraped up my knees so badly I could barely walk. He didn't say much, just told me to stay quiet. I didn't trust him, but I didn't have a choice."

Her eyes flickered with the remembered fear, the uncertainty of those moments. "He hid me in a culvert and told me to wait for him."

She gave a long, mournful pause.

"I heard the helicopters. The screams. And I just waited there, hiding, waiting for a man who helped Saddam kill my family. Before the tanks rolled in and they closed the town, he picked me up in one of those beat-up, old black sedans they had. I still remember the smell—sweat and cigarettes and duct tape that had baked in the sun."

"Where did he drive you?" Annie asked.

"Baghdad. It took hours. He took back roads, avoiding checkpoints. I didn't know where we were going. He said they were mobilizing forces toward the eastern front, so we had to be careful."

"Did he talk to you much during the drive?"

Maya's lips pressed together, and she shook her head. "He said to say I was his niece if we got stopped. He was afraid. His hand trembled as he held his cigarette."

She paused, looking down at her own trembling hands, her face contorted in agony. Annie made no attempt to hurry her.

"He talked, but I think he was having a conversation with himself. He said he signed up to protect Iraq, not to murder children."

She paused again, then lifted her eyes and looked at Annie.

"At one point, he pulled over to the side of the road and walked around the car with his pistol and pulled at his hair. I think he was debating whether he should kill me. I think… he was… the risk he was taking… I think he was brave. He was a complex human being. In him, I first glimpsed what would take me decades to understand, that we are all contradictions, and it takes courage to face that complexity."

⌘

"Do you want us to stop?" he asked, delicately wiping a single tear falling down her cheek.

The cool fabric beneath her felt like silk spun from moonlight, its smoothness accentuating the heat rising from her skin. The contrast was intoxicating, pulling her further out of her head and into the temple of her body, where every movement, every kiss, and every whisper seemed part of an unspoken liturgy. Time dissolved in the cadence of the night—the ocean's steady percussion, the soft rustle of the jungle breeze, and the mingled sighs of those who surrounded her.

Her gaze traveled upward, her body still trembling in the aftershocks of desire as she took in the sight of him. He loomed above her, his silhouette outlined against the velvety expanse of the night sky, where stars seemed to shimmer in rhythm with the pulse still echoing through her body. The faint sheen of sweat on his chest caught the starlight, his muscles taut and rippling with the effort of restraint and release.

His eyes locked onto hers, their blue intensity softened now, almost reverent, as though he were memorizing this moment, taking a snapshot to save and to cherish. The warm breeze teased through his hair, and she thought of how the air itself seemed to caress him, as if it, too, were drawn to him.

Her fingertips itched to follow the paths of light and shadow across his body, but her arms felt deliciously heavy, her form pressed into the bed. He kissed her temple, the gesture achingly soft, and in that instant, she felt cherished, like something rare and precious.

A trembling exhale escaped her lips, and she blinked up at him, her gaze steady despite the tear she had just shed.

"Green," she whispered. "Please don't stop."

∽◦⌁◦∽

"How did you get from Baghdad to Kuwait?" Annie asked.

"A Bedouin smuggler," Maya said. "May I have some water?"

"Oh, of course." Annie gestured to someone off-camera. Moments later, Jeremy appeared with a bottle of water, handing it to Maya with quiet efficiency.

"Thank you," Maya said. She took a few sips, her fingers tightening around the bottle as if grounding herself, and handed the bottle back to Jeremy to take off set.

"I think it was common during the war—the smuggling, I mean," Maya continued, her tone contemplative. "The officer knew him. I think they had some kind of history scratching each other's backs. I don't know what the arrangement was." Her eyes unfocused, her gaze drifting somewhere far beyond the studio lights. She blinked, shook her head faintly, and refocused on Annie.

"He put me in traditional clothing, something stained with dirt and sweat. I wasn't his only cargo. Some drugs, I think. We moved under the cover of night. He seemed to know where the military patrols were, but the war was chaotic. Unpredictable. It was a different danger every night." She hesitated, her voice growing quieter. "He wasn't kind to me."

Annie leaned forward slightly, her body language gentle and empathetic. "Did he abuse you?"

Maya shook her head, her lips pressing into a thin line. "No. He treated me like cargo. I was a burden." Her voice faltered for a moment. "I don't know what the agreement was, but I remember the moment it fell apart."

Annie stayed silent, giving Maya space to continue.

"We stopped at a phone booth in Kuwait," Maya said, her voice trembling faintly. "He made a call, spoke in hushed tones. When he hung up, he looked… different. He told me the officer was dead. Arrested, tortured, and killed—all because of me." Her hands clenched in her lap, knuckles whitening. "He said there was no point taking me any further. I wasn't worth anything to him anymore."

Maya paused, her breathing shallow, as if reliving the moment. "He told me that everyone who ever tried to do anything for me was dead. He told me I was on my own. He told me not to trust anybody ever again, and he told me to start running before he shot me, and to never look back."

She looked up at Annie, her voice breaking as she continued, not bothering to wipe the tears that fell down her cheeks. "I stumbled into Kuwait City, starving, dehydrated, and barely able to walk. *I don't even know how I made it.*"

A heavy silence hung in the air, punctuated only by the faint hum of studio equipment. Annie's eyes remained fixed on Maya, her expression a mix of empathy and quiet admiration.

The air feels heavier with every step, dense and warm, like walking through the breath of an ancient beast. She reaches instinctively for the weight of his watch, her fingers brushing against its smooth surface.

They move through the towering trunks, their bark ridged and ancient, the fronds overhead murmuring in a language older than memory. The whispers coil around them, indistinct at first, then clearer, dissolving into the faint echoes of bangs—three distinct gunshots.

He squeezes her hand tight, grounding her. The sound does not press forward. It unspools backward. The echoes fade, unwinding, unwriting themselves. The orchard thickens around them, the ground softening beneath her feet, and the air shifts, scented now with sweet dates and jasmine. A breeze stirs, weightless and familiar.

Somewhere ahead, children laugh.

Her steps slow. The tension in her body unravels, strand by strand, as the night sheds its menace, peeling away like the husk of something long hardened and left to dry. The orchard is no longer an uncertain threshold.

It is home.

The rigid grip of the palms loosens, their order dissolving into a clearing bathed in golden light. The sound of a distant oud emerges, weaving through the laughter, a single thread of melody connecting her to something she hadn't dared to remember.

And then she sees them.

The light gathers at the edges of a courtyard, soft and golden, not harsh like memory, but warm like the stories left behind. The low walls of her family's home breathe with familiarity, their whitewashed surfaces dappled in shifting shadow.

Her father sits beneath the shade of a palm, his hands repairing a small wooden chair. His face, so often serious, wears the quietest of smiles, his voice humming an old tune that she suddenly knows she has never forgotten.

Near the garden wall, Qasim crouches, his round face lit with mischief, his dark eyes gleaming in that way they always had when he had hidden something of hers and made a game of her finding it.

Her mother kneels in the garden, her hands buried in the dark, rich soil. The folds of her hijab frame her face, and when she turns, her expression is open, radiant with love and pride, as if she had never left at all.

She exhales, the breath long and unshaken.

"Are you afraid?" her mother asks, her face serene despite the weight of her question.

She nods, honest in this sacred space. "Every day." She feels Richard squeeze her hand, supporting her.

Her mother's knowing smile holds both pride and sadness. "When they silence one voice, a hundred must rise to take its place."

❧

Maya's fingers trembled as they rested on the edge of the table, but her gaze held steady, her coal-dark eyes reflecting the light of her own projection on the big screen.

Annie leaned forward slightly, her voice softening but losing none of its intensity. "You are proof that no act of cruelty can erase the light of those who dare to defy it."

The crowd in the dining hall was silent, every person hanging on Annie's words, their faces alight with a mix of awe and emotion. Maya swallowed hard, her throat tightening with the weight of her own voice. She glanced to her left, where Richard sat, his hand resting on hers, steadying her as he always had. Across from her, Hannah's eyes glistened with unshed tears, her lips pressed together as though holding in a cheer.

Madison leaned forward, her expression one of reverent focus, while Elizabeth Lang, stoic as ever, nodded subtly, as if granting Maya silent permission to take the moment for herself.

Maya inhaled deeply, gathering the courage she had spent a lifetime searching for. "My mother," she began, her voice clear but tinged with emotion, "taught me that courage isn't the absence of fear. It's standing up anyway. I've spent years running away from her legacy, thinking I wasn't enough to carry it. But maybe it's not about being enough. Maybe it's just about standing up."

Annie's expression softened into a smile, but her eyes held the same piercing intensity. "And here you are, standing up. What do you want people to take away from your story, from your candidacy?"

Maya hesitated for just a moment, then spoke with quiet conviction. "That we can be more than what the world tries to reduce us to."

The screen cut to black, the interview ending with a simple "Maya Russell for Senate" tagline. Beneath it read "Oppression: She Will Bury You." The room remained charged with the energy of her words for several moments before, like a wave cresting and crashing, applause erupted from the crowd. A standing ovation followed, the sound swelling as though the collective emotion of the room had taken physical form.

At her table, Maya's chest heaved, her heart pounding with the weight of it all. Richard stood beside her, clapping, his face split with a wide, proud grin. Hannah reached across the table, grabbing her mother's hand, her tears spilling freely now. Madison wiped her eyes, smiling through the flood of emotions whose names she would have to look up later on the Feelings Wheel. Even Lang, standing now with slow deliberation, let her hands come together in a measured, approving clap.

Maya let out a slow exhale, stood up, and with her stilettos still echoing off the marbled floor, walked to the microphone by the screen.

ACT 4:
RESOLUTION

THE MOST POWERFUL
THING IN THE WORLD

In the open cabana, they lounged in a loose, almost languid camaraderie, each grappling with the aftershocks of the night in their own
way. The air was thick with the scent of charred remains from last
night's fire curling lazily in the damp breeze. The wooden beams
above them creaked with the shifting weight of the world waking
up, while the ocean, ever watchful, murmured its endless hymn as
it stretched to the horizon.

The long banquet table, once a stage for indulgence, now lay
in elegant disarray. Scattered plates bore the ghosts of their feast:
smears of chili paste, forgotten crumbs of qatayef, the glistening
remnants of slow-roasted lamb. A tipped wine glass wept its last
dark streak across the linen, a silky imprint of excess left to dry in
the warming air. The mingling scents of cinnamon and cloves still
lingered, traces of the lavishness that had filled the night before.

Soft lantern light pooled in golden circles over the floor. Somewhere in the distance, a lone seabird called out, its cry sharp and
solitary, cutting through the hush of morning's arrival. The night

still clung to the edges of the sky, but dawn had begun its slow, relentless unfurling.

And still, they waited.

Julia sat cross-legged, chin propped on her hand, fingers drumming lightly against her knee, a slow, thoughtful rhythm, as if she were keeping time to a song only she could hear. She had a way of reading a room, of understanding the spaces between words, the subtle pauses that carried as much weight as the things spoken aloud. Her past adventures had taught her to see past the surface performances, past the masks men wore even in their most vulnerable moments.

She'd developed an eye for the desire behind the desire, the real hunger that drove them, the ache they couldn't name. And sitting here in the golden half-light of dawn, she could see all of them with crystalline clarity.

The Ex-Husband sat with his elbows on his knees, cradling a lukewarm mug of coffee like it might anchor him to earth. Julia watched his fingers trace the ceramic rim in endless circles mapping invisible constellations. This was a man whose deepest desire had never been control or conquest, or even the comfort of understanding. What he craved most was wonder—pure, childlike awe at the mystery of existence. He was the kind of man bored by answers, smart enough to build an entire career through questions. Here, now, waiting for something miraculous to unfold, she could see the boy in him again, the one who still believed in magic.

The Italian reclined with that practiced European nonchalance, one eyebrow slightly raised as if to suggest that whatever was about to unfold was merely another pleasant diversion in his collection of worldly experiences. The pose was perfect—effortless, magnetic, the kind of casual elegance that whispered of Roman afternoons and Venetian terraces.

But Julia had spent too many years reading the spaces between performance and truth to miss what lay beneath, the precision with which he ran his thumb over the mug's handle, the almost imperceptible tension in his shoulders, the quick glances toward the others—measuring, comparing. There was a stillness in him that had nothing to do with his cultivated cool and everything to do with being genuinely moved by something larger than himself. His deepest desire, Julia realized, was to be worthy of beauty, to deserve the kind of transcendent moments that transformed men into better versions of themselves. He was performing nonchalance because he was secretly, profoundly inspired, and his old defenses couldn't quite contain the wonder blooming in his chest. For once, his charm wasn't a strategy but a shell cracking open.

The Brazilian sat adjusting his shirt collar, but his eyes kept drifting toward the temple steps with an intensity that had nothing to do with anticipation and everything to do with devotion. Julia recognized this, too. She'd seen it in clients who came to her not for domination but for connection, for the electric moment when boundaries dissolved and souls touched.

His desire was communion, not just with bodies (though Julia suspected he was exquisite at that) but with the universe itself. He understood rhythm the way most people understood breathing, as something essential, automatic, sacred. His whole being seemed tuned to frequencies others couldn't hear. He wasn't waiting for something to happen; he was feeling it happen, cell by cell, breath by breath.

And the Chef was the most fascinating of all. He leaned back with that satisfied smile she'd seen on artists after they'd created something transcendent, his foot tapping an unspoken rhythm against the wooden floor. Of all of them, he seemed the most present, the most at peace, not with complacency, but with the quiet knowing of a man who understood *process*, who had long ago learned that the most profound flavors, like the most meaningful moments, took time to deepen.

His desire was for the alchemy of transformation itself, the mysterious way simple elements could become something greater when touched by heat and time and intuition. He'd understood last night before it happened, had tasted its essence in the preparation. While the others were still processing, he was already savoring.

Then, at the top of the temple steps, she emerged.

She moved slowly, deliberately, as if testing the weight of herself. Each step was an unveiling, her body caught in the flickering glow of the torches, their flames bending toward her like silent witnesses. She was wholly, unshakably naked.

The torches cast ribbons of gold and shadow over her skin, light twisting around her like silk unraveling from a forgotten past. Darkness clung to her in soft currents, retreating and returning, as if reluctant to release her entirely. The firelight kissed the hollow of her throat, skimmed the arc of her hip, pooled in the valleys between ribs and curves as if trying to mark her, to make sense of what she had become.

With each step, the world gave her back to itself.

The soft curve of her collarbone gleamed beneath the fire's glow. Her breath, slow and sure, rose through the swell of her breasts, unbound and unapologetic. The lines of her bare legs, long and effortless, carried her down the temple, step by step, her descent both ritual and reverent.

And then, the scars.

Not hidden. Not diminished.

Illuminated.

Torchlight flickered across her skin, the flames casting restless patterns, shifting between shadow and revelation. The rising fingers of dawn reached tentatively over the horizon, pale and hesitant at first, then bolder, tracing the ridges of her body like a sculptor rediscovering their creation. The light did not smooth her, did not erase her. It etched her anew, gliding every mark with the reverence of something earned.

A slender, silvery arc on her hip, a crescent moon poised before vanishing, its glow catching in the dim firelight before surrendering to the blush of morning.

A jagged etching on her thigh, a fracture in time, the ghost of something sharp and unforgiving, now softened at the edges, no longer a wound but a signature, proof of survival rather than destruction.

A faint line beneath her breast, so delicate it could be mistaken for a trick of the light, a whisper of pain past, rewritten not in erasure but in resilience.

The scars did not mar her. They inscribed her, each one a chapter, a map of endings and beginnings, a testament to the flesh's defiance of forgetting, and perhaps, the body's quiet, steadfast belief in redemption.

And then she was among them, stepping onto the cabana's wooden floor. She did not speak. She did not need to. Her coal-dark eyes shimmered, reflecting not just the rising sun but something brighter, something wholly her own. She stood among them, whole in a way she had never been before.

Julia arched an eyebrow. "This," she said, amusement and admiration shining through her eyes, "will make one *hell* of a story.

www.ingramcontent.com/pod-product-compliance
Lightning Source LLC
Chambersburg PA
CBHW030342120726
47901CB00007B/1873